Skulls
&
Roses

Skulls & Roses

*AN EPIC OF THE ROAD
INSPIRED BY THE MUSIC OF
THE GRATEFUL DEAD*

Sea Gudinski

Dedicated to the staff and frequent patrons of Jamian's Food and Drink—and its most magnanimous proprietor who provided the endless supply of cocktail napkins that contain the majority of this manuscript.

Table of Contents

FORWARD

Let my inspiration flow in token rhyme, suggesting rhythm

That will not forsake you, till my tale is told and done

While the firelight's aglow, strange shadows from the flames will grow

Till things we've never seen will seem familiar

Shadows of a sailor, forming winds both foul and fair all swarm.

Down in Carlisle, he loved a lady many years ago

Here beside him stands a man, a soldier from the looks of him

Who came through many fights, but lost at love

While the story teller speaks, a door within the fire creaks;

Suddenly flies open, and a girl is standing there

Eyes alight, with glowing hair, all that fancy paints as fair

She takes her fan and throws it in the lion's den

Which of you to gain me, tell, will risk uncertain pains of hell?

I will not forgive you if you will not take the chance

The sailor gave at least a try, the soldier being much too wise

Strategy was his strength, and not disaster

The sailor, coming out again, the lady fairly leapt at him

That's how it stands today. You decide if he was wise

The story teller makes no choice. Soon you will not hear his voice

His job is to shed light, and not to master

Since the end is never told, we pay the teller off in gold

In hopes he will return, but he cannot be bought or sold

Inspiration, move me brightly. Light the song with sense and color;

Hold away despair, more than this I will not ask

Faced with mysteries dark and vast, statements just seem vain at last

Some rise, some fall, some climb, to get to Terrapin

Counting stars by candlelight, all are dim but one is bright;

The spiral light of Venus, rising first and shining best

On, from the northwest corner, of a brand new crescent moon

While crickets and cicadas sing, a rare and different tune

Terrapin Station

In the shadow of the moon, Terrapin Station

And I know we'll get there soon, Terrapin Station

I can't figure out, Terrapin, if it's the end or beginning, Terrapin

But the train's put it's brakes on, Terrapin

And the whistle is screaming, TERRAPIN

While you were gone, these faces filled with darkness

The obvious was hidden. With nothing to believe in

The compass always points to Terrapin

Sullen wings of fortune beat like rain

You're back in Terrapin for good or ill again, for good or ill again

\-   ***Terrapin Station,*** **Jerome Garcia and Robert Hunter**

I

Bertha

I blame Bertha.

I always have, and insofar as I can tell, I probably always will. Although, when it comes right down to it, who does a man truly have to hold accountable for the dastardly course of his life other than himself?

More than once in my day, I have found myself in the audience of self-proclaimed pious men talking at me about the merits of morality. I never listened. I can't honestly say I've thought too much on the subject. The question of the difference between sin and righteousness never much concerned me. The only governing principle I ever ascribed myself to was the question of whether or not a man was deserving of his fate. If I'd known the word in my day, retribution would have been my mantra. When I was just twelve years old, my brother kicked me in the groin; that night, I took my father's peacemaker and shot him in the foot. But before I get too far ahead of myself, let me tell you about Bertha.

She was the county sheriff's daughter—and quite a looker at that. Let's get one thing straight: Bertha wasn't just another pretty face; she was just about the prettiest face I ever did see—in all of Oklahoma or anywhere else, for that matter. She was far less favorably endowed when it came to brains, but that wasn't of any great concern to me. I met her in the summer of 1925, and it was right around then that all my troubles started...

It was in the city of Tulsa that we made our acquaintance. Tulsa was supposed to be a stop on my way east. Now it's the reason I never got there. But, the reason I ended up staying so long is as apparent to me now as it was then.

In those days, it was what we now call the Roaring Twenties. The Great War—the war to end all wars—was over. The Anti-Saloon League and the Women's Christian Temperance Union had spoken their part, and prohibition was on. Gin trickled into towns throughout the backcountry by way of homemade stills and corn mash fermenting in bathtubs while rivers of bootleg liquor ran through every city in the Union. Speakeasies popped up overnight like crabgrass and were just as hard to uproot. All numbers of good, honest, hardworking citizens turned into scofflaws by the stroke of a pen.

It was a German railroader on the Union Pacific with a real taste for bootleg Pabst who told me that New York City was the place to be. He spun me—an impressionable young man of twenty at the time—all these wild tales of underground taverns, scores of short-skirted, loose women called flappers, southern Negro jazz in Harlem, and dance halls with no shortage of gyration. He told me that the Dries called New York 'Satan's Seat,' and that's when he sold me. After all, a friend of the devil is a friend of mine.

By that summer, I was getting pretty bored of just straight traveling all the time. I hadn't had a permanent address in over five years or any real spending money to speak of. I'd already been just about everywhere east of the Pacific and west of the Mississippi, all the way from Minneapolis to San Diego and Seattle down to Houston. Those first five years were by far the most uneventful of all the time I've spent on the road. I passed the time drifting in and out of oil boom towns, hanging around all-night poker games, leaning over back-room roulette wheels, and trying my luck at faro bank—never staying too long in any one place. In the meantime, I'd had quite a few laboring jobs—been able to call myself everything from a fence painter to a graveyard plot salesman. I'd been given the slip from every job I'd ever worked before my first week was up with the exception of my stint as a six-by-three salesman. I took that particular job in Topeka, and in the morning, the boss man had given each of us selling men a nickel advance to ride the streetcars. So rather than do all that hard walking up and down the streets selling plots and having all numbers of angry housewives slam their front doors in my face, I just slipped that silver nickel into my trouser pocket and hopped on the next freight outta there. As my Ma used to say, "Jackie-boy, you'd rather steal a penny than work hard for an honest dollar." I never was too ashamed of that; after all, as my Pa used to say, it's a "dog-eat-dog world." And if New York really was as wealthy, decadent, and organized as that old rail man said, I figured once I got there, I might be able to exercise my real skilled occupation—gambling.

From the tracks, Tulsa was nothing more to me than another Midwestern oil-boom town. By that time in my life, I'd already been in dozens like it, and I could give a convincing description of the place without ever leaving the boxcar I was in:

When I got off at the depot, I'd walk about two blocks past the railroad workers' shacks and find myself on the only paved road in town—Main Street. There'd be a barber shop and a beauty parlor, a grocer and a five-and-dime, trinket and trunk shops, a couple diners and eat'n places, and a couple saloons masquerading as diners and eat'n places. There'd be the Tulsa post office on the corner, the mercantile store, and the telegraph office next to that. There'd be two or three churches depending on the density and denomination of the congregation, a police station and a firehouse, a funeral parlor, and the adjacent bank.

A couple blocks down, you'd find your blacksmith and cobbler and your boarding houses with rooms to let. There'd be the doctors and optometrists, druggists, newsstands and apothecaries, and maybe even the schoolhouse. If you continued on down the road, the buildings would become lower and older, many sorely in need of a new sign or a whitewashing. This is where you'd find your neighborhood skid row—the pool halls, all-night bunco games, and houses of ill-repute where the oil-field workers gambled away their hard-earned pay. If you took the time to look up around this part of town, you'd be able to see the five-and-six-story apartment houses and the factories jutting up just behind them, poking their dusty red brick facades out from the thick, black coal smoke that curled from their smokestacks twenty-four hours a day—their fuel in none too short supply, delivered daily by big, black sooty train cars that rode in from the countryside, determined to build this country up quick and right. And, for every coal car that pulled into town, two tank cars pulled out—headed east direct from the derricks; those quiet, stoic masterminds out there in the prairie pulling the strings behind all this booming, bustling industrialization. They'd sprung up like vast oily militias across the Union—pumping out liquid gold—black as night and as precious as a quarry of diamonds.

There was nothing special about Tulsa. It was the same old dog and pony show I'd seen in every town from Austin to Zanesville. There was no particular reason I'd stopped in Tulsa, and likewise, there was nothing there of any much interest to me. However, it was a convenient place to stop and knock some of that old coal dust from my clothes and get a decent shave and some greasy 10¢ hamburgers before I headed out on the next train east to New York.

However, it wouldn't be long before I discovered Tulsa had much more to offer me than a two-bit shave and some lousy burgers. In Tulsa, no less than a fortune awaited me, and this wasn't no fortune you had to sift out of the river silt with a pan; this fortune came already printed up on green-on-one-side-gray-on-the-other bonafide Uncle Sam dollar bills. It was the kind of easy money that hard-traveling freight train migrants fancy they can only dream about. And—what's more, the folks in Tulsa were just itching to give it away.

Of course, I didn't know a word of this when I hopped off the train just before the depot. All I knew was that those ol' railroad bulls would surely be hanging around down there, ready to razz any traveling men they could find, so I just waited 'til that old engine slowed past the junction, then swung down the ladder and landed with both feet on the cinders. I straightened up my old dirty cap as the train let out a big hot breath of air from her breaks and began to shudder to a slow halt. By the time the train pulled into the depot, I'd already jumped a few sets of tracks and was on my way into town. A couple of other bums who'd spent the last hundred miles or so dangling from freight cars dropped off and started heading in the same direction as me, dragging their old dirty bindles and bedrolls behind them. As for me, I didn't have so much as a gunny sack when I rolled into Tulsa, just a few odd coins jingling around in my pocket and the loaded dice and marked deck that were my meal ticket.

The first thing I did upon arriving in town was get myself that shave—a good decision which was only the beginning of the luck I was to have that day. From the start, I was right about Tulsa. Everything was as I'd imagined it back on the train, except, I remember, there were three blocks from the tracks to Main Street, not two.

Even from the first few blocks alone, it was clear that the boom chasers had hit Tulsa hard and stuck there. Tulsa, to them, seemed like the only place in the whole damn country where they'd laid their bets and won. When you're on a winning streak, you don't exactly get up and leave the table, so the oil field layers and all those who came with them filtered in by the thousands. They came in droves, and the builders, carpenters, masons, farmers, bankers, and undertakers all jumped to their feet to accommodate them. Tulsa was just full of construction at that time. It've been a pretty sure bet that if you'd swung a dead cat, it would've landed in a pool of freshly poured concrete.

Even so, Tulsa was a quiet sort of town—during the day, that is. Most men were hard at work in the factories or the oil fields, and the women were at home, except for those who were out running errands and had brought their tots along with them. A few little boys and girls had their noses pressed up against the storefront glass, creating clouds of fog with their breath as they begged their mothers for the velocipedes or tinker toys they saw in the window. School clearly hadn't let out yet, because, apart from a handful of Negro kids playing stickball in the alleys, the streets were clear of the little scamps. As in all boomtowns, the women dressed fine in voile dresses and wore hats that perched precariously on the back of their heads with a high-tone air as they strolled past men like me who had nothing better to do in the world than watch them go by.

I was walking along the sidewalk, taking my grand old time, watching those big, white clouds drift across that wide-open sky and the coal smoke that rose up to meet them. The sun was shining on my freshly-shaven face, wind burnt from having spent the last few days riding atop a reefer car. I remember lighting up a cigarette with my eyes still upturned and then immediately colliding with something short but upright, sturdy but soft, and surprised but humored.

"Oh, pardon me!" she exclaimed as I stumbled forward and she swept into my arms.

At first glance, I could hardly believe what I saw. Her voice was as sweet as fresh golden honey and fit for a goddess. Her face made all the good and useful parts of this man's brain turn to mush at the sight of it, and as hard as I tried—although admittedly, I wasn't trying very hard—I couldn't pull my eyes away. Her features were as delicate and perfect as a sculpture, her skin as smooth and white as alabaster. Her wide eyes were the same color as absinthe, and her hair fell around her face in soft swirls of caramel and looked much the same as Ballantine's looks when you pour it into a glass. Her lips were as red as grenadine. She couldn't have been more than seventeen.

"No, pardon me!" I responded once I'd found my voice, "It's my fault. I wasn't minding myself, I'm pleased to say. What's a pretty young thing like you doing out here alone? Seems like these streets are a mite more dangerous than they look with big ol' mindless men like me blundering about."

"It's no trouble. I'm not hurt," she replied with a giggle. "I just had some supper at Joe's lunch counter. He makes a terribly good roast beef sandwich. His egg crèmes are tasty, too."

"Is that so?" I replied, feigning interest and shooting a glance toward the swinging glass door she'd just stepped out from when I'd run into her.

"That's right," she answered, "Tulsa's very best. Everybody knows that. You must be new to these parts," she observed.

"That's right. Just arrived by rail," I told her.

"Stayin' long?" she asked.

"Long enough to buy you an egg crème or two."

She blushed and hid her face.

I introduced myself then. "I'm Jack," I said.

"Bertha," she replied, extending a dainty hand in my direction. It was as delicate as a bird's wing and had pink paint on the fingernails. I kissed it.

"The pleasure is all mine," I told her as I met her emerald eyes.

"That's what you think," she replied coyly, starting off in the other direction. "I'll be seeing you around, Jack." She winked at me.

My brain turned back into gelatin immediately. I watched her until she rounded the corner, her full hips moving underneath her light summer dress—she was just dreamy. Once she drifted out of sight, the very next thing I did was step into that diner myself to see if there were any more like her inside.

There were three men and not much else inside the establishment. Two were seated at the counter, and one was standing behind it. Once I was sure there were no ladies present, I let out the breath I'd been holding in since I first ran into Bertha, and as I did, a whole bunch of words came out with it.

"Woo-wee! Did you see the chassis on that dame who just walked out of here? Hot damn, she was fine—a perfect specimen of the female sex! She had these gams—boy! I could just neck with her until the sun comes up! She was making eyes at me too, can you believe it? A dame like that? I reckon she thinks I'm the bee's knees!"

While I was carrying on, the two customers had spun around on their barstools to face me, one bearing a look of significant disapproval, the other turning all shades of red as he tried to hold back a mounting tide of laughter. The man behind the counter was as white as his apron and frantically signaled me to pipe down as the other two had their backs turned to him. Needless to say, I did. One of the two men seated at the counter stood up, and from his uniform, I could plainly see that I'd evidently overlooked the fact that he was a cop; and not just any old cop—for he had the county sheriff's badge pinned to his chest.

He was an inch or two taller than me and balding—with a sparse ring of colorless fuzz encircling his head just above his ears. He was nearing retirement age and portly, but he had a double-action Colt revolver and a baton hitched in his gun belt, and that was more than enough to make me clean up my act right quick. When he spoke, he was painfully serious.

"We don't approve of that sort of language in this here town," he told me sternly.

I figured it was just my luck that I'd gone and flapped my gums in front of the oldest, most proper rube in the whole city. "Pardon me, Officer, but you must've seen her. In this particular circumstance, I do believe strong words were called for."

The old bull just stiffened his gaze, "Young man, in this here town, we believe it is never appropriate to drool over a lady as though she were a choice cut of meat!"

I didn't want any trouble, so I decided to look offended. "I agree with you entirely, Sir; I wouldn't dare talk about a woman that way. My own mother was a woman, after all. My Pa taught me to admire women like a fine painting in a gallery, painstakingly made beautiful by countless hours of delicate work."

He narrowed his eyes some more; he wasn't buying my whitewashing for a minute. I was thankful I had gotten a bath and a shave, or he might have pinched me for vagrancy on the spot. "You ain't been in Tulsa very long, have you? I'd've known for sure if you were. What's your name?"

"Just made it in this morning. Name's Straw, Jack Straw," I told him.

—After all, why tarnish a perfectly bad reputation with flattery?

I stuck out my hand for him to shake. He didn't take it and continued interrogating me instead. It went something like this:

"I am Sheriff J.L. Steele," he announced, puffing out his chest. "Where are you from, Mr. Straw?"

I replied with the last place I'd been, "Kansas, Sir, Wichita."

"How long do you intend on staying here in Tulsa?"

"Oh, I don't know, it depends."

"On?"

I wanted to make another mention of Bertha, but I figured a crack like that was hardly in my best interest. Therefore, I told him, "work."

"What kind of work is it that you do, Straw?"

"Oh, just about anything," I replied, this being the first remotely veritable thing I'd told him thus far, and even that was only true in regard to occupations that included cards, dice, or booze. "I'm a regular Jack-of-all-trades."

He didn't laugh, "Where are you lodging?"

"I don't know yet; I already told ya I just got in."

"I'm going to arrange some accommodations for you with Ms. Perkins. She has a boarding house two blocks down this road here."

"That won't be necessary, Sir," I replied, "I ain't even sure I'll be staying 'til the evening." This was most assuredly untrue, especially with Bertha running around single and all.

Sheriff Steele left his tender on the table and started toward the door.

"I insist," he told me severely and then called out to the other two men, "Good day, gentlemen!"

As soon as that little bell on the door quit chiming, the big, burly, red-haired harp who'd been sitting next to the sheriff let out the peals of laughter he'd been suppressing since I'd first opened my mouth. Nearly hysterical, he held his belly and howled. He was laughing so hard he could barely speak, and even when he could force a few words, his brogue was so thick I could barely understand him.

"Ah boy! You've really done it now, boy!"

I was somewhat peeved at the man. I'd just gotten chewed out by this self-righteous sheriff, and he was laughing like the whole thing was funny enough to be in pictures.

"What! What's so funny?" I snapped at him.

"Ah boy! You dahn't know, do you boy?"

"Know?" I asked, "Know what?"

"What Mess Bertha's surname is!"

I shared a glance with the man wearing the apron, and suddenly it all made sense, "Steele." I said with conviction as I sat myself down on the barstool next to the chortling Irishman.

"Dat's right, boy," he said, wiping a tear of laughter from his cheek and clapping me on the back, "you're carryin' a torch f'r de sheriff's daughter, mate!"

I shook my head and stared down at the table. I couldn't help but laugh at my own stupidity now.

"Don't worry yourself too much about it," the man behind the counter said, "That old blue-nosed bull ain't about to run you out of town on a rail for insulting his daughter. That is, if you stay away from her."

I made it perfectly clear to him that was not at all my intention.

"I dahn't blame you," the young harp told me, "Just dahn't let de sheriff catch you cashin' in."

"Man..." I shook my head, "Man, I could use a good belt of giggle water right now. You know of any place in this lousy town where a man can quench his thirst?"

The two of them looked at one another for a moment in silent conference, and then the man behind the counter asked me, "What'll do you?"

I looked all about me; this had to be the most unsuspecting juice joint in all of the Midwest. "You mean to tell me I'm sitting in a speakeasy right at this very moment, on Main Street?"

"That's right," the man behind the counter confirmed, "Anywhere else would arouse suspicion."

I pointed at the door, "You mean to tell me that there bull who was just in here don't know he was sitting at a liquor counter?"

He nodded.

"By Harry, I guess I am in luck today," I murmured, and then told the barkeep, "I'll have anything you got, excepting that coffin varnish; I ain't fixin' for this to be my last drink."

The barkeep reached down below the counter and pulled out a good-sized pitcher filled with a clear liquid. "No coffin varnish here," he said as he filled my glass up about a quarter of the way, "just pure Rocky Mountain gin."

Those words caught my attention right quick. Having grown up in Colorado, I'd known the taste of Rocky Mountain gin since the cradle. "Give it here," I told him, "I'll let you know if that's Rocky Mountain gin or not."

Sure enough, it was.

"Tastes just like the stuff my Pa makes," I said, downing the evidence.

"That'll be four bits," he said.

I pulled a half dollar from my pocket and laid it on the table.

"Do you fellas mind telling me where you acquired this fine batch of rotgut?"

The two of them exchanged another glance.

"Say Straw," the big harp replied, "You dahn't look like no lawman to me, so we's goin' to let you in on a wee little secret. Besides," he added, "I like your style."

Since we were being right with one another, I decided to come clean on my own to show them I was on the level. "My name ain't Straw," I told him, "but that's what you'd better call me from here on. My real name's Jack Jones. I only told that bull Straw to keep him from getting the goods on me. I ain't friends with no lawmen if you know what I mean."

"And how, oi, while we's doin' dis introductin', me name is Shannon Todd."

The man behind the counter poured me another shot from his pitcher. "I'm Joe McDunlop," he told me, "and I'm the head of the bootleg ring in Tulsa."

I took a good hard look at him then, with some very real doubts about what he'd said strong in my mind. Now, Joe McDunlop—from what I'd seen of him so far—was one of those Caspar Milquetoast characters: shy, retiring, quiet. At about forty years of age, he looked like he'd spent the entirety of his life up to that point behind a lunch counter. He was tall and scrawny with bony hips, a pale complexion, and thinning hair. His arms were about the same size as kindling wood. He was both sole proprietor and sole operator of Joe's Lunch Counter—both owner and soda jerk. If he was the head of Tulsa's bootleg ring, I was Davy Crockett.

"Oh, don't be a wiseacre!" I told him, "Level with me now—give it to me straight. One of your customers brings it to you, right? Doctor Hall, who has his practice down on skid row—he charges you three bucks a bottle, and you just serve it and don't ask any questions. I know how these things go."

There was not a shred of jest on the man's face; in fact, he had such a serious nature that even smiling might have pulled a muscle. "I am giving it to you straight," he replied, "I'm being right honest with you."

"Come on, Joe, why should I believe you?" I went on, "Why would you tell me all this anyway? I'm nobody, a stranger. You'd be risking your cover—even the most brainless bootlegger is smarter than that."

"He's a stubborn one, ain't he," Joe said to Shannon, pointing at me, "I'm telling you all this, Sonny, because I've seen enough young and hungry men in my day to know you're no different from me."

With this, he caught my attention. I narrowed my eyes, "How's that?"

"You're a traveling con artist, a boomtown hustler—permanently on the take and looking to line your pockets with as much coin as possible."

I raised my suspicious eyebrows, "What is it that you're getting at?"

Joe, the soda-jerk-turned-bootlegger, reached beneath the counter and pulled out a rolled-up newspaper tied in brown twine and laid it down in front of me. "What's this?" I asked him.

"Open 'er up," he instructed me.

I untied the bundle, and as the folds of newsprint fell away, a pint of gin in an unmarked glass bottle was revealed. I looked to Joe for an explanation.

"My brother owns one of Tulsa's three highly competitive newspapers. However, after January 16, 1920, the Tulsa Chronicle has plenty more readers than it had in the preceding years. Every morning, roughly 6,000 Tulsa residents wake up to the Chronicle on their doorstep. For around 2,000 of them, the news goes down a mite easier with a gin chaser. I lost one of my delivery boys last week to Steele—pinched him for picking pockets while he was off the clock. I need to break in somebody new before the demand outweighs what I can supply. I need somebody unsuspicious, unassuming, and unfamiliar; somebody who ain't got any other obligations and who don't mind staying up late nights and shirking the law. I think you just about fit the bill, Jack. What do you say?"

I knocked back the rest of that shot and stood up from the counter, "What do I say?! What do I say?! Well, I'll tell you what, Mister, I say you're screwy! What did I ever do to you that you want to get me thrown in the clink? Steele will be watching my every move until I beat it on out of this town! I'm going to have a hard enough time putting the moves on Bertha with that puritanical prune pit breathing down my neck without getting involved in any bootlegging caper! Besides, what's in it for me?"

Joe immediately reached into his top pocket, as if he'd anticipated my outburst, and laid a crisp, new hundred-dollar bill on the counter. "How's that for a week's pay?" he asked me, "a bit better than what you'll turn working out in them oil fields, eh?"

The power of the almighty dollar can never be overstated, especially when you have the opportunity to get your hands on a couple thousand of them—all entirely tax-free. The offer was far too keen and the temptation far too great for me to resist it.

"When do I start?" were my next words to Joe.

His face bore an expression that might, under careful scrutiny, be described as a grin as he informed me of the address where I needed to be that evening at midnight.

Shannon Todd, conversely, grinned freely and clapped me on the back to welcome me aboard. In doing so, he just about knocked me flat on my face. It wasn't so apparent when he was sitting down, but standing at his full height of about 6'3", Shannon was unmistakably hard-boiled, with muscles that stretched the seams of his corduroy shirt and a neck so thick it demanded the separation of his two top buttons. His hand was so big it just about reached across my whole upper back; the width between his thumb and pinky measured the distance from shoulder blade to shoulder blade. He was built like a brick factory and was certainly not the kind of fellow you'd ever want to get into a fight with. However, he was most certainly the kind of man you'd want by your side if you were a working scofflaw like me.

From the start, I took quite a liking to Shannon Todd; in fact, we got along famously. At that time in my young life, I'd never met a man quite like him before. All men like us are taught from boyhood that in order to amount to anything at all in this life, you've got to be in the business of something—whether it be soldiering or buying or selling or laboring or traveling don't matter so much as the fact that you are indeed in business. Well, the only business Shannon Todd seemed to concern himself with was smiling. All things considered, the man didn't appear to have a care in the world. He walked around day in and day out wearing this enormous grin on his broad Irish face, and his fat, round cheeks bore a consistently rosy hue. Although this tendency of his was due to his natural endowments, a great deal of it, undoubtedly, was the result of gin. Insofar as I could figure it, the only trade the man applied himself to was drinking, and whereas liquor makes some men interested in brawling, Shannon just smiled. Upon drawing a losing hand, the average gambling man will cuss and swear until his luck changes, and when he starts winning again, he will cuss even more. But if Shannon and I were sitting around the poker tables and he lost $50 to the biggest pot of the night, he'd just laugh at himself in that raucous chortle of his and say something like, "Oi, I guess I've dahn it now! Plumb broke I is! Ah, well, you can't wen dem all!"

The man was so uncompromisingly good-humored it was hard to fathom, and since I never did enjoy the company of gloom-mongers anyway, his company was even more welcome. Moreover, he was so resolutely loyal that he rivaled a collie. If we were down in one of the pool halls or gathered around a game of faro bank and one of my more perceptive opponents accused me of cheating, Shannon would take him aside and tell him, in effect, that if he didn't apologize to me, he'd be spending the rest of the evening looking for his teeth. On all but one occasion, they did—and understandably so. When somebody tells you they're going to use your face as a punching bag, you don't usually call their bluff, especially when the fellow threatening you is roughly the same size and shape as a British tank. And, in that one instance when my accuser decided to try his luck, that poor sonofabitch hit the floor so hard I was sure he'd cracked the tile. Meanwhile, Shannon was back smiling even before the man he'd laid out had regained consciousness, as if nothing at all had transpired.

Men had this remarkable tendency to keep their distance from him, as if by irresistible force. Smiling or not, he was downright intimidating, and this charm of his worked just as well on the cops as it did on regular men. No self-respecting officer without a death wish would even attempt to arrest Shannon Todd unless he had the full force of the Tulsa Police department at his immediate disposal. As long as I stuck with Shannon, not only did I have a gay companion, I had immunity.

II

The work, although I hesitate to call it that, started the next day. I've never put in an honest day's work in all my earthly living, but I've sweated and slaved more hours in the name of contraband and larceny than most men have toiled long and hard for. In the end, I must admit, it hasn't amounted to much—I've been at it nearly forty years now, and I ain't got much to show for it except a rich crop of stories and a whole lot to think about. There are a number of things I'd change about the course of my life if I could, but it hasn't been all bad. Although, for all intents and purposes, the very beginning of my bastard life began just then, even though I hardly knew it at the time.

"Grown men deliverin' papers!" I remarked to Shannon as we beat it on downtown to the newspaper office, "What a thought!"

Shannon chuckled, "Well, we ain't your standard-issue newsboys. We're 'and-picked."

"Hand-picked, huh," I mused, "McDunlop picked me because I'm a scofflaw. Why'd he pick you?"

"I reckon 'e picked me because I got dese 'ere muscles." Shannon stretched and flexed his arms until his biceps bulged like softballs.

"I guess in his business, the more men he has who can fight, the better," I figured.

"Nah," Shannon scoffed with a smile, "McDunlop could tell by me second glass dat de only way I got dese 'ere muscles was by bendin' me elbow!"

We showed up at the newspaper office near about midnight. The office of the Tulsa Chronicle was a neat three-story brick building bordered on one side by a bank and on the other by a mortuary. From one end of the empty block to the other stretched a line of shiny black automobiles—Ford Touring cars from the look of them—all of them that model year or last. Under the streetlamps, I could see that each and every one was stuffed to the gills with newsprint.

"By golly, do all them automobiles belong to McDunlop?" I asked Shannon, waving my arm over the narrow street.

"Dat's right. Jim McDunlop, dat is, de brother."

"Shoot! That must've set him back...why...." I took a minute to total up the sum on my fingers, "maybe twelve or fifteen thousand dollars!"

Shannon let out a hoot, "Jack, you ought to double dat and den some, twice dis many cars left 'ere an 'our ago."

I shook my head, awed at the notion of such wealth. "No wonder he can afford to pay us gin-runners a hundred dollars a week."

"Why do you think dey built de paper office so close to de bank for, eh? It's so dey wouldn't 'ave so far to carry der loot!"

"Boy, Shannon, I'd like to be rich like that someday," I remember telling him. "Rich enough to buy myself a fleet of Henry Ford's finest, just because I'm aiming to. I could drive a different car every day of the month! Ain't too easy getting rich off half-a-buck-ante poker games, 'specially when you're losing last night's poker winnings on tomorrow's faro game! You've got to be rich to win big. Money comes to money."

"Ah, you keep on at dis gig fahr long enough, Jack, and you'll 'ave enough dough to play in de real tourneys. Thousand-dollar pots...satin shirts...any dame you want..."

"You're a gambling man too, I take it?" I asked.

"Only on days dat end in Y," he affirmed.

"Shannon," I said, eyeing him the same way a connoisseur eyes a thick Cuban cigar.

"Yeah?"

"We're going to have us one hell of a time before we're through!"

Shannon just laughed.

I followed him as he led me down the block to one of the last cars in line. For two men taking part in a sizable degree of illicit business, we talked and laughed openly—and we weren't the only ones. The alley practically buzzed with activity under the street lamps as thirty or forty men called to one another across the rows of cars, flagrantly cracked jokes, and arranged plans for later in the night. There wasn't a shred of subtlety to the whole affair. If there was a man present who was even the slightest bit concerned about interference by the law, he didn't show it.

The whole thing was perfectly businesslike. Two men were assigned per car, each containing a list of addresses where the papers and the liquor were to be delivered. A wiry, chipper little man with a pen and a clipboard went around to the cars and solicited the signature of each of the men before they drove off. When he arrived at our car, I signed my name as Jack Straw. Shannon signed his as Dinky Doodle. The little man, whose name I later learned was Dan Tabor, chuckled when he saw Shannon's signature. "Last week, he was Weakheart," he told me before hurrying away down the block.

Shannon turned the key, and the car roared to life. As unbelievable as it seems today, in a world where automobiles and their corresponding infrastructure cover every inch of the American landscape, at that time in my young life, I had not yet driven an automobile of any kind. Shannon asked if I wanted to drive, and I declined, citing this.

"I 'adn't driven before I started workin' fahr McDunlop either," he replied. "I did part o' me growin' up in Dublin, de rest in 'ell's Kitchen. I seen more cars den I ever did 'orses, but I only ever knew one man personally who owned one."

Seeing as it was the one place I had made up my mind to go, I asked him many questions about New York, and we talked it over thoroughly as we drove down the darkened city streets, headed for the residential districts. We traveled in a kind of convoy with several other delivery cars for a while, but before long, they broke off from us, and each went their separate ways. When we reached the upscale midtown neighborhood known as Maple Ridge, Shannon eased our car to a crawl, and we began keeping our eyes peeled for house numbers. The houses built along the wooded boulevards and avenues were nothing short of mansions, many surrounded by wrought iron fences and neatly manicured lawns. Shannon informed me that these were the residences of some of the most prominent and influential oil tycoons and robber barons to ever set foot in Tulsa County, some of whom paid upwards of $20 a bottle for their bootleg gin.

It didn't take me long to realize that what the McDunlops had going for them was a real racket. The more influential and well-known the customer, the more the price of liquor spiked. The customers we delivered to in Maple Ridge were getting the same bottle of gin that the ranchers and oil field workers down by the river were getting, but the business magnates and politicians were paying four or five times the amount. The need for silence and a light touch figured tremendously into the price. As I've realized over the years, the harder and more plentiful the work, the less a man comes to earn. I didn't do a fraction of the work the man getting paid $10 a week was doing, but I was making exponentially more simply by keeping my mouth shut and my nose clean. Other than that, there wasn't all that much to the job, to be perfectly honest.

Shannon navigated us from house to house, and upon arrival, I did all the leg work. I'd check the post box for the liquor money first and, whereupon finding it, would slide the whole parcel—paper and bottle together—through the mail slot in the customer's door. On about a dozen occasions each night, the box would be devoid of cash, and I'd slip the bottle free of its wrapper and toss the paper up on the front stoop. The first of these unsolicited bottles would typically find itself nestled in the coat pocket of myself or Shannon, where we would later retrieve it in-between stops to relieve the tedium and monotony of the evening. The route usually took us about four hours, and by the time we arrived back at the newspaper office with one gunny sack full of cash and one full of surplus liquor, we were usually powerful drunk. Dan Tabor, who signed in the cars and collected the bounty, was well-aware of our deviance but never said a word, and on more than one occasion, I caught him extracting a stack of bills from the sack and slipping it into his own coat pocket.

That first night was no exception. When we rolled up to the curb alongside that stout brick building, we were just howling, laughing about the devil knows what. We were one of the last cars back; dozens of others were already parked along the side of the street, still and quiet, their engines cool, dormant until midnight tomorrow. Dan Tabor swept over to us, collected our signatures and our sacks, smiled knowingly, and went on his way.

The whole thing was one great big con from start to finish. The bootleggers conned the clerks, the clerks conned the McDunlops, the McDunlops conned the customers, and the customers conned the law. The clerks knew full well they were being conned by the bootleggers and cooked the books, taking extra pay for themselves as compensation. The McDunlops knew full well they were being conned by the clerks, so they marked up the liquor to stay in the black. The customers knew full well they were being conned by the McDunlops, but they couldn't do a thing about it if they wanted to keep up the guise of being upstanding citizens. The only group being conned that was still in the dark about the whole thing was the law, and the longer it stayed that way, the more profitable it was for everybody else. The customers didn't mind paying double to the McDunlops because it kept them on the right side of the law. The McDunlops didn't mind the thieving clerks because being able to get a couple dollars over on their employers kept them loyal, and the clerks didn't mind the boozing bootleggers because it kept us sated and out of the speakeasies.

The bootleggers were by far the most delicate cog in the whole operation, but the McDunlops seemed to have covered all their bases. Hand-picking their drivers ensured them of the character of their employees, which was, in just about every case, rotten. Running two men in each car warded off stool pigeons, and the obscenely high pay kept us motivated and quiet. The McDunlops raked in money with one hand and had us by the cojones with the other, but at the same time, we had them by their purse strings. If they quit paying us, we would squeal. If any of us quit working or started acting shady, they would have us replaced. And, if, for some unholy reason, one of us brought the law down on the whole operation, he would most assuredly be lynched by an angry mob of unemployed bootleggers before he reached the edge of town. It was quite a brilliant system to be a part of.

In addition to the residential deliveries, Shannon informed me that Joe McDunlop also ran a ring of drivers who delivered wholesale quantities of liquor to the dozen or so speakeasies that had secreted themselves around downtown Tulsa. A good number of these speakeasies could be found lurking in the basements or backrooms of pool halls, cigar shops, cordial stores, and just about every otherwise legitimate business run by residents of Italian or Irish descent. Even one of the local Catholic churches, The Church of the Most Precious Blood, had a so-called speakeasy operating out of the chapel, courtesy of a fully-stocked confessional. McDunlop's product could be procured in various other high-traffic locations throughout the city as well, doled out by the pint or quart to desperate individuals eager to pay the extra dollar or two for clean Rocky Mountain gin in place of their customary jolt of Jamaica Ginger. According to Shannon, McDunlop's imported liquor flew off the shelves faster than the delivery drivers could supply it, and after my first week in Tulsa, that came as no surprise to me. Generally speaking, the harder a man works, the harder he drinks—and those oilmen worked up quite a thirst! For what had officially been declared a dry state more than a decade before prohibition was enacted nationwide, Oklahoma was most assuredly wetter than the Arkansas River.

That first night after we finished our rounds, Shannon brought me to what was another common incarnation of the speakeasy in those days. Its patrons called it the Devil's Hat-Rack, and it was about equal parts gambling house and blind tiger, both illicit institutions and neither any sight short in demand. It was located on the top floor of the Wilson-Cavett paint factory, in a space that in 1918 had been intended solely for accounting offices. However, by January of 1920, the floor had been thoroughly retrofitted and contained not only a thirty-foot oaken bar and brass rail but a tap that filled its customers' glasses nightly with Canadian beer supplied by a twenty-thousand-gallon water tower on the roof.

The Devil's Hat-Rack was the oldest post-prohibition speakeasy in all of downtown Tulsa—meaning, of course, that it was the best concealed. Wilson-Cavett was a reputable company; its employees worked eight-hour days, its vice president was a committeeman, and it was the first factory in the city to stop employing children after the new edict was enacted. It was bordered on both sides by apartment buildings, and the door to the back stairwell opened into an alleyway secluded enough to accommodate heavy foot traffic at all times of the night and wide enough to accommodate a large vehicle, such as, say, a tanker truck full of Canadian beer. Every time I frequented that particular saloon, I never saw less than a dozen people inside—and that number stayed constant whether it was two in the afternoon or four in the morning, as it was that day.

"Tell me something, Shannon," I remember asking him in-between swallows from our pocketed bottle, "is that there lunch counter the only wet establishment in this balled-up town, or have you got a real speakeasy here?"

Shannon's yellow teeth glinted under the streetlamps in some kind of crooked, ossified smile, and he slapped me on the back with roughly the same force as the clapper in the Liberty Bell. "Say, Jack, if dat ain't fancy thinkin', I dahn't know what is! See dat big 'ole yellow block buildin' about three blocks down?"

"Yeah, I see 'er all right."

"You're gonna go in through de back door, walk up two flights, and ask fahr Patsy. If 'e gives you a 'ard time o' it, you tell 'im Shannon Todd sent you. I'll meet you dere, but first I's got'a iron me shoelaces."

Apparently, Shannon had a reputation that just wouldn't quit because when I spoke his name to the grouchy, irritable old bouncer who'd told me to blow, that door opened up for me so fast you'd have thought I'd laid a stick of dynamite against it.

Inside, the Hat-Rack was nothing fancy. It was solid brick, red from floor to ceiling—but I couldn't rightly tell that from my first impression alone, on account of all the smoke. The Hat-Rack didn't have any windows, and by dawn on any given day, that cigar smoke hung just about as low and thick as mountain fog on a humid summer night. Why, most times, you couldn't even tell what the man at the table next to you looked like.

There were several speakeasies in Tulsa. With Shannon, I frequented all of them, but none nearly as much as I did the Hat-Rack. There was something special about the place that drew me to it. There weren't any trap doors or hidden liquor cellars that so many other speakeasies of the day fashioned, but what it did have was just about the biggest, orneriest, meanest clientele this side of Colorado. What I mean by that is, while Tulsa wasn't nearly as organized as Chicago or New York, there was no shortage of men willing to fight for their rights—rights both real and imagined—and most, if not all, of these men imbibed those self-proclaimed rights at the Hat-Rack. An old Winchester hung on the wall behind the bar, amongst others secreted about the place, and though I never saw it in use, Old George, the bartender, would pull it down from its perch and take aim at any suspicious or threatening characters who'd gotten past Patsy just often enough so that it never gathered any dust.

I'd already found my way to the bar and was halfway through my first glass of beer when Shannon arrived.

"So Jack, whatcha think?" he asked me.

"Shannon," I told him, "I think it's about time to win me a little money."

Gambling is man's oldest and most fortuitous social institution, and poker is by far its most lucrative pastime. I first became enamored with the game as a child; the raw thrill of it gripped me at a young age, and now more than forty years later, I can say with certainty that it hasn't loosened its hold. To succeed as a gambler, you must possess a certain degree of patience, subtlety, skill, and luck. I am a very lucky man. Roughly nine out of every ten times, I walk away from a poker game with somebody else's hard-earned money in my pocket. However, as it is with some men, I'm not too fond of waiting for luck to come to me. I'm not a very patient man, except when I have to be. When I feel I'm running a little low on luck, I just make some of my own. Some less imaginative men call what I do for a living 'cheating.' I prefer to think of it as 'manufactured opportunity.' As long as there have been games of chance, there have been ways of improving the odds. Any real gambler knows how, and any man who's played more than a dozen games has either cheated or been cheated. In the art of separating a man from his money, I am as close to a professional as one can get. If you spot me fifty cents, I can hand you back a fortune in an hour, all of it ill-got. I suppose I could've done well for myself without weighting the scales, but I can't imagine why I would've ever wanted to try.

The first rule of sharping—or sharking as it is now called—is never to cheat in the first round—unless you like looking up into the muzzle of somebody's gun. The game that first night at the Hat-Rack was an exception to the rule. Generally speaking, it is considered suicidal to try to pull anything before you've adequately sized up your opponents. Besides, it's impolite to take a man's money before you've even had the chance to buy him a drink first. However, one combination of factors makes for irresistible circumstances—time and inebriation.

When I arrived at the saloon that evening, it was past four, and the three men sitting at the table closest to the bar had been blottoed since long before. Their spirits were as high as they were, each deal was accompanied by fraternizing and laughter, and the dead soldiers and deadwood were piled amongst one another. They were ripe and ready for picking and, most importantly, unarmed.

I pulled up an empty chair with a smile and was greeted cordially by all three men. I took a moment to look them over the best I could through the smoke. They wore overalls and flat caps, each covered by varying amounts of dirt, and I figured them for laborers. They invited me to the game, which was quarter ante, and after I dealt—and won—the first hand, I bought a round of drinks for the table. Shannon stood off to my right and leaned against the bar drinking his beer and watching the game with mild curiosity.

I stuck to my usual routine of calculated wins and engineered losses. I won the next two hands, lost the fourth and fifth, folded on the sixth, and returned with passion and vengeance on the seventh. The time it takes the deck to move around the table once is more than enough for the skilled gambler to become acquainted with each player's habits. At this point, I usually begin to work them over, but when my opponents are roaring drunk, it tends to change the procedure a bit. Drunks are never patient, never subtle, and rarely skilled; however, once in a while, they do get lucky. I've been scalped by my own carelessness more than once in my day and forced to watch reluctantly as another man staggered away from the table after shoving into his pockets the sizable pot I'd just spent the last hour or so building up.

Usually, I keep two cards up my sleeve; one is rarely of much good, and any more than two are likely to be noticed, although that night, I doubt if any of them would have noticed if I had so much as half the deck in my sleeve. I didn't make off with much that evening—if I remember correctly, the biggest pot paid just over forty dollars—but in two hours, I'd taken them for enough to carry me for the next week or so with enough left over to buy them another round of drinks. Drunks, especially jolly ones like this bunch, are much more obliging following a loss if you soften the blow with a pitcher of cold beer.

Shannon and I left the Devil's Hat-Rack just after daybreak with bellies full of Canadian brew and sleep in our eyes. The rest of the town was just stirring. The teamsters were out, having been fired up and cussing since before dawn, the milkmen were delivering in their wagons and trucks, and the newsboys working for Tulsa's other two newspapers had just begun their hawking. Shannon stretched, yawned, and tossed our empty bottle of gin into a barrel of garbage on the corner.

"Ye know Jack, Tulsa's got a mighty peculiar way about 'er, mighty peculiar indeed. She's got a way o' makin' ya feel at 'ome and like a complete stranger at de same time," he told me.

"She's home enough for me already," I said. "With the sheriff on the lookout for me now, I might as well be back in Denver—or in one of the couple dozen places I've been in since."

Shannon threw up his hands and scoffed, "It ain't de sheriff you need to concern yourself about, it's dat old bird who's putting ye up."

"You mean Ms. Perkins?" I asked him.

"Ye know it!" he replied.

"How's that?" I inquired. "I met her yesterday afternoon. She seemed harmless enough. She's just an old widow—ornery some, but I've got her matched there."

"Sheriff Steele dahn't 'ardly do any work at all, not with dat ole maid on de beat."

"Just what are you getting at, Shannon?" I asked him.

"What I mean is, Ms. Perkins 'as got just about de biggest boardin' 'ouse in all o' Tulsa, and she's got it right on Main Street," he explained. "Most travelers who come into Tulsa go right to 'er place, and most o' de trouble around' ere comes by way o' bums and drifters. Why, de sheriff makes it 'is practice to send any new face in Tulsa right to 'er front door where she can keep an eye on dem. Fahr an ole stool pigeon, she sure does sing like a canary."

While I doubted him quite strongly at the time, it wasn't long before I learned that Shannon's assessment of Ms. Perkins' character had been true down to the very last word.

III

The days were long and leisurely, as summer days often are. I slept through most mornings and afternoons in my bed in the boarding house and paid my room rent to my increasingly suspicious and ungracious landlady once a week. Shannon had not exaggerated the grim extent of Ms. Perkins' watch. If I was lucky, I could get cleaned up and out of the block without running into the witch, but unfortunately, that was usually not the case. Nine out of every ten afternoons, she could be found sweeping the sidewalk in front of the house, keeping her hawk-like eyes peeled over the town. Despite my manner of work, she regarded my daily routine as perfectly unnatural and reminded me of that as often as possible, along with her great displeasure at the fact. However, she was a much greater pestilence than she was a danger, and I went on playing the charmer anytime I was in her presence, even though I was well aware it wasn't doing me a shred of good. Just so long as she never found out about the true nature of the McDunlop's business, the several-hundred-dollar bankroll under my mattress, and my affair with Bertha, no matter how many times she told Steele of her persistent misgivings, I remained untouchable in the eyes of the law. Although, in the end, it wasn't Ms. Perkins' testimony that sent me to prison, but Bertha's.

From the moment I first laid eyes on Bertha, the image of her pretty face had never left my mind—and understandably so, considering the nature of our initial happenstance outside the lunch counter. She'd been in my arms once, and I was resolutely determined to have her there again. Therefore, every evening around five o'clock, I would stroll over to the drug store across the street from Joe's lunch counter and get myself a malt and a newspaper, and just like clockwork, every evening at five sharp, Bertha Steele met her father, the sheriff, for supper. Once about an hour had gone by and the sheriff had filled his belly and smoked his cigar, he'd head back to the station for the night shift, and I'd make my way down to the lunch counter and buy Bertha an egg crème. She was tickled pink when I pulled up a stool next to her at the counter that first evening, which made me feel a whole lot like a fox that'd given the farmer the slip and found a way into the chicken coop.

After just a few minutes of sitting at that counter, I noticed something about Bertha that hadn't been so apparent when I'd run into her on the street. I'm certainly not an educated man, but it is my considered opinion that Bertha was inordinately dull. I mean, this dame was so stupid she couldn't pour water out of a boot if the instructions were on the heel. Until that point in my life, I'd thought you had to work at being that stupid, but to Bertha, it came perfectly naturally. Her IQ was two points above a brick and one point below an ass. In fact, I wouldn't be the least bit surprised if, when the Good Lord was handing out intelligence, Bertha thought they were playing blackjack and decided to stick at 18. Women are simple creatures to begin with, and those insipid chronicles of everyday life they titter about amongst themselves when they gather in storefronts or at church socials are hardly of any interest to a man. However, the sight of her plump, red lips moving and smiling and her bright eyes dancing around the room was quite a beautiful sight to behold, even if her words were not. She'd sit there jawing, and I'd sit beside her, watching her and pretending to listen. Every so often, I'd grunt or nod to make it seem like I was paying attention, and McDunlop would pour another jigger of gin into my coffee cup, so all things considered, our meetings were quite enjoyable.

Every evening just before dark, once Bertha had run out of things to say about the quilt she was knitting, the wash she'd hung out that morning, and her chickens—a subject I endured more conversation about in one sitting than any man should be privy to in a lifetime—she left me with a peck on my cheek and a feeling in my chest that could only be remedied by a stiff drink and a hard run around the block. McDunlop provided me with the first necessity. The second brought me to the basement staircase of McEnearney's Pool Hall—an establishment where I spent a great number of my nights that summer and lost a great deal of my pride. Pool is just about the only gambler's delight that I could never get a bead on. To this day, I play pool with roughly the same degree of skill as I did the first time I held a cue in my hands. My fascination with the game has hardly lessened as the years have ambled on, but nevertheless, I reckon I look just as keen in the cool, calculating eyes of a hustler today as I did forty years ago.

The first evening I found myself at McEnearney's, I lost every dime I'd won the night before at the Hat-Rack, leaving me without even one red cent to my name. To make matters worse, Shannon—who likely could've played against Willie Hoppe without insulting his skill any too severely—walked through the door just as I paid up.

He greeted me with an incorrigible grin and a clap on the back that nearly sent me clear across the room, "I reckon ye best stick to poker playin', Jack 'ol boy, and leave billiards to dose o' us who can rightly 'andle 'em!"

"Aw, lay off Shannon, you don't know the half of it—this here tinhorn hustled me!" I griped, pointing at my opponent, who was swaggering out the door with my thirty-seven dollars.

Shannon let out such a hoot and a holler that I swear the rafters shook, "Jack, de last time I saw ole Sherm Whittler collectin' it was from a fifteen-year-ole farm boy who was blind in one eye! Dat bein' said, I rightly believe you couldn't shoot no worse if you were blind in both eyes!"

If there hadn't been any pool halls in Tulsa, I likely could've left that town a rich man. However, my dignity was on the line, and in the tradition of every disgraced man in history, I gambled away pretty near half of every week's pay down in McEnearney's trying to prove myself, despite the undeniable fact that I couldn't recoup my losses—let alone my pride—even if I played there every afternoon until five o'clock on Doomsday. Determination has always been my finest attribute, but sometimes I just don't know when to quit. Each time I strolled into McEnearney's with full pockets ready and willing to spoil some long-standing reputations, half a dozen men walked out richer, and every evening at quarter-to-twelve when Shannon came to collect me, a whole string of hoorahs and wisecracks followed us down the street. I nursed my defeat on McDunlop's unclaimed gin and threw myself into Bertha's sweet and sympathetic arms. In the business of forgetting troubles, there is no better remedy than the touch of a loving woman, and she was certainly a most suitable anodyne.

As you can well imagine, it wasn't long before the time we spent sucking down egg crèmes at the lunch counter wasn't nearly enough to slake our desire for one another—and despite the misgivings of this man's rationale, I resolutely decided that I must see more of her, no matter the cost. Needless to say, Steele hadn't forgotten that I was in town. More than once, I'd locked eyes with him on the street, and no words needed to be exchanged for me to know that he had my number. Luckily for me—and Shannon too—Steele worked sunup to sundown most weekdays, nights alone on Fridays and Saturdays, and on Sundays enjoyed the luxury of repose with Bertha by his side. I tried my best to stay out of his way, and to my knowledge, he never caught sight of Bertha and I together; however, his suspicions had been aroused, and that made me no less guilty in his mind than if he'd seen us necking in the back of McDunlop's struggle buggy. Therefore, I found it necessary to resort to measures far more keen on risk than reward if I wanted to spend any time alone with her, especially if I wanted to do so in a place where we weren't forced to sour the evening with conversation. And so, one night during our paper route, just before the gin began to take hold, I became the author of a mad idea.

"Shannon…" I spoke into the darkness, "where does Sheriff Steele bed down for the night?"

Shannon, somewhat startled as he questioned the basis of my inquiry, responded verily, "Well, de sheriff lives just down Utica Avenue, about 'alf a mile from 'ere. Why d'ya wanna know? What's cookin' in dat devilish mind o' yours?"

"I'd like to see if Bertha wants to meet me for a midnight rendezvous."

Shannon eased the jalopy to a halt in front of the next house and met my eyes. "Jack, you dog," he admonished me as I gathered up yet another loaded newspaper out of the gunnysack, and despite any misgivings, when I returned, he drove on.

A few minutes later, we pulled up alongside a modest, single-story ranch house a couple of blocks from city limits. It had faded yellow clapboard siding and was encircled by a thick hedge nearly as tall as the roof that concealed it from the roadway. Steele's shiny, black police wagon was parked in the drive. As we approached, Shannon cut the motor and shut off the headlights.

"Dahn't dally now," he told me as he looked around him, evidently nervous, "and for god's sake man, dahn't get caught!"

"Don't worry," I assured him. "I have absolutely no intention of getting caught luring the underage daughter of the county sheriff out of his house and into a car filled with bootleg liquor in the middle of the night—I'd rather serve a life sentence in the penitentiary."

Shannon was unamused, "If Steele catches you, you *will* serve a life sentence in de penitentiary!" he whispered.

"I have no intention of that, either," I hissed as I snuck through the hedge on the furthest corner of the yard.

On the other side of the hedge, it was dark. The house loomed before me, quiet and menacing, with all numbers of untold horrors—and one very voluptuous reward—inside. I slipped the half-empty bottle of gin out of my coat pocket, took a swig, steeled my nerves, and crept along the hedge until I reached the back of the house. In the moonlight, I could just about make out what appeared to be a large chicken coop surrounded by a low wire fence and bordered by a pump and trough. Careful not to trip over any pails or other hidden objects that were likely scattered about the yard, I shuffled through the grass until I came to stand beneath an open window. The bottom sill of the window was just above my head, and upon looking up, I could see a long pair of drapes rustling in the slight breeze that blew in from outside. I glanced about me once more. Thus far, my presence had gone largely unnoticed. The house remained dark and still, and apart from the uneasy clucking of a chicken or two, the night was silent. Following a couple more deep breaths, I wrapped my hands around the window frame, planted my feet on the side of the house, and pulled myself up.

In all honesty, I had absolutely no idea whether or not the room on the other side of that window belonged to Bertha. However, I knew from her stories that Bertha and the sheriff were the only two occupants of the house; therefore, I had a fifty-fifty chance of picking the right room—and for a gambler, those are pretty decent odds. As soon as I peered past the drapes, I knew I was in luck. The window opened into a bedroom, and as the figure in the bed evidenced, it was indeed occupied. However, the rear of the house was already in the shadow of the moon, which meant it was nearly impossible to make out anything else inside the room. I remained frozen there for a moment as I scoured the darkness to no avail. I could see a tall bureau and nightstand on either side of the bed but nothing that distinguished it as Bertha's. Finally, there was nothing more left for me to do other than try my luck. I ducked down below the window and braced myself to run.

"Bertha..." I called softly in a trembling voice, "Bertha!"

The figure in the bed began to stir but then turned over and remained asleep.

I called again, slightly louder this time.

The figure murmured something unintelligible and slowly rose.

Immediately, the two-pound knot in my stomach vanished and was replaced by butterflies. Unless the sheriff had gone undercover as Aphrodite, I had most assuredly chosen the correct room.

"Pa?" Bertha asked, looking about the darkness in confusion.

"Bertha, it's me!" I whispered.

"Me?" she repeated, beginning to sound alarmed, "I don't know anyone called Me! How do you know my name?!"

"Shhh!" I whispered urgently, "Bertha, it's me, Jack! I'm outside!"

Bertha let out a sigh of relief as she lifted her robe from the bedpost, quickly slipped it on, and padded over to the window. "Oh, Jack! What are you going around calling yourself 'Me' for? You sure know how to confuse a girl, don't you!"

My eyes rolled so far back into my head that, for a moment, I thought I saw my brain.

"What are you doing here, Jack? It's the middle of the night!"

"Well, Shannon and I were out on our paper route, and I got to missing my favorite girl," I replied cheekily, "I don't suppose you'd be interested in accompanying me on a moonlight drive now, would you?"

Bertha leaned out the window and kissed me. "Just give me five minutes to get decent," she replied.

It took me five minutes to remember what my name was.

After the allotted time had passed, Bertha reappeared at the window as promised, looking far more stunning than decent. I helped her to the ground, and then we both took off running toward the car and tumbled breathlessly into the backseat—and just in time too. When Shannon caught sight of us running, he started up that car so fast that we barely made it in before he floored it and took off up the street. We were nearly back to the newspaper office before any of us spoke a word—mainly because Bertha and I were otherwise occupied.

"Jack, 'ave you gone daft?!" Shannon berated me as he pulled off to the side of the road and turned around to face us, "We've got 'er; now what? It's nearly four in de mahrnin, and if de two o' you are plannin' on playin' lover's lane back dere, I sure as 'ell ain't gonna be yer chauffeur!"

Bertha giggled; Shannon's severity was as lost on her as it was on me, and to my surprise, she answered him, "I know a place to go," she said.

Shannon and I exchanged a baffled expression but didn't press her, and in-between kisses, Bertha provided Shannon with directions until we were parked directly outside the Hat-Rack. I looked at her and raised one eyebrow, waiting for an explanation. Bertha provided none; instead, she simply took my hand and led us around back. At the top of the stairwell, Patsy greeted her by name. At the time, I was shocked, but when I think about it now, I believe I should have known better. After all, I've never met a child of a lawman who didn't break the law or a child of a preacher who wasn't a sinner.

Almost immediately, Bertha proved a beneficial addition to my nightly gambling. I'd often bet heavy with a beautiful broad wrapped around my neck, but there was never a woman more effective in weighting the odds than Bertha. She could entice a man just enough to distract him and let his senses run away with him—but she never encouraged them. I never had to swing a punch on Bertha's behalf—which came as a mighty surprise to me in those days—although I'm sure the fact that she was the sheriff's daughter made her seem even more like forbidden fruit to most men than her figure did to begin with. To this day, despite my misfortunes, I deem myself a brave man when I consider the depth of my involvement with her and the tenure I earned on the other side of the line.

Needless to say, that was not the last evening Bertha accompanied Shannon and me to the Hat-Rack. Every weeknight thereafter provided us with new opportunities for wickedness and debauchery—except for Fridays when the sheriff was on the beat. Come quarter after three, Bertha would be awake and waiting for me in some flouncy gown that accentuated her curves with enough elegance to make her the envy of Lady Godiva. I'd crawl through the hedge and call out our signal, that of a nightjar, and she'd respond in a chirping little voice to let me know that the coast was clear—at which point I'd rush over to the window, help her down, and whisk her away to the car that Shannon would leave idling on the other end of the street.

Down at the Hat-Rack, my poker games quickly became the hottest around, and iron workers, oilmen, mule skinners, and straw bosses from all over Tulsa who were holding a little extra came to try their hand. At the Hat-Rack, I encountered hustlers, swindlers, and tinhorns by the dozen, but none who were a match for me. After all, with Bertha's beauty and Shannon's fists, I couldn't go wrong!

The games became a nightly extravaganza; men brought their harps and guitars, women brought their panty-girdles and pumps, and Old George poured beer all night long. Old George didn't talk much—he mainly just stared down newcomers with eyes of steel and collected tabs—but one evening near about dawn, that old mustached stiff broke his stoic silence. He told me that in the month since my arrival in Tulsa, he'd sold more beer than he had in all the time since prohibition had driven them underground—and as I was the purveyor of the Hat-Rack's turn of good fortune, he would henceforth allow me to drink free of charge. I accumulated so much money after that I had to start another bankroll and pry up a portion of Ms. Perkins' floorboards to stash it.

The excitement hardly ended with the evening, either. The first time we drove Bertha back to her house just after sunrise, we found the sheriff's car absent from the driveway and therefore gone for the remainder of the day. So rather than ride back to the newspaper office with Shannon to return the car and explain our truancy, I remained behind with Bertha. I no longer had to crawl in through the bedroom window; Bertha let me—a gambler, bootlegger, and all-around rotten apple—right in through the county sheriff's front door. After Bertha got through feeding her chickens and counting her eggs, the time alone afforded us opportunities not often enjoyed by virile young men of that time. Although the first time I suggested doing the devil's dance together, Bertha was uncharacteristically reluctant.

"Oh, Jack, you know I'm keen to," she'd replied, following a heavy sigh, "but I'm afraid I just can't until we're married."

"Why's that?" I asked, wrapping my arm around her delicate shoulders as we sat side-by-side on her bed.

"Well, my Pa raised me to be powerful religious, you know," she explained, "and I wouldn't dare do nothing the Good Book tells me I can't."

I considered inquiring how she supposed the rest of her nightly escapades would go over with Saint Peter—let alone the big man upstairs—but I figured it wouldn't do my case any good.

"I thought you said you couldn't read," I replied, "you ain't committing a sin if you can't read the Good Book."

"But my Pa reads me the verses and the preacher does."

"Don't matter none," I insisted, "after all, they could be lying."

"Lying?" she echoed, "now, why would they do that, my father and the preacher both?"

"Why, it's simple," I told her, "so they can make sure you don't do nothin' they don't want you to—to keep you from running off with a man like me, to keep you servin' 'em and doting on 'em and to keep you from havin' any kind of fun."

Bertha thought hard on this for a moment, and I could tell from the look on her face that the very act required a great deal of effort. "You can read, can't you, Jack?" she responded finally.

"Sure can."

Bertha rose from the bed and strode toward her nightstand. She returned with a large, leather-bound volume in her hands. "Then...well...you can read the Book to me, can't you? You can read it and tell me if it says anything about...you know...I know you wouldn't lie to me."

I took the Book from her and opened it on my lap as I thumbed through the pages. "It don't rightly say nothing I can make out," I told her after a while, "—just a lot of thee's and thou's and shalt's and hast's and something here about women always obeying their men...."

My eyes left the page and tracked over to where she stood before me, nearly ecstatic. "Oh, thank goodness!" she exclaimed, clasping her hands together and flying to my side, "the temptation nearly killed me!"

After sixty years of life, a man can call to mind scores of memories that have made the whole ordeal seem nearly worth the time. When I think back amid the haze of gin and smoky backroom bars, there are a few shining moments that are enough to keep me going when the road gets long and the nights get cold, but there's not even one that comes remotely close to that midmorning's bliss with Bertha. There are many things a man remembers, but few that set his soul on fire. The days that subsequently passed did so as if in a dream, and paradise was revisited again and again. However, as wakefulness arrives to halt all men's dreams, that inevitable pause was imposed upon us, and the time formerly spent in our carnal engagement was instead filled with conversation.

Bertha's words comprised most of our discussions, and for a girl whose mind was filled so abundantly with nothing, some of her offhand words were enough to strike a great deal of fear into the heart of a bachelor like me. There were words such as 'husband,' 'marriage,' 'children,' 'forever,' and one she used quite freely, 'love.' —Little did I know that it was the lattermost of these words that would land me in more trouble than all the rest combined. Before very long, it began to dawn upon me that Bertha was settling in for eternity while I considered the whole thing to be nothing more than a mad fling, a fact that created as much discontent in Bertha's mind as it did comfort in my own. In fact, I had no idea how much of a hole I had dug for myself until I stood at the bottom of it and looked up—and it was at that point when I turned to Shannon for help.

"Why dahn't you marry 'er? After all, she is de prettiest girl either o' us 'as ever seen," he suggested after I'd hashed the whole thing out for him over a game of pool at McEnearney's.

"Marry Bertha Steele?!" I nearly shouted as the cue ball jumped the table for about the third time that game and rolled across the concrete floor before it came to rest near Shannon's foot.

"Why naht?"

I laid down my cue, "First of all, the sheriff would have me drawn and quartered if I ever dared to do such a thing, and besides, I'm just a young buck—born to be a bachelor, as it were. The last thing I need in this world is to be hitched to an old nagging ball and chain for the rest of my damned life—especially one as dumb as Bertha."

"You dahn't strike me as de kind o' man who cares 'ow smart 'is woman is," Shannon replied, retrieving the ball from the floor and placing it back on the table, "Fifteen, corner pocket."

"By golly, I don't—that is, normally. I may not be the sharpest tool in the shed myself, but Bertha is about as sharp as a ball-peen hammer. It don't bother me none that she can't read nor write, but she thinks that white eggs come from white chickens and brown eggs come from brown chickens. Every day she runs around the henhouse with a broom, trying to find and shoo the brown chicken she thinks has been sneaking in and laying her eggs!"

Shannon guffawed so loudly that every head in the room turned toward us, "Oi! If dat wee lass were a man, I reckon she could run fahr president and stand a good chance at winnin'! —Eleven, side pocket."

"Now you see my problem," I told him, turning back to the game and eying up a shot, "any other time, I wouldn't think twice about leaving town, but between McDunlop's pay and the Hat-Rack, it's an awful shame to leave on account of one rotten tomato."

Shannon watched the ball deflect off the side of the table and began chalking his cue, "Maybe naht," he cracked, "After all, it's just more fahr you to lose in 'ere—game ball, corner pocket." Shannon took his shot—the eight-ball rolled deftly across the table and vanished into the pocket while the cue ball stopped dead in its place. "You know, Jack, dere's some-in' I've been studyin' on fahr quite some time now, and I believe it may be de solution ta all yer troubles."

"Shoot," I said.

"Every night, McDunlop delivers dousands o' dollars' worth o' liquor, right? Well, where does all dat liquor come from? Joe told me it's Rocky Mountain gin alright, which means dey've got ta ship it down from Colorado one way o' another—and in-between de shippin' and deliverin' dey've got to store it somewhere. If we can find out where, well, we'd 'ave a gold mine in our 'ands. And, while it's naht a 'undred dollars a week, if you can find a way to, er, allow say a truck full o' dat liquor to accompany you out o' Tulsa, I'd say you wouldn't be too worse for wear. If you get away wit it, by golly, I may just try it meself!"

I met his eyes, "Shannon, old boy, I knew there was a reason I liked you."

IV

I spent the next two days trailing the McDunlops, first Joe and then Jim, under Shannon's careful direction. This attempt at sleuthing proved unsuccessful, whereupon I turned my attention toward Dan Tabor, who was far more incriminating. While smoking a cigar on the stoop of the apothecary across the street from the newspaper office, I discovered that each day around noon, he signed out three trucks that returned several hours later, filled from bed to brim with boxes, crates, and sacks labeled paper, ink, and typeset. The following day, Shannon made arrangements to borrow a buddy's flivver, and together, we trailed the three trucks out of town. We followed them at a distance for several miles as the seemingly endless rows of homes and businesses began to slow until they ceased entirely. Ranchland replaced the sidewalks and shops, and barns and silos emerged. Just past the bend in the Arkansas, the three trucks slowed and turned off down a steep, heavily-wooded path that extended down toward the river. We watched them until they were swallowed by the trees and then drove on.

That evening following our paper route, Shannon dropped me off at the top of that same hill with a bottle of gin in one hand, a bag of eats in the other, and a sack of smoking in my trouser pocket. The moon was nearly full, providing ample light as I made my way toward the river. I followed the path as it wound down the hill, careful to remain hidden from sight behind the tree line as I kept an eye out for watchmen and oncoming cars. At that point, I was still entirely unsure of what I would find at the end of the path, but I expected some sort of liquor storehouse and hoped that it was unoccupied—at least long enough for me to poke around and get some idea of what I was up against. What I discovered, however, was far more promising than I could've ever anticipated.

The packed dirt road led right down to the riverbank. Apart from a large, run-down barn, the entire area appeared to be vacant and utterly unassuming—hardly characteristics one would attribute to the headquarters of Tulsa's booming liquor trade. I even began to question if I'd followed the right road, but after checking the barn and finding the windows boarded up and a suspiciously large padlock on the door, I decided to stick around for a bit. I nestled myself down in a thick clump of brush about twenty yards from the barn, popped the cork out of the bottle, and settled in to wait.

No more than fifteen minutes after I'd concealed myself in the brush, a series of headlights appeared farther up along the path and grew brighter and brighter as they approached the barn. When I caught sight of them, I laid flat on my stomach and pulled my coat over my head. When they reached the bottom of the hill, two of the cars cut their engines, and a third nosed up to the embankment and flashed his lights over the moonlit water five times. A moment later, from upriver, the sequence of flashes was returned by lantern, and a small fishing boat began quietly puttering toward the shoreline. Immediately, about half a dozen men emerged on the scene. Car doors were slammed in succession, and a flurry of voices erupted to breach the silent night. The barn was unlocked, and the heavy wooden doors swung open as the men stepped inside and retrieved hand trucks.

Intrigued, I watched as the boat drew near the bank and the two crews greeted one another before they began offloading sacks and crates onto the shore.

"Are we still on for tomorrow night?" one of the boatmen asked.

"Sure are," one of McDunlop's men replied, "and Joe wants another shipment Thursday night too, same time—that is, if you guys can handle it up there. He wanted me to have you tell your Sawatch boys to pump up production—we're thirsty down here!"

Another one of the boatmen laughed, "We'll pass the message along, but you know how those mountain men are—they'll only send us a batch of booze after they've drunk at least half of it to make sure it's up to scratch!"

The rest of the time I spent staked out on the riverbank was otherwise uneventful. The three cars departed soon after the men had carted the liquor into the barn and relocked the door, and the men in the boat preceded them. The lure of sleep, encouraged by the cool night air and half a pint of gin, became irresistible shortly thereafter.

Noon arrived the next day, and the puttering of engines roused me from my slumbers. Like clockwork, three truckfuls of men roared around the bend in the road and pitched to a halt directly in front of the barn. Laughing and cussing, they commenced work and passed the boxes and sacks of liquor along to one another as they loaded their mislabeled cargo into the holds of the trucks bound for the newspaper office—and later that evening, the vestibules of some of the wealthiest men in America. Of course, before it arrived there, it had to be transported by the delivery men, and when Shannon picked me up at the top of the hill around midnight so that we could do our share, I recounted everything I'd seen.

"From what yer tellin' me, Jack, dis sounds like just about de easiest 'eist around," he said as we headed back toward Maple Ridge. "All we've got ta do is wait until dey've offloaded de boat and left—dat way, we know we won't be disturbed—den we'll peck de lock and 'elp ourselves. McDunlop'll never know we were even dere!"

"There's only one problem," I told him, "where are we going to get a truck?"

A big gap-toothed grin spread across Shannon's ruddy face, "Dahn't worry yer wee 'ead about it," he replied, "I got it covered."

When that fateful day finally came, I checked out of Ms. Perkins' boarding house around noontime. I bid the old witch adieu—a statement she received with particular pleasure—and then it was off to do the dirty work—informing Bertha of my intentions. As much as I was enamored with her, the more she expressed her love for me, the further away I wanted to be. I never could quite tell why. There really is no explaining a man's desires; maybe it was the thrill of the chase, dread of commitment, or utter disinterest in ducking Sheriff Steele any longer—or perhaps it was just pure, unadulterated greed. I suppose I'll never truly put a bead on it, and I guess it doesn't really matter, either. After all, she'd already given me the greatest gift a woman can, and, really, how do you follow that? As far as I was concerned, it was all over but the crying and the whining, but Bertha had other ideas.

"What do you mean you're leaving!?" she cried, crestfallen, "We're going to get married, start a family...." There were tears in her big green eyes.

"Bertha, honey, listen to me." I tried to reason with her, "Your father hates me more than a cat hates water. He'd shoot me outright before he agreed to let me marry you."

"Well," Bertha sniffed, wiping her eyes, "Then why don't we run away together?"

"Silly girl!" I exclaimed, "You don't think I'm the kind of man who'd have a girl run away with him without having a place to go, do you?"

Bertha shook her head weakly.

"I'm going to leave town for a short while, just long enough to make some preparations for us. Besides, if I leave, your father may just forget how much he hates me by the time I come back."

Bertha pouted, unconvinced.

"Don't worry, I'll be back before you know it. I've just got to ask you one small favor—whatever you do, don't come after me."

She wiped her eyes with the back of her hand, "Okay," she moaned reluctantly, "but before you go, why don't you give me something to remember you by?"

My eyes drifted to the clock on her wall. "It's nearly five, Bertha," I told her, "ain't you supposed to be meeting the sheriff for supper?"

Bertha shrugged, "Knowing you, we won't be too long."

For all her practical disadvantages and intellectual shortcomings, she was irresistible.

It's a man's world, undoubtedly, but women have their ways. For a man so eager to leave not an hour before, ready and willing to bid his enchantress a final goodbye, I was awfully comfortable in her presence. So comfortable, in fact, that it was Bertha who alerted me to the sound of footsteps on the threshold and the imminent possibility of danger at hand.

"It's Pa!" she gasped, jolting upright in bed like a shot.

I've never put on pants so fast in my life. When I climbed out that window, I had one shoe on, my shirt half-buttoned, and a couple thousand-dollar bankrolls bulging out of my pockets. I had one leg in and one leg out when a sound knock was placed upon the door.

"Mind what I said now," I hissed, "bye, Bertha!"

Bertha was in tears again, as women often are, and without even a hint of subtlety, she shrieked, "Bye, Jack, I love you!"

At once, all my carefully laid plans became unraveled. The door flew open, splintering from its hinges, and the angriest county sheriff the world has ever seen burst into the room. Still hanging from the windowsill, feet dangling precariously above the ground, I froze as if held by force. For a moment, everything was still—as if in that second of sinking realization, even the breeze held its breath—and then all hell broke loose. Steele rushed the window, Bertha screamed, and I dropped to the ground and ran, tripping over myself and the chickens as the unmistakable whine of a police siren sliced through the evening air. I threw myself through the hedge and took off like a bat out of hell, bobbing and weaving my way in and out of residential blocks and alleyways as I tried to lose him—yet that siren continued to blare, hastening my step and heralding my doom. The Steele homestead was over two miles from anywhere safe and familiar, and that being the case, I think I hopped every fence and tore through every yard in Tulsa County. My heart was beating so hard in my chest that it felt like it was two feet in front of me, and my left shoe was still nestled in the grass outside Bertha Steele's bedroom window. This wasn't the first nor was it the last time I was fervently pursued by the angry father of a former lover, but it was the first and only time that her father was within his legal right to shoot me—and that certainly put a skip in the old step, to put it lightly.

Steele trailed me for hours. What should have been a short walk straight up Utica Avenue turned into a two or three-hour wild goose chase in which I was the fowl. The sun was nearly down by the time I finally lost him, and as I was rounding the corner onto Main Street, in a gesture representative of both my lingering terror and complete incredulity, I turned around to ensure that the sheriff was not, in fact, still behind me. As I did so, I ran smack into a tree at a full sprint. The ricochet sent me flying back into the gutter, where I regained consciousness shortly after as a group of concerned bystanders helped me to my feet. I had a purple shiner above my eye the size of a misshapen baseball and a pounding headache that felt like I'd been listening to Jack Benny play the violin for the last two hours. As I staggered away downtown toward the nearest cobbler shop, sullen, bruised, and none too happy, I could hardly wait to fill that truck with booze and take off for the next state.

When Shannon came to collect me, I was settling debts at McEnearney's—a task that did little to improve my mood and a lot to shrink my holdings. After he was through poking fun at my appearance and listening to me recount my tale of woe, I pulled him aside to confer about our undertaking that evening.

"Is everything set for tonight?" I whispered as I attempted to stay out of earshot of the other men.

"Sure is," Shannon grinned, "say, dose are some mighty fine boots you've got dere," he observed.

"Sharp, ain't they?" I replied, moving into the light of a bare bulb fixed in the pool room ceiling, "the cobbler said they're made out of a rattler that was shot in this very county. They set me back a C-note, but boy, ain't they fine? And would you look at that heel there? Sort of a heart shape, ain't it? Never seen boots quite like 'em. I guess when you consider these 'ol shit-kickers in with the rest of it, today hasn't been entirely rotten."

"I'd say naht," Shannon agreed, "and getting' some from Bertha can't be forgotten either."

I thought of her supple lips and tender kisses and sighed, "she sure was an ace where it counted... it's too bad she was a dud everywhere else."

"Ah, dere'll be more like 'er—although I dahn't know 'ow many you'll be likely to find in Oklahoma."

"Well then, it's a good thing I'm aimin' to be outside the state lines before breakfast—come on, let's blow this joint."

With that, I bid a hasty adieu to the snooker tables and pool sharks that had cost me my ill-got gains and told them that we'd have a rematch when I saw them in hell—I figure by then I'll have learned to play with a loaded cue. The sound of roaring laughter and every cuss ever uttered by man followed me out of the hall as I took to the stairs after Shannon in hot pursuit of that week's foolproof scheme.

To my surprise, the first thing I saw when I made it up to the street was McDunlop's car idling on the corner.

"You already signed out the car?" I asked him.

Shannon nodded as he stepped over the door and eased himself into the driver's seat. "Well, I figured as ye ain't comin' back t'night, it'd be a mite suspicious if we both went down to see Dan together, so I went alone."

"Ah, Shannon, old buddy," I commended him as I dug into the gunnysack and pulled out a bottle of McDunlop's gin, "you surely do think of everything, don't you?"

Shannon, as usual, just laughed.

I hit that bottle hard the whole way out of town. Shannon was in unusually good spirits, respiring mirth and merriment with every breath. Meanwhile, my mind was occupied with giddy boyish excitement as I imagined the night ahead. It wouldn't be two hours before we'd heisted all the liquor a nascent bootlegger could dream of into the waiting truck and I'd be off to the next state towing a load of more high-quality gin than even the old Genna brothers themselves could shake a stick at. As Shannon regaled me with tales of glorious former heists, car chases, and beer chasers, I mapped out the route I planned to take that evening out of Tulsa and into the promised land of riches and revelry. Kansas was my first objective—I figured any state that'd been dry since before the prohibition amendment was enacted surely must have one hell of a market for bootleg liquor. From there, I figured I'd keep on heading east—through Missouri, home of the late great king, Anheuser-Busch, and up into Illinois—keeping as far from the streets of Chicago as I could. Then, I'd move on to bone-dry Indiana, Ohio—the territory of the great George Remus, King of the Illegal Liquor Trade, Pennsylvania—the seat of Philadelphia, the so-called Bootlegger's Elysium—and finally, into New York City. By then, I hoped to have a sizable bankroll, a thriving business, and, above all, a reputation.

Before I realized it, I'd downed half the bottle and was scrounging around on the floor for the cork when Shannon suddenly killed the headlamps and pulled off the road and down the embankment into the brush. We were about a quarter-mile past the path that led to McDunlop's barn, and with myself in the lead, we ankled down the hill in near-total darkness, feeling our way through the trees and keeping a careful distance from the roadway. After we'd walked further than I'd anticipated, right around the time I began wondering whether or not we were lost, a pair of headlights that foretold the arrival of a barreling Ford appeared at the top of the hill. Within seconds, the car sped past, not fifty feet from where we were cutting a trail for ourselves through the undergrowth. The two of us froze, bristling.

"Keep your 'ead down, mate," Shannon warned me, "We ain't alone."

"The boat must be down yonder," I told him, "They're getting ready to offload now."

Sure enough, I was right. Once we reached the tree line just outside the clearing, we got down on our bellies and crawled through the brush until we had a clear view across to the barn and were within earshot of the men.

"Whoa! Elverson, Dudley!" one of the men called as he stepped from the car to greet two shadows that emerged from under the barn's eaves, "What are you two doing 'round here in the middle of the night?"

"Guard duty, Moss," the shorter of the two fellows spoke up. "Somebody's been watching us. Another one of the boys found a pile of cigarette butts and an empty bottle of gin out in the bushes over yonder," he turned and gestured toward our hiding place in the trees, "looked to me as if he was camped out there most of the day."

"We've had fellas snooping before," the other watchman explained, "but none that sat around and waited. It ain't the law, so McDunlop reckoned whoever it was planned on coming back to rob him. That's where we come in. He ain't none too cheery about it neither—he said watchmen always have a way of stirring up trouble, but he didn't reckon he had much of a choice."

My stomach sank as his ominous words reached my ears, and I could feel Shannon stiffen beside me, "Dey're on ta ye, Jack, you gobshite," he tried his best to whisper, "Some spy you are!"

"Like you would've been any better!" I hissed accusingly, "They would've seen you across the river with your red hair!"

To my complete and utter dismay, I watched in pained silence as the liquor was unloaded, transferred, and stored under the attentive gaze of the watchmen who, as luck would have it, remained behind to guard the storehouse after both the boatmen and drivers had departed for the evening. At that moment, it felt like all my good fortune in Tulsa had finally run out. However, one fact remained in my favor: the key to the barn was nestled in the top vest pocket of the watchman named Dudley.

We initially intended to lift the liquor without McDunlop becoming any the wiser. Neither watchman was particularly intimidating, but confronting them incited the potential for unintended consequences, either for Shannon or myself.

As the boat's wake faded into the moonlit water and the two men who remained behind lit cigars and settled in for what they evidently expected to be a long and uneventful evening, I turned to Shannon and whispered, "What now?"

The two of us deliberated in hushed voices until we had hashed out a plan that we both agreed upon. We waited nearly an hour for the excitement of the delivery to ebb and the watchmen to relax—lulled into inattentiveness by the gentle stillness of the night and the bubbling and lapping of the calm river water against the rich, fertile bank.

Once they'd seated themselves on empty crates and eased back into the warm fabric of their coats, eyes barely open, and all conversation faded into companionable silence, we moved in. Patiently and silently, we picked our way back up the hill, crossed the well-worn path, and inched our way toward the rear of the barn. The two men sat with their backs to the door, the riverbank on one side of them and the only point of entry—by automobile, that is, on the other. I had no doubt in my mind that both of them were armed.

Just as we were about to emerge into the barn clearing, Shannon bent down and whispered in my ear, "You go in first, Jack. I dahn't want dem seein' me face. Soon as you gaht 'im in a clench, I'll jump de other one."

Our proximity to the two watchmen didn't leave me much room for rebuttal.

Cautiously, I stepped out from the tree line and crept into the shadow of the barn. The hair on the back of my neck stood as straight as porcupine quills, and my breath was trapped in my chest. Both men remained unaware of my presence as I rounded the corner of the barn. I drew a few feet closer until I could just about reach out and touch the taller of the two. The Colt .45 hitched in the shorter one's belt did not fail to catch my eye. Innate fear aside, I was sure of myself and certain that Shannon would be close behind me.

With a yell loud enough to wake Rip Van Winkle, I lunged forward and plowed into the man who stood before me, knocking him from his perch upon the wooden crate and landing in the dirt with my hands firmly around his throat. I dug my toes into the damp soil and leaned forward with all my strength as I attempted to press his face into the ground and avoid his flailing arms and legs. I had only seconds to secure my grip before the second man jumped up—obviously bewildered—and, swearing, grabbed me by the shoulders and attempted to pull me off his comrade. Though shorter, he was considerably strong, and had Shannon not arrived at that very moment to drag him off, I believe the fight would have become instantly hopeless. Free of my burden, I deftly slid my right arm around the man's thin neck and pressed my left hand into the back of his head as his strength fled him. Moments later, his gasping and sputtering ceased entirely, and his body went limp beneath me as I temporarily relieved him of consciousness. A heavy thud several feet behind me was evidence enough that Shannon had had little trouble with his own quarry.

I released the watchman, and his head dropped into the dirt without so much as a grunt. A rush of adrenaline flooded my body, and I immediately sprung up and rolled him over, my hands flitting from his coat to his trousers as I separated my victim from his valuables. Unfortunately for me, the man did not carry a wallet and had nothing in his pockets other than a book of matches and some silver; however, he wore a handsome ruby ring on one hand and a gold wedding band on the other. I searched him thoroughly for a gun, but he carried none; rather, he had a bowie knife with a carved wooden handle in a leather sheath strapped to his belt. I examined it briefly as I called to Shannon behind me, "did you get the key?" I asked him breathlessly, my voice cracking with excitement.

"I've got it!" he called back as he hurled the watchman's gun across the clearing, and it landed in the water with a final, satisfying plunk, "Let's see what we've gaht 'ere now."

"No doubt this fella's been working for McDunlop for a while," I laughed as I slid my plunder into my pockets, "I got his rings and about four bucks in change—ain't that luck!"

Shannon didn't reply; instead, he jammed the key into the padlock on the barn door and, upon opening it and peering inside, let out such a hoot that the birds roosting in the trees above us stole away across the river in haste.

"Hurry up, go and get the truck!" I implored him as I struggled with the snap on the leather sheath of the bowie knife.

"Dere ain't no truck."

His reply was cool and matter-of-fact. It contained none of the jollity usually present in his voice and was followed by the unmistakable sound of a gun cocking.

My blood froze in my veins. When I looked up, it was into the barrel of a .38 special. Shannon stood behind it. For the first time since I'd met him, he wasn't smiling. Instead, he reached into the inner pocket of his coat and produced a copper badge. In the dim moonlight, I was able to make out the words 'Bureau of Prohibition'.

Suddenly it all made sense.

"Why you no-good two-timing four-flusher!" I spat, enraged. "You've been letting me do all your dirty work while you sat around collecting dough! And now I suppose you'll bribe the McDunlops—strongarm them for all they're worth!"

Shannon shrugged absently, "If you were in me position, Jack, I 'ardly doubt dat you'd 'esitate in doin' de same. As fahr me methods, well, a man's gaht a right to size up 'is target. Acceptin' a bribe o' $1,000 from McDunlop would be like 'oldin' up a jewelry store and only stealin' de lookin' glass."

"I ain't leaving without that liquor," I spoke gravely.

Shannon sighed, "Jack, dere's a million and one men like you in dis country—a scofflaw, lookin' to duck de law, 'and out a small fortune in booze, and get rich quick. Yer exactly what de big-time traffickers in charge o' de whole operation call 'disposable.' 'Owever, to me, ye are important. Dere are men in charge o' dese syndicates who are rakin' in more money dan de national trust, and dey're who I'm after. After dese last few months wit you, I've found de lead I was lookin' fahr, and if McDunlop dahn't pay me what I tell 'im to, I'm blowin' de lid off o' de whole din."

"You're a rat!" I snarled, "But I don't care what you do to McDunlop, just as long as I leave here tonight with that liquor!"

Shannon chuckled as if he found my dogged persistence exceedingly comical, "No, Jack, ole pal, if I let you leave wit McDunlop's car, I wahn't 'ave nothin' to drive, and moreover, I'll 'ave a contingency. Now get out o' 'ere!"

Most men would've cut their losses and run like hell, as instructed by the Brobdingnagian who was threatening to shoot them point-blank and likely would've done so without any great remorse; however, I was far too angry to act rationally. Instead, I stood up defiantly, the muzzle of his gun mere inches from my face.

"You ain't a man," I taunted him, "you're nothing but a coward, hiding behind that thing! I ain't got no gun, so what are you pointing that thing at me for? Are you afraid of me?"

Shannon practically howled with laughter. "De Bureau gave me dis gun and told me to shoot anybody interferin' wit me investigation; but Jack, I like you, so I'm goin' to give you a fair fight—if you're willin' to gamble. Deuces are wild; winner takes all." Shannon uncocked the gun, slipped it back into the holster strapped to his chest, and smiled.

As he rolled up his sleeves, my mind was racing like a jackrabbit. *You've really done it now, Jackie-boy, you've really done it now,* I thought to myself. I had as much chance of winning a fair fight with Shannon Todd as I did playing chicken with a train, so I tried like hell to think of alternatives.

I grew up with seven older brothers—anybody who thinks I'm a stranger to brawling is mighty stupid indeed. My mama used to tell me I came into this world throwing punches, and with my disposition, that's likely how I'll go out. Although I can tell you that to date, she hasn't been proven right.

—Though on that fateful evening, as Shannon towered over me like a small mountain, it would be a falsehood to say I was unaware of the grave danger I was in. The ol' Grim Reaper was on the scene that cool September night, casually leaning against the side of the barn with his arms crossed and a devilish little smirk on his mysterious, shrouded face. In fact, I saw him quite clearly right about the third time Shannon ricocheted my skull off the ground. Although, at that moment, I was far too incensed to be any too afraid. The last few months of friendship and camaraderie had instantly turned into a violent, raging desire to beat the ever-living daylights out of him. He was the enemy—and despite my glaring inability, I was utterly determined to take him.

With all rational thought crowded into the deep recesses of my vengeful mind, I flew at him with doubled-up fists and uncontrollable rage in my heart. I aimed for the side of his head with a wild haymaker, and when my fist collided with his flesh in what would've been a debilitating strike against any other man, Shannon barely budged. It was as if I'd gone after him with a goldarned feather brush. He grinned, an expression now far more sinister than jolly.

"Looks like you're fixin' to make dis real easy fahr me, Jack," he sneered with a quick jab to my left ear.

For a goliath, he had the reflexes of a cat. My legs buckled upon contact, my vision blurred, my head rang like the bell in the Old North Church, and the very next thing I remember was a mouthful of dirt and a strong sense of foreboding. I shook off the blow and struggled to my feet as Shannon lumbered toward me. Ducking, weaving, dodging, and exchanging blows, we fought viciously, like animals—though even my most calculated strike failed to inflict any more than a fraction of the damage he did. I spent most of my time hopping about like a rabbit, trying like hell to evade his flying fists, and when one did inevitably land, the result was devastating. After a series of futile attempts, I was able to clip him with a low blow to the kidney that produced some measurable effect. Though rather than injure him, it seemed only to anger him, and before I could get out of range, he caught me in the shoulder with a shove from his outstretched hand. That blow knocked me a good dozen feet backward and sent me sliding through the dirt face-first as my chin bounced off the ground and the sickly sweet taste of fresh red blood slid down my throat along with a small, hard lump that I suspected to be one of my teeth. Coughing and sputtering with my eyes stinging from the mud and my jaw pounding, I attempted to scramble away. Still, I was far too slow, and pain unlike any other I'd ever experienced before tore through my body as his boot collided with my spine, and he sent me rolling away.

If my grim fate had not been evident to me before, it sure was now. I had not the strength nor the ability to stand as Shannon came after me and dragged me to my feet by the back of my coat.

Panting and aching, I steadied myself before him as he stood taunting me, "What o' me naht bein' a man, eh? You call yerself a man, Jack? You should see yerself—you're about a sight short o' dead, and you ain't 'urt me none yet! Some man you are!"

Finally, in a rash attempt to silence him, I threw a wild, uncalculated punch at his jaw. Having clearly anticipated my action, Shannon grabbed me by the wrist, twisted my arm behind me, doubled me up, and stomped his foot three times. The first facilitated a knee to the groin, the second landed square in my stomach, and the third and final blow caught me in the face. I was finished. Shannon shoved me backward again, and I hit the dirt breathlessly as the world around me faded in and out. I was laid out on my stomach, spread-eagled before my foe, and in-between ragged gasps and waves of squalid nausea, plan B began to form in my mind. I knew full and well it was impossible to beat him in a fair fight, so I decided to play the card I had up my sleeve—or rather, hitched to my belt.

As Shannon loomed above me, gloating, I was able to take quick stock of my physical condition, which, as far as I could tell, consisted of the following: mouth bleeding, nose bleeding, head pounding, ears ringing, vision blurred, organs bruised, left shoulder possibly dislocated, and what angered me most of all—up until that point in my life, I'd prided myself as one of the country's finest fighting men who still had all of his teeth. Desperate, I slid the bowie knife I'd just acquired free of its sheath and kept it concealed against my body as I rose, my arm dangling at my side, a mere shade from useless. I drew toward him, weak and unsteady, and once I was within a suitable distance, struck out with my other fist in a last-ditch effort to distract him. When he responded with an equally fruitless strike, I lunged toward him and buried that blade in his shoulder up to the hilt, then jumped back to avoid his swinging fist.

Swaying on my feet and struggling to see straight, I watched as all the air left Shannon's body in a massive exhalation. His eyes widened in pain, and he staggered backward, his hands rigid as they grasped at the weapon that pierced him. To my great surprise, he did not retaliate, and as I braced myself to run, he did not reach into his coat to retrieve his gun as I expected him to. In fact, as he continued to backpedal, he did something equally surprising—he fell.

I stopped and stood for a long moment, bristling and contemplative, as I examined the scene before me. Vague suspicion began to set in, accompanied by overtones of snide satisfaction. However, after a few more seconds of witnessing Shannon's undeniable struggle, macabre curiosity drew me nearer—whereupon, in the scarce moonlight, I was able to observe that I had, in fact, stabbed him not in the shoulder as I had intended, but square in the chest. Dark blood streamed from the wound as he struggled to rise from his place in the dirt, his body trembling, his eyes darting from side to side, pained, fearful, and unfocused.

"I should've known better," he fought like hell to speak as he sunk back into the mud, "Sho-should've known b-better dan to pick a fight w-wit d-de devil. I should've killed you w-when I...'ad...d-de...c...cha—"

A violent tremor passed through his monstrous form, and just like that, he died. Silence followed his final vow, and it was deafening—bringing with it a striking sense of relief and a number of questions—the most pressing of which was, '*Now what?*' After all, I'd never killed anyone before.

This question, though initially troubling, was answered rather quickly as one of the two downed watchmen began to stir. Determined to keep them from witnessing the grisly scene I'd just produced, one by one, I took them by the arm and dragged them inside the barn. I lit a lantern just inside the doorway, then located a length of rope that I used to bind their wrists together and treated each of them to a swift kick in the head, just for good measure. After all, the last thing I needed while figuring out how to dispose of a body was for the other two men I'd accosted to come around.

Luckily for me, as the result of finding a spade resting against a crate of liquor, the problem of hiding Shannon's body didn't take all that much figuring. Spade in hand, I blew out the lamp, bid a painful adieu to the mountain of liquor that would never be mine, and relocked the door to the storehouse. It took all the strength I had left in me, but somehow, I was able to drag Shannon's colossal corpse from the clearing over to the bank of the river. With my left arm and shoulder in sorrowful shape and the rest of me not much fitter, I decided it was impossible for me to dig him a fitting grave, so I pulled about two feet of river silt away from the bank where it was soft and wet, then removed the knife from Shannon's chest and gave the body a shove. Heavy and limp, it crashed through the brush and landed in the shallow channel. Eager to get the hell out of there, I threw just enough dirt over the body so that it was indistinguishable, then hi-tailed it back up the hill and to the car. Once in the driver's seat, a whole other set of questions arose—mainly due to the fact that I'd never piloted an automobile before.

By then, dawn was close to breaking, and I had another decision to make. Leaving the state and my sins behind had an unmistakable allure, but fleeing from the scene of a murder by daylight in a stolen car without papers filled with bootleg gin seemed to invite a significant possibility for undesirable repercussions. With that option off the table, I seemed to have but one course of action, and if I worked it just right, I could retain not only my freedom but what was left of my dignity.

Once I'd recovered my half-empty bottle of gin from under the passenger seat and filled my belly with all that remained, I drove the car, bucking and sputtering, back into the city of Tulsa and returned it to the alley behind the newspaper office. Dan Tabor met me on the sidewalk as I pulled up.

"Where's Shannon?" he asked me as he eyed up the back seat, still full of undistributed papers, "he signed it out."

"Shannon picked me up at my room," I told him breathlessly, "I dropped him off near his."

Dan took a long look at my swollen, bruised, dirt-and-blood-stained face. "He was tired, eh?"

"Dead tired," I replied as I slowly stepped down off the running board and began to hobble downtown, one arm wrapped around my stomach and the other hanging limply inside the sleeve of my tattered coat.

V

I made it to the back door of the lunch counter just before the sun rose over the city. The street lamps were still lit, and early morning fog ensconced the avenues as the skinners and teamsters made their way from the rail station to the oil fields. The heavy odor of wood and coal smoke hung low in the air and provided a strange sense of security despite the peril that loomed so close behind me. I rapped on the door with a heavy hand, and a young, worried-looking maid arrived at the bottom of the stairs leading to the upper floors. She winced when she saw me and hurried anxiously away when I asked after her employer. McDunlop appeared in her place about ten minutes later, wearing a heavy cotton robe.

With my finest attempt to appear distraught and flustered, I told McDunlop the whole story: how Shannon had brought me with him down to the barn that evening, how he had jumped the two men and locked them inside, and how after seeing the liquor stored there, revealed that he was a Federal Prohibition Agent and that I was to testify to what I had seen, or he would shoot me dead. I told him how Shannon intended to bribe him and his brother, and finally, in the most mournful tone I could muster, I told him how I had fought gallantly in his honor and, finding myself outmatched, killed Shannon in self-defense.

McDunlop listened to the whole story without so much as a grimace. There was no exclamation, no interrogation, and other than pursed lips and a furrowed brow—which was his default expression to begin with—my account engendered no discernable reaction. He continued to eye me suspiciously, as he had since I'd arrived on his stoop, then turned and called out an unintelligible message to his maid. She returned in a hurry with a leather billfold, accompanied by a youth a few years my junior.

"Ernie," McDunlop told the youth, whom I presumed to be his son, "go on over to Uncle Jim's. Tell him we've been compromised. Tell him to get every trace of liquor over to the newspaper office pronto—I want all shifts working, you understand? And get word to Chester—I don't even want his boat in the water for the next week—got it?"

The youth nodded seriously, and McDunlop continued, delineating a list of instructions dealing with particularities I did not understand. He kept his narrow, skeptical eyes trained on me the whole time he spoke.

Once the youth hurried off posthaste, McDunlop turned to me and extracted a thousand dollar note from his billfold.

"Get out of town," he told me severely, then stepped back over the threshold and closed the door, leaving me alone on the stoop.

As per his instructions, I began heading north to the railway station, feeling particularly satisfied with myself. I had intended on taking the first train east, but once I found myself halfway there, I realized something. With McDunlop in control of the situation, I had nothing to worry about. The law wasn't after me, I wasn't suspected of anything, and moreover, no sane conductor would ever let me on a passenger train in my condition. And, with that said, considering my innards were still rolling around like loose marbles from the beating I'd just endured, the last thing I needed was to be bouncing around on the iron floor of a freight train for the next twelve or more hours. With all due respect to my victory and success in getting off scot-free, I decided a stiff drink was at hand—and if nothing else, it would at least aid my aching head.

I arrived at the Hat-Rack just as the morning regulars shuffled off down the street, nursing their livers on their way to the mundane toil that consumed their days. A few stragglers remained at the bar, and to them, George, and Patsy, I recounted my harrowing and heroic tale. They received me with handshakes and slaps across my ailing back as they treated my wounds and poured whiskey in me and over me.

In an hour's time, the news of Shannon's treason and my 'Victory over Volstead' had hit the streets, and every patron who arrived seemed to be already abreast of last night's escapade. Patsy had gone down to the pawnbroker and redeemed the gold band and ruby ring I'd removed from the watchman for cash, my ragged, blood-stained coat had been replaced, and I'd been informed that the next passenger train to New York City was in two days—giving me ample time to clean up and rest up. The thought that I'd just killed a man played little on my mind, and I was more than happy to hunker down at the Hat-Rack and enjoy free drinks and my proverbial fifteen minutes of fame until my train rolled in.

—That is, until the next morning.

Right around dawn, a scrappy little iron worker came bursting through the door toting a freshly printed newspaper and a parcel of bad news. I could feel the desperation closing in as the words rolled off his tongue, and the rest of the men in the bar fell silent as he broke this most unfortunate news to us. Apparently, I'd underestimated the depth of Shannon's treachery. Long after nightfall the previous evening, two more Federal Prohibition Agents had arrived in Tulsa and enlisted half the police force in anticipation of a major liquor bust down near the river. According to the paper, they'd arrived on the scene packing heat, ready to confiscate and apprehend, but instead were greeted by a red herring and a dead body—the dead body of the same prohibition agent who had notified them of the tip. And, printed in big, black letters at the end of the article was the name of the man who Sheriff Steele had declared as the prime suspect, Shannon Todd's notorious companion—yours truly, Jack Straw.

This shocking news certainly came as a blow; however, it did little more than delay my exodus from Tulsa. After all, I was staked out in what was likely the safest, most inconspicuous joint in the city. No man who knew of my whereabouts would dare speak a word of them outside the Hat-Rack's walls, lest he lose both his watering hole and the respect of his compatriots. All I needed to do was wait until the din died down and the agents left town. And, until that time, I remained well-informed of all goings-on because every fifteen minutes, another parched scofflaw would come panting up the stairs and provide me with a detailed bulletin of the ongoing outrage that was afoot outside.

It became immediately evident that it was not in my best interest to leave the confines of the Hat-Rack anytime soon. According to the prevailing word of mouth and the papers alike, all of Tulsa was in a complete uproar. Prohibition agents from all over the state were sniffing for alcohol in just about every corner of the city. The cops were raiding cat houses and gambling halls. The railroad bulls were working double shifts at the depot, arresting bums by the dozen. And, whole posses of morally upright citizens who had carefully stowed away their cache of liquor at home had taken to the streets in pursuit of the heinous killer. The word murder was on the tip of everyone's tongue. The perpetrator, on the contrary, was nestled in a cloistered barroom far above the scandal that ravished the town, living a life of luxury—for a time. Little did I expect that I would find my grand reprieve shortened considerably by the end of that day.

The witching hour was accompanied by its customary merriments. I was seated at a table covered in idle cards and surrounded by an eclectic array of men as I smoked a four-bit cigar and retold my story for the eight-hundredth time in two days when, suddenly, there was a commotion at the door. Immediately, a burst of paranoia flooded the Hat-Rack. Men jumped up from their chairs, drinks were cleared, wagers were hustled away, weapons were drawn and pointed, and a flustered, red-faced, teary-eyed Bertha Steele stumbled into the room.

"Oh, Jack! Oh, Jack!" she cried frantically as she rushed to my side, "the whole town is out looking for you! Pa wants to lock you in prison and throw away the key!" She embraced me passionately and then, remembering herself, stepped back away from me with a shiver.

"Tell me you didn't do it!" she beseeched me, "tell me you didn't kill Shannon!"

Every red eye in the bar was on me as I reassured her of my innocence. "Of course not!" I scoffed, trying my best to sound genuinely offended.

"How do I know you didn't do it?!" she insisted, her eyes narrowing to meet mine.

"I was here gambling all night!" I declared, and a few good sports raised their voices in agreement.

"And how do I know *that!*"

"Because I'm telling you I was here, Bertha!" I retorted, "I couldn't have killed and buried Shannon Todd if I was here hiding from your Pa the whole goldarned night!"

Bertha recoiled, satisfied with my apparent candor. I've always been adept at rephrasing the truth—Mama used to tell me that when the Lord handed out consciences, I'd lied and said I'd already received my share.

"But then why is your name in all the papers!?" she whimpered, her accusatory tone changed once more to distraught confusion, "has the whole town gone mad?!"

I laid my hand on hers, "Bertha, your Pa has it in for me, you understand? I'm going steady with his daughter—and we both know that he don't like that. He'll arrest me sure, no matter if he knows I'm innocent or not—it don't matter none, as much as he hates me."

Bertha burst into tears and buried her face in my coat, "Oh Jack, we'll run away together. I'll help you!"

"I can't leave, Bertha. If I did that, I might as well turn myself in! And I sure as hell ain't taking you with me! The sheriff'll really be after me then...." I peeled her off my chest and held her at arm's length, "You have to get out of here, Bertha, and don't come around here anymore!"

"I'll talk to my Pa," she begged me, "I'll tell him that you're innocent! He'll listen to me!"

"Bertha, I'll be back for you," I urged her, "it's like we talked about; now get out of here!"

It took a great deal of leveraging and convincing, but with a helpless whimper and a heavy sob, she reluctantly left—and half the patronage followed in her wake. Those who remained were clearly nervous, and all conversation resumed slowly and cautiously. I breathed a sigh of relief and turned back to the table to continue my tale when I felt something hard and metallic prod me in the back. Old George stood there with the Winchester in his hands, its muzzle trained on my feet.

"McDunlop may own some of the lawmen around here, but that ain't the case with the sheriff," he told me gravely. "He ain't got no pull against what Steele sees with his own two eyes. He knows that if you're still in town, Bertha's gon' find you—and she can't find you here! I'm sorry, Jack, but you gotta leave."

He didn't leave me much opportunity for rebuttal. The room had fallen deathly silent for a second time, so after a moment's pause, I stood, retrieved my hat, finished my drink, walked to the door, met his eyes, and left without a word.

It was dark and raining when I made it out into the alley. Whatever moon there was remained hidden behind the clouds, and the streets were devoid of both automobiles and pedestrians. I spent a good few minutes peering out at the sidewalk, mustering up the courage to leave the safety of the Hat-Rack. Finally, eager to get out of the weather, I pulled my coat up around my ears and my hat down over my eyes and made it for McEnearney's. However, to my grave disappointment, I found that no other establishment, no matter how crooked, would let me in with my infamous reputation. Finally, drenched, exhausted, and void of alternatives, I pulled the rotten planks off the back door of a vacant pub that opened into a narrow alleyway on the east side of town.

I'd chosen the place with the vain hope of finding something promising, but once I got inside and located a candle, it was obvious that it had been boarded up long before prohibition. There was an abundance of dust and cobwebs but not very much else. The bar was empty of liquor, the mirrors had been shattered, every table and chair in sight had been overturned, and shards of glass covered the entire floor. In fact, the whole barroom was smashed up so bad it looked like Carry Nation had been through there twice. I hunkered down in one of the back rooms, turned open the soggy newspaper I'd found on the sidewalk, and settled in for a long, uncomfortable wait.

That morning's latest murder news included Shannon's autopsy results. According to the county coroner, I couldn't have hit him more square in the heart if he'd had a medical diagram printed upon his chest. A single, fatal stab wound had felled the 6'3", 300-lb Shannon Todd, and the cold-blooded killer was still at large. Unfortunately, I knew exactly where he was—huddled in the storeroom of a burned-out pub, hungry, thirsty, dry, and sick to death of being forced into hiding.

I lasted two days there, and on the morning of the third, I decided to make it for the train. I left the shelter of the pub just as dawn broke, put my head way down, and lifted it up only to glance at the street signs. After two days of solitude, I was as hungry as a dog, my swollen tongue felt as dry as sandpaper, and the scents of numerous untold morsels wafting up into the early morning air from the confectionaries and bakeries was nearly enough to drive me mad. I couldn't get to the railyard and out of Tulsa fast enough.

I was within two blocks of the tracks when I heard an all-too-familiar voice behind me. I scurried another whole block before the gaining footsteps from behind nearly overtook me, and I spun around to confront my pursuer. As if excerpted from my worst nightmare, it was none other than Bertha Steele, carrying her basket of eggs on her way to the grocer. For me, it was a most unfortunate happenstance, as the woman had absolutely no concept of subtlety and continued to shout my name, even after I'd turned around. No matter how much I gestured and urged her to be quiet, she only ceased screeching once she'd flung her arms around me, sending eggs splattering all over the street. Panicked, I tried like hell in a bucket to pry her off me and run like the devil, but it was too late.

As if they'd been following her, a covey of cops from every direction descended upon us. They surrounded us instantly, bent me down over an automobile parked at the corner, wrenched my arms behind me, and locked me up good and tight. Bertha was dragged away, kicking and screaming, and pandemonium immediately flooded the streets of Tulsa. Sirens wailed, fire whistles blew, and every occupant of every home, business, and apartment house within ten blocks flocked to the scene to gawk. Men in robes, women in aprons, and children in nightgowns lined the sidewalks, gasping, whispering, and pointing as they witnessed the spectacle. I knew the jig was up, and I had nothing left to lose, so I bluffed and started yelling, hollering, and making an awful scene, much to the delight of the onlookers.

"Test me! Test me!" I shouted, "Arrest me, why don't you! The real crook is still out there! You'll see! That sick sonofabitch who killed Shannon is still out there roaming these here streets! Nobody's safe! Women, take your children home and keep 'em locked indoors! These here coppers are 'rrestin an innocent man!"

It was an impressive display, but as I might've expected, it proved futile. When the Black Maria pulled up to the corner, they stuffed me down inside, and I rode on over to the jailhouse with a revolver pointed at my head. You see, cops have a nasty habit of not believing much—even when you're telling them the truth, they're skeptical, let alone a naked lie.

And so, with a whole lot of prodding and shoving and not very much conversation, I was led into the sheriff's station where they confiscated the contents of my pockets and the watchman's infamous knife, grilled me thoroughly, and for the first time in my life, I had my picture taken in jail. They even took away my shiny new boots.

Once they were through booking me, they rustled me on up to the calaboose, where I stood like a newly broke stallion. That was not the first time I'd been locked up; however, it was the first time I'd ever been arrested for a crime as egregious as murder. In the past, I'd been jailed for gambling, fighting, and sleeping in the street, but I'd been tried and served my time without suffering any too severely. Though, in this instance, the future seemed markedly more uncertain and far from hopeful.

For the first twelve hours, I stood at the iron door, hoping that each time the guard walked by, he'd open it up and tell me I was free to go. Of course, I didn't expect it, but it's certainly what I wanted, and despite its futility, that's what I hoped for. It may sound foolish to you, but most men who find themselves incarcerated assume the same position that first evening. Even I—who was no stranger to jails by that time—didn't so much as touch that lousy bunk until long into the night. As any man who has ever faced a harrowing sentence knows well, the true hopeless gravity of imprisonment rarely comes at the moment of apprehension. Rather, it arrives sometime later and is accompanied by a burdensome weight so unbearable that it knows no equal in all the world. For me, grim reality accompanied the deputy as he made his rounds to each of the cells that evening, carrying with him a stack of cold metal trays containing some foul-smelling colorless gruel and a piece of stale bread. He took one look at me when he entered the cellblock, then shook his head and chuckled irreverently.

"You'd best make yourself comfortable, Mr. Straw," he told me as he unlocked the cell door and handed me the tray, "you'll call this cell home until the sun goes down."

I dropped the tray on the bunk and sneered, "I knew you ol' coppers couldn't hold me without evidence—I'll be a free man by tonight!"

The deputy looked humored as he slammed the big iron door behind him, "no, no, sonny, you'll be here for life, you see, until the sun sets in your eyes and you retire to the six-foot-three—which will be altogether roomier than where you'll be living out the rest of your days."

Until you've been stripped of your freedom, until you've felt the tight fist of the law close hard around you like the coils of a snake, until you've been forced to sacrifice all the joys and pleasures of life in exchange for the same toil and drudgery reserved only for beasts and watched from behind iron bars as the dreams you'd built up for years took to the sky like coastbound birds, you cannot know the despair that fills these jails and hangs over men like a pendulum blade.

At that moment, the despair that I'd so valiantly warded off for such a time flooded upon me at once. To a man of such tender years, life appears as a great sea immeasurably full of opportunities bobbing distantly in the tide. The profound vastness of such an epoch greatly comforts the adolescent mind and instills in him no lack of cocksureness and invincibility. For a boy, hardly a man, to be faced with a notion as elusive and disturbing as eternity is often vain and its grandeur taken wholly for granted. However, pair the imperceptible gleam of eternity with the stark fear of doing time, and suddenly that same young man, having known no degree, no lyceum, and no seminary, finds himself subject to a breadth of understanding that has perpetually eluded all the scholars, philosophers, and parsons of old, barring those who at one time or another found themselves imprisoned.

Some men, when faced with such a grisly fate, despair at length and are subsequently relieved of hope, but lo the resilience of the young man's will, for I cannot number myself among them. Following my hearing, the veil of despair which had so thoroughly cloaked my faculties and ravaged my mind changed at once to anger. It was conducted at the county courthouse and so heavily attended that in order for all the interested parties to catch a glimpse of that year's most notorious criminal, the entire audience was subject to rotation each time a new witness was brought to the stand. The stir-steerer who had been granted to me by the court in exchange for fifty dollars spoke little on my behalf, and his statements professing my innocence were cleared from the courtroom floor as quickly as if they had been a mess of dreck tracked in from outside.

Ms. Perkins was the first to grace the stand. She regaled the court with her observations of my character, or lack thereof, as revealed during the three months I spent as a boarder in her entrapment—and did not fail to mention that I had terminated my stay there on the morning of the murder. To my great surprise, she was followed by Dan Tabor, McDunlop's clerk-turned-bagman, who held up his right hand and swore before the court that neither Shannon nor I had reported to work at the newspaper office the night he was killed—entirely eliminating my hope of an alibi. Sherriff Steele picked up where Dan Tabor left off, testifying that he had often seen Shannon and me together at the lunch counter and on the street. And, before the judge dismissed him from the stand, Steele did not forgo the opportunity to disclose the fact that on the evening of the murder, he had caught me sneaking out of his house after a sordid rendezvous with his daughter. While he remained vehemently adamant that I was guilty of the current charges levied against me, he made it quite clear that he was also entirely in favor of having me tried for trespassing and attempted kidnapping in addition to homicide.

By the time Bertha herself took the stand, I was already well aware that even the most cunning stir-steerer would have a hell of a time beating the case—and that was before she opened her mouth. Those same plump lips that had only a week before taken me to heaven and back proved to be an indispensable asset to my conviction. Though she spoke passionately of my innocence from the witness box, as she recounted to the court every unbelievable lie I'd ever told her, any hope of my acquittal became less and less plausible.

The final nail in my coffin came directly from the hand of the prosecutor who presented before the court and those assembled an array of evidence so insurmountable that a clearer picture of the crime could not have been envisioned even if I remembered the events of that night to them myself. He spoke of my having accompanied Shannon to the site of the supposed 'liquor bust' and that upon failing to heed Shannon's orders—proposedly due to my involvement in the bootlegging activity—I initiated a physical confrontation which ended with the fatal stabbing. He even presented the watchman's knife—complete with its blood-stained wooden handle—to the court as evidence. As if that were not enough, he went on to provide a startlingly accurate account of how I'd attempted to conceal the body and concluded his oration as he announced triumphantly that the soles of my snakeskin boots matched exactly the unusual prints left behind on the muddy riverbank.

I was beaten and defenseless. I had the opportunity to make a statement myself, but as advised by the stir-steerer, I refrained. After less than a minute of deliberation, the judge declared, "the defendant to await the decision of the grand jury."

Despite the din of the crowd, Bertha's broken sob could be heard across the courtroom.

Two harness cops appeared beside me, and I was marched up several flights of stairs to the county jail, which was located on the top floor of the courtroom. The irons were removed from my wrists, and I was handed a bar of soap and locked in without a word from either of them. To my surprise, I saw that a copy of that day's newspaper had been left on my bunk.

I've never been in this life for fame, although as a boy, I remember being told that seeking fame ain't the way to acquire it, that most times it just leaps up and slaps you across the back of the head when you least expect it. That being said, it was a typical case of sick irony that my mug was printed up on the front page of the Tulsa Chronicle that fateful day. All those quiet, unassuming city folks who unwrapped the folds of newsprint from their bottle of Rocky Mountain gin that morning before they poured it into their coffee had no idea what the front-page felon had done so that they might get their buzz.

II

Mama Tried

What followed in the ensuing weeks was the swiftest trial in Oklahoma history. Within just a few short months, my case had been tried and disposed of, the verdict fated to live infamously on in the city archives, and the criminal sentenced to a lifetime of sorrow. Because of the nature of my crime, my trial was held at the federal district court before a hardnosed judge by the name of Kennamer and a jury that was far from sympathetic. I plead not guilty on the grounds of self-defense, but Tulsa was Steele's jurisdiction and he would've made right sure that I went to prison even if that old wicked Shannon Todd had shot half a dozen bullets into me before I killed him.

In the eyes of the prosecutor, the whole incident appeared to be perfectly premeditated, and motive didn't seem to be much of a concern when there was that much evidence stacked against me. I was even suspected of being a bootlegger myself, but my 'legitimate' job as a delivery man for the Chronicle and Ms. Perkins' testament to my daily habits saved me from that judgment. Though, in the end, it really didn't do me very much good, and I was still convicted of the first-degree murder of a federal prohibition agent.

I had long been privy to the stories of travelers, bums, thieves, and the most unfortunate of average men bewailing the corruption and malfeasance of the law. However, it was not until my extended stay in the Tulsa county jail that I became the object of it. Following my hearing, the stir-steerer who had 'represented' me demanded the balance of my money held in the office as a retainer. At the time of my arrest, my pockets had yielded a total of $2,200. When the shyster called to collect his fee, only $400 remained, the rest having been divided amongst the upstanding officers assigned to protect it. Disappointed by the size of his payoff and reluctant to provide counsel for a suspect implicated in such a despicable crime, he waived our defense when faced with the mounting tide of evidence against me, leaving me penniless and prey to the inequity of the justice system.

The night before my sentencing, Sherriff Steele himself arrived at the jail. He strolled down the long hall with a striking air of victory and stood before the iron bars of my cell with an expression of complete and utter contentment upon his pale, fleshy face. I rose from my cot with an unflinching grimace and stood before him. He remained silent for several minutes as he looked me over with satisfaction and contempt. Scowling begrudgingly, I stared back at him until he finally broke the silence.

"Mr. Straw, you have no idea how much it warms my heart to see you behind bars," he announced proudly, "Never again will I have to worry about you laying your filthy hands on my daughter. The poor girl has been crying for weeks; having to appear in court has certainly made her wan—however, I am sure that as soon as you are put away, her spirits will naturally improve. She'll forget about you before very long, but you'll still be here rotting away, right where you belong."

For the only time since I first laid my eyes upon him at the lunch counter, I saw him smile. The expression, so unnatural for a miserly old coot such as he, stretched crookedly across his face as his muscles balked at performing such a foreign task.

I remained silent, my own sullen expression unchanged.

"You haven't had very much to say for yourself, Mr. Straw," Steele taunted, continuing his schadenfreude, "—not at the hearing, not at the trial, not even when given a chance to defend yourself."

My gaze stiffened, and my teeth clenched, but I stayed silent.

"You know, Mr. Straw," he spoke blithely, "under federal law, first-degree murder is a hanging offense." He paused then and stepped closer to the cell door, his voice changing instantly from loud and decorous to low and guttural, "—and nothing would please me more than to see you swing."

In the face of his provocation, I retained my silence; however, if looks could kill, Steele would've been stone dead faster than Shannon Todd on the bank of the Arkansas River. My heart was racing; I could feel the blood rush through my body like a torrent, tearing a searing path through my veins as it pounded in my ears and coagulated in my fingertips. I was sweating like a stick of dynamite, and it took every ounce of self-control I possessed to keep myself from flying to the door, reaching through the bars, wrapping my fingers around Steele's throat, and choking him to death.

With his eyes fixed on mine, he stepped away, his voice once more returned to its usual, unequivocal lilt, "Mr. Straw, I reckon that you'll be seeing my face in your mind every day until you die—and I thought it would be only right to let you know that I'll be smiling."

Steele smiled then, a big, wide, ugly smile that hung on tenaciously like a scar, and utterly pleased with himself, he started down the long dim hall toward the stairwell that led outside to freedom.

When he was about halfway down the corridor, I just couldn't contain myself any longer. I rushed to the door, grasped the iron bars with all my strength, and hollered at the top of my lungs, "STEELE!"

As if he anticipated my outburst, he gradually drew his steps to a halt, and slowly, deliberately, he turned partway to face me.

"Steele," I spoke, my voice shuddering with rage, "Steele, you mark my words. I vow to you right here and right now that one day I will stand on your grave, and I will do so as a free man. You'll turn so hard under the ground that I'll feel the earth move beneath my feet—and you won't be able to do a damn thing about it!"

Steele didn't say a word. Rather, his cold, callous eyes met my wild ones for a moment before scanning me thoroughly. He looked me over with the same morbid intrigue as a larcenous yegg eyeing up a soft target. He examined my ragged breath, my hardened jaw, and my trembling hands before letting his gaze linger for a moment on my neck. It was as if he was imagining the hangman's rope tight around it, choking the life from my body as my feet twitched and shuddered, dancing in the air three feet above the ground.

Slowly, his eyes climbed to meet mine again, the corner of his mouth rose in a smirk, and he turned on his heels toward the door. He strode down the length of the hall and exited the cellblock without a glance behind him, leaving me gripping the bars of my cell red-faced and drenched in sweat until my knuckles turned white, my fingernails cut into my palms, and a trickle of blood streamed down my wrists. My head pounded as anger rocked my body—and the pain only fueled it. I was breathing hard, dizzy with murderous rage, and filled with such wicked, vile thoughts they would've killed any rightly moral man.

Like most men, I prefer to regard myself as notably resilient—physically strong, mentally tough, and emotionally indifferent to any troubles that may rise to assail me—the kind of man who can look a hangman in the eye and spit in his face. However, following Steele's visit, I felt as if every virtuous claim I could make to my character fled me. I felt as if I'd been engulfed by fear as dark and inescapable as the prison walls that surrounded me and would surround me for the rest of my life. It was no colder in the cellblock that night than any other; the chill of the stone walls and steel floor gripped me with no greater tenacity, and yet, I shook. I shook with fearsome intensity, my whole body quivering like an autumn leaf in a harsh breeze, terrified of being swept away. I felt that noose around my neck as verily as if Steele had placed it there with his own two hands. I was so assured of my imminent death that I did not loosen my grip on those iron bars until the next morning, petrified that if I had, a trap would've opened beneath my feet, and I'd have left this life dying in the worst way a man can.

This grim, almost mad utter certainty that overcame me lessened none in the twelve hours I remained there. Even after the guards led me away to the courtroom dock, I stood like a sentry before my demise. The proceedings were carried out as callously and methodically as legal proceedings always are, and once again, the courtroom was packed solid as the ghoulish population of Tulsa anxiously awaited the declaration of my punishment.

The judge reviewed the case briefly, after which the jury was sent out to deliberate in the next room. They returned in under twenty minutes, and fortunately for my neck, the twelve of them could not come to an agreement as to whether or not I should be hung. Therefore, when that gavel came down, I was condemned not to the gallows but to life in prison.

It is said that a man's true nature is revealed to him at the moment of his condemnation. When my sentence was pronounced, it felt like a red-hot lump of coal was dropped into my throat and burned straight down through my insides, searing my stomach and boiling my entrails. Agony is a word I have used to describe it in the past, but it's never entirely summed it up. For all its horror and grave anguish, this invitation of torment, suffering, and living hell met me first with a striking sense of relief.

My remand came to the marked dismay of Steele, who would've gleefully handed me over to Rich Owens—Oklahoma's own Jack Ketch—

without so much as an afterthought, and if nothing else, that instilled in me some small sense of vindication. Of course, it was fleeting, as all victories are, and left me in a hurry shortly after the guards led me out to the garage behind the courthouse and proceeded to beat me mercilessly within an inch of my life. They left the irons on both my arms and legs and inflicted upon me a series of devastating blows that made my conflict with Shannon feel like nothing more than a sparring match between friends. For many years it remained the worst beating I'd ever received until a Negro trombone player and his praetorian band exceeded the damage in a back alley off of Bourbon Street some thirty years later. Despite the benign nature of my sentence, I arrived at McAlester far closer to dead than alive, with a face so swollen and bruised that even if my mother could recognize, she surely couldn't love.

I spent the first three weeks of my incarceration confined to the third-floor infirmary under the care of an extremely gay cat named Gary Thorpe. Thorpe had done time for malpractice and, after his sentence was up, had been appointed the chief medical officer at McAlester. Though he'd been pardoned by the state, after spending nearly a month in his quarters, I still had my doubts. He was crass and inattentive, and at no point during the three weeks I spent under his care did he ever give the slightest indication that he had any idea what painkillers were.

In-between fighting off bouts of unconsciousness inflicted by my massive concussion and cursing Thorpe's incompetence, I spent the balance of my time nursing a hatred so deep and foreboding that the devil himself would've had a worthy challenge comprehending the sheer depth of my fury. Harsh and unforgiving recriminations sank their teeth into my soul and drained me of all my love. Ailing as I was, I was forced to consider the most unpleasant notion that I may be somehow responsible for some degree of my misfortune. However, no self-respecting unlucky man with so much as a thought to his own preservation of mind will blame himself for his bad turn. Instead, he will most certainly shuffle off that most demoralizing burden upon the closest and most susceptible target. In my case, that accountability fell entirely upon the supple bosom of Bertha Steele, who, despite her ignorance, had become my worst enemy—and the sheer malice I bore on her behalf even outstripped the rage I felt toward the sheriff himself.

Needless to say, it wasn't long before I relieved myself of any fault whatsoever, which, if I am to be brutally honest, was quite a load off my mind. After all, why should I bear the weight of conviction upon my guiltless conscience when it was Bertha who was to blame? I'd killed, but I'd done so in self-defense—at least, that was what I told myself and anyone who asked. The fact that I'd been planning to rob a bootlegger of illegal goods and that the man I'd killed, corrupt or not, had been enlisted by the federal government to stop me didn't seem to factor into my deduction.

It took me several weeks to arrive at that fitting conclusion, but once I did, I rested easy, and by the time they released me from traction, in my eyes, I was an innocent man, wrongly convicted and screwed by the system. And, that being the case, I toted around with me the characteristic hubris that all self-proclaimed innocent men assume, accompanied by a supercilious haughtiness that was to land me in a world of hurt more than once during my stay. Some men are stripped of their pride when confronted by the necessity of enduring situations half as deplorable as those I encountered in McAlester. I was not one of them. Being the only innocent man in a prison full of unrepentant convicts doesn't make the beatings any less severe, the labor any less grueling, the food any less disgusting, or the confinement any less excruciating; however, it does posit you as the victim, rather than a man unwilling to accept the punishment he is owed in return for his wicked deeds, and once you can lie convincingly to yourself, it matters far less if you actually succeed in persuading anyone else.

To a youth unaccustomed to even so much as the concept of restraint, life in prison was quite an adjustment, to say the least. In the years following its establishment, the Oklahoma State Penitentiary was considered a marvel of its time. And as if to prove a most vulgar point, its treatment of prisoners was of utmost severity—unfortunately for those of us who were inmates there. Unlike the Tulsa County Jail, where I remained confined to my cell, in McAlester, our cells were unlocked shortly after daybreak, and we were not returned to them until late at night. I believe if the governance of that prison could hang its hat on any one policy, it would be work details. They had a detail for everything: laundry, KP, farming, woodworking, tobacco-stripping, delivery truck offloading, livestock-tending, floor-scrubbing, rock-breaking, mattress-making—hell, if the warden needed to take a particularly heavy shit, I wouldn't have been surprised if at least a couple fortuneless men were assigned to accompany him. Warden Schaffer's philosophy—as he told it to the papers—was that hard work made for more efficient rehabilitation. However, considering a hefty percentage of the inmates there were serving life sentences, his efforts appeared ludicrous and futile.

Of all the prisons I've spent time in, McAlester was, by far, the most stringent. From what I'd heard through the bars of the Tulsa County Jail, McAlester was no playpen, and from the first, it was very obvious to me that what I'd heard was gospel. It was a stately and imposing building with a façade that offered no suggestion as to the conditions within its walls. It loomed over the valley, dark and ominous, and fanned the flames of fear that licked at the soul of any doomed man destined for the mercy of its horrors. The place occupied approximately the same landmass as a proper town and annexed all the surrounding farmland for as far as the eye could see—which, from inside, was not very far at all. The penitentiary was surrounded by big gray stone walls so high and insurmountable they might as well have risen halfway to heaven. Nothing makes a man feel smaller than reducing the size of his world, and when the walls of McAlester swallowed you up, you felt just about as insignificant and powerless as an ant under the lens of a magnifying glass held by a child in the noonday sun.

If the very thought of prison doesn't cause you to tremble, then you don't know the first thing about prison. If you failed to salute an officer before speaking at McAlester, you'd spend your next twenty-four hours in solitary confinement. If you stepped out of line when being led through the rotunda, you'd be shot by any one of several aerial guards that patrolled the gun walk. And god forbid you got the notion to escape stuck in your craw—even if you made it past the dozen guard towers and managed to scale the twenty-foot wall, you'd be french-fried by the 400-volt electrified fence that encircled it long before you ever saw freedom again.

According to some older inmates, the all-white east cell house at McAlester had been built to house approximately 650 men. By the time I arrived fifteen years later, something like 850 would be a conservative estimate of how many men were actually confined there. Each cell in the east cellblock was no wider than I am tall and occupied by a minimum of two men. The floor and walls were solid steel, frigid cold in the winter and searing hot in the summer. Windows were limited to the corridors alone, and if you were unfortunate enough to have one directly outside your cell, as I was, just standing at the door in August was enough to burn your feet right through the soles of your shoes. Considering how overcrowded it was at the time of my incarceration, with the new cell house not yet completed, trusties were allowed to sleep in the hall. However, with the guards having to step over men all night long as they prowled the corridor with their felt-soled shoes in search of disciplinary offenders, most times, three men were confined to a cell, despite the fact that there were only two bunks, one atop the other. As the last man in and the youngest of the three, I was made to sleep on the floor most nights, except during the summer when the cool steel served as the only respite from the sweltering heat.

We were permitted only what the warden provided and nothing more. The only contents of each cell that a man could rightly call his own were the mattress, pillow, sheet, and towel that were given him. We were allowed but one jumpsuit, one pair of shoes, a pair of long underwear, and a coat in the winter months. Contact with the outside world was, by and large, forbidden. Letters could be written once every three weeks, but though they left our hands sealed, they were undoubtedly reopened and censored before they were mailed. Having no one to visit me and no one to write, these policies affected me far less than the other men, who'd been separated from their wives and families. That being said, the sheer monotony and boredom that prison offered me ate away at my soul like a cancer. The only non-prison-issue items we were allowed came from the commissary, and to obtain them, you needed money in your account in the warden's office. Since I came into McAlester penniless, despite occasional generosity on the part of my cellmates, I was in want of most everything. Contraband of any sort was a bygone fantasy, and even the trusties couldn't be bribed. Not even the guise of freedom was allowed.

The only reprieve we were given was on Sundays when the prison chaplain held a compulsory mid-morning service in the dining hall. For me, the service itself was not much of a joyful circumstance, considering I had more dirt under my fingernails than I did religion about me. However, following the minister's final blessing, we were released into the courtyard for a few hours, where we were permitted to indulge ourselves in card and crap games to our hearts' content. Immediately, the scourge of prison despair lifted, and laughter was heard—an utterly foreign sound in such a setting. Decks of cards and dice were produced from the pockets where they were stowed away during the week, cigarettes and matches were divided up amongst those assembled to use as bets, and the prior week's debts were called up out of the recesses of the convicts' minds.

No man anywhere in this world has a better memory for any subject than a man in prison. The mind of a convict is perpetually full of numbers—equations, problems that need thrashing out, and solutions that need ascertaining. A convict, especially one in my position, need not concern himself with the affairs of the outside world. For him, prison is his world, the whole of his universe, and above all, his home. With nothing of circumstance to distract him, his mind becomes endlessly more receptive to any information given it. I've been quoted more dates by twenty-year men than I've ever been by a historian and heard recalled by lifers strings of statistics and figures that would even evade the ken of a mathematician. To survive in such a hostile environment, a man has no choice but to abandon his concern for the fields and streams of home. They, to him, are nothing but a dream and just about as useful. As a result, his senses become heightened, finely tuned to the patterns of his surroundings. Any inconsistencies are immediately noted, analyzed, and determined if they are a cause for concern. His wit becomes invigorated, and his mind tenacious.

Due to my financial hardship, my only hope of procuring some small articles to provide me comfort and refuge was by winning them on Sunday afternoons. Now, I've been a gambler for over forty years, and I tell you verily that I had a tougher time separating hardened criminals from their cigarettes and talcum powder than I ever had with the high rollers in the Nevada casinos later in life. Although, that may be partially due to the fact that most of the underhanded tricks I employed on the bettors I learned in prison. I arrived there already boasting an impressive repertoire of knavery, but the level of skill I displayed by the time of my exodus far outstripped any petty confidence tricks and wobbly sleight of hand that I'd relied upon up until that point to keep me fed. Now, not only did I know how to steal plays in poker and stack the deck in high-low-jack, I'd been given an introduction to every kind of backroom swindling that man had concocted in his devilish mind over the last few centuries. No longer did the beguiling mystique of faro or craps elude my cunning eye, and I'd been outfitted with every device similarly invented to separate a man from his dollar. I'd been instructed in the art of past posting and perfected the method of making loaded dice, a technique famed in both song and story.

Of course, there were other ways of making money in prison—some even legitimate. One of Warden Schaffer's most notable experiments during his time at McAlester—or at least the one that got him the most press—was the concept of rewarding particularly hardworking inmates with a chance to accumulate money on their own merit. If an inmate completed his daily duties, he could choose to undertake a secondary task for which he would be monetarily compensated. Of course, he wouldn't see a cent of it until it was time to go out into the world again, but he could use it for canteen items or send it off to his dependents, if he had any. Of course, one may presume that if I was in want of money, my appropriate course of action was obvious. However, I'd never gotten up a hard day's work outside of prison, and I'll be damned if I had any intention of doing so while I was in prison. I figured I wasn't getting out anyway—so what did I have to gain? The work details were implemented primarily to forge skilled and disciplined citizens out of felons. I'd never be awarded the chance to prove myself as a good citizen, as a productive member of society; rather, I'd be a taxpayers' burden until I grew old and died—and hell be bound if I was going to do so with a shovel in my hands.

That being said, my supreme lack of motivation was not much appreciated by the guards. They started me off in the broom factory, and though working conditions were, by and large, better than I would've expected from a prison factory, I'd had more than my fill of broom-making by the time my first eight hours were up. I lasted an additional few months at that tedious chore until I decided enough was enough and chose to relieve myself of any further responsibility in that camp. Breaks, other than when sanctioned, were not permitted, nor was smoking while working. So, it was understandable that when I leaned back on my stool with my feet propped on the binding machine and lit up a smoke, I was shortly thereafter descended upon by several guards, all of them madder than hell. For that infraction, I spent three days in the hole. I don't suppose the fact that when I flicked my ashes, a whole pile of unfinished brooms caught on fire did anything to help my case, either.

The second job they assigned me to was shirt-making. About fifty sewing machines were laid out across two dozen workbenches in the upper room of the overall factory building, and no less than two hundred men applied themselves to the trade. Having been raised in the manner I was, I had no use for so-called 'women's work', and little to no skill therein. I protested my reassignment immediately and repeatedly but to no avail. I lost nearly all my privileges in the two months I worked at that commission, and by the time I decided to put up a strike against it, the guards had had more than their fill of my insubordination and nailed me with another three days in the cursed hole. When I was released and led back to my cell, I found the gray denim uniform I'd first been issued changed for a striped jumpsuit—the raiment of captured escapees and inveterate disciplinary offenders—and this was all before my first six months were up.

By the start of 1927, I'd been reassigned once more to the brickmaking gang, that arduous and meritless duty reserved for those inmates deemed troublesome. There was a whole host of reasons why this particular assignment was the worst of all the details at McAlester. First and foremost, it was the most heavily guarded detail at the prison. By itself, that instance would have been bad enough, but it was made worse by the fact that the brickmaking plant was located about a mile from the prison proper. Each and every day, we were marched out to the wagons in our fetters and chains and proceeded to be shown the vast hopelessness of our situation. For those intimately familiar with the inside of McAlester, being shown the outside was arguably even worse. Even if one could avoid the spotlights and the shower of machine gun fire and scale the walls without being shredded to ribbons or electrocuted, he'd still be doomed. It was nearly impossible to escape past the two-thousand adjacent acres of farm, fields, and cemetery belonging to the prison. The guards were keenly aware of this, and they made right sure that each new morning we were duly reminded of our desperation—and that was all before the work began.

Work at the brick factory was grueling, dirty, and bitterly cold in winter. At the urging of my cohorts, for the first time in my life, I decided it was in my best interest to keep my head down and the work flowing. As it was explained to me in so many words, if you fucked up on the brickwork detail, there wasn't much further down you could go. The last poor bastard who shirked his duties in the brickyard—sometime last spring—was purportedly still in the infirmary. The brick factory was, in every aspect, the end of the line for both inmates and prison personnel. The guards assigned to that post were dispensed there after the number of complaints filed against them on the grounds of cruelty and barbarism exceeded the number deemed suitable for officers of the law—which was another reason the brickyard had been built so far away from the prying eyes of inspectors, board members, and the visiting public.

I had even less of a desire to bunk with Gary Thorpe again than I had to work, so work I did—until my hands were stained the color of red clay and my skin was so cracked and dry that I couldn't even make a fist to strike out against my oppressors. If I had, every crease in my hand would have split wide open, and streams of fresh, red, angry blood would've spilled out into the dust. The nature and pace of the work were so punishing that before my first week was up, I found myself mired in jealousy over my cellmates—one of whom pulled perpetual KP, the other relegated to the Oklahoma license plate factory—the cushiest job in the whole prison.

My cellmates were a colorful bunch, and though we got on passably, their presence never did all that much for my spirits. Both of them, like me, were in for life. At about 35 years old, the eldest, Tennessee Jed, was the more remarkable of the two, and by remarkable, I mean strange. He was about 6'0" and less than 170 lbs. He was as skinny as a beanpole and the possessor of a pair of shoulders so narrow that if they were any closer together, they'd be single file. In fact, the only fat present on his body was confined to his head. He was smarter than Bertha, albeit marginally, and about as dull as the day is long. His face was as long as a stallion's, his nose as spindly and sharp as the point of a knife. His ears stuck out so far from his head that when we were out in the yard and a stiff wind came tearing through, two men had to take hold of his arms in fear that he'd be swept up in the midst of it and get tangled in the electric fence atop the gray stone walls. I reckon that if they ever left us out in the yard when there was a tornado brewing, all Tennessee would've had to do was take off his cap, and he'd be halfway to Memphis before the alarm bells even rang.

Tennessee arrived at the prison already toting his moniker; however, he had no doubt earned it due to his incessant yearning for home. According to his life story, which I was spared no detail of within twenty minutes of being assigned to his cell, his main regret was not the murder of his swanky but demeaning employer, nor was it his failed attempt at shirking the law, which inevitably resulted in the injury to his back that left him destined to peel potatoes in the prison kitchen for the rest of his sorry existence—rather, it was simply his decision to leave home.

"A'ways been poor, a'ways," Tennessee explained to me that first night, "Reck'on that ain't suprisin' as there was fifteen of us. Pa row corn, taught us how, but rowin' corn ain't gon' feed no fifteen grown chill'n. I left Memphis at seventeen, an' that's tha worst decision I e'r made, been sorry fo' it all ma life. Ain't no place in the world like Tennessee, least ain't none that I seen—and I been all the way to Tishomingo. Tishomingo, Tishomingo... that's where it all happened, in blamed Tishomingo...."

Over the course of Tennessee's wandering tale of woe, I learned how he had ultimately landed himself in McAlester. Due to the peculiarity of his accent and the fact that he was missing most of his teeth, several portions of his recitation were largely unintelligible. However, Tennessee was as stalwart to his story as the tail is to the back of a cat. Whatever details had escaped me the first time he told it undoubtedly became clear during the three years that followed. Tennessee never tried to pass himself off as an innocent man, but he made it his life's purpose that everyone within earshot of him was as well versed in his sorrows as he was. I will not presume that with age, most men lose their longing for their childhood home as I did, but there are many in this country that can count themselves along with me. Tennessee was, absolutely and irrevocably, not one of them.

According to his story, when he first left the cornfields of home just past the south bend of the Mississippi river right outside of Memphis, he moved to the city and procured a job as a sommelier at a theatre called the Minglewood. According to the prevailing word of mouth amongst his workmates, the best jobs were the ones proffered by the big bankers and oilmen in Oklahoma, where all of Memphis seemed to be relocating to.

Oklahoma's first oil boom hit in 1901 when the Red Fork gusher blew her top just south of Tulsa. The intervening years between then and 1907, when Tennessee arrived to swell the ranks of that new state's burgeoning population, consisted of an economic bonanza. As in Tulsa, those magnates into whose pockets the money flowed came last to Tishomingo and dominated huge swatches of previously undeveloped land with their private mansions, swimming pools, and tennis courts. It was in one of these aforementioned residences where Tennessee sought—and found—work as a butler in the employ of one Mr. Charlie Phogg.

According to Tennessee, Charlie Phogg was what they call 'a real bad man'. After the grievous injuries Tennessee had suffered on his account, I would've imagined he'd use some stronger adjectives, but as Tennessee was the epitome of humble Arcadian heritage, even after all Phogg had subjected him to, Charlie Phogg remained in his mind as simply, 'a real bad man.' Apparently, these were the same words Tennessee used to describe him as he stood trial for his murder.

'A real bad man' in Tennessee's world was characterized by the following affronts, described to me at length upon my arrival and innumerable times thereafter. For one, Phogg was incessantly cruel in every way a man could embody the term. He was also nouveau riche and compelled by an endless supply of pomposity as he sought to cement his position in his newly adopted class. As an unsurprising result, Tennessee and the other servants with whom he worked were subject to no lack of degradation.

For a man as tolerant and mannerly as Tennessee, these conditions did not sodden his resolve; however, the nearly constant abuse and twice-or-thrice-weekly beatings he endured as a result of his incompetence did wear away at it in time. All men have a breaking point, even those as dull and acquiescent as Tennessee Jed. Harried as he was, after about six months of meritless toil and wanton brutality, Tennessee decided that he'd had enough, and in a fit of rage, he beat Mr. Phogg senseless with the chain formerly reserved for use on himself. At the conclusion of this episode, when Tennessee saw the gory result of his actions, he fled the mansion to avoid persecution. As per his stunted intelligence, he determined a boarding house half a mile into town would be able to provide him with adequate protection. As is easily foreseeable, this was sadly not the case.

When the maid discovered Phogg bruised, bloodied, and ruptured on the floor of his chamber and found Tennessee was gone, she sent for the police, who sure enough came rushing into the boarding house no more than two hours later. Sentient enough to realize that the stampede of angry footsteps up the stairs foretold the arrival of something other than his neighbor in the adjoining room, Tennessee lit out down the rear stairwell as fast as he could. As a result of nothing other than utter misfortune, this proved to be a fatal mistake. For as far as he could tell, he tripped over his own size fourteen shoes and went tumbling head-over-heels down four flights of metal stairs. He was apprehended shortly upon landing.

As it turns out, Tennessee did a worse number on himself than he did on his employer and spent the next two months in the hospital with a broken back, incongruously chained to the bed by his wrists to prevent his escape. Once he was well enough to stand trial, he was ungraciously received by a jury of Phogg's peers, each affiliated with one or another of his financial or political interests. After a malicious public defamation by Phogg, who had fully recovered from his injuries, the judge severely reprimanded Tennessee and sentenced him to one year in county jail.

As urged by letters from family and friends, Tennessee steadfastly resolved to return to Memphis on the day of his release. But alas, as it seems to be with men of incorrigible bad luck, on his way to the train, he encountered none other than his former employer, Charlie Phogg. It was readily apparent that the malice Phogg bore him had not lessened during that intervening year. As Tennessee told it, Phogg marched right up to him on the street, cracked him in the head with his walking stick, doubled him up with a Dutch winder to the eye, and kicked his feet right out from under him before brushing off his coat and strolling into the nearest tavern, leaving Tennessee gasping and winded on the Tishomingo sidewalk.

Most men would have followed Phogg with the intention of laying on him the beating he so richly deserved. However, as Tennessee could not retaliate following his injury, after he crawled away into an adjacent saloon and imbibed half a dozen drinks as consolation, he made up his mind to shoot him. A gun was easy to come by at the price of fifteen dollars, and henceforth, crippled though he was, Tennessee made quick work of Mr. Phogg. Those in attendance said he likely killed him with the first shot, but that didn't stop Tennessee from plugging him five more times before he hit the ground. Allegedly, the cops arrived before the gun smoke even cleared. The rest was history. Tennessee concluded his lament with a pitiful sob and spoke wistfully of the fine life he'd left, the poor family he'd shamed, and the beautiful state he'd never see again. Even now, some forty-odd years later, I can still hear his doleful voice ringing in my ears.

That was Tennessee Jed—then there was Dupree. Randolph Dupree was his name. He was a short, scrappy, beady-eyed fellow. Everything about him was dark; his countenance as well as his soul. He was swarthy, sported nappy hair, and had eyes so dark and shifty you had to stand within inches of him to see that he had pupils. The most striking detail of his appearance was that the vast majority of his face was covered by hair. Most men shave in prison; it is cathartic, ritualistic, familiar, and real. Few activities in prison resemble those one remembers from their former life, and the most basic human habits transform grotesquely upon incarceration. Shaving was one of the few rites that maintained its dignity, and the only men who went wooly-faced in prison had already resigned themselves to their fate.

Dupree had only been in prison two years, yet already he was fast becoming an incorrigible jailbird. He looked after his own hide, polished his own opportunities, and severely lacked almost every form of basic human decency—although I believe this was an accident of birth rather than a consequence of institutionalization. He'd rave with the chuck horrors one minute and bend over backward to appease the guards the next. He regarded his privileges as the breath of life—as most hardened convicts do— and I am certain that he would have much preferred gruesome death over losing them.

To be quite frank, despite his prodigious character flaws, as a cellmate, he was far less objectionable than Tennessee—mainly because he kept to himself and rarely spoke unless spoken to. Dupree had a list of grievances a mile long; however, he made mention of them once, only once, and spent the rest of his time gritting his teeth and waiting for chow—or a fight, whichever came first.

Dupree was chronic. He was hardly older than I was and oozed larceny and bad will from every cloying pore. Upon meeting him, you'd be inclined to believe he was born a felon. I was wary of shaking his hand the first time, unsure I'd still have all five fingers when I got it back. Unlike Tennessee, he'd arrived at McAlester unsolicited; every poor choice and rotten turn that'd led him there had been of his own making. He was born to a fine family in Nashville—his father was a doctor, and his mother a former debutante. Dupree had never been in want of a nickel, yet every aspect of his character yielded to crime. If he could've stolen the whitewash off the walls of our cell in order to make a buck, he would've without hesitation. The yarn he spun me is as follows, and I am inclined to believe every word of it, for as criminal as his tendencies were, he was positively incapable of lying.

Dupree told the tale of his road to McAlester unashamed and unrepentant to the last. I've never been a man to assume very much moral clarity, but Dupree was a member of that breed of men to whom the voice of reason never calls. He had been a killer from his earliest years. Small animals numbered amongst his first victims, and they were quickly followed by more significant and praise-worthy game. I'd bet every last dollar that ever passed through my hands that his bedroom was adorned by the heads and skins of animals he had relieved of life with utmost enjoyment. In those bygone days of gunslingers and pistoleros, he would have been hailed as a legend. Steel-nerved to the last, he could fell a man and walk away without a second thought—and he did just that. It was the murder of an Oklahoma City jeweler he stood trial for, and a unanimous jury had declared his punishment to be life—for death was too sweet and too swift a reward for such a soulless man.

If Dupree had killed another human person before the ill-fated jeweler, he was not caught; however, I doubt that he had. For, as Dupree surpassed his adolescent years, his lecherous mind hinged on another formerly unknown desire: women. Dupree was one of a peculiar class of men who have all but sold out to the undying and unwavering wants of women. If the man had been born queer, he would've never been sentenced to life in prison; alas, his love of women, however warped, compelled him from the first.

I will not go so far as to say that it would've been impossible for Dupree to win the affection of a woman without lavishing her with wealth and treasures, but I imagine that it would have been considerably harder for him to know the joys of the fairer sex if he had to rely on his looks and personality alone, and I have reason enough to believe that he never tried. Privy to the family trust since boyhood, Dupree never had a reason to seek work or practice money-consciousness, and it was not until he had spent more than his share that his father cut him off. Of course, as logic rarely dictates in any young man's mind, rather than find employment in some seedy den of inequity consistent with his slimy disposition, in order to continue to meet the demands of his beloved Viola Lee, he turned to thievery.

What began as petty shoplifting soon developed into a string of department store robberies that resulted in Dupree walking out with a mink stole and floor-length rabbit coat, amongst other spoils. This seemed to placate the insatiable Viola Lee for a short while, but before long, Dupree was out on the route to riches again. Night prowling and bank robbery took the place of retail theft. However, as these endeavors required considerably more cunning and tact, several close calls quickly proved that burglary was not the right racket for Dupree, who was about as subtle as a howitzer. From there, he served a short term as a counterfeiter, after which he moved on to terrorizing jewelry stores—the crime that would pin Dupree's freedom to the fence for the rest of his life.

Apparently, he'd walked into a Diamond Palace in downtown Oklahoma City just before closing time and, with his pistol in hand, demanded the clerk fork over the largest diamond he had. When the clerk hesitated, Dupree blew his head off—with pleasure, I am sure. Unfortunately for the unknowing Dupree, the clerk's last act had done him dirty. While Dupree was stuffing his pockets with the contents of the jewelry counter, that silent alarm blared through every precinct in the city. He never even made it out of the block with his loot.

The judge who presided over his trial was so appalled by the remorseless nature of the defendant that in addition to all the crimes Dupree did commit, he hung on him every lingering cold-case burglary in Oklahoma County. This left Dupree with a sentence of one hundred and thirty years, in addition to two life sentences—one for armed robbery and one for murder. As Dupree told it, his darling Viola Lee had wrung her hands before the judge and begged for mercy on her suitor's behalf. Still, it had done Dupree no good at all, and two months after he was shipped off to McAlester, the news reached him that his sweet little Viola Lee had married the very same judge. Invoking his family influence, Dupree had written letters, appeals, and petitions and mailed them off to every office in the country, but it was to no avail. Dupree was doomed like the rest of us and doomed to stay.

The former is a tale that has been told in every rank dungeon, stonewalled prison, and skookum house in human history, and I do believe that if it weren't for women, the men of this world wouldn't need prisons at all. The stories of Tennessee Jed and Randolph Dupree stand out not because of their singularity but simply due to our frequency of interaction throughout all those long years of forced proximity. There were other men about the prison with whom I became well acquainted, especially those I gambled and worked with, but their stories are too numerous to recount, and their names long since receded into the annals of my mind. There ain't a freight ride long enough for me to tell you all that happened there, and likewise, with all the years that have passed now, I suppose I'd even have a hard time remembering.

II

Confinement works on a man in strange ways. I've already attempted to describe, in part, the toll prison takes on a man's senses, on his habits, and on his mind. However, there are other casualties of incarceration—far too many to mention—that befall a man's perception. Generally speaking, all those who rightly deserve to be confined to a sanitarium must have previously served some enduring stretch behind bars. When imprisoned, even the sanest man alive is susceptible to awakening one morning and finding his mind neatly divided into its component parts. No man is spared the prison horrors, not even the short-timers, and every man who emerges from prison does so permanently changed in some fundamental capacity. His history hangs on him like a brand and influences every aspect of his free life forevermore. And, if he is never again permitted to experience the outside world, he lives the rest of his life psychologically deranged in one way or another.

Men subjected to bodily torment and mental stagnation have a marked tendency to develop attachments to the most mundane and unusual forms of deliverance. Some men take up reading and become experts in bizarre fields or master foreign languages they'll never have the opportunity to speak. Some men collect rocks; others, newspaper clippings. Still, others occupy themselves with rehashing their ill fortune, like Tennessee, or grind their fingertips to the bone writing requests for pardons like Dupree. Despite the variety of manifestations, all of these methods achieve the same result—they all take up time, the common enemy of every prisoner. I learned early on that the surest way to stay sane in prison was to go crazy. To allow yourself to be utterly consumed by some extraneous endeavor of little or no use to you on the inside was the only way to keep the walls from closing in and the despair from alighting upon you. In almost all cases, a distracted mind is a sane mind, as an idle mind is far more subject to cracking up.

However, I did not read books on organic chemistry or write letters to my congressman, nor did I spend my yard time examining pieces of shale or recounting every detail of my misfortune. Instead, I listened to the train. The northern spur of the Katy railroad that connects Kansas City to Fort Worth runs straight through the town of McAlester, and though I never saw the train itself, I could hear its whistle in every corner of the prison. Before very long, I had compiled a complete mental schedule of those freighters. Not only that, following several well-directed inquiries, I knew where each train was bound, from whence it had come, and when it was due. By the time my first six months were up, I could tell time by rail; and whether I was working down at the brick plant, in my cell at night, or confined to solitary, when I heard that whistle, I knew exactly the time of day.

I'm not sure what the sound of that whistle did for the other men or if many of them even paid any attention to it at all, but for me, it marked the difference between self-possession and attempting to crawl out of McAlester through the drainpipe in the sink—especially at night. The first night you spend in prison is irrefutably the hardest, but all the nights that follow aren't exactly duck soup either. Night in prison is endless, indefinite, and, to be perfectly honest, terrifying. Every man develops his own method of fending off its harm. Some men count the seconds until morning—or until they become comatose—others tarry away at escape plans or play the harmonica. I tried every one of these approaches and several others, but none of them worked. I did take up playing the harmonica shortly after my arrival but quit before very long—the sound of it never failed to make me shiver. For all the delight it brings men on the outside, the sound of the harmonica in prison is drab and lonely—as if the walls themselves are crying. On the other hand, the whistle of that train gave me solace; it was safe, predictable, and above all, familiar. Rather than allowing my mind to marinate in fear of the future and despair in the present, the sound of that freighter rolling by brought back more memories than I could ever begin to count.

One thing prison is designed to do that it actually succeeds at is making men think. The contents of those thoughts may not always be the consequences of one's actions, as the legislators who spend their lives screaming 'reform' suppose, but an imprisoned man certainly does spend a great deal of his time thinking. I can say with absolute certainty that I thought more during those three years in prison than I did for the rest of my life. When you've got all those hours and nothing to do, nowhere to go, and seldom to ponder other than your own rotten luck, you get to thinking, and thinking hard. To remember is to journey, journey back down the roads that you took to get where you are now, and when I'd stretch out my stiff back upon the lumpy mattress that laid across that cold iron floor and ease my head on down, I'd think back, way back...

Most often, I found that my mind brought me back to memories of my childhood: of my Ma and Pa and brothers...of our two-story clapboard house peppered with BBs and .22s...the still out back where my Pa was born and died...the old bay horse, Buck, that all eight of us rode, double-rode, and triple-rode...of the gully where I spent the better part of my earliest years and the train tracks that I played on and around during just about every other waking moment in between. In those days, at only twenty years old, there wasn't much more than this to remember, but now it feels like half a dozen lifetimes ago...

I did most of my growing up just outside of Five Points, Colorado. That's a neighborhood in Denver, just past the depot and close to the Negro district. I attended the schoolhouse in Five Points—or at least I was supposed to—and as a youngin', most of my friends were colored. I never could tell much difference between me and my Negro friends other than on account of our color. We walked the same, talked the same, threw the same, sat the same, ate the same, and shot the same—and after all day playing out in the hot sun and dust and down in the muddy river bed, there was no telling us apart at all. My Ma and Pa were what you'd call indifferent, but most of the other white folks in town would tell us boys not to play anymore with the 'picaninnies' and to mind our place. I went right on playing with them anyway. I never was any too good at minding what other folks told me to mind, and I figured if I was going to treat another man like he was a low-down rotten scoundrel, I at least had to know the reason why before I did. After all, there aren't many men in this world who're more of a low-down rotten scoundrel than me.

Maybe if I'd been born someplace else, I'd've struck out upon a different course in my life. After all, if I'd pursued any measure of legitimate business with the vigor I've pursued the illegitimate, I may have rounded out my life as a very wealthy man. However, no fully sane person who can rightly say they've got their wits about them ever moved out to Denver, at least in the early days. Denver was, from the first, a hopeless town full of dirty, desperate, despicable people killing themselves to make a living. Both my grandfathers came for the gold and kept up their digging, shoveling, sifting, panning, and praying until one day, they fell down dead face first in the dirt with as much gold to their name as the day they set foot in the territory.

By the time I was born in 1905, the thrill of King Oil and its breath of change had yet to reach us. In the mountains, the fruits of the earth still reigned supreme, miners were still considered the coming race, and in many ways, we regarded ourselves as one of the last bastions of the old world. Denver was one of the few places known to our great nation in which a man could be both a somebody and a nobody within the same postal code, carry a gun and gamble, drink freely and openly, and, more oft than not, live to tell about it in the morning. It was the locale where the silver standard heaved its final dying breath and the swan song of the Wild West was played upon Victrolas. It was the sanctuary of the fugitive, the backyard of the traveling yegg, and the confidence man's seventh heaven.

Apart from drinking, betting was the chief form of entertainment in Denver. The vast majority of the natives were well-versed in all the gamblers' tricks and the bunko men's cons, but the visitors, newcomers, and greenhorns were as big a bunch of suckers that ever struck out toward shore, and the natives could hardly resist having a bit of fun with them. Unless he was a fast learner, those who arrived in our humble town uninitiated in the schemes of our land generally found themselves plucked as bare as a prairie chicken in a pot. Just about every man in Denver was a sometime gambler and lost just as much as he won when he answered the call of the fickle goddess of fortune.

My Pa, through some stroke of brilliance, dumb luck, or opportunity, became a logger instead. He spent six months out of every twelve up in the mountains, and in his time with us, he took to moonshining. For him, it was more of a habit and a hobby than a source of income, but he brewed a batch of rotgut so fine that everyone who tasted it wanted a jar for themselves. He sold it to the neighbors, their neighbors, the town doctor, the constable, and anyone else who was passing through and wanted a taste of something that could really 'cut the dust' as they say.

Pa was a quiet man, not quite shy and certainly not dull—not quite observative, but certainly not disinterested. He had sandy hair the same color as the clay along the embankment. He wore it longer than was customary at the time and kept it hidden under a black Stetson hat that he rarely removed—in all the years we lived together, I can count on my fingers the number of times I saw his scalp. He looked out at the world through a pair of narrow blue eyes that were perpetually thoughtful and framed by deep furrows and laugh lines that made him look quite a few years older than he was. His mouth was encircled by a ducktail beard, and his lips were nearly always clamped around the stem of his pipe or the rim of a Ball jar. Mostly, I remember him out back by the still in the grove of hydrangeas just before the gully, checking his barrels of mash and waiting for the old keg to start thumping. Out of all my brothers, I'm the only one who shares a name with him—John Sampson Jones. I suppose after having seven sons, he and my Ma ran out of original names—but besides my prodigious drinking habits, that's where the similarities between us end.

He was the breadwinner and kept us grubstaked and well-off but otherwise kept mainly to himself. He spent half the year felling timber up in the Arapaho Forest and the other half drowning his aching back and boredom in quart jars of gin. He didn't speak often, and when he did, you considered yourself both lucky and forewarned. For a man who spent a good part of his life with an axe in his hand, he was awfully gentle. He owned just one pistol and always told us boys, "A shot fired in anger is a waste of a bullet." Now, don't get the wrong idea; my father was by no means a particularly religious man, nor was he the preaching type, but many folks have told me over the years that he was wise. To this day, I can't see where they came to figure that. If a life spent in tedious labor by day and gin stupor by the lesser light makes the words of a drunkard wise, then no less than a prophet am I.

In the winter months, our home was full of dedicated imbibers. Many were retired locals who, tired of the same old crowd in the saloon day after day, sought out my old man. Others were fellow loggers who spent the off months visiting their friends and family. Even though ten of us lived in our three-bedroom house ordinarily, Ma always found a place to put everybody, no matter the time of year or how many of them showed up at once. Ma could turn out work faster and more efficiently than any woman alive and did so without a single complaint. There was a constant stream of pies that ran from the oven to the windowsill to the growling stomachs of any number of insatiable small boys at all times. She could mend, wash, cook, serve, and clean simultaneously—each chore completed to perfection—and still have one eye reserved for looking after her brood.

Ma's eyes were a rich, dark brown—as brown as the loam that covered every inch of farm country in the springtime when the farmers turned over their fields for the first time each season. They were always kind, always understanding, and never harsh. They danced and smiled and were good-humored to the last. Her face was fine and fair and radiated beauty and warmth. Her hair was coal black and soft enough to wipe away any child's tears.

Never in all my years have I met a woman more adept at corralling the band of rascals in her charge than my mother. Of course, having been to the rodeo seven times before, by the time I was up to the gate, my mother thought she had a bead on all the devilry that spawns inside a small boy's mind. I wasn't more than knee-high to a grasshopper when she realized she'd thought wrong.

Being the littlest of eight rough-necking brothers, I got all their hand-me-downs. Every shirt, pant, and darned sock I owned had been patched and mended so many times they should've been made into rags three brothers ago. Being the littlest, Ma got to feeling sorry for me always having to wear my brothers' old worn-out clothes and would go on over to Woolworth's and buy me a new pair of britches or a new shirt. I'd strut around proudly for the next week until all my rough and tumbling caught up with me, and then there'd be no telling the difference between my new clothes and my brothers' old ones.

Getting new clothes ahead of my brothers wasn't the only perk of being the youngest. My Ma seemed to have a soft spot for me, and although I deserved it more often than not, she never raised a hand to the back of my head or a belt strap to my rear. To Ma, it didn't matter how ragged I ran her, for I was her littlest boy, and she was determined to raise me up right, altogether better than the others. However, by the time I was four years on this earth, my Ma probably up and wished she could rightfully call me her bastard child about a hundred times.

From the day I was born, it just wasn't in the cards. I remember being an ornery little scamp and hearing the folks in town talk in hushed down voices about how my father's seed had soured over time, although none could be too certain if the dip in quality had been due to age or all that rotgut he poured down his gullet in the offseason. Granted, not everyone in town was convinced that my father was to blame. The dairyman, blonde-haired and blue-eyed like yours truly, had acquired quite a penchant for Mrs. Delilah Jones during the logging season past. He even made two daily trips to the Jones homestead to ensure all seven little ones had all the milk they needed. I was born the following spring, shortly after Pa returned to the mountains—two whole months ahead of the rest of my brothers. Despite my mother's ardent protestations, it took several years before my father was fully convinced that I belonged to him—and by then, I rightly think he would've been relieved to pass off all responsibility for me onto the milkman.

Considering the vast wildness of the country where we lived and the unruly nature of its inhabitants, it is quite remarkable that I am the only one of my brothers who turned out as an incorrigible ne'er-do-well. Believe it or not, all seven of them turned out to be fine, upstanding men, as humble-hearted and mild-mannered as they come, despite their childhood scrapes.

My two eldest brothers, Jerry and Ronny, were twins. Though alike in birth and countenance, they were different in nearly every other way. Jerry was the firstborn of the two and the pride of the family. He was bighearted, hardworking, nurturing, and selfless to the last. When it came to hereditary scruples that my folks passed down to us boys, Jerry got nearly all of them and left Ronny holding the bag. If there was a compliment to be had, no matter the source, it always seemed to find its' way to Jerry—and he was never a sight short in making himself available to receive it. Whenever there was a chore to be done, Jerry was first in line, and he didn't discriminate—whether he was hanging out the wash as a favor to Ma or splitting cordwood for Pa, he never complained. He was the sort of kid who would hang around the grocer's all day, not to chew gum and gossip like the other youngsters, but so that he could carry baskets for elderly shoppers—and for no other reason than the satisfaction of having done a good deed.

Jerry was the talk of the town and the pride of Five Points from the day he was born. He had Ma's heart and Pa's brawn. He was a proud, chesty marvel who strutted through his world full of strength and conviction and yet maintained that if he needed to hoist it all upon his back, he could still stand. Atlas himself would have had a friend in Jerry. There was never much that all of us boys could agree upon together, but it is no surprise that it was unanimous amongst all seven of us that Jerry was our favorite. He could concoct games that made him the preferred playmate of every child in Five Points and conducted himself with such modesty and graciousness it made him the envy of every mother. As a babysitter, he was the tops, and with Pa in the mountains six months out of the year, he taught us just about everything we knew about being boys in a man's world. That is, all except one thing—and that's fishing.

With the South Platte River right in our backyard and the railroad tracks just beyond it, as boys, one of our favorite recreations was laying on the bank with a fish pole, waiting for the train to come in and the trout to bite. I remember countless occasions in which Ma, fed up with our pestering and horseplay, chastened us to the river with the stipulation that we were not allowed back in her sight without first producing a fish that she could fry up for supper. Although, considering the richness and abundance of the South Platte in those days, such a task could keep a small boy busy for no more than an hour—no matter how poor a fisherman he may've been. Often, we found ourselves running back to the house with a whole line of fish strung over our shoulders before Ma even had a chance to clean up the ruins of our last debauch.

However, one thing was a near certainty. No matter what time of day you went down to the bank of the South Platte, in rain or shine, spring or fall, during school hours or after, you could find Ronny there. While Jerry was out practicing chivalry, Ronny was cloistered on the bank, inventing new and improved ways of romancing trout. He could tie flies so enticing that when the fish saw him coming down the gully, they'd practically sit up and beg. He'd make all his poles and lures from scratch out of materials he collected around the yard and in his travels about town. One Christmas, Ma and Pa scrimped and saved and bought him a brand new five-piece split-cane fishing rod that came by train all the way from New York. Though, Ronny, peculiar as he was, found himself afraid to sully this most precious gift. When he returned to the river the next day, he did so with a carved maple bough he'd cut from a limb in our backyard, and the beautiful split-cane rod remained untouched in its case under his bed, coveted by the rest of us for as long as I can remember.

We all thought it was a powerful shame, but Ronny didn't need much help catching fish anyway, and the fact is, he was happier with his crude rods and homemade lures. It didn't take all that much to make Ronny happy, and I can say with conviction that he would've lived out his life quite contentedly had he been left alone in solitude on the bank with a fishing pole in one hand and a can of chewing tobacco in the other.

Before I was born, Ronny was regarded as the black sheep of the family, although not so much on account of his antics but rather his attitude. He was, in essence, a loner and altogether quieter and more unassuming than his magnanimous twin. Of course, having been raised in the shadow of charisma incarnate, it is no wonder why. Ronny played varsity in the Five Points hooky league since elementary school, but even so, Ma found it hard to reprimand him—after all, you don't bite the hand that feeds you, even if it belongs to your own truant son! To be frank, the most heinous affront Ronny ever committed was shirking his boyhood responsibilities to pursue his passion, a passion that remitted some very handsome rewards about the home. And so, really, what was Ma to do?

There were a few women around town who disagreed with her methods of child-rearing, but all respected her tireless efforts. I suppose one of the main reasons Ma was so fair to us boys was because she had no choice but to pick her battles. She couldn't expect to punish us for every minor infraction of her rules, as there weren't enough corners in the house to send us all to!

Unfortunately for Ma, boys three and four were twins as well—and born only a couple years after the first two. I reckon the day they came on the scene was just about the proudest of Pa's whole life. Whereas Jerry and Ronny had Ma's thick black hair and dark brown eyes, Hunter and Phil were spitting images of Pa—and so identical in appearance to one another that even we had trouble telling them apart. Both of them inherited Pa's quiet, industrious nature in addition to his physical characteristics. If Ma contributed anything to their genetic makeup, that fact remains to be seen.

Both of them were mental marvels. The firstborn, Hunter, was endowed with an inherent knack for carpentry. If you gave him two rotting logs, a length of rope, and half a dozen nails, Hunter could build the best gang fort in all of the southwest territory. Boys from across the county enlisted his services every summer when school let out and the necessity for an appropriate meeting and fighting place for each neighborhood gang became apparent. In the summer of 1908, at just nine years of age, he built the back porch on our humble homestead and, at fourteen, was accepted into an apprentice school run by a local union outfit. He was an innovator par excellence and possessed such a resourceful nature that his practical abilities seemed to excuse his scholastic shortcomings. For all his ingenuity, he had the attention span of a gnat when it came to any subject that did not capture his immediate interest, and all attempts at schooling and book learning were, by and large, lost on him. Educational pursuits typically involve spending a significant number of hours indoors, and as Hunter saw it, that was simply not an option. He was as adventuresome as they come and had he been born a century earlier, he would have made a fine pioneer. In the warmer months, Hunter even slept outside. Eventually, Ma put up a fuss about wild animals and fever and other misfortunes that have been known to befall a man who sleeps out under the stars, so Hunter acquiesced and returned to bed. However, unbeknownst to Ma, during the following weeks, he built a small platform on the roof above the dormer window in his bedroom that he would climb out on after everyone else had fallen asleep. It even had railings around the perimeter to keep him from rolling off in the midst of a dream.

His twin, Phil, was what you'd call a tinkerer. If it whirred, puttered, or sparked, it was Phil's paramour, and if, by chance, a mechanism with wheels or gears of any kind arrived in his purview, he would be wholly enamored for weeks at a time. Due to his proclivities and the nature of his interests, he was the first son upon whom Pa bestowed the honor and responsibility of keeping his still running through the logging season—and from 1913 on, Pa's still thumped, gurgled, and bubbled gleefully year-round. He also had an insatiable penchant for guns. Besides his collection of cap-pistols and BB guns, by trading with schoolmates and other shady characters around town, Phil was able to amass such a wide assortment of arms it would've made a militiaman drool. On one auspicious occasion, by means he never revealed, he was able to get his capable and expedient hands on a box of grade A bona fide dynamite. He kept it hidden for months until one summer evening, after a grueling and indeterminable wait, while Ma and most of the neighbors were at town hall celebrating the election of the new mayor, us boys decided to blow up the river.

The seven of us watched with bated breath as Phil dug into the bank and cautiously placed the charges and then, with the most dignified and ceremonious air a twelve-year-old could muster, struck a match and lit the fuse. We all ran like hell and huddled together on the porch, eagerly awaiting the blast. After what was only about ten minutes but felt like forever, once we had all prematurely concluded that the box of 'dan' had been a dud, then came the roar. Pats of mud flew in every direction, and a massive cloud of dust and smoke billowed up between the trees and into the dusky evening air. We all rushed down the bank and discovered to our surprise and glee that the gully was a good five feet wider, and the channel was a foot or two deeper. From that day onward, every barefoot boy in Denver County wanted to go fishing in our backyard, while Ma and the neighbors stood around dumbfounded as they marveled at the alarming and unprecedented rate of erosion that had occurred in our section of the South Platte that summer. Phil walked around with his head held just a little higher from then on, and I believe it was that fated evening when he discovered his true calling—explosives. That being said, neither Phil nor his wingman, Hunter, were ever suspected, nor was any dynamite ever implicated.

No child is exempt from the call of temptation—especially boys by nature—and Hunter and Phil were no exception. However, this was largely an isolated incident, and between the two of them, it is difficult to determine who possessed more patience and virtue. I hardly remember an instance when either of them was in any kind of real trouble. They were both cooperative and reserved, which got them in good with the grown-ups, yet they possessed boundless curiosity and ingenuity, which made them compelling playmates for us kids. I suppose it was the relative docility of all four of her boys that led my mother to believe that it was a good idea to have more children, and the next three of my brothers were born each consecutive year from 1900 on—until there were seven Jones boys altogether.

Mick was the first 20th-century Jones baby, and though he boasted our mother's sable features, he had a personality that was all his own. Even as a youth, he was tall and strapping, brutally handsome, and the inheritor of Pa's piercing blue eyes. From his earliest years, girls of every age swooned when they saw him, and the rest of us made it a practice not to bring home any girls whose affections we were unsure of—lest we lose them to Mick. He was never in want of female company, and wherever he went, he was typically seen linked arm in arm with a lass—oftentimes one several years older than himself. Having known and enjoyed the pleasures of girls from a young age, he led a life that heartily enabled their companionship. Mick was the sporting type and went in for swimming, tennis, and baseball, ran track and field for the school team, and wrestled in the recess yard. As a result, he was as svelte and muscular as any of his peers and the object of infatuation for many of the neighborhood's young women.

Of course, as with those born favorably endowed on all other fronts, wit typically completes the package. Mick had wit in spades. He was a whiz in school, spewing figures, formulas, and verb tenses with twice the speed and half the effort of every other student in Denver. Teachers praised and commended him, and principals applauded his ability. The civics professor who ran the high school debate team even went as far as to say that Mick was the best pupil to pass through his class in the twenty years he'd been an educator.

Mick grew up right quick—and his pride grew right along with the rest of him. He was out of knickers and into long pants before he was ten years old and strutted around town toting a pipe and a hip flask with one girl hooked in each arm at the age of 13. He became a man before any of us— or at least that's how the citizens of Denver saw him. At home, he met our fraternal envy with nothing short of arrogant conceit, and the rest of us did our best to knock him back down to our level. After all, Hunter wasn't about to go around widening all the doorways in town just to accommodate the size of our brother's big head. Plus, there's nothing like watching a red-faced, teary-eyed, six-foot-tall teenager dressed in a bowler hat and smoking jacket run blubbering to his mother to bewail the unfairness with which his brothers had accosted him.

The ringleader of these crusades was usually our brother Robbie, the younger, shorter, duller, and testier version of Mick himself. Since the other four had arrived upon this earth in pairs and Mick and Robbie looked so similar and were so close in age, many folks naturally assumed that they were twins as well—and then they wondered why Robbie was so stunted in comparison. That just about burnt Robbie up, and Mick never hesitated in taking delight in that particularly backhanded compliment. Consequently, in due time, Robbie became exactly what he turned out to be for most of his childhood: a freckle-faced rabble-rouser with a surly expression and a left hook that could've flattened Jack Dempsey. I don't think a week went by in Robbie's life from the ages of five to fifteen that he didn't have a black eye, a fat lip, or some other ugly, imposing bruise somewhere on his body—and more likely than not, most of those came from me. Robbie and I were nearly inseparable from our earliest years, yet, even so, we were constantly bickering, shoving, hair-pulling, name-calling, and sucker-punching one another. In fact, I believe I was personally responsible for loosening each and every one of his baby teeth, and he popped out most, if not all, of mine. However, for all the abuse we levied upon each other, if another boy in town attempted to inflict similar treatment on either of us, the other would rally to his aid with unparalleled vengeance. The first time I came home from school crying after a bloody scuffle in the recess yard, Robbie went out and whupped every boy in sight until he got to the kid who had pummeled me, and then when he got back, beat me doubly hard for crying.

Make no mistake about it, Robbie could hold his own in a brawl no matter who his opponent was, and by the time I was twelve years old, he'd taught me how to fight so well that I was considered one of the best journeymen scrappers in all of Five Points and second only to him. Robbie's most esteemed point of pride was that he remained undefeated in every schoolyard brawl from the fifth grade through high school. His skills were so refined, and his record so impressive that even some adults around town kept tabs on his bouts. After all, in those days, a boys' brawl outside the corner store in Five Points drew just as many grown men as spectators as it did adolescents. As in many other western towns around the turn of the century, men settled their disputes as men, and in those locales where gunplay was outlawed, men's fists flew hard and often. These displays captivated us boys to no end and Robbie most of all. He was a veritable disciple of bare-knuckle pugilism, and it is my considered opinion that though a featherweight and scrappy, he stood a fair chance of whipping any man that ever stood up against him. In fact, it is thanks to Robbie and the twelve years' worth of beatings I bore at his hands that the first strike Shannon Todd served up against me didn't kill me on contact.

Apart from me, Robbie was the only one of the Jones boys who was routinely in trouble. In fact, I don't think the sun ever rose two days in a row when neither he nor I weren't being bawled out by Ma for some transgression. Frequently, the offense was an affront one of us had committed against the other—for the two of us were masters of petty revenge. As a boy, he was wanton and unruly and had a sense of rascality and bedevilment that rivaled my own. Yet, for all his mischievousness and cunning, Robbie had a nasty streak of morality.

Ma sent all eight of us to Sunday school every week, but Robbie seemed to be the only one on whom the preacher's sermons made any lasting impression. In fact, he was so wicked that it was perfectly laughable to imagine that he would be the first one in line for the chapel, and I truly believe that he intentionally misbehaved during the week just so that he could pray harder on Sundays. Robbie knew his catechisms forward, backward, and upside down and could spout scripture from memory just as well as the preacher himself. On Sunday mornings, he'd transform himself from a rowdy, boisterous scamp into a youth flawlessly dressed, groomed, and conducted—a perfect picture of WASP heritage—and during the service, when any of his brothers would pinch or jostle him in an effort to incite some tomfoolery, Robbie stood firm before the Lord. On Sunday mornings, Robbie was incorruptible. He even read the whole Bible—cover to cover—at least three or four times.

The only other one of us who ever endeavored to open a book without it being wholly obligatory was Billy. Billy, my youngest older brother, was born three years before me and probably the only reason Ma didn't go after the town doctor when she found out that I was on the way. If the word meek ever had a personification, it could be found in Billy. He was soft-spoken, shy, and the closest Ma ever got to the daughter she never had. He was essentially Ma's shadow for most of his early years and had no aversion to learning how to cook or mend or any of those domestic tasks women consume themselves with throughout their days. He was of a slight build and had Pa's tawny hair and Ma's round, dark eyes. His face remained pudgy and pneumatic until long after puberty had unveiled the chiseled features inherent in the rest of us, and he entered adulthood with a scar on his cheek where I'd shot him with a BB as a child, and it had gone clean through and knocked out one of his teeth.

Despite the laud and acclaim that Mick received for his high marks in school and the amazement with which Hunter and Phil were regarded for their creations, Billy might have actually been the smartest of the brood— but you'd never know it. He was observant in a quiet, contemplative sort of way and rarely shared his impressions with the rest of us. He possessed the same sense of goodwill as Jerry, enjoyed peaceful solitude just the same as Ronny, could tinker and build right alongside Hunter and Phil, made marks nearly equivalent to Mick's, and when push came to shove, could swing a wallop that would leave Robbie smarting for a week. However, because he could do it all and never found a niche all his own, hardly anyone noticed that his aptitude in just about every endeavor he undertook was, at the very least, slightly above average. The one pursuit that was unique to Billy alone was reading. The kid was a fiend for literature. He devoured books the way other boys scarf down candy with a sense of enjoyment that was almost criminal. He was a regular at the town library and frequented the school library so often that the librarian allowed him to take out up to a dozen books at once. His passion for the written word completely eluded the rest of us and generally resulted in him becoming the subject of our pestering and ridicule. However, it may've been all that time he spent reading that imparted to him his most precious gift.

For all of Billy's timidity, it didn't take much to rope him into a scheme, and it was in these instances that he exhibited his greatest talent. For a small boy, Billy had a considerably heightened conscience. Whatever the situation, Billy could turn it over in his mind and examine it from all angles. He could point out every contingency and consequence that any given action may produce and devise apt methods to circumvent them. In all the scheming and conniving that filled our adolescent days, Billy was rarely a perpetrator, but more oft than not, he was the brains behind the operation. Of course, as an adult, it is clear to see that the only reason Billy had the corner on the graft market was because he thought before he acted—something most young boys conveniently forget to do—and all my life, I've found myself wishing that I'd been born with his sense of discernment. Actually, to be fair, any of my brothers' meritorious qualities would have served me well.

When I came along in May of 1905, I was a fair-skinned, ice-eyed, tow-headed marvel—a genetic anomaly, that is, assuming the milkman didn't actually have anything to do with it. I was stubborn and obstinate from the first, and despite our differences in age, I terrorized my brothers from the time I was able to crawl. Mick used to tell me that babies came from storks who would leave their precious, swaddled cargo on the front stoop for elated families to love and adore—which had been the case for all seven of them. However, he said my stork must've been either drunk or fed up with carrying me because rather than gently placing me on the porch, he'd dumped me in Pa's mash barrel instead. According to Mick, the only reason Pa fished me out was because he didn't want me to foul up the whole batch of gin. I remember slugging him at least a dozen times after that insult. After Mick went and stooled on me, Ma would drag me in the house kicking and screaming, where she'd lecture me on proper conduct and the golden rule and then leave me to go sweat out the rest of my afternoon in the corner of the kitchen where I'd bide my time contemplating the sweetest method of revenge.

Of course, if it was Mick or Robbie or any of the rest who were in trouble, Ma would've taken them out behind the still and given them a good tanning, but I alone was spared this fate. Sometime during the three years between Billy and I, Ma had heard that spanking children wasn't effective discipline and, therefore, resolved to raise her last boy in the best way she saw fit. Of course, since she'd already considerably tanned the hide of all seven of my brothers, she figured they were already accustomed to that sort of punishment and therefore made no motion to suspend the use of the strap. Only the Lord knows if I would've turned out better if Ma had whipped me silly every time I made a wrong turn, but I'm fairly certain I couldn't have turned out worse. In fact, it became quite clear early on in my life that if I was to make proper use of myself in this world, I'd best go in as a poster child for the seven deadly sins.

First off, I was lazy—as Pa said, lazier than a broke-back old hound dog sitting in one-hundred-degree heat. Getting me to do an honest day's work, even with good pay, was like getting a pig to lay eggs. I haven't earned one good, clean dollar in all of my earthly living yet, but I've slept between more silken sheets, drank more fine imported wine, shot more pearl-handled pistols, and ate more rich, fancy dinners than any good old god-fearing honest working man ever has.

Pa always told us boys that there are only two certainties in life, one being suffering and the other being death. As an impressionable youth, I took that to mean that the whole of life was absent of purpose and, when left to direct its own course—like a clipper adrift in a shoreless sea—was devoid of joy. Therefore, due in part to the meritless advice of an old cynic, I turned bad. Although, as a rule, I would never count myself amongst the mean-spirited or the cruel, I simply sought pleasure at every turn. A woman I once knew called me a hedonist. It was years before a freight-hopping ascetic explained to me what that meant. I still take it as a compliment.

After all, it is the cornerstone of my character. At suppertime, I'd waive the formality of chewing my first portion just to have a chance at seconds. Whenever a rash of gluttony and stomachaches broke out amongst the Jones clan, it was usually because I'd burglarized the candy store or broken into the gumball machine outside the soda fountain, and one of my brothers had found out and blackmailed me into sharing my spoils. I'd had more cavities drilled by the age of eight than most have in their entire lives.

Of course, I did not stand much of a chance regarding my penchant for greed, as that was largely innate. For what other earthly reason would my grandparents have abandoned the homes of their forefathers to set out upon a fabled, dusty track riddled with doom other than to follow the call of riches and wealth? Greed is in the blood of all Denver men, and I am by no means anemic. Certainly, growing up in the company of seven other budding Denver men did nothing to quell my inborn vices, either.

As any man with brothers knows, living with them is about equal parts love and hate. I do not believe a single day passed when I was not angry with at least one of them for some fleeting transgression—sometimes for no other reason than for being better than me. When one of my brothers was praised for a job well done and I, in the same breath, was scolded, it goes without saying that he would be the unfortunate recipient of the balance of my wrath until someone else surpassed their grievance with a more dastardly deed.

I, too, wanted to be wreathed in the laurels of my parents' praise, but as I had no talent to speak of that rivaled the likes of my brothers, I decided I had no choice but to nurse my pride elsewhere. I figured that if I couldn't succeed at being *better* than them, I'd try my hand at being *worse*. If Ronny cut school three days in a row, I'd cut school for a week. If Hunter refused to come inside at bedtime and Ma had to go after him in the backyard, I'd run out to the front. If Mick got reprimanded for climbing too high up in a tree, I'd climb one twice as high. If Robbie refused to take a bath and wash behind his ears, when my turn came, I'd protest twice as loud. All the ladies about town—and even some men—would be shocked and appalled when they heard of my antics, and the more they swore and exclaimed, the more it tickled my fancy. Newcomers to Five Points would clam up and point when they saw me coming, chicken-hearted classmates who were afraid of getting in Dutch with their folks would cross over to the other side of the street, and then, of course, there were the girls...

All seven of us were jealous of Mick's prowess in the art of courtship, but I was captivated by females entirely on their own merit. From the time I was no more than five years old, I'd sneak into town and peer under the swinging doors of the saloons along Broadway to watch the b-girls saunter about as they served drinks to the vociferous imbibers seated at the tables. Having been raised surrounded on all sides by men, the curiosity I attached to women from my earliest years should come as no surprise, and I began pursuing them just as soon as the concept of such an endeavor took form in my randy young mind.

Most men speak of the accompaniment of an angel on their right shoulder and a devil on their left, but I am not so fortunate. I was born with two devils instead of the customary one, and both of them continually rally for superiority. I do not know whatever became of my angel, but it has always occurred to me that somewhere in this wild world walks a man bestride by two angels, himself a prime candidate for Saint Peter's court, while I have been destined for perdition from the very first. In fact, Shannon Todd was far from the first man to refer to me as the devil incarnate—long about 1915, half the neighborhood of Five Points shared his sentiments.

Growing up in Denver, there was no shortage of mischief for a wily scapegrace like myself to become entangled in. The earliest memory I can recall is the sound of the five o'clock freight passing just outside my bedroom window and the excitement with which I rushed outside behind my brothers to watch it go by. The tracks crossed the South Platte just before our house and ran parallel with it until they reached the freight yards and the depot. There is no describing the wonder and curiosity that the railroad and its itinerant travelers evoked in us boys—and myself especially. As a child, the idea of being a bum was positively glorious. To lead a life in which rouge traveling, adventure, and the unknown reigned supreme beckoned us on like the summer wind—but in the end, I was the only one who answered the call.

The bums were a staple in Five Points, and as our house was only a few miles from the freight yards, it became a bit of a landmark for the chronic drifters. Hanging a ride to the end of the line, especially in the daytime, was a sure-ticket way to land yourself in the stir for ten to fifteen days. Therefore, the most thoroughgoing bums would drop off a mile or two from the depot, and when riding into Denver, that put them right in our backyard. Yeggs, tramps, bindle-stiffs, hobos, and bums of every other varietal would swing off the freights almost daily, and we'd wait beside the tracks and watch for them with wide-eyed anticipation. Oftentimes, they'd want to bum a meal or else work for one, and on these most auspicious occasions, my brothers and I would spring into action. One of us would raid the icebox while another retrieved the jar of Pa's gin that we'd hidden in the hollowed-out stump of a tree. A third would hunt up a sack of smoking, and if it was summertime, Robbie and I would make a fast run down to Farmer Willard's next door and steal a melon or a shirt-full of blackberries, all in hopes that the man would stay awhile and reward us gallant boys with the greatest pleasure of all—a story!

On our way home from school each week, we'd drop by the freight office and check the schedule for the coming days. When we knew there was a freighter coming in from Dodge City or St. Louis—or better yet, Chicago or New York—half the neighborhood boys would be gathered in our backyard. Generally speaking, it doesn't take much prodding to get a bum to start talking, and as long as the supply of vittles and white line hold out, once you get them going, it is nearly impossible to get them to quit. The regular travelers were the best of all. There were bums we knew by name who stopped by every time they rode into Denver. They knew they were guaranteed a meal and a jolt, and we knew we were guaranteed an entertaining anecdote. There was Cowboy Pete, who recounted fighting tales of every town from Port Arthur to Puyallup. Then there was Blackfoot John, a 6'9" Saskatchewan Indian who'd gone up to Alaska after the Klondike and come back broker and meaner than any man before him. My personal favorite was Salt Lake Smitty, a notorious night prowler who spun us hair-raising tales of narrow escapes, unexpected windfalls, and jailbreaks that kept us rapt in attention and left us speechless.

Of course, these traveler's tales did more for a young boy than simply widen his horizons. At school and in the gang house, the Jones brothers became known purveyors of stories so rich and exciting they were hardly believable—and depending on which brother you heard them from, some embellishment was to be expected. Daydreams of faraway places and the fantastic experiences I imagined having there crowded my young mind and spurned a desire for travel and exploration that continues to gnaw at me to this day.

The bums were not the only thrilling thing about having the railroad in our backyard. Even during those days and weeks when we had no transient visitors, the train alone held more than enough excitement to adequately fill our halcyon days of boyhood with mirth and adventure. Sometimes we'd pretend to be the train, other times, we'd pretend to rob the train, hop the train, drive the train, or fight the train. And, there were countless lazy afternoons when we'd fallen asleep on the lip of the gorge with our fishing rods between our feet as we waited for the train so that we could wave to the men riding her and petition the engineer to blow the whistle for us.

When we got bored of playing on the tracks, the South Platte River occupied much of the remainder of our time. Now, the South Platte was no more than a gurgling stream ten feet wide at that stretch, but for a bunch of boys who could find a whole day's worth of enjoyment playing in a single muddy puddle, that stream held years' worth of adventures. We knew every shale and stone in that gorge and what was underneath them. We were on a first-name basis with every toad, bird, and beetle that called the river home, climbed every tree along its bank, and whacked one another with every downed branch that landed in its tide. The closest thing we ever had to a bath in the summertime was when we played in that old river—although our feet were always permanently brown with mud. Wearing shoes was considered by every boy in Five Points to be the surest form of torture grown-ups had ever devised.

Ours was not the only house that backed up to the river, and on days when we found our yard particularly uninteresting, we'd set out in search of greener pastures. We'd go after Phil's arsenal, arm ourselves with bb guns and cap pistols, and play war in Farmer Willard's fields next door. We'd set up our camps on opposite sides of the gorge, map out the 'territory' that was ours to defend, and take one another's produce prisoner. In the summertime, hardly a week passed when Ma wasn't dragging at least two of her blackberry-stained boys by the ears down to Farmer Willard's to apologize for raiding his crops. And, when we weren't stealing fruit or trampling on his vegetables, we were down in the gorge behind his barn where he'd dammed up the South Platte to provide a source for his irrigation pump. Through his arduous efforts, he'd created a pool about a dozen feet deep and nearly twice as wide. It made a magnificent swimming hole, and fishing there was so effortless it was almost criminal. Of course, after pillaging his means of subsistence, Farmer Willard got a little sore at us boys hanging around his property, and not a summer passed when he didn't send one of us running home with a backside full of rock salt.

Fortunately for crotchety old Farmer Willard, the appeal of his land faded with the warmth and sunshine, and we spent the snowy winter months on sleds, careening down the hill in the yard of Ms. Johnson, our neighbor on the other side. Apart from Ma, Ms. Johnson was just about the kindest and prettiest woman I had ever met in Five Points. In all the years, I never heard her raise her voice, even to her own children, and she had a parcel of them. Her two older girls were the same age as Jerry and Ronny and generally kept to themselves, but she had three younger sons and one daughter who were some of our most regular playmates.

Between the four of them and the eight of us, we got into more capers than I can remember—and as long as we played on the bank, our antics were observed and chronicled by one Widow Tabor, who lived directly across the river from us. Widow Tabor, the patron saint of stool pigeons, spent most of her time sitting on her back porch watching us like a voyeuristic hawk and reporting our shenanigans to Ma and Ms. Johnson. She was a batty, bible-thumping bigot who'd been scraping a living off the bank of the South Platte long before Five Points ever sprung up beside it. Having no children of her own, she was under the impression that boys were descended directly from the devil himself, and she made every effort to quash our revelry. Of course, this sentiment of hers was only strengthened when we retaliated by leaving frogs and dead worms in her mailbox or shooting down her bird feeders from blinds secreted along the gorge.

All things considered, we spent more time on that riverbank than we ever did inside any four walls, and the only time we voluntarily left the bank was when we had houseguests. Southern hospitality never had a thing on Ma, for regardless of the responsibilities that she was yoked with daily, she routinely went out of her way to produce the most extravagant spread possible whenever we had visitors. In a flurry of flour, basting, and powdered sugar, Ma would set forth upon the supper table a feast fit for old King George himself. Plates and tins full of pies, cakes, braised beef, sugar-cured ham, and just about every other delicacy a growing boy could imagine were strewn across the table in such enormous quantities that they just about hung off the edges. However, even with the luxuries that guests afforded us, the novelty wore off fairly quickly, and within two or three days, we would be back in the gorge rattling Widow Tabor's cage. In fact, the only time we confined ourselves to our own yard for any length was when Uncle John came to visit.

Uncle John Cassidy, Ma's only brother, would come into Denver and stay with us a few times a year, and when he did, I'll bet anything that our neighbors got down on their knees and thanked God for it. Although, that being said, apart from us and Ma herself, I can't imagine any other soul rightfully thanking God for Uncle John. He was a free-spirited opportunist with a nose for expediency and graft that outstripped the likes of any other I have ever encountered. He was a big, beefy son of a gun who brought a hurricane with him wherever he went. He was as loud and boisterous as Daniel Boone and had a raucous laugh that carried so far that we could hear him coming back from a tear in town when he was still a mile off. He was dark and swarthy like Ma and hard-bitten from many a cold winter that he'd weathered in elements too harsh to tell about, but at the same time, he was permanently youthful. In fact, his eyes still held the same glint of mischief that could be found in any of us boys.

Uncle John always arrived in one of two states. Either he was fringe-laden in a hand-cut calfskin vest, grizzly and half-crazed from having spent the last few months crawling through the wilds of every canton in the west, or he was clad in shirt-sleeves and a bolo tie toting saddle bags so filled with riches that he could hardly buckle them shut. No matter how he arrived, Uncle John always had a twenty-dollar gold piece dangling from his watch chain, and there wasn't a time he dropped by that he didn't come bearing gifts. We didn't grow up particularly poor by any stretch of the imagination, but by the time you got to dividing Pa's paycheck between the ten of us, there wasn't very much left over for frills. Therefore, when Uncle John came to town, it was like Christmas, and he had a bag of tricks that rivaled that of Kris Kringle himself. He'd bestow upon us wide-eyed boys toy soldiers and hoops, glass marbles and shooting irons, and he always remembered what each of us liked. He never once crossed our threshold without having a book in tow for Billy or a new lure for Ronny—and once I began to show interest, he never set foot in the house without a new card game in mind for me. Ma and Pa weren't absent from his benevolence either, and on nearly every occasion, he would bring a pretty new dress for Ma and a bottle of what he called 'good whiskey' for Pa.

Pa never took much of a shine to Uncle John. Of course, as kids, we figured that was because he'd insulted the finest homemade hooch in all of Denver County. Pa clearly resented Uncle John's insistence in bringing over his 'good whiskey' to avoid drinking Pa's gin, but once the new bottle was drained and the mason jars had been cracked open, the two of them seemed to be just about as chummy as a couple of sailors out on furlough. At the time, we were too young to understand alcohol's curious ability to make friends out of enemies and vice versa—and there was something else we were too young to understand: Pa didn't trust Uncle John.

Even as children, we were well aware that Uncle John lived a heedless and wild life, for that was apparent as soon as he opened his mouth. To hell with Billy's dime novels, Uncle John told stories even more fantastical than the railroad bums themselves. He regaled us with riotous tales of bare-handed encounters with mountain lions, perilous journeys through Indian Territory, and the utter abandon with which he carried on in town when it was all over. Uncle John called himself a prospector, but as I came to learn later, his prospects often went far beyond what could be unearthed with a shovel or pickaxe. I believe the kindest term for him would've been a gambler; however, throughout his life, he could've checked every box from crook, womanizer, bunko man, and perpetual schemer all the way through to sometime bum. Of course, he never divulged all this to Ma and Pa, and they thought his primary source of income was a particularly lucrative sustenance farm he ran down in Leadville, in addition to his wintertime trapping.

In reality, cards and dice were his meal tickets, so it is no surprise that he was always abreast of the latest and most exciting games. As kids, he started us off with chuck-a-luck and euchre and then turned us on to high low jack and all fours. I quickly became a fiend for such lucrative excitement. I immediately turned my sights toward my brothers and schoolmates, betting with Cracker Jack cards and cigarette posters, marbles, stamps, and every other article that young boys treat as currency.

My skill at the games commanded me a great deal of attention in the schoolyard, and by 1917, I was known throughout Five Points as an enterprising young gambler. The other boys would gather around to watch me beat the pants off my opponents and then beg me to teach them the tricks I'd used to secure my victory. I never said mum about my methods, but I was usually able to hustle at least a few boys a day into a game. As a result, I quickly amassed waist-high stacks of baseball cards, more marbles than I knew what to do with, and every cereal box prize ever invented. In fact, I accumulated so many desirable collections that I began selling them to the sons of monied folk for considerable sums. No longer did I have to pester Jerry and Hunter for nickels so that I could buy penny candy at the five and dime; I could support my habits on my own living wage—and I never needed to exert even an ounce of sweat or labor to achieve it.

Once I realized my propensity for the craft and the spoils it brought with it, I was met with an entirely new outlook on life. I thought about Jerry working six days a week at Woolworth's to keep up the mortgage on the Curtis Park home he had bought for his new wife and young son. I thought about Hunter swinging a hammer eight hours a day for a dollar's profit. I thought about Pa and the twenty years he had spent slaving away in the mountains...and for what reward? Rheumatism? Enervation? A quick route to old age? None of those consequences sounded particularly appealing to me; therefore, at the tender age of eleven, I decided that rather than work, I would spend my life touring every saloon and gambling house in America.

One would assume that Colorado's enactment of statewide prohibition in 1916 would have put quite a damper on my plans, but in some ways, it only served to foster them even further. With Denver declared legally dry, Pa began cranking out gin at an unprecedented rate. At first, he only endeavored to quench his own thirst, but pretty soon, others around town began calling on him to outfit them with a stash of their own. Moonshining was illegal in Colorado before the teetotalers took over, so Pa didn't have any qualms about keeping up his riverside distillery post-prohibition. However, distribution proved to be a bit of a nuisance. Pa didn't want every parched resident of Five Points banging on our door day in and day out, so instead, he enlisted the assistance of us boys. Robbie, Mick, Billy, and I were his usual accomplices, and every day after school, we would load up our wagon with as much booze as we could pile in and make our rounds about town. Once a week, we'd deliver a whole wagon-full to Pike's—a gambling house on downtown Market Street. Usually, I'd leave all that tramping around to my brothers, but whenever we had to make a delivery to Pike's, I always tagged along. None of us were old enough to be allowed into such an iniquitous establishment, but because we were the bearers of their sweet libations, the proprietors made an exception for the Jones boys, and I cherished every second I spent there like it was the moment of my last breath.

The gambling that went on at Pike's differed entirely from what I'd witnessed in the saloons around town. At Pike's, the men were silent and serious. The laughing and fraternizing that characterized the saloons was absent, and the stakes were considerably higher. The dealers' nimble fingers flitted between checks and cards as quick as the wind, and their eyes never left the table. If any man endeavored to cheat, he needed to first be possessed by enough impetuous gall to make him immune to the fear of knowing full well that he'd be shot dead if caught.

I held my breath when I stepped into the parlor and stood as still as a board, trying my best to blend in with the wall as I poured over the layouts and studied the techniques those most mythical men employed to bring themselves such wealth and acclaim. And, once we made it home, I wasted no time practicing those same techniques myself as I tried to beat my brothers out of the money Pa paid them as recompense for their time.

As long as Denver's prohibition held out, so did Pa's supply of gin, and every week when delivery day rolled around, I headed the expedition. As a result of my observations at Pike's and the bi-annual tutelage I received from Uncle John, I got very good, very fast. I soon found there was hardly a treasure in all of Denver that I couldn't lay my larcenous hands on—all I had to do was find a way to win it, and it was mine for the taking. However, there was one object I sorely desired that all the cunning bets in the world couldn't win me, and that was Katie Mae.

Katie Mae was the daughter of a prominent high-tone family that lived in town. Her father worked at the First National Bank of Denver, her mother ran the Denver chapter of the WCTU, and Katie Mae herself was about as clean-cut and respectable as a debutante. So, of course, as the disrepute son of a moonshiner, I was just bound to be sweet on her.

Although, it must be stressed that I didn't just like Katie Mae; in fact, I'll even go as far as to say that she was my very first love. I followed after her as dutifully as the moon follows the sun, bestowed upon her trinkets and curios that I felt sure would impress her, and did everything in my power to turn her attention toward me. I yelled, I fought, I dunked her ponytail in the inkwell, I walked on my hands and somersaulted and spit, but alas, not one little thing I did piqued her interest. Despite my very best provocations, Katie Mae went right on avoiding me like I had typhoid fever—and not only did she avoid me, she flat-out ignored me. She ignored me like I was a pebble in a gold mine, and the more she ignored me, the more desperate I became. Although, if I could treat my grieving ego with any consolation, it would be that Katie Mae ignored most boys' advances.

Katie Mae was just about the most conceited girl I've ever met. It wouldn't have mattered if her Pa owned the bank, all that was in it, and every oil well in Texas; she would've conducted herself just the same. She was as proper as a duchess, never tardy or rude, and would never even dream of playing with us boys. The idea of getting down on her knees and shooting marbles or catching caterpillars simply appalled her, and all I ever saw her do in the recess yard was stand around and gossip.

But, despite all her haughtiness, I found her to be completely enchanting. She was as pretty as a picture with harvest moon eyes and chiclet white teeth. In the wintertime, she wore a blue bonnet and, in the spring, a little straw hat with yellow ribbons, and she'd stroll about town with her chin in the air and those yellow ribbons streaming down her back bestride her long brown ponytail. I saw an awful lot of that ponytail, mainly because I followed her to and from school every day. In fact, after my heart got stuck on Katie Mae, I never missed another day of school again. I was in the classroom every morning by the first bell just so I could sit behind her, though my grades showed little improvement despite my better attendance. After all, I was far too busy daydreaming about the wondrous life we would have together once I'd discovered the best way to get her attention to pay any mind to my schoolwork.

I reckon I could've been the scholarly type if I'd made up my mind to do so, but academics never did take to me too naturally. Stuffy classrooms, rote memorizations, strict school teachers, and the knuckle-bustings they offered ornery children like me did nothing but turn my thoughts to more exciting endeavors. Ma begged and pleaded for me to do better and cautioned me that if I didn't, I would end up a railroad bum with nothing ahead of me but roads fraught with hardship. As growing up to be a bum was my loftiest aspiration anyhow, her dire warnings were all but lost on me. Even Pa tried to impress upon me the importance of education and how even as a logger, he made use of principles he had learned in the classroom, but it was to no avail. As neither of them placed any stock in my promising career as a gambler, they both challenged me to think of a single profession in which schooling was unnecessary. By late spring of 1917, I had the answer for them.

In the early part of that same year, the Huns torpedoed several American vessels, and outraged, our noble country had flung itself headfirst into war—bringing four million of our boys along with it. The week of my twelfth birthday was accompanied by news that shocked the nation and changed our family forevermore. Conscription was a word I'd never heard before that day. However, from then on, it seemed to make its way into just about every conversation I heard—especially after my two eldest brothers, both age 21, received conscription letters in the mail. Jerry and Ronny were given mere weeks to settle their affairs before being shipped off to Camp Meade in Maryland, followed by deployment in France. Upon turning eighteen in September, Hunter and Phil followed in our brothers' footsteps and joined up as soon as possible, eager to serve their country and flaunt their newly attained manhood. Initially, all four of them were infantrymen, but Jerry, typical of his illustrious character, went one step further and volunteered to train as a bombardier. I remember waiting out near the mailbox for hours after school for their letters from training camp to arrive and reading the exciting accounts they held. The idea of marching and fighting all day long and camping out every night captured my boyish imagination, and shortly after their deployment, I announced to Ma that I had decided soldiering would be my life's work. After all, I surely didn't need to learn my multiplication tables if I was going to be clobbering the Germans for the glory of our great nation.

Before long, I was spending weeks on end up on the roof of the house picking off anything that moved with my BB gun—including squirrels, rabbits, birds, my brothers, and the wash Ma hung out to dry on the line. For those weeks, all aspirations of being the country's shrewdest gambler faded into the back of my mind, my school attendance dropped off completely, and even my devotion to Katie Mae dwindled. But to me, none of it was of very much consequence anymore. If I was going to be a soldier like my brothers, I needed to train, which meant that the rest of my great aspirations would have to be put on hold for the time being.

—Though it is perfectly astonishing how quickly passion can resurge when provided the proper impetus.

A bright, balmy early summer afternoon is hardly an apt time for an ambitious future soldier to be sitting idly indoors rehearsing spelling words, so once again, I gave school the slip and retreated to Hunter's abandoned blind on the roof. I was lying flat on my stomach, BB gun in hand, picking off leaves as the wind blew them in my direction. The sun was warm on my back, the breeze cool through my hair, and I was convinced that I was close to becoming the best soldier the world had ever seen. Pa had left for the mountains, and Uncle John was visiting from Leadville, so Ma was occupied inside and oblivious to my truancy, and I was left to pick off my verdure enemies undisturbed. That is, until Robbie came home from school.

100

I was in the midst of reloading when I peered over the peak of the roof and spotted Robbie strolling up to the house, arm in arm with Katie Mae. Immediately, I dropped the can of BBs I was holding and lit out over the roof. Ma and Uncle John must've thought it was raining water buffalo. When I reached the front porch, I shimmied down one of the posts, landed on the railing, and confronted my treacherous brother just before he opened the front door.

"What the hell are you doing with my girl?!" I shrieked, red-faced and mean.

Both were startled by my sudden appearance but seemed amused by my outrage.

"I'm taking Katie Mae to the nickelodeon," Robbie shrugged, beaming with pride.

"Oh no you're not!" I bellowed, "You know I'm the one who's sweet on Katie Mae!"

"Then why haven't you taken her to the nickelodeon?"

"I—because I—she—you...." I stammered. It was just too much for my fragile young heart to bear at once.

"You traitor!" I blubbered, flying at him.

Katie Mae jumped out of the way and ran behind the railing as Robbie and I lunged at each other, belting one another with savage blows as we went to war for her love. I fought honorably and valiantly for her, but Robbie was four years older, a whole head taller, and—as much as I hated to admit it—a far better fighter. He wore me out in mere minutes; I could feel my strength failing me and my head and flesh pounding. Desperately, I struck out with my leg in an attempt to trip him, but he side-stepped my trap and employed one of his own. Robbie had never before been one to fight dirty, but in this battle for honor, he stooped to the epitome of low blows and, while I had my legs apart, kicked me so hard between them that I threw up. By the time Ma and Uncle John caught wind of our struggle on the porch, I was lying flat on my face at the foot of the rocking chair, writhing and wailing at the top of my lungs. Uncle John hoisted me up and whisked me inside, where he deposited me on the sofa in the parlor with an ice pack and a gag bag. While I tried my very best to compose myself and keep from bawling, Robbie somehow managed to convince Ma that I'd been the one in the wrong. To my shock and dismay, she let him off the hook, and he and Katie Mae hurried away into town.

When I saw Ma step back through the door without Robbie in tow, I felt the weight of every crippled boyhood dream come crashing down upon me. I laid motionless on that sofa for the next several hours, just as depressed as a boy could be. All of my glory had flown away from me, and my pride still lay mortally wounded on the front porch. I had failed as both a soldier and a man, and my best friend, my own brother, had humiliated me in front of the girl I loved, the girl he had taken for himself. When Robbie returned, Ma made him apologize, but I refused to even look at him. Both she and Uncle John tried to console me, but I mutinied against their efforts. At suppertime, the seven of them dined and laughed at the kitchen table while I lay there dejected, staring up at the mantle above the fireplace where Pa's peacemaker sat in its gun box. And, by nightfall, a sly and nefarious idea had begun to form in my vengeful young mind.

Once everyone else had gone up to bed and Ma had draped my despondent form in a quilt and kissed my aching head, I snuck across the parlor and stood before the fireplace, my eyes fixed on Pa's gun box. Pa's peacemaker had once belonged to his father, and it was strictly off-limits to all of us boys—even Jerry and Ronny, who were grown. None of us had ever handled it or would dare to, though we dreamed of it often—for it was a dandy gun, and Pa showed it off to all his friends when they came to visit in the wintertime.

It felt as if I stood there half the night, staring up at that box. I imagined reaching up on the mantle and removing the hallowed weapon from its cask, turning it over in my hands with care, and depositing a smooth, new .45 caliber bullet in each of its chambers. I pictured myself grasping the gun in both hands and creeping up the steps, silently pushing open our bedroom door, and standing before Robbie's bed, the muzzle of the pistol trained on his forehead.

—And after I worked up enough courage, that's precisely what I did. Although once I made it upstairs and drew the gun before his unconscious form, a moment's hesitation resulted in a marked change in my plans.

At first, I had only intended to scare him with the weapon. I figured I'd prod him awake so that when his eyes snapped open, he'd see my malicious grin and the sinister barrel of the gun. I thought maybe I'd fire once out the window just so he knew it was really loaded, then make him beg for his life, apologize for betraying me, and swear to never lay his eyes on Katie Mae again. But, as I crept closer to his sleeping form, I saw something that I hadn't previously imagined: his foot. I stood stock still for a moment as I stared at it incredulously. That was the foot that had kicked me, the foot that had caused me such agony, the foot that had so thoroughly embarrassed me in front of the girl I so badly wanted to impress—and it was sticking out from under his warm cotton blanket, cool and serene while he slumbered. I just couldn't help myself. I turned the muzzle away from his face, released the safety, and pumped two rounds of heavy lead into Robbie's right foot.

The roar from the weapon shattered the peaceful silence of that idyllic night and woke the entire house immediately—and Robbie's blood-curdling screams woke the neighbors shortly after. Mick jumped out of bed first, grabbed me from behind, and wrestled the gun out of my hands. Billy was close behind him and snatched it up from where I dropped it on the floor as the door swung open with a crash, and Ma, Uncle John, Phil, and Hunter charged into the room.

At first, there was a great deal of shouting and confusion, but it didn't take long for them to see what I had done. Ma ordered Mick and Billy to take me downstairs and keep me there while Uncle John and the other two worked to bandage Robbie's foot. It all happened so quickly that I didn't even get a chance to see the results of my handiwork. However, the severity of Robbie's wound was immediately apparent as Phil fled down the stairs and out to the barn so he could hitch old Buck to the wagon and drive Robbie to the hospital in town. Hunter followed him down within minutes, Robbie's crippled form trembling in his arms. Still dressed in a housecoat, Ma was right behind them. But, before she hopped into the wagon with my brothers, she paused before me with tears heavy in her eyes and told me in the saddest and sternest voice I'd ever heard that if I moved so much as an inch before she returned, she'd thrash me so severely that I'd wish I was Robbie.

I was never very good at taking orders from anyone, but I was well aware that I'd outdone myself—and in the spirit of self-preservation, I sat inert on that sofa until the next morning. When Ma returned, her face was pale and tear-stained, and she moved as if she was in a dream. She did not acknowledge me when she entered the house; instead, she immediately took to the stairs and called for Uncle John. I could hear the two of them talking in raised voices, and there was some opening and closing of the heavy bureau drawers in my room, but beyond that, her actions were a mystery to me. Several minutes later, she reappeared, holding a suitcase in her hands. Ma dropped it at my feet and morosely explained that she was sending me away.

Apparently, my fancy gunplay had done quite a number on Robbie's tootsies. His pinky toe had been shot off entirely, and there was a gaping hole in the bottom of his foot. The doctor said he'd have to stay off it for months, and even after he started walking again, he would likely limp heavily for the rest of his life. My actions, she said, were incomprehensible, and their consequences, however dire, were required to be equally harsh. Therefore, my punishment, the most severe and draconian she could think of, was to ship me off to Uncle John's farm in Leadville.

"It's time you learn what life is really like," she told me gravely in a voice thick with emotion, "and working with Uncle John will teach you just that. You must realize that every action you take has a reaction—and it's not always what you want it to be. I've tried my very best to raise you boys up right, but you, Jack, have fought me tooth and nail every step of the way. I suppose if your father didn't spend half his time away from here, you would've turned out better. You need discipline; you need a man in your life, a good man like your father. You may think Uncle John is all stories and games, but you don't meet with success in life, as he has, without putting in a great deal of effort. You're going to learn that, Jack, you must learn that—because you cannot come back home until you do."

Ma reached out and enveloped me in a hug then, and it was the strangest hug she ever gave me. It felt as if she yearned to hold me forever, and, at the same time, it felt as if she was an automaton, cold and emotionless as she pulled away. In a daze, she handed me the suitcase and led me out the front door to where Uncle John was waiting in his car. She stood on the front porch with her hands on her hips as we pulled away and waited until we were nearly out of sight before she broke down and began to cry.

It was about a four-hour drive to Leadville, and Uncle John and I rode in silence for the first three. Despite the significant part I had played in deciding them, the events of the last twenty-four hours stunned me, and the true implications of my actions had yet to fully emerge. My mother had banished me from home without allowing me to say goodbye to my brothers or even apologize to Robbie. The thought of living away from them was paralyzing, and the idea of having to work and go to school every day was even more so. Remorse and regret flowed through me earnestly, and I very nearly caved in and began begging Uncle John to turn around— however, once I remembered Robbie's treachery and Ma's unfairness in treating it, I remained stoic.

When we were about thirty miles to Leadville, while I was still assailing my grieving conscience with a host of self-recriminations, Uncle John decided to break the ice.

"Say, Jackie-boy, what do you see on the horizon?" he asked me without averting his eyes from the road.

His question eluded my literal young mind, and I answered him sober and verily, "pines...mountain tops...road...why?"

Uncle John laughed at my response. It was a light-hearted, raucous laugh that sounded like you were shaking a parcel of rocks in a paper bag.

"No, boy," he answered, "what do you see in the future—your future? There'll surely come a time—and it's coming right soon—when you won't be able to spend your days runnin' round and shooting your brothers—sad as that is. When that day comes, what do you want to make of yourself? What do you want to do with this life of yours?"

It was just about the most fatherly talk Uncle John ever gave me, and its influence was far greater than he or I could have ever imagined.

"Up until yesterday, I wanted to be a soldier...." I told him as I shifted uncomfortably in the hard leather seat, "but I'm not so sure anymore. I suppose I'll just have to be a bum now."

"No, no, no, Jack," Uncle John shook his head disapprovingly, "you don't want to be neither. Listen, we're going to be spending an awful lot of time together from now on, and if you take to learning what I know, you'll be fixed for life."

Of course, I hadn't the foggiest idea of what he meant when he first uttered these words, but it didn't take long for me to catch on.

I suffered more for my transgressions during that car ride than I ever did after we arrived at our destination. Little did I know at the time, the summer of 1917 was to be the very best I'd ever had and would set me upon my path of knavery and deceit faster and more assuredly than any other experience in my life. It was not long before I learned that Uncle John Cassidy was considered to be one of the most notorious bunko men in the state of Colorado. He was also known to be full of a fair amount of balloon juice. Some of his sensationalized talk even managed to get by my perceptive mother, and, as it turns out, the hardscrabble farm I was destined to sweat and slave upon for the foreseeable future was a twenty-square-foot sustenance garden akin to the one we boasted in our own backyard. As soon as I laid my disbelieving eyes upon the meager crops that grew there and the sagging chicken-wire fence that encircled it, I realized that there had been considerable miscommunication somewhere along the line.

"This is your farm?" I asked Uncle John doubtfully.

Uncle John laughed again, this time heartily. He slid his arm around my shoulders and asked, "You disappointed?"

"Well, no!" I replied hurriedly, "but I thought Ma sent me here to work for you."

Uncle John reached into his top pocket and pulled out a fat Cuban cigar which he subsequently lit. He took a few puffs, then knelt down beside me and exhaled a massive lungful of the thick, sweet-smelling smoke.

"Smell that, Jack? You ever know your Pa's cigars to smell that sweet?"

I shook my head.

"Y'know why that is? That's 'cause you don't get to enjoy no good living when you're making it by breaking your back. Ain't no farmers 'round these parts smoking these puppies—no ranchers or miners neither. But, you see, not everybody can make money the way your Uncle John does. You've got to have the knack, you've got to have balls, you've got to take chances—an' if you can't do that, you better keep your day job because your night job just ain't gon' pay." He paused to inhale another huge breath of smoke. "You've got to think about these things now, Jack, or you're bound to end up like all the rest of them—dying before they're barely born—" He exhaled, "Delilah sent you here to learn. She s'pects you to learn to work the land, and you will. You'll hoe the garden and pick the vegetables and carry water from the pump, and you'll do it just the way I tell you to. Know why?"

I shook my head, both curious and wary.

He leaned in real close and looked me in the face, his dark, bushy eyebrows raised and his soot-black eyes narrowed. "See that parcel over there? That's only one itty-bitty part of the land I own. If you disobey me, I'll make you till up another just the same size, lay in a crop, and tend to it. An' I know' 'Lilah ain't never thrashed you, but she ain't here, an' that's the way I was brung up; I don't know no other. I got a strop hangin' on a peg by the door with your name already on it. So, I don't want no funny business. 'Lilah also 'pects you to go to school, and you'll do that too. The first time I find out you played hooky, you'll be turning up another parcel of land. And if you think I'm just funning with you and that you're gon' carry on the way you have been, I swear by Harry that this place really will be a farm by the time I decide to send you back to Denver."

As he uttered these words and stood back up to his full height, I felt my heart sink. That little spark of hope that ignited when I first caught sight of the garden had been snuffed out entirely, and the smoke it produced caused my eyes to water. I turned away and quickly wiped my face on my sleeve, but the intense look of disappointment that remained could not be concealed.

"Come on, Jack," Uncle John spoke, his voice filled once more with its usual levity, "into the house. That was one hell of a trip, and boy, am I parched!"

I followed after him listlessly, dragging my feet in the dirt as I went. Inside, Uncle John ushered me to a crude wooden table in the kitchen, where I sat sullenly with my arms crossed while he rummaged through a cabinet in the pantry. When he returned, he placed two tumblers on the table. In his fist was a bottle of Four Roses.

My despair was immediately changed to bewilderment, and I watched disbelievingly as he casually uncorked the bottle and poured each of us a snort.

"Like whiskey?" he asked me. "Well, of course you do!" he continued before I got the chance to reply, "If you're at all used to the taste of that shit your father makes—Phew! I'd rather drink turpentine myself, but to each their own."

Even at the tender age of twelve, I was no stranger to alcohol. I'd watched Pa make it my whole life and even assisted him on occasion. Pa had been known to give us boys a swig from the jar on holidays or when he was in a particularly good mood, and we'd all been known to sneak gulps when we could, but never in my life had I drank store-bought liquor from a glass all my own—and when the opportunity presented itself, I could hardly contain my excitement.

Uncle John raised his glass in a toast, and I followed suit, watching intently as he tapped the glass back on the table, raised it to his lips, and drained it of its contents. I did the same. The seemingly innocuous liquid hit the back of my throat like hellfire and burned all the way down. My eyes watered like a leaky faucet, my stomach churned violently, and yet, somehow, I resisted the all too tempting urge to spit it back in the glass. I thought the taste was rancid and the kick was fierce, but I did my best to take that belt like a man.

"Ahh!" Uncle John exclaimed after he'd placed his empty glass back on the table, "nothing like it! And look at you! I told you this stuff is better than that rotgut you get at home—and you better stick to it. Your Pa's gin will knock you for more of a loop than a gunpowder toddy." He paused to refill our glasses, and, bracing myself, I reached for mine.

"Uh, uh," he cautioned me, "this one is for sipping now. This here's 100-proof—tastes like heaven, I know, but drink it too fast and it'll slip you under the table real quick."

I set the glass back down in relief.

"Do you know why we tap the table with our glass after we toast?" Uncle John asked me.

I shook my head, intrigued and ready to savor every tidbit of this manhood's sneak preview.

"It's out of respect for all those we've outlived."

"I didn't know that," I replied, repeating the ministration as I endeavored to take a single, careful sip out of the tumbler.

"You're going to learn an awful lot of things you didn't know in the time you spend here, Jack," he told me as he rose from his seat and pulled out a drawer in a rickety end-table nearby.

He returned with a pack of playing cards in his outstretched hand. Elation gripped me immediately.

"You've always been keen on card playing, Jack. How about I learn you a game?"

I voiced my agreement enthusiastically.

Uncle John sat down and immediately began to deal. He expertly turned through the deck and extracted three cards, which he showed me. They were the king of clubs, the king of spades, and the ace of spades. He laid them face up on the table between us.

"I'm going to turn these three cards over and shuffle them up. Do you think you can pick out the ace of spades?"

"Sure, I can," I told him.

I watched intently as he rearranged the cards, then pointed to the card I believed to be the ace. He turned it over, and I was right. Excitement flooded me, and Uncle John smiled.

"Think you can do it again?" he asked.

"Of course!" I replied, utterly sure of myself.

"Would you bet on it?"

"Sure, I would," I replied, "but I don't have any money."

"Alright then, we'll just pretend. How much would you bet?"

"I'd bet a dollar," I told him.

Uncle John smiled mischievously, "pretty rich for a boy your age," he told me.

I shrugged proudly. "But not for me," I replied.

"What if I told you I wouldn't accept a bet of less than $5.00?"

"I'll bet five dollars; I can pick out that card lickety-split!" I announced.

"Ok, five dollars then," Uncle John agreed as he shuffled up the cards again. I kept my eyes trained on that ace, and when he let them lay, I turned over the proper card.

"You're quicker than I thought you were," he praised me, "alright, you've already beat me out of six dollars; how about double or nothing? Twelve dollars."

"You're on!" I exclaimed, and the process was repeated again. Uncle John shuffled, and I kept an eagle eye on those cards. Plenty sure of myself, I pointed to the same card I had the first two times, except this time, when he turned it up, it was the king of clubs. I froze.

Uncle John clicked his tongue at me as he attempted to stifle a grin. "Now, now, Jack, let's not be hasty. Didn't I teach you never to place big bets unless you're sure of your chances?"

"But I was sure!" I protested, "I watched that card like I'd bet my life on it!"

He laughed. "They all do," he sighed, "and yet, they all lose. It's all in the deal," he explained, "it don't matter how close you watch 'em or how long you spend choosin', when the dealer's got the knack, you don't stand a chance. Watch again."

I paid close attention as he shuffled and dealt those same three cards a dozen more times. I focused so closely on the ace that my eyes began to cross, but even so, sometimes I guessed right, sometimes wrong.

By the end, I was frustrated as hell and feeling a little jingled from the booze, but my curiosity could not be dulled.

"Let's try this another way, shall we, Jack? Let's make it fool-proof," Uncle John ventured as he turned up a corner on the ace. "Even a blind man could win now."

Reassured of my ability, I watched him throw the cards again. This time, I guessed correctly.

"Not so hard now, eh?" he asked, "Let's go again."

Once more, I turned up the correct card.

Feeling chancy and confident, I reached into my trouser pocket and pulled out the toy bomber that was my most prized possession.

"I'd like to bet for real," I told Uncle John as I pushed it into the center of the table alongside the three cards, "my plane against your five dollars."

Uncle John's eyes widened in thorough amusement. "Are you sure?" he asked me.

I nodded my consent. After all, the corner of the winning card was turned up, and I couldn't lose.

—Except, following the deal, when I selected the card with the bent-up corner, it was a king. Panic coursed through my adolescent mind, and I reached out instinctively to grab my toy. Clearly anticipating my response, Uncle John swept his hand across the table and snatched it up before I even got close.

"No reneging!" Uncle John chastened me as he deposited my precious plaything into his shirt pocket.

"But that's not fair!" I cried accusingly, "I picked the card with the turned-up corner! It was a sure bet! You cheated!"

"I did?" Uncle John asked innocently.

"Yes!" I declared.

"How?"

I opened my mouth to return a scathing reply and then closed it again.

"Unless you can prove that I cheated, the bet stands."

I sunk into my chair, defeated.

"It just goes to show you, Jack, that you never really know. All of life is one big con from start to finish. Nothing is what you think it is, and you can't trust no one. See now, I'm a gambler—been a gambler for ten good solid years—and I've come to find that gamblers are some of the most honest men in the whole country. You see, everybody knows that gamblers always have a trick or two up their sleeve and that they approach life from the other side of the coin. There ain't a man I've ever known who's gone through life without cheating a time or two to get ahead, but the difference is, everybody who ain't a gambler endeavors to convince everybody else that he's honest."

I listened, but I didn't respond; I was still sore over the loss of my plane.

"Oh, come now, Jack," he remarked in an attempt to rally my spirits, "grab that bottle over yonder and pour us another round; I'll give you a chance to win back your bomber."

I was still angry with him, but curiosity about the mystifying game got the better of me, and I did as he said.

It was that fateful evening that I learned my first short con. Monte is the

110

game's proper moniker, but Uncle John insisted I call it Rocky Mountain Euchre instead.

"After all, monte's been around for over a century now, and even the most brainless suckers are beginning to catch on," he explained as he taught me the proper technique for seamlessly switching cards on the deal, entirely unbeknownst to the bettor.

Rocky Mountain Euchre was far from the last game that Uncle John taught me in my apprenticeship there, and every new day brought another lesson in sharping. Sleight of hand was Uncle John's claim to fame, and he tutored me in every conceivable method of trickery. I absorbed this most intriguing schooling like a sponge and responded to it with unparalleled enthusiasm. The morning's work in the garden seemed trifling and insignificant when set against the excitement that awaited me if I did a good job. And as a result, my days of ostracism were largely pleasant and replete with new experiences.

Once I'd completed my chores, I was free to explore the town completely unchaperoned, and I peered into every corner of it with glee, spurred on by that blithe curiosity that only boys of a certain age know. Leadville was smaller than Denver, but what it lacked in size, it more than made up for in excitement. The lawless element that Leadville had played host to since its inception had faded with the silver and gold, but what remained was a whole host of men as rugged as the pines and as tough as hardtack. They were men in the wildest and most grandiose sense, and watching them toil in the daytime and take to the streets at night left me awestruck. By that year, an upsurge of morality gripped both the state and federal governments, and all the pleasures that men of the world enjoy most—wagering, whiskey-drinking, and whoring—had been made illegal. However, just like in Denver and other prominent western towns, the men of Leadville heeded the voice of government just about as regularly as they heeded the voices of their wives, and underground saloons, false-front gambling halls, and red-light boarding houses flourished as a result.

About two weeks into my residency in Leadville, I accompanied Uncle John to my first speakeasy—a cloistered, makeshift dive bar disguised as a stockroom behind the general store. I stood nearby—drink in hand—watching him kibitz with the regulars as they scared up a game. Recreational games between acquaintances were considered a low-stakes skill-sharpening activity designed to pass the time until an out-of-town sucker could be landed and given a proper fleecing. I watched these matches in attentive silence as the men cast their bets, collected their checks, swapped tricks, and conned one another silly. Sometimes I watched them all night long, and when last call came around, Uncle John always made right sure that we ordered two drinks apiece.

On days we didn't spend sousing in the stockroom, we played at home, as Uncle John endeavored to instruct me in every hustler's fancy that man had ever devised. We'd spend long evenings wagering by candlelight with a bottle of whiskey and several dog-eared decks of cards between us. Each time we bet, Uncle John placed my toy bomber on the table with the stipulation that if I won, I'd get to keep it. He played against me as shrewdly and unrelentingly as he would Bat Masterson—and needless to say, I lost every serious game we played for the first two months I stayed there. The frustration was fierce and mounting, but dogged persistence kept me at it, and at last, in mid-September, in the final hand of a game of five-card draw, I put up a spade flush against his full house. Uncle John was floored by his unprecedented loss and utterly baffled by how I'd delivered it. I collected my plane as recompense and, wholly pleased with myself, reveled as he praised me and toasted to my accomplishment. Of course, Uncle John was unaware that I had pulled the fifth spade from behind my ear, where it'd been stuck in the band of my cap. Though if he had known, I'm sure he would've been doubly proud.

The next day, when I was supposed to be in school, Uncle John took me down to the haberdasher and had me fitted for my first pair of slacks, shirt-sleeves, and waistcoat and then brought me around in succession to the barber, cobbler, and milliner. He likely spent a small fortune, but by the end of that afternoon, it was no question that I was the best-dressed twelve-year-old that Leadville had ever seen. Considering I'd never known my wardrobe to consist of much more than patchwork hand-me-downs since the day I was born, I was prouder than a peacock swaggering around in my new duds and wished more than anything that my brothers could see me.

That evening, after I'd visited just about every store in town showing off my new clothes, I accompanied Uncle John to the cigar shop. Before we went inside, he paused outside the door, looked me up and down like he was eyeing up a crap shot, stuffed a four-bit stogie between my lips and a wad of bills in my pocket, and ushered me in through the front door. Before I even got a chance to ask him what was going on, he hustled me through the shop to the walk-in humidor in the back. As soon as the heavy wooden door swung open, I suddenly understood his intent. No shelves lined the walls of the tepid room, and the partition in the back had been removed, creating an area twice the size of the original space. Several smooth, round card tables had been assembled in place of the customary merchandise, and a faro layout had been erected in the corner. The electric lights were dim, the air was stale and thick with smoke, and the handful of men present were perched like vultures upon their stools when we arrived.

Uncle John removed his hat and greeted those assembled coolly and cordially—then he introduced me, his nephew, the prodigy. Apparently, some of the men there knew Uncle John even better than I did, for they immediately scoffed and shook their heads incredulously.

"I got to hand it to you, Cassidy; this one's certainly original," a portly English chap declared.

"No doubt more so than the last," a second man with a scar on his cheek spoke up. "Say, boy," he asked, turning to me, "where'd he find you? Did he pick you up off the street or nab you out of the cradle?"

The whole bunch of them laughed callously.

When I explained to them that I really was his nephew, it only seemed to arouse more confusion.

"Any mother that'd rightly let her boy go off with you must really be a sap. We all find our way here one way or another, but why dress up a boy his age in such a way and bring him here, to this place? For what gain?" A third, older and far more somber man asked.

"Oh, my sister's a peach," Uncle John replied casually, "but her opinion of me is a bit dyed-in-the-wool. You see, fellas, I was relegated to set this boy straight. He's here doing time with me for shooting his brother with a .45. Yessir, purty near blew his whole damn foot off. This poor soul's been destined for the penitentiary since he drew his first breath, and that still may be where he ends up, but at least this way, he'll have something to do when he gets there—and if he does preserve himself from that life, he'll meet with more fortune than he ever would otherwise."

Despite Uncle John's candid account, the bunch of them were not easily convinced, and I held my head up proudly amidst their digs. They meant me no disservice, surely, and likely pitied me as well. Once Uncle John finally convinced them to let me play that evening when the rest of the men and their marks arrived, I used every ounce of their skepticism to my advantage.

Gamblers, as a class, consider themselves to be more honorable than any other men of money in the country. Though scorned by their equals in wealth, they continually count the best of them amongst the most generous, charitable, and moral men that have ever walked the earth. They consider the fate of the victims they've bested to be no fault of their own and collect the debts they are owed with the same calm sense of entitlement as the infernal taxman. Most of these men had no qualms whatsoever about beating a twelve-year-old boy, but they were doubtful that the twelve-year-old boy actually could, in fact, beat them. Though a novice, I quickly won the respect of Uncle John's compatriots, along with a good deal of their money. Granted, they, like he, were professional gamblers who made their living off of other men's misfortunes—misfortunes that were oftentimes artificially inflated—and I immediately realized that I still had a great deal to learn.

Every day after school, I hightailed it to the humidor, where I learned the secrets to every game under the sun. The hours I spent in the classroom sped by like water in a torrent and were occupied chiefly by thoughts of the night to come, tricks that needed polishing, and schemes I could hardly wait to enact. Although, as per my understanding with Uncle John, I attended every class and was never tardy. I may not have made high marks by any means, and homework of any form was still entirely out of the question, but the marked change in my performance was enough to appease Ma.

I began receiving letters from her the same week I arrived, and they continued in a regular fashion throughout the time I spent there. Her first letters were dire and somber as she recounted the critical weeks Robbie spent in the hospital, peaked and delirious from a dangerously high fever that lasted for ten whole days before it finally broke. Her distress was raw, but as Robbie regained his strength and Uncle John reported my strict obedience and diligence in work and school, her tone gradually recovered its usual cheerful concern. She made sure to forward me all four of my brothers' letters from the war in addition to the notes that Mick, Robbie, and Billy occasionally sent along.

In October, as the ominous winter chill began to alight upon the land, I plowed under the wizened remains of the summer's bounty and was free to devote nearly all my time and attention to gambling. By the time winter recess was declared in December, I felt as much like a man as any other. I weathered the holidays away from home considerably better than expected and spent most of the Christmas season drinking mulled wine on the corner of 6th and Harrison with Uncle John and his band of miscreants, watching the lady shoppers and whistling as they strolled by.

All things considered, life was perfectly grand. I'd become well-known amongst the residents of Leadville and regarded as a bit of a boy enigma. Thanks to Uncle John's intervention, my reputation as a scamp and a troublemaker had not followed me there, and accounts of my remarkable skill as a card sharp spread through the Colorado underworld like an oilfield fire. Sharpers from other parts of the state stopped by the humidor to try their luck against me, and to Uncle John's pride and delight, I never stepped down from a challenge. No cards were ever dealt in the humidor that I didn't have a stake in, and each time my turn to deal came around, Uncle John's cautionary words rang out clear and true in my mind, guiding my hands and fueling my exploits.

In the six months I stayed with him, I never broke a single rule, never became personally acquainted with the strop in the doorway, and never had to till even one additional inch of land. As a result, Uncle John and I became fine companions, trusted confidants, and a pair of speculators to be reckoned with. For Christmas, he'd gifted me my very own watch and chain with a twenty-dollar gold piece affixed at its terminus, and as the new year dawned, I set my sights on a future replete with prosperity.

<h1 style="text-align:center">III</h1>

However optimistically I regarded the year to come, 1918 seemed to have a far more dire fate in store for me. In the week following Christmas 1917, tragedy struck the Jones clan. A wire from Denver arrived at the telegraph office in the early morning hours of January 1st, and the Western Union man knocked upon our door as Uncle John and I fought off the lingering aftershocks of the previous night's debauch. The message it contained struck me as violently as a kick in the chest and immediately ended my tenure in Leadville. My brother Jerry was dead. Unlike the amenable holiday cease-fires of earlier years, no such truce had been imposed, and his plane had been shot down over a German encampment on none other than Christmas Day. Ma was utterly devastated by the news and mournfully beckoned me home from my exile. Tears have stained my memories of our reunion, and grief imbued the ensuing weeks as the whole town mourned Jerry's loss.

Uncle John stayed with us until Pa left for the mountains. At home, I continued to be my same saintly self, much to my family's disbelief, and in the evenings, Uncle John was my key to Denver's speakeasies and gambling dens. When he finally returned to Leadville in April, he fixed it with his acquaintances at Pike's to let me gamble there unaccompanied as long as I presented a signed slip from my teacher each afternoon. I thought that added condition was utter hogwash, but having little choice in the matter, I remained in school. I told the teacher the slips were for Ma as proof of my attendance and therefore was allowed to relish in the delights of cutthroat backroom gambling as frequently as I desired. However, school proved even more dull and uninteresting than before. I'd become as much a man as a twelve-year-old can in the preceding months and, therefore, no longer partook in the joys of boyhood. I avoided my old gang of friends, sold off my collections of marbles and cards, and began to keep company solely with men. And I was not the only Jones boy to do so. As it turns out, in the eventful half year that'd passed, all of the Jones boys had become men.

I suppose I'd been foolish to imagine that my life would return to its former glory following my return, but at that time, I'd known nothing else and therefore knew not what to expect. Even after the shock of Jerry's death wore off and we all tried to resume our daily comings and goings, the sense of home that Five Points had always provided before never returned. I felt like a stranger in the very place I'd been born and raised, and my family, though welcoming of my return, regarded me with a good deal of mistrust and treated me as a bit of an outsider. As much as I had grown and changed in the brief time I'd spent away, so had my brothers.

When my four eldest brothers answered the call to war in 1917, none of us ever imagined that only one of them would return, but in the end, only Phil came marching home. Guilt-ridden and shell-shocked from his time in the trenches, he abandoned his childhood calling of working as a blaster in the mines and became a traveling merchant on the Mississippi. Mick graduated from high school in the summer of '17 and had been accepted into Boston College, from which he had returned for Jerry's service and for which he again departed thereafter. Billy, too, had left home and, following my return, took up smithing under the direction of a mentor in Auraria. However, it was Robbie who'd changed the most. Billy's love of study had infected him during those two sedentary months, and religion had become foremost in his mind. For Robbie, there was no more tumbling along the riverbank, no more street-corner brawls, and no more mischief-making. He'd given up drinking, chewing, and even delivering Pa's gin. His trauma had inspired in him a profound change of heart, and as a result, he distanced himself from my devilry. As a good Christian, he'd forgiven me for my egregious assault but was nonetheless wary of me from that day forward. He'd become quiet, reserved, and pensive, and before the end of that decade, took a steamer east, bound for a seminary in New England. The banks of the South Platte were now silent; the whooping and caterwauling of boisterous youngsters faded into the placid memory of time. Before I knew it, I was the last son who had not yet left home to pursue worldly concerns. As for myself, being too young to have fought in the war, too dull to have become a scholar, too wicked to have become a clergyman, and too lazy to have become an apprentice, like a disciple of Casey Jones, I hopped on a freighter after the death of my mother and became a tramp, akin to the men I'd watched ride the rails all my life.

Ma died in 1920. I was fourteen years old. It was December when it started snowing and February by the time it stopped. Sometime during those forty days, Pa and I awoke to the sound of our world crashing down. We'd both fallen asleep at the kitchen table, a handle of the youngest gin I'd ever tasted between us. We found her in her bed, buried in snow; one of the biggest, heaviest beams that'd ever held up any roof in any house in the country laid right across her. Pa and I tried like hell in a bucket to free her, but it would've taken all my brothers and ten more men like us to move that old beam so much as an inch. It'd been one of the first cut in Colorado nearly one hundred years ago, and before that, it had grown up in the ground for twice as long. It took three men eight hours the next day to saw clean through it and six of us to haul the pieces down to the gully where they'd never be seen again. The doctor said she'd died instantly.

We buried her exactly two months before Pa returned to the mountains. That gave us time to repair the roof and put up a few more batches of gin. I spent most of those two months by his side, and in all that time, he never spoke more than two dozen words to me. He never was quite the same. He never said a word about the thing, and though I never saw him cry, he did more talking with his eyes than he ever did with his mouth. He'd spend all day minding the still, just sitting and staring at it, a quart jar in his hand, eyes bleak and empty. He made more gin in those two months than in any previous season—after all, he needed to, for he was drinking far more. He'd swill that hooch from sunup on, and when night came, he'd go over to the stove in the kitchen, where he'd light a fire and heat up a can of beans. No, he never said a thing about it, but you never did see a man heat up a can of beans and look so forlorn. He never showed it all that much when she was living, but he must've loved her something fierce. When she died, so did he. His body kept living just the same, but his spirit went on ahead to the grave. For Sampson Jones, Death had no mercy at all—for it had stolen his three eldest sons from him, and then it had taken his bride.

He left in April when the snow melted, and I stayed behind. I cut hickory in the daytime to keep that gin boiling up, and I drank it on down at Pike's in the evenings. I kept on that way for a month or two until the warmth of summer impressed upon me its allure, and then I turned my sights east. By that time, I was bored and hungry and itching for adventure, ready and eager to leave Denver behind. So, I packed up a gunny sack, crossed the river, and walked the tracks until I made it to the railyards. When I got there, I hopped on the first outbound freighter I saw, and after five years of drifting along from here to there, I found myself in Tulsa, which would prove to be the bane of my existence for the rest of my life. However, I've always been a man of action, never one to complain. I always figured if you've got time enough to complain, you've got time enough to change.

I turned 21 in prison, doing life without parole. There was no chance of getting out early on good behavior, so I figured there was no reason to follow the rules. I was sent to prison for fighting, and that being the case, I didn't think there was anything worse they could do to me for fighting while in prison. Boy, was I wrong.

Solitary confinement doesn't mean a thing to you until you've done that kind of hard time, and the words hard time don't mean a thing until you've been in solitary. The first three days are the hardest. After that, you begin to lose track of time. Going mad is the surest way to stay sane in there. If you try to hold on too tight to your mind, that's when it slips away from you. I know some youngins who've done time and told me that solitary hadn't rattled them. As soon as I hear them say things like that, that's when I know they're lying. There isn't a man alive that time spent in the hole doesn't touch. You find yourself wishing to live every painful and ugly moment of your life over again—a hundred times if necessary—rather than spend another hour, another minute alone in the dark. Maybe it wouldn't be so bad if the walls weren't so close together or the floor wasn't so hard and cold. Perhaps it'd be sufferable if they fed you something other than bread and water, or if you could wash or shave or take a civilized shit—but there ain't a warden alive who'd ever stand for you to find out. I don't know how the other men did it, but I know full well the only reason I made it out without caving my head in against the wall was because of the whistle of that train. I strained and listened for it all day long—counting the seconds—mapping out its track in my mind. Anticipation can bring a man through hell and back, and every time I heard it, that whistle removed me from the horrors of reality and whisked me up into the world of my memories. It saved me; I have no qualms about admitting it. And in addition to preserving me from the imposing fate of death, it also made me think; not only of the past but of the future—a future of my own making.

I stayed in that lousy prison for three years and four months, a good half of which I spent in solitary. After my last stint in there—two whole weeks for bashing a guard over the head with a chow tray—rather than repent and reform my evil ways, I decided that I'd had enough. I knew I couldn't bear to spend the rest of my life living inside those same old gray walls, eating the same old gray slop, and staring into the same old gray faces of the other inmates who'd been dead inside for so long and were just waiting for their bodies to catch up. I vowed that there was no way I would grow old in that prison; there was no way I would be one of those ragged old coots carving another dreary line into those old cell walls. It was either bust out or die trying, and the idea of dying didn't sit too well with me, so I had no choice but to find a way to escape.

Many men in the past had attempted to escape from McAlester, both through the use of force and subterfuge. Some had been successful, but most had been sought out and recovered, and a good number of them had returned prostrate, destined for a slab in the infirmary. I never had any intention of counting myself among them. Many men in my position considered this undertaking an impossible feat. However, self-reliance is a virtue—likely the only one I can claim to possess—and the combination of ample time and desperation has the tendency to spur some remarkable ingenuity.

Escaping by use of force—intercepting a guard and stealing his weapon, taking him hostage, and threatening every last living soul standing between me and the front door to freedom—certainly aroused my faculties. But the level of security, however slight, that was guaranteed by subterfuge edged out ahead in the end. As I've mentioned, escaping McAlester on foot was entirely out of the question. There were only two other ways into the prison, and therefore, only two ways out—by truck and by train. Miles of track cut across the grounds as trains passed through McAlester weekly, bringing in raw materials for the various industries housed there and transporting the prison's wares to the free market. Freighters were continually being loaded and unloaded on sidings throughout the compound, and every time I stepped into a car, the beckoning call of liberty invaded me with maddening intensity. The temptation to stow away amidst the pallets of new bricks was nearly impossible to deny, but I knew the odds of successfully slipping the bonds of my confinement in that manner were incorrigibly low. The most glaring obstacle was that no train pulled out of McAlester until all the inmates on the detail were accounted for—a procedure that was as demeaning as it was disheartening.

Of course, escaping via automobile was nearly as damning. Delivery trucks, grocery trucks, mail trucks, and several others entered and exited the prison throughout the day. Because the details assigned to offload them were considerably smaller, the guards were somewhat less attentive, focusing instead on the articles being delivered to ensure that no contraband was being introduced to the prison. It might seem like slipping into the back of one of these trucks when the guards' backs were turned was an obvious method of escape—but as a rule, all incoming and outgoing vehicles were thoroughly searched at the gate, making an attempt of that nature even more fruitless. However, to every rule, there is an exception.

After spending three years in that prison, I was well-versed in the schedules of most of the guards and had intimate knowledge of their personalities. I knew which guards were sons of bitches, which bent regulations to allow the inmates small pleasures, which were devilish taskmasters, and which were criminally lazy. I knew I had no chance of getting by the young guards, the hotshots eager to supplant their rookie status; however, the older guards were another story. Those veterans who'd been at McAlester when it was built and who, after twenty years of toting a badge and a gun, could taste the sweet breath of retirement in the breeze were where I concentrated my efforts. They were the ones who I knew were capable of missing a trick—especially if it was played by a master.

I threaded through my plan for months, hashing it out with as much foresight and cunning as I could muster. I sought to predict every potentiality and manufacture methods to combat them. I rehearsed my escape day in and day out—as I loaded bricks into the kiln, ate in the mess, lay on my dirty mattress at night, and served my time in solitary. I may've put my head down and churned out work as was expected of me, but I gritted my teeth and swore to God and the devil that I would not die there. I had far too much potential as a desperado to spend my life as an involuntary anchorite. I had far too much virility and charm to live out the rest of my days as a celibate, and I certainly had far too much good, strong vinegar running through my veins to die an early death. I would've never supposed that I was destined for old age, but I was most certainly of the opinion that no red-blooded Denver man should give up his earthly stake and claim his seat in purgatory while idly doing time.

In the brick plant, the sweltering estival days dragged endlessly on and left me scalded and crimson, my skin as hard-baked and dry as the clay I handled year after year. It was miserable, backbreaking work. I'd curse the sun each morning with as much spite and malice as a condemned man curses the rope. Under my breath, I'd curse the guards every minute of every day as I kept my eyes peeled for inconsistencies, opportunities, the slightest hint of hope, the vaguest shred of chance—and always, I remained vigilant. You see, some men make this world, and some men just live in it. I've always preferred to make the world I live in and yield to no man. There have been times when the world has won out on top, but theirs is the battle, not the war, and it has consistently been my conviction to fight until I die. This dogged determination eventually resulted in circumstances breaking in my favor, and when opportunity knocked, I answered the call with bells on.

On October 20, 1929, I broke out of Oklahoma State Prison in the back of a grocery truck. I had a couple busted ribs on the mend that took quite a beating crashing around in there and one mighty sore back from a tuck-and-roll at forty miles per hour, but all in all, it was a hell of a lot better than having to yield to the tight fist of the law for the rest of my god-damned life, and it took a lot less planning than you might think.

The altercation that warranted my two-week residency in the hole earlier that month had ended with the guard I'd assaulted bludgeoning me into submission with a baton on the floor of the mess hall. I spent two weeks in solitary with three broken ribs, cramped in a space that made it impossible to lay down, struggling through blinding pain to suck in short gasps of wretched, dank air so squalid that if I could've gone the two weeks without so much as a breath, I would've abstained entirely. It was then I vowed that would be the last time. Never again would I suffer so in the bowels of the prison, bound and tortured with dysentery and soul-rotting dampness that lingered long after I returned to my cell.

When I was finally released from torment, after a few days in the infirmary, I was temporarily assigned to KP duty alongside none other than my insipid cellmate, Tennessee Jed. The work was banal and tedious, but it afforded me a chance to heal and, in the end, to escape. Although, when I finally worked up the gall to give old Warden Schaffer the slip, the form my exodus took differed almost entirely from how I'd envisioned it. In fact, the opportunity seemed to present itself with such immediacy that I hardly had time to think.

That fated evening just before sundown, a grocer's truck, stuffed to the gills with vegetables, pulled up to the loading dock behind the kitchen. The guard on duty was Galen Donohue, one of the most senior but careless guards at McAlester. He handed us a list of the various quantities of carrots, potatoes, and parsnips that we needed to offload and proceeded to lean on the truck's fender and absently chat with the driver until we'd completed our task. They talked freely and largely ignored our presence as we limped back and forth from the truck to the stockroom dragging fifty-pound sacks of root vegetables behind us. Considering our physical maladies, it is no wonder Donohue let his judgment slacken with us in his charge. However, it was his disregard that afforded me the opportunity of a lifetime.

The thought of that evening's escape was hardly present in my mind until, amid the course of shuffling amongst the boxes and sacks stacked in the back of the truck, I noticed a foreign article wedged between two sacks of parsnips—a pocketknife! A tidal wave of adrenaline washed over me and practically knocked me off my feet. I snatched it up and immediately deposited it into my pocket, my heart pounding. Such a find was akin to a diamond in a coal mine, and my mind immediately began churning out schemes. However, before I had a chance to enact any of them, providence arrived in the form of a second guard who stumbled across the loading dock, doubled over and clutching his gut.

"Donohue," he called out, green in the face, "you gotta take my post at the gate. I got it—that damn rancid stomach bug. Flannery had it, Dobson had it, Michaels had it, and now I got it. Got it bad."

"Are you two cripples almost finished with that?" Donohue asked as the second guard careened toward the head.

Tennessee peered out from the back of the truck, "yessir," he replied, "just fo' mo' boxes here."

Donohue sauntered over to us as we hoisted the final boxes to our shoulders and examined the inside of the truck. Finding everything in order, he called out to the driver, "when they're finished here, I'll let you out the front gate. Can't leave that post vacant. Even sick as a dog, Johnson should've never left—Schaffer'd have his head for that."

As soon as Donohue turned and strode briskly away toward the front gate, I sprang into action. I ran into the stockroom and swiped an empty fifty-pound sack from the shelf, then grabbed a bewildered Tennessee by the arm and dragged him back to the truck, hissing murderously in his ear that if he did not follow my exact instructions, I would personally ensure that he'd be back in Tennessee within days—lodging at the family plot up on Boot Hill. Knife in hand, I climbed into the sack and told Tennessee to tie it shut as quickly as possible.

"Listen to me," I growled under my breath as he clumsily looped the twine into knots, "when you shut that door behind you, don't turn the handle all the way, leave it only about a quarter down, so the latch is just barely caught. Do you understand?"

"You're crazy, Jack," he stuttered, "you knows they check all these here trucks. They's gon' catch you sure."

"Shut up," I ordered him, digging the tip of the knife into his stomach through the bag, "and if you screw up and I end up back here, I swear by Harry I'll rip your arm off and beat you to death with it!"

"Ok, Jack," he whispered, flustered, as he lumbered out of the truck, "have a good trip, Jack."

Over the pounding of my heart, I heard the truck doors bang shut and the handle turn a quarter of the way. Hope, long buried under years of despair, radiated in my chest. I could taste liberty as surely as I was alive, but I refrained from jumping to any hasty conclusions. The hardest part of the journey was indeed still ahead of me.

As the truck approached the gate, dizzying, paralyzing fear gripped me. The gate was no more than a few hundred yards from the loading dock, but at that moment, it felt like miles. Huddled inside the bag, I closed my eyes and tried to become as still as death and one with the darkness.

Gradually, the truck slowed to a stop in front of the gate. The moment of judgment had come. I wrapped my arms around my aching side and took breaths so shallow I felt as if I was hardly breathing at all. If another guard was on duty, he would've climbed into the truck with a flashlight and taken stock of the cargo, potentially even kicking a few of the closest sacks to ensure they actually contained vegetables and not fugitives. However, somehow, I knew deep down in my soul that Donohue would not so much as unlatch the door—and in a few moments, that gate opened up, and the truck returned to motion again, commuting my sentence and delivering me to freedom. The relief that ran through me was so great I nearly passed out. I felt as if I was drunk on my own incredulity, and rejoicing to myself, I swayed with the rocking and bumping of the truck as it picked up speed and rode past the outer wall, past the cemetery and the brick plant, past the trusty building and the farmland and into the free world.

Unsurprisingly, between the emotional cocktail of exhilaration and disbelief and the darkness that enveloped me, I lost all conception of time. I had no idea where I was, the direction I was headed, or where I was going to end up. I only had minutes before my absence was discovered and hours before my escape was confirmed. The panic that'd taken a brief hiatus resurged with a startling intensity as I groped for a plan in terror. At that exact moment, the whistle of the seven o'clock freight resounded across the plain, closer than I'd ever heard it before. Not only was the truck carrying me away from the prison, it was bringing me nearer to the train!

Reanimated with determination, I cut my way out of the sack and fought to stay on my feet as the truck rolled and bounced down the road with the same carefree abandon as a two-ton tumbleweed. As soon as I got my bearings about me, I lit out with a tremendous flying kick and struck the doors. I tumbled to the floor in excruciating pain, and the doors remained closed. I had to muster the strength to repeat the action three more times before the latch finally gave way and the doors burst open, sending me flying out the back as the truck bumped and crashed over a series of potholes and left a billowing cloud of dust behind it, with me in its wake. For a dizzying, agonizing spell, I lay prostrate in the tall, dry weeds beside the road and dug my nails into the dust as, winded, I cursed God and all creation.

I immediately thought there was no way my dismount had gone unnoticed. But, as I collected my faculties and took stock of how many patches of skin and hair I'd left plastered across the roadway, the sound of the grocery truck, my Trojan horse, faded off into the distance and the whistle of the evening train sounded again, beckoning me on like a siren song. With immense effort, I struggled to my feet and, in the light of the crescent moon, began to hurl myself through the prairie grass in the direction of the whistle. With eyes narrowed toward my objective, all pain and blood loss momentarily ignored, I made it to a clearing through some wiry scrub trees and crept up the embankment toward the big iron beast as it chugged along. Attempting to mount a moving train under cover of darkness is generally considered by novices and seasoned bums alike to be a death sentence, but I was desperate. So, with a leap comprised of far more faith than skill, I caught hold of the ladder on one of the last cars as it reached me. With a final, desperate clamor, I swung up into the belly of the empty boxcar and, utterly exhausted, crawled on my hands and knees to the rear corner, where I sat with my back against the wall, breathing hard and chuckling incredulously at myself.

All of a sudden, I was right back at home. Vast swathes of familiarity, joy, and wonder overtook me, and I sighed. No more cold iron prison cell, no more grueling manual labor, no more choking under the pressure of the guards' boots across my throat, no more half-rotten suppers in the company of men tormented by the threat of mortality and the promise of death. All I had to concern myself with was getting as far away as possible and finding a change of clothes. After all, a man in a striped jumpsuit can't exactly walk into Sears and Roebuck and purchase a pair of overalls on time. But for the remainder of that evening, though I did not sleep a wink, I rode easy, lulled into a state of satisfaction and peace by the rhythmic clapping of the iron wheels over the rail joints.

The next morning, as the sun reached its first gentle tendrils of light above the horizon and through the wooden slats of the car, I peered through the shadowy half-darkness and saw the crouching figure of another man leaning against the opposite wall. I tensed up immediately when I realized I was in the company of a stranger and readied my knife in my hand. Across the foggy divide, I watched with bated breath as he stood, stretched, and ambled toward me. He was thin, wiry, old, and grizzled—a chronic drifter and veteran of the road. He carried a worn gunny sack across his back and donned an army-issue cap atop his grey head.

"I thought I heard you climb in here huffing and puffing long about last night," he told me as he knelt down near me. "Looks like you were in an awful hurry."

Still startled by his presence and naturally suspicious of his magnanimity, I did not respond.

"We passed out of Oklahoma a few hours ago," he continued, "figured you might want to know that. This car's billed to Wichita; should be arriving just after sunup—you might want to start thinking about making your exit."

I cocked my head at him, still wary, "what're you, some sort of talking timetable?" I sneered, "How the hell do you know?"

The little bum laughed, "Boy, I've been up and down this line 'bout a thousand times before you were a dirty thought in your daddy's mind—and unless you want an express trip back to where you came from, I'd advise you listen."

I gave him a good hard looking over and concluded that stool pigeons and those engaged in other such finkery rarely made it to his age.

"In that case, do you happen to have some rags to spare for a fellow down on his luck?" I asked.

He eyed me crossways and scoffed. "Where your luck is concerned, boy, I'd say you're riding pretty damn high," he retorted before digging into his sack and unearthing a spare set of duds for me. The pants came up to my ankles, and the shirt was more a collection of patches than it was a shirt, but they were warm and inconspicuous, and I couldn't have been more pleased. We hopped off together just before daybreak and hunkered down a few hundred yards from the tracks, where we boiled coffee over a fire made from stray kindling and my prison jumpsuit.

"You'll be doing a lot of running," the little bum cautioned me as the fire engulfed the last of the fabric and crackled in the purple dawn.

"Yeah, but I'll be running free," I told him.

III

Big Railroad Blues

I spent the better part of the next decade on the move. I'd spent three years in prison under the watchful eyes of those whose job it was to keep me there. I spent the next three years in virtual obscurity. I hopped from boxcar to boxcar on slow freighters and rode the rods on fast passenger trains. For those three years, I never saw the inside of a city in the daylight. I sprung into boxcars or dropped down into reefer cars and slept during the day. At night, I slipped away into the towns and cities to gamble and scalp the natives for whatever coins and small bills might buy me my next meal. I kept away from the streetlamps and the good parts of town, confined myself mainly to the all-night pool halls and gambling joints, and only hung around the most inconspicuous and well-dug-in speakeasies.

When I gambled, I always kept the odds in my favor, but I did so with greater tact. I kept a low profile and even fixed it so I'd lose every few hands just to convince my opponents that I was on the level and not on the take. I took far fewer chances and kept my odds fair and my pots small, never walking away from the tables at night with more than any one of the players could afford to lose. Small winners, especially migratory ones, are never talked about or remembered. But big winners, especially when they are migratory, seem to find themselves the subject of legends and will, at one time or another, arrive in a town where their reputation has arrived first and alerted both the locals and the law to their presence. Poker players are an especially shrewd bunch; if you swindle them, they will remember your face and name just as clearly as they would their own mother's. After all, if you wound a man's body, it'll heal in a week or two. But, wound a man's pride, and he'll carry his hatred for you into the next life.

I wanted no part of any such talk. I kept away from any and all illicit business except drinking and crooked gambling. When I hopped freight trains, I did so carefully and in good taste, keeping off the caboose and away from the baggage cars. I confined myself mainly to boxcars and away from other bums who might make trouble for me. Once five or more bums congregated in the same car, I slipped away to another part of the train where I might travel unseen and undisturbed. When I did ride the passenger trains, I did so on the brake rods—slung across the trusses, constantly peppered by rocks and cinders, mere inches away from certain death.

If someone had tracked my course across the country during those three years, it would've looked much like the way a moth flies around a flame. I back-tracked, side-tracked, and just plain train-tracked in so many different directions and poked my head into so many different towns I couldn't possibly remember them all. And, that big old spot in the middle that I got close to but never did touch was none other than Oklahoma— because I knew if I showed up anywhere inside that Panhandle border, I'd be as hot as the moth that flew right into the fire.

On the whole, I made no trouble for anybody during those years. Yet, despite my efforts to stay out of the way of the law, I still felt highly uneasy when I would pass the express office or police station and see the bulletin board out front all lit up, displaying the scowling mugs of killers, crooks, escapees, and yours truly. I walked some faster when I came by these places, pulled my hat down a little further and the collar of my coat up a little higher, and headed for the darkest alley or the most jam-packed gambling house where my face would be seldom seen and soon forgotten. Other times, I was so frozen, so weary, and so hungry I contemplated turning myself in just so I could sleep on a straw mattress near a warm stove and leave the cold iron floor of the freighters forever behind me.

As a precautionary measure, I began carrying around working papers that documented John Sampson Jones Jr. as my legal name and Denver as my place of birth. I started keeping a beard and combing the coal dust down into my hair to darken it. After all, it's a great deal harder to see the blond-headed, blue-eyed, clean-shaven face on the wanted poster under all that black soot and facial hair. The poster also listed my height as 5'7" and my weight as 150 pounds. Now, I couldn't do anything about my height, but while Oklahoma State Penitentiary wasn't exactly what I'd call good living, after that first year out on the road, I dropped thirty pounds and wasn't much more than skin, bones, and a mess of dirty blonde hair. There were empty spells when I would've sold my soul for a tray of prison slop and rightly killed for a chance to eat my mother's cooking, but those days were long gone.

There are certain realities a man becomes accustomed to after any extended period on the road. As a fugitive, those realities are considerably harsher and more pervasive than they are when encountered by the average bum. For example, a seasoned traveler is never full. No matter how readily available the meal, he'll never fill himself up to the point of satiety. After he's been hungry once, with not even the faintest idea of where his next meal will come from, he makes sure that he squirrels away some morsel to carry him through the periods of despair and drought with at least a crumb of hope nestled in the corner of his shirt pocket. Even during my years of surfeit and abandon, I refused to embark upon the long road to anywhere without a few crackers or strips of jerky secreted within my clothes.

The only real difference I can spot between man and our fellow animals is hunger. With a full belly, man can think and speak intelligently and concern himself with matters greater than his own sustenance and livelihood. He can endeavor to create, learn, and better himself and his world. But a hungry man is of no more use to his fellows than a feral beast. No higher callings rustle in his bosom. No altruism or humanitarian endeavors strike his fancy. No benevolence occupies his strangled thoughts. He is single-minded to the last and intent on satisfaction, on remedying the pangs in his stomach and the maddening dull ache in his head. To be three or four days empty is a curse I would not wish on my worst enemy. It is a condition I have endured more regularly than I could've ever imagined while sitting at the loaded-down supper table with my family, stuffing my face—entirely unaware that such a wretched state existed.

Hunger, in its various forms, is one thing that likens all travelers to one another. On the road, conservation and resourcefulness are key. Those freighters pass many a Harvey House—but try finding one that'll let you in without a coat. Therefore, I've found that the realm in which hoboes have displayed the most striking ingenuity is in their means of creatively acquiring food. Traveling this way is rarely lucrative, even in my chosen profession, and nourishment is a constant concern. DD'ing—or pretending that you're deaf and dumb—is a method that will forever strike me as particularly clever. As for myself, I never could get the act down just right and have been chased off unfriendly porches by angry homeowners twice as frequently as I ever successfully scored a meal. I usually had better luck bumming my vittles off the railroad workers' wives.

Although I made it a practice never to cast any of my bread upon the water, there were times when providence did deliver. I've found myself on freighters out of California stuffed to the gills with wine grapes headed east and eaten so many that my tongue was stained purple for a week. I've sprung into stock cars full of chickens and made off with a couple of the fattest ones stuffed down in my shirt—the thought of roasting them over a fire causing me to be nearly half-crazed with desire as I waited ravenously for the train to pull to its next shuddering stop. For all the long years of dearth and near-starvation that I endured on the road, there seemed to be a number of fortune moments that arrived just in the nick of time.

I remember one time when I was just coming off a summer on the poultice route in southern Utah. For three whole months, I'd had a full belly warmed with greasy sackfuls of generosity handed out by simple, charity-minded housewives. I'd lived almost exclusively in hobo jungles, which, despite their humble trappings, were a stark contrast to the poverty that followed. My evenings were characterized by purple passages, the kind that can only be had when convened around a campfire under a star-washed sky with ten or twenty other traveling yeggs sipping on Old Chock and telling highly embellished stories of places we'd never been and experiences we'd never had. Once all the wheat had been cut, the vegetables picked, and the fields plowed under, the migrant workers headed south to the lands of perpetual plenty, and I—a fool—headed north. My decision had been in an effort to shirk the bulls that always flocked en masse to freighters headed south just after the picking season ended. They were notorious for busting in on empty cars loaded with travelers and shaking them down—their few meager dollars earned after months of backbreaking toil traded in for a chance to escape being jailed for vagrancy. I wanted to be as far from such extortion as possible, so I decided to lay low along the Canadian border for a while. Of course, after my summer in clover, I'd forgotten what fun it is to freeze your nuggets off with your hands shoved up in your armpits riding in a slat-sided stock car amid the great northern winter.

After the first snow hit Kellogg, I quickly decided that I'd rather try my luck with the bulls than keep hustling the smelter workers for sums that amounted to starvation wages before they even gambled a portion away. However, when I left, I was flat broke. I'd spent my last lonely jit on a gallon of port wine to keep warm with on my trip and couldn't have sold every stitch of worn, torn clothing on my back for so much as a can of WWI surplus hash. By the second frigid night of the journey, I and the little bum who'd left with me had consumed half a gallon of wine but nothing else of any consequence, and we were beginning to get woozy. When our train pulled into the railyards at Boise, we had every intention of throwing our feet in town, but the next freight south—billed to Cedar City, Utah—was leaving as we got there, and there was a storm bearing down. Hunger took a backseat to expediency, and clutching the leavings of our gallon, we sprung into one of the last cars in the line mere minutes before the whistle blew and our great iron steed crept into motion.

It's pitch black at night in an iron boxcar, but with the help of a few dry matches and some hands-on investigation, you can get a general sense of what you're riding with. In this case, when we began to feel around, we discovered our car was stuffed to the gills with sacks of potatoes. Gleefully, we filled our pockets and bindles with as many of the little golden wonders as they could hold, and come daylight, when we crawled out, we stole away with probably twenty pounds between us. Ravenous as we were, we could've eaten them raw, but with only a few hours to morning, we'd held out, and when we lit up a campfire and cooked those babies over it, it was one of the best meals I've ever eaten—beluga caviar included. After all, everything tastes better when you're hungry.

Procuring a meal was certainly my primary concern, apart from being apprehended and carted back to Oklahoma, but it was far from my only worry. One would assume that a bum's life would consist of a whole lot of nothing, considering how that word has come to be used amongst the monied folk these days, but believe it or not, I lost more sleep those three years I spent as a fugitive than I did at any other time in my life. In cold climes especially, I'd beg for a meal with money in my pocket just so I could go back to a room with a real bed to eat it. In the summer months, sleeping out under the stars was about as close to comfort as I could hope to get—but even then, when within city limits, I did so with one eye open, ever vigilant to the ministrations of wild animals, displeased townsfolk, and overzealous coppers. Sequestered in a full boxcar on a long haul was really the only place where I could sleep deeply and feel secure—however, sleep on a freighter is essentially an oxymoron. When your head is bouncing off the cold iron floor, and your teeth are chattering away louder and faster than a typist's keys, counting sheep just doesn't cut it. Many nights, I laid awake with my head resting on my balled-up coat as I vainly tried to cushion the blows, cursing my wretched misfortune and thinking of Ma and Pa and all the various attempts they'd made to spare me from such a life.

Bathing, too, was not so easily accomplished. Such luxury could cost up to a dollar at a tonsorial parlor, and unless I was holding some extra, I considered such an expense to be a rank waste of money. Considering that I shied away from society whenever possible, most times, a dip in a creek or a long, hard downpour were the closest thing I got to a regular bath—although there are instances when I've gotten pretty creative with gambling house sinks as well. Like most bums, I made it a point to carry soap and a razor as often as possible so I'd be well-prepared whenever the opportunity arose.

Granted, no matter how diligently I tried, I nearly always looked like a bum. I could leave a town with a hundred clams in the pocket of a new suit and, by the next night, look just as ragged, sooty, and dirty as the hobo who'd been hitting the rails for the last thousand miles. Thoughts of vanity rarely enter the mind of a traveling man, but the problem was that I drew eyes. Men sized me up as I shuffled down the street, women shot me scornful glances and turned away, and cops took one look at me and invented any excuse to throw me in jail or run me out of town.

Therefore, I had one more reason to confine myself to the wrong side of the tracks—where the bad element presided, and I blended in. In most places, if you traversed these parts with an upright walk and straight hat without dragging a dirty, stinking bedroll behind you, most cops would ignore you, their eyes peeled for more conspicuous offenders. When I lived on the road, I carried a bedroll as often as possible but stashed it somewhere close to the railyard before I broached city limits. About half the time, it was there when I returned—those were desperate times, after all. That's not to say all bums are thieves—on the contrary, the Johnsons of the road were, in fact, some of the most upstanding travelers I've ever met. They'd rob the jewelry store man, the insured homeowner, or the station master blind but wouldn't touch a man's bedroll unless given license by the owner himself. I never could count myself amongst them. Most of the bedrolls I've slept in throughout my life have been stolen.

Living on the edge the way I did in those days required a great deal of horse sense and not much talking. Fugitives are hardly loquacious, and when I spoke willingly to those outside my own kind, the conversation was almost exclusively comprised of inquiry. Of course, I had to ensure that I asked the right questions to the right people—for any misgivings aroused were doubly dangerous for newcomers who looked like me. My affinity for booze nearly got me in Dutch several times—after all, I'd only killed one prohibition agent—the rest of those Izzy and Moe types and the cops that backed them were still rampant everywhere I went. Therefore, suspicion was paramount in my mind at all times. When I cast my eyes upon any street in even the most idyllic town, every soul I saw assumed the character of a copper, stool pigeon, fink, shyster, or otherwise objectionable snitch deemed mortally treacherous until proven otherwise.

Fairly often, in reflecting upon his bygone years, a man finds that his periods of plenty take the sting out of his spells of destitution. In hindsight, he may find it hard to remember those troublesome times of insolvency and ruin, their severity ever so paled by the abundance and fortune that followed in their wake. It is not so for me. I spent the vast majority of my time on the lam cold, weary, and half-starved—and there have been few years since that have been altogether absent of those sordid conditions. Every ice-covered boxcar, every long walk down endless desert road, and every pang in my empty stomach are as real to me now as they were then.

After the Idaho debacle, I decided it was best to remain south of the snow line. I divided my time between Arizona, New Mexico, the Texas Panhandle, and when picking season came around, anywhere west of Barstow. Pickers, being so unfamiliar with superfluous cash, especially during the Depression years, often found themselves in my clutches. But temporary affluence aside, I always felt like I was under the gun. There wasn't even a fleeting moment when I did not feel the iron fist of the law snatching at my coattails. A constant sense of loneliness pervaded those years, and no matter how many willing women of the evening and commiseratory fugitives I ran across in that time, it persisted.

Contrary to my romantic nature, I surrounded myself almost exclusively with men—and my interactions with them, on the whole, were merely transactions. I formed no friendships, but I made no enduring enemies. Their vittles, suits, and billfolds kept me traveling on, and I sought nothing more from them. All desire for companionship, I felt, was decidedly second to wearing my stripes on my arm rather than across my chest. However, I sure did miss women.

Following my remand, there was not a man I met who I trusted, but there were some I grew to like. On the other hand, women are irrefutably dangerous creatures, themselves having the tendency to land a man in utterly ludicrous instances of ill-befitting treachery without even the slightest malicious intent whatsoever—as I so painfully learned back in Tulsa. Therefore, I swung wide around the red-light district, crossed the street when I came to the local whoopie parlor, and stood pat with arms folded when the dame beside me at the speakeasy began crying in her gin over some old flame. But, as it is with all men, I could only withstand so many batted eyes and tight bodices before I broke down—and when I did, I made sure that I left town the same night. After all, the last thing I needed was to sacrifice my liberty in exchange for some post-coital kissing because I just so happened to spend the night with some self-professed single moll who'd decided to snub her boyfriend that evening.

—And where that left me, more often than not, was in a constant state of dissatisfaction. At times, I felt the loneliness to be terminal. I longed for love on the interstate, yearned for affection amidst those frozen nights, ached for the touch of a woman—the brush of a skirt, a gentle kiss—anything other than the hard clank of cold, lifeless steel, cold, tasteless meals, and cold, hard stares. The few moments of intimacy I found, driven predominately by lust, lacked entirely the feminine warmth and adoration I craved and further sullied my ego.

The worst of all such moments found me mulling along Howard Street in San Francisco on one particularly bleak evening. I'd blown in on the southbound freight earlier that morning and was running short on funds, opportunity, and hope. As usual, without making any real effort to find it, my senses had steered me toward the nearest thriving skid row, and in San Francisco in the early thirties, it was a doozy. Like every other neighborhood of its kind, it had all the regular fixtures. On the nearest respectable corner could be found the credit union, its façades adorned by the overdue and the rejected, their pained expressions partially obscured by cigarette smoke as they stared across the corridor into the void of the unknown. About a block north stood the first of several dozen hock shops—its dingy plate-glass windows lined with watches and wedding rings and its sidewalks lined with trollops and snide-eyed racketeers. A spattering of five and dimes, drug stores, and soda fountains followed. Some of these were clearly less reputable than the others, as evidenced by the staggering drunks that littered the street, their empty bottles of Jamaica Ginger, patent medicine, and bootleg hooch rolling in the gutters along with the least of them. And, where there were drunks, there were pool halls; the wild commotion within often spilling out onto the street, where I'd step around a brawl and dodge the ghoulish crowd only to trip over a trembling hophead passed out at the base of a lamppost.

No matter how many cheap flophouses there were to a block, there was always a disproportionate number of hypos, lushes, criminally misfortunate, and otherwise insane denizens sleeping on the street. Breadline refugees and cast-outs from the unemployment office trickled in from alleyways amid the stench of lye soap and chop suey. And, as they arrived, they were dutifully watched by the vague, expressionless eyes of bedraggled housewives as they hung their battleship-grey sheets on tangled clotheslines suspended above the narrow, squalid streets. If you were unlucky enough to appear well-groomed or otherwise out of place, hucksters materialized out of the gloom to pitch you thread and matches, and barefoot little kids with dirt-streaked faces pestered you for nickels. And they did not come alone: beggars accosted you at the end of every alley, babbling fugitives from the sanitarium began to spin you their contrivances on world peace, and if any of the former did not get you, the hookers did.

All of my life, even in the most unlikely of circumstances, I seemed to find myself an apt target for these advances, and that evening in San Francisco was no different. As I shuffled through the midnight gloom listening to the rank calls of pimps and gangsters and shifting my last ninety cents around in my sock, a figure from the shadows approached me. She was an old, gnarled harpy of a woman, aged at least fifty and ridden hard and put away wet a good number of those years. Her dress was beaded nylon, her cloche hat heavily starched, and an imitation fox stole draped loosely over her narrow, gaunt shoulders. Her hair was bleached, and the smoke from her cigarette had caused the curl to drop. She had the eyes of a nebbish and the voice of a tugboat captain. There were more lines in her face than there are on the highway.

"Evening, Honey," she crooned as she sashayed up to me and slid her arm around my waist, "would you like some company for a while?"

"No," I told her outright, sullenly picking up the pace.

"Miserable evening. Feels like the smog is just reaching down and pulling the breath right out of you," she replied, undaunted, matching my step.

I averted my eyes and ignored her.

"Where are you headed?" she asked, "I'll walk with you."

"I don't want your company," I responded forcefully, "now get away from me."

"Oh, you don't mean that!" she exclaimed playfully, hooking her arm in mine and pressing her head against my chest, "who else is going to give you what you really want tonight...what you really need?" I could feel her hot, heavy breath on my neck.

"Get the hell outta here, will you!?" I shouted, shoving her away with a glare. As I did so, under the light of the streetlamp, I suppose she got a good look at my face for the first time. Startled, her eyes widened, and she flew back to me, all coquettish pretense dropped.

"You look like my dead husband!" she cried, clinging to me in the middle of the sidewalk and gazing into my eyes.

"Then I suppose your husband was a very fine-looking man," I responded dryly, unaffected by her emotional display.

In an instant, she erupted into a mad fit of laughter, "no, Sonny," she cackled, "he was about as fine-looking as a dead minnow in the sun, but boy was he rich!"

I stared back at her, partly exasperated, partly embarrassed, and partly intrigued by her novel approach.

"I ain't rich," I told her.

"I don't care," she replied.

Whether she just wanted a few minutes of shelter from the cold or if I really did look like her dead husband, I'll never know, but I kept my ninety cents, and we both got a little warmer.

Towns, rooms, schemes, money, marks, women—they all passed in and out of my life with as much tenacity and predictability as a whirlwind. The only constant of my life in flux was the train. It was the only last gleaming vestige of hope I had at a new start. It was my only subterranean means of escaping one bad stint with a chance of a better turn at the other end of the line. When set against the alternative, all the discomfort and despair became largely inconsequential. The train made me a shadow, a ghost. It kept me safe, and just like when I was back in McAlester, it kept me sane.

To this day, I love the sound of that train approaching—the click of her wheels rolling over rail joints, the high-pitched trill of her whistle—I always walk toward it, never away. To me, it's like a lullaby—and Lord knows it's the only one I've had for a long time. Even after all these years, riding the rails has retained its allure and mysticism. The trains, the roads, the depots—they've all become like old friends. And, in that very same fashion, the relationship we maintain is one of both love and hate. Aside from Bertha, I do not believe there is any other element of my life I've cursed more than the train. In my dealings with flat-wheeled boxcars, rough grades, rawhide hoggers, petulant brakemen, and hardnosed bulls, I've used more expletives than a whole team of mule skinners pulling a heavy load uphill in the snow. However, I've yet to experience a moment of solidarity equal to that which is had while riding through the sandy Georgia wilderness in a side-door Pullman at dawn, feeling the early spring breeze rustle through my clothes and the Blue Ridge mountain air soak into my lungs. In such moments, with a full belly and a good coat, you feel just about as free as you're ever going to get.

Especially on a long haul in the west, when stations and towns could be a hundred miles apart with nothing in between except water tanks and emptiness, a man finds himself clinging to the train like she was his woman and regarding her as such. Since the dawn of the industrial age, men have flocked to the rails with the same fervor as they pursue gold, silver, and oil. Railroads are the rivers of the modern world. They are life-bringers and life-changers, but unlike the rivers, their course is entirely dependent upon the will of men. Towns, cities, livelihoods—they all come and go with the roads. All of society's excrement can be found along the tracks, rusting and rotting—reminders of a torrid history teeming with both progress and shame. They are the bum's sanctuary and the scavenger's delight. They are the dreamer's chariot and the adventurer's passport. For a fugitive, they were both an Elysium and a nightmare.

As long as we were moving, I felt relatively comfortable. However, every time we pulled into the depot or the yards, the hair on the back of my neck would stand up. As soon as I emerged from the safety of my niche, there was no telling what would be there to greet me.

A commercial depot was far more perilous than the marshalling yard. There, the eyes were more prevalent, the bulls were tougher, and there were fewer places to hide. On the other hand, the yards were a labyrinth of switches and signal towers, lights and sidings, with so much activity for a man to get lost in that you could become almost invisible. However, this asylum was far from guaranteed, and unless I rode in under cover of darkness, I'd swing off just outside the yards and catch it out on the run. This approach was common to most of us tramps, and outside larger towns where the hobo jungles thrived, when that freight would start rolling up a grade, a whole wave of men would rise out of the weeds and run toward it.

Most of these men spent their time in-between trains inhabiting the jungles—shaving, cooking, sleeping, recuperating, shooting the shit, polishing their shell game, or just getting drunk. There was always some old cloudy-eyed buzzard stirring a pot of mulligan over a fire surrounded by drying shoes and dripping laundry. You could also expect to find one or two runaway road kids who, in making a temporary home out of the jungle, were relegated as errand boys. The advantage inherent in freckle-faced youth and apparent innocence was valueless to a bunch of dirt-caked, rut-faced, down-and-out sots living in tree-lined groves beside the tracks and for their trouble, the kids always ate well and were looked after. The jungles were oases for migrants goaded by trouble, and as long as you didn't make any while you were there, you were generally welcome to stay for as long as you wanted.

However, as for myself, I hated the jungles. I found them to be overwhelmingly depressing places, despite their solidarity. In my early years of traveling, they'd served as a necessary means of networking, honing my trade, and learning about this strange and dangerous world I'd chosen to enter. But during the Depression, their prevalence grew tremendously, and their population changed significantly. The rise of the fruit tramp and the dust bowl refugee—both classes without the slightest capacity for dereliction among them—made me even more of a pariah than I had been before. I wanted to keep on the move, but when I was in dire straits, the jungles became a necessity. They offered shelter, sustenance, and humanity. Granted, in those days, I had little use for humanity.

I found safety and solace in those places where other men found loneliness and despair. Traversing the Kansas prairie or the Colorado Plateau once the train has passed and not a soul is stirring for miles on end is a condition of mind and body that often sends shivers up men's spines. The sense of utter aloneness that overtakes you, the quiet, wordless fear that creeps in, the sublime knowledge that you could scream for a century and nobody would hear you often make such tracks miserable for most men. But contrary to most men, I wasn't afraid of the weather or wild animals or going a few days without a good hot meal. Rather, I was afraid of men, specifically those who had the unrestricted authority to tell me that I was to spend the rest of my life pounding salt and hauling clay. I trusted no one and watched my back—because there wasn't anybody else who was going to watch it for me. Although, as some scarce instances proved, there were exceptions to my cynical mistrust.

The first time I traveled to Seattle was after swinging onto the blind end of a baggage car in Dryden and holding it down all the way out. It was early summer; the logging season was in full swing, and I knew those men would be itching to spend some of their hard-earned money soon. With high hopes of setting myself up in an oft-frequented dive and living large on their losses, I beat it north from Yuma and was on the last leg of my journey. At that time, I'd yet to find myself west of the Cascades and, to my great pleasure, was heading there fast on the BNSF mainline. I had a fresh sack of smoking with me and, safe from the wind, had settled myself in with the makings and begun rolling cigarettes by the dozen. I was so immersed in the task that I hardly noticed when another tramp climbed onto the platform beside me a few miles from our last stop.

He was hardly more than a boy, maybe seventeen or eighteen at most. He wore a broad-brimmed straw hat, patched corduroy overalls, and a pair of mud-caked boots that looked like they'd seen Civil War service.

"Howdy, pardner! Where ya hailin' from?" he asked breathlessly as he knocked some soot from his clothes.

I eyed him hesitantly and continued rolling my cigarettes without reply.

"Say, can a body git one o' them?" he requested sheepishly, "ain't got no 'bacca myself. Ah boarded 'er out from tha' jungle jus' past Berne. Gon' see if ah c'n hold 'er down 'til she hits Seattle. Headed out ta Tacoma myself—got a sister thar. Been married pert' near a year now. She's got a youngin' named after Paw, you see, he's dead now—had an awful mess of that sugar trouble, Paw did—an' I'mma goin' f'r to visit them out there for a good while and...."

"Oh, here!" I shoved a smoke into his outstretched hand, hoping it would shut him up for a while, but he just rambled on.

"...her husband works f'r one of them there meatpackers unions an' is gonna see 'bout git'n me a job. Things down on the farm ain't been all too good lately, an'—say, pardner, you never tole me where yer hailin' from!"

I crushed the loose end of a cigarette between my lips and stood up, "I don't think that's rightly none of your business, pardner." I replied with a sneer. In those days, a talkative bum had just about the same appeal to me as dysentery, and I headed for the ladder to the deck.

"I wouldn't ride 'er up there," he cautioned me, "tunnel a' comin'. Coal smoke'll get ya."

I paused in my ascent only to scoff, "A little coal smoke don't bother me none!" I shouted back to him, "I ain't no sissy."

I seated myself on the deck, shaking my head at the exchange that had just taken place. Some gay cats have an insatiable need to flap their gums, and they were hard-pressed if they thought they had an audience in me.

From atop the train, I surveyed the lush, green Washington landscape. An endless expanse of sky-grazing pines covered the hills and ridges of that mountain country, rising and falling, dipping and twisting around the narrow railroad grade. It was a clear, cloudless morning in the great virgin wilderness, 14,000 feet high. The air was pure as crystal, and I drank it in like cold sparkling water rushing forth from a bubbling spring. Riding the deck in such climes imparts an unshakable feeling of invincibility to a man, no matter his ails. With the boundless power of that iron beast beneath you reaching speeds of eighty miles per hour or more and vast expanses of unmolested, primeval scenery soaring past, one can't help but feel their heart swell with both the humble admiration of a frontiersman and the pride of a king. But, the Road allows no false impressions, and she never permits you to sit on top of the world for long. In fact, it seems that she requires you to pay handsomely for such sublime pleasures.

Several miles down the line, I noted with pique that the gay cat had been accurate in his prediction: the gaping maw of a tunnel loomed ominously in the distance. In a decision comprised almost exclusively of pride, I shifted to my stomach but remained atop the blind. I'd held down trains through tunnels before, and while it was far from the most leisurely riding, it was surely preferable to remaining on the platform below with such disdainful company. Or so I'd thought. Little did I know the Cascade Tunnel measures nearly eight miles long.

I was atop the first blind—the car directly behind the tender on all passenger trains—and when we hit that tunnel, the smoke immediately laid flat across the tops of the cars. With the clearance above measuring only a couple to three feet, it had nowhere else to go. This I expected. What I did not expect was its duration. The hogger halved his speed upon approach and took the tunnel at a calm and unhurried twenty-five miles an hour. This would have been perfectly tolerable at a shorter stretch but enveloped by the impenetrable darkness and the spectral glow of the headlamp, I began to get that sort of creeping, tingling anxiety that only overcomes a man when he would prefer nothing more than to crawl entirely out of his skin. My eyes burned with such stinging intensity it felt as if lit matches were being held against them. My lungs instantly filled with the dense black smoke, and the more I coughed, sputtered, cursed, and gasped, the more it got to me and the faster my throat closed up. I tried to hide my face in my shirt, but such an attempt was fruitless. I clamored for breath like a drowning man caught in the current, straining with every fiber of my being for a lungful of that beautiful clean air that'd been so profusely abundant mere moments before. And, as I lay there suffocating, my consciousness began to take leave of me. Fear's ghostly black hands tightened increasingly around my throat as my heart swelled and pounded in my chest. To pass out on the deck almost certainly spelled death. Panicked, I inched my way backward in the direction of the ladder, thrashing about wildly with my feet as I felt for it, the stone roof of the tunnel hurtling by mere inches from my skull. I never made it to the end of the car. Those moments of boundless terror are the last that I remember.

When I regained wakefulness, it was with such a heavy tightness in my chest that I wished I hadn't. The meager sips of air I drew in were clean again but accompanied by such painful discomfort that I felt like I was breathing through a hypo. As I struggled to recapture my breath, I realized with a start that I was no longer sprawled helplessly atop the deck of the blind. Rather inscrutably, I was piled against the door on the platform, wheezing pitifully. The farm kid sat silently across from me. It was clear what had transpired. That rangy little bum had single-handedly climbed up the ladder and eased my pathetic, inert form safely down to the platform of the blind. And, rather than take the opportunity to deliver me a heap of well-deserved contempt, he offered only the earnest inquiry of, "you a'right pardner?"

Heaving, I solemnly thanked him, and as a token of eternal gratitude for his magnanimity, I gifted him the balance of my tobacco. I did not smoke again for a year. Nor have I decked a train through a tunnel since—though every time I enter one, I think of that itinerate Hoosier. He'd been right, after all. Tunnels will get you—blame coal smoke.

The former is just one example of the many ways of dying on the road—some of which I encountered daily. That's not to say there weren't good days; they were scarce but not altogether absent. Every so often, the gods would order up a beautiful day—an unobstructed sunset, a cool breeze on a balmy afternoon, or after endless weeks of breathless heat and drought, rain so hard that you thought the sea and sky had traded places. Or sitting in an empty boxcar with your legs hanging out the door on a midnight tour of some star-swept wilderness where the crickets and bullfrogs are so loud they rival the low moan of the whistle. Or among confidants in the jungles, swapping stories and grafts, sharing the wealth of the hour, and relishing in the great unbounded freedom of the traveling man.

The most raucous expression of this great unbounded freedom occurred during hobo conventions. A convention was called to order when a dozen or more hobos with an ample supply of money, booze, and dirty laundry flopped in a jungle at the same time. They were often spontaneous affairs and could run anywhere from a day to a week depending on how long the food and fuel held out and the constable stayed away.

The longest convention I ever attended lasted twelve days. It took place in the jungles just west of the quaint little Kansas hamlet of Olathe. Grapes and apples had just come into season, and hobos from all over the map began heading west. The Santa Fe depot at Overland Park and the yards in Kansas City were just northeast of Olathe, and those jungles became an auspicious waiting spot for those looking to catch a train out.

This was in the days prior to my conviction, when my capacity for sociable malingering was just as great as that of any other bum on the road. So, when I walked over the crest of the hill above the jungle and saw two dozen men strung out along the creek, I knew I was in for quite a jamboree. At the bottom of the hill were bum chieftains and tramps royale, along with all the other strange denizens of the road. I saw the traveling con-men of my own camp mingling amongst the ever-present cripples, alki-stiffs, and lungers. There were the brass peddlers and hucksters who battered the privates and threw their feet on the drag for their meals. And, of course, there were the migrant pickers, strong, wiry, bronze-skinned hopefuls eminently riding the crest of optimism's wave. They numbered the most, and despite their general contempt of the listless bums that so sullied their hardworking image, even they, at times, were due for a night of debauchery.

By nightfall, the population of the jungle swelled to rival that of the town, and its inhabitants were growing hungry. Blankets were unrolled, shoes were removed, and we all contributed whatever makings or money we had. Believe it or not, the smallest towns are often the most bountiful to the beggar, and the road kids lit out on the procurement tour and returned with a feast. Shares were divided equally. Square-faces of fortyrod whiskey were passed around, jew's harps and banjos were produced from the bindles that concealed them, and the convention was on. With the constant influx of new arrivals headed west, there were enough means to carry the convention well over a week—until the town whittler returned from his fishing trip and, at the townspeople's urgings, promptly put the kibosh on the whole affair.

Hobos and their camps have always been execrably plagued by John Law—this, of course, being a source of great indignation to the hobos. Most men out on the road are generally peaceable. We live by our code, just as you live by yours. We even have our own justice system—though it is too straightforward, sensical, and insusceptible to corruption for it to ever be adopted by society at large. Considering the vast numbers of men who took to the roads, the accounts of violence, vandalism, and insurrection attributed to us were significantly less than expected. Most of us simply chased wanderlust and opportunity whenever the whim struck. We'd willingly rejected the stifling clasp of society and had no use for its ludicrous regulations. For the other faction—those who'd hit the road out of necessity—quite the opposite was true; society had rejected them. It may well seem like society has everyone's best interests at heart, but try telling that to a man jailed for vagrancy because he didn't have the price of a flop or one sentenced to hard labor for begging because he hadn't eaten in two days.

The most pervasive stumbling block for the hobo is his tendency to be misunderstood. His face is unshaven, so he is disdained. His clothes are dirty, so he is contemptible. He is different, so he is shunned. He is a stranger, so he is feared. And god forbid two hobos are seen together—for they are most certainly a dangerous gang worthy of immediate arrest. Jail is simply a fact of life for the hobo, whether he is an honest migrant or a morally bankrupt swindler like me. For many, pinches are commonplace and sometimes even seen as a convenience. Being fed for free three times a day for anywhere from a week to two months was as appealing to me as it was to the next man—quality notwithstanding—but with my history, I could little afford such digs. Miraculously, I managed to almost entirely elude jail time during that three-year stint. Granted, that was principally due to my constant diligence, persistent fear, and the fact that I could run awfully fast. This was a blessing in many ways, but mainly because I would have rightly killed any bull or constable who'd attempted to apprehend me and found myself swinging on the end of a rope.

I know the cops were only doing their job, and yes, I am a murderer—but so was Saint Peter. Yes, I killed a man—and I feel no remorse. I killed a man—but I didn't mean to kill him. And, I defy that any man in my hopeless position that fated evening would have acted any differently. The same goes for the matter of apprehension. After three years of veritable hell, let's see if you submit any too quickly to the man who promises to return you to such torture. That is what I mean about hoboes being misunderstood. Do you think that the man who's been trembling half-frozen in the ice compartment of a reefer car in the dead of winter is going to think twice about knocking on the back door of your nice, warm establishment and asking for some scraps from yesterday's supper? —Of course not! But to society, he is not a man in need; he is, at best, a nuisance and, at worst, a threat.

That's the thing about men who live outside the towns and cities of life, men who ride—who curse and sing and gamble and work, who scratch and claw at a single strain of light like it is a golden nugget sitting atop a stout elm—there aren't any men like that where you live, because men like that don't have an address. There aren't any full-blooded traveling men buried on your Boot Hill because men like that, men like me, die along the tracks of life. They move and keep on moving because they don't know anything else—and don't want to know anything else. And when that freighter rolls through, we see the town stirring in the early morning hours, we know the habits of the city folk and the homesteaders, but they don't know us; they don't see us. We are shadows that drift through towns like ghosts and are gone with the morning dew. We are strangers to you because we are strangers to every town and every city. We aren't familiar to you because we aren't familiar to anyone—that is, anyone but ourselves. There is a strength and pride possessed by every bum you've ever ignored on the sidewalk or denied a meal. We have been tempered by circumstances and hardened by conditions so severe that they would quickly kill any lesser man. We know what we've endured and what we've survived, yet we keep traveling on. Rejection, disappointment, hunger, discomfort, persecution— they are our cross to bear...and yet, we keep traveling on.

II

After I left McAlester, I remained within eyeshot of the tracks for three days. Only after I was several states away in Kentucky and so tired and hungry that one good tall breeze with any gumption would've laid me flat did I slink into a town. I did so amidst the evening rush when all the local working men were headed home to their wives, too busy dreaming of supper and nursing their aching backs to look closely at the face of the man walking toward them on the street.

I've never been one to needlessly indulge fear, but I knew full well what they'd do to me if I was ever discovered and sent back to Oklahoma. With those shudder-inducing thoughts firm in my mind every waking moment, my nerves soon became so brittle they'd've been far better suited as kindling wood. I was so tightly wound you could hear my ass rattling four blocks away in either direction. I jumped a foot any time a car backfired, and whenever I heard a siren, my legs up and carried me into the next county before my brain had any conception of what my body was doing.

The first time I found myself somewhere even remotely safe was in a basement barroom under a fresh fish market on the riverfront in Detroit. I sat there with my boots on the rail, caressing a tumbler of gin like it was the finest woman I'd ever loved. I was one of the only men there at the time, and the jointist, a wiry little chin wagger, kept trying to scare up a conversation.

"Don't talk to me; I'm trying to get drunk," I cautioned him as I raised my glass to my lips and he sauntered over.

Predictably, he recoiled. "That's what we're all trying to do here. You ain't gotta be such a prick about it. What, you and your dame have it out or something?"

I went on sipping my drink, paying no attention to him.

Regrettably, he went on, "I ain't never seen a drinking man so averse to company. And the way you're draining them glasses, you'd think you haven't had a good snootful in years."

"Bingo, Bub," I snarled in reply, "so shut yer damn trap and let me enjoy it without having to hear your miserable yammering."

Curious and undeterred, he slithered up to the bar and eyed me like a hungry rat, his eyes glinting as he sniffed after the juicy hunk of scandal he could sense darting about just behind my eyes.

"You've been in the clink, eh?" he asked knowingly, "What'd they nail you for? Armed robbery? Bootlegging?"

"Ain't been in no clink," I protested, trying my best to sound genuinely offended as that familiar knot of dread began tightening in my stomach, "I've been on the wagon."

He squinted back at me with his rodent eyes, positively unconvinced, "yeah, the paddy wagon."

Enraged at my own transparency, I stood up from my stool, threw the remainder of my drink in his face, grabbed the bottle he'd been pouring from, and hurried up the stairs and onto the street.

Though despicable, I had no doubt he was well-connected in the neighborhood. Eager to get out of that troublemaking operator's stomping grounds, I tucked the open bottle into my coat and caught the first streetcar headed in my direction. After seven hours of zig-zagging, double-backing, and cross-cutting while I took quick glimpses over my shoulder for any cocky-looking gangsters quick-stepping down the sidewalk toting a tire iron with my name on it, I crawled through the broken window of a long abandoned railroad pump house, settled myself down in the warm, dry sand, and drank that bottle to the dregs without wasting so much as a drop.

The former was only the first of many paranoid encounters of this caliber. It got so that I became instinctively reticent. I even tried my luck on the DD route—although I didn't have much success. I chose my acquaintances wisely and sparingly. On the whole, I traveled and worked alone, but there were short stints during which I shared my company with a carefully selected cast of characters. I often resorted to these sociable measures only in periods of dearth—the rate of success of four feet being thrown for breakfast being eminently more than two. However, the instances in which I had the pleasure of assistance in obtaining my needs were pitifully infrequent. I was terminally jealous of the jockers I encountered with their dutifully loyal prushuns but did not dare think of endeavoring to find my own. Prushuns were undoubtedly a cure for loneliness, but if I jockered the wrong boy, I'd most certainly find myself in a world of trouble. So, I carried on alone.

The first five months after I escaped were the coldest, hardest, emptiest, and loneliest. After the initial rush of freedom, the shock and fear began to ebb into a constant heightened awareness of my surroundings. Despite my diminished liberties in the outside world, I was still eminently happier living like a shadow than behind bars. However, as the dreary winter days wore on into spring and I shuffled between nameless towns, smoky backrooms, and fortuneless snooker tables, my mind began to take a different turn. This change followed a perilous run-in with a guileless brakeman who arrested my course and claimed the reason he'd found me clinging to the ladder of the baggage car in 30° temperatures as we charged across Rollins Pass was because I was planning on sabotaging the train. After I'd explained my innocent intentions to the conductor—who is wholly the reason I was not jacketed by the bulls and sent directly back to McAlester—I realized traveling in that way without a shred of identification was just about the most dangerous thing I could do. And after I'd settled myself comfortably in a hotel in Boulder, satisfied with my winnings for the first time since I'd escaped, my thoughts began to turn toward home.

I certainly wasn't homesick by any stretch of the imagination. Still, I longed to be somewhere I didn't constantly have to look over my shoulder and force my identity upon the locals. I wanted to be in a place where everyone knew me as Jack Jones without question, and the only place where that was irrevocably the case was in Five Points. I thought about writing Pa, but after having been gone nearly a decade and silent for its entirety, my abrupt return would be regarded as strange and suspicious. While he wouldn't turn me in, I knew I could expect no quarter, and far too many years had passed for me to even attempt to track down my brothers. Therefore, I bypassed all contacts in my immediate family and sent a friendly and inconspicuous letter to Uncle John, who was at that time and still remains the only man on this earth who ever understood me. I hung around Boulder for two weeks, waiting anxiously for a reply, but goaded continually on by the fugitive's itch, I gave up and moved on to Coal Creek, where I folded and wrote Pa in Denver. To my complete and glad surprise, my uncle answered promptly from this address. He informed me that Pa had already left for the mountains and asked him to come up north from Leadville to fix up the house in his absence—which, even from afar, I knew really meant cook up enough gin so that he'd have an ample supply when he returned.

And so, with the comforts of home strong in my mind, I headed south, and for the first time in nearly a decade, I came walking home. As soon as my boots lit on those crisp Denver cinders, I could feel the change. I could smell it in the air, taste it in the water from the fountain, and feel it on the dusty street beneath my feet—I was home. Honest familiarity enveloped me, eager anticipation alighted me, and a creeping sense of relief was close at hand. The change of years was evident there, but even so, I could've made that twenty-minute walk from the depot blind drunk. And, when I reached the corner of my yard, a smile like one I hadn't known in years spread across the same face where my old convict scowl had threatened to take hold.

The place looked generally the same. The bushes had gone wild and grown up to the second story, and the old clapboard siding was sorely in need of whitewashing, but the carved names of the Jones brothers were still there just as clear as they'd been the day I'd swung aboard that eastbound freighter and left such dreams behind. Before I even reached the back porch, I could hear the old still thumping away in the brush. Uncle John was splayed across my father's armchair, sunburnt from his brow to his potbelly. I tended to the still before I roused him—if there's one thing Pa instilled in me, it's "first things first." And—to be entirely forthcoming—I was the slightest bit hesitant. Ten years had passed—I was a grown man, a felon, a blown-in-the-glass tramp—but when Uncle John awoke mid-snore, his uproarious outburst of "Kid! Hey, Kid!" assured me that all my uncertainty had been in vain.

He, too, showed signs of age. His black curly hair had greyed somewhat around his temples, and his beard somewhat around his mouth. His paunch had grown over the years and evidenced that homebrewed beer had been added to his usual whiskey diet. There were lines around his eyes and across his cheeks that I'd never seen before, and his nose had been so badly broken it looked like his face was signaling for a left turn. Of course, bodily, I was even more drastically changed, and he started asking questions before I could get any in myself.

"Where the devil have you been, Jack?" he exclaimed in delight.

"Aw, here and there, you know how it is..." was my sheepish reply.

"Oh, come now, Jack!" He guffawed and slapped me across the back so hard I almost fell over, "what have you been doing with yourself? Can't rightly be anything too promising—you look about as skinny as a signpost."

"Slingin' bricks does wonders for the waistline," I replied dryly.

"San Quentin? Folsom? Territorial?" he asked knowingly.

"McAlester. Three years."

His response was a flinch and a grimace, "what the hell did you do, boy, kill somebody?"

I just stared back at him, unblinking.

"Cheat? Tinhorn?" he inquired.

"Dry agent."

Uncle John shook his head and poured himself another jigger of bootleg, "well, I hope you remembered what I told you when you were a boy—you didn't look into his eyes, did you?"

"No, I didn't look at his eyes—I was more concerned with his chest."

"His chest?"

"That's where I stabbed him."

Uncle John shook his greying head again and offered me a snort, "Why ain't I surprised, Jack Jones? Born a bastard, ain't never gon' be any other kind of man...they only stuck you with three years for shivin' a fed?"

"Well, not exactly," I explained as I choked down the whiskey he'd poured, "I'm out on the sightseeing tour."

This time, he couldn't hold back the laughter. The deep, resonant *haw-haw* that had been the soundtrack to so many of my glorious, mischievous childhood evenings echoed all the way down to my toes and brought a touch of warmth to my frostbitten soul.

Once Uncle John had exhausted his covey of questions, I asked some of my own. He filled me in on the whereabouts of my family, caught me up to date on the litany of scams he'd embarked on in recent years, and, most importantly, gave me the rundown on the local gambling scene. As expected, I was the only one of my brothers out sifting the cinders and bucking the law. Phil, that terminal bachelor, had worked his way up to captain his own merchant ship and sent a letter or two every half year or so. Mick was married with a couple of daughters and was working as an assistant professor of anatomy at Yale. My rascally brother Robbie was living in Hoboken and had become a fully ordained pastor with a congregation of his own—last Uncle John had heard, he and his wife were expecting their first child. Billy was the only Jones brother who remained in Colorado. Consistent with his scholarly nature, he'd started out as a prodigious blacksmith, but after he tired of that, he became a defense attorney and moved out to Colorado Springs. He, too, was married and had almost eight kids himself.

According to Uncle John, when Pa came home from the mountains in the fall of 1920, he wasn't surprised to find me gone, but as years passed without word, whenever they all got together, they'd speculate as to my whereabouts.

"—you were always one of the finest topics every Christmas—where you went, what you'd been doing, the conniving schemes you pulled as a kid, and whether or not you were still living. I never had no doubt in my mind about that last one. I always knew that you were just like your uncle, so hell-bent on living that you weren't gonna release your hold on life until somebody fresher, meaner, and more hell-bent himself came along and made you give it up."

"There've been a couple close calls, but ain't nobody licked me yet," I replied, feeling the liquor begin to take hold, "Now, tell me, how's Pa?"

"Ah, you know he ain't been the same since your Ma..." he began, "don't hardly ever talk—not that he ever did much anyhow. Never has anybody visiting no more, hardly keeps the house—that's why I'm here."

"I thought you were here for the gin."

"As far as Sam is concerned, that's all I'm here for. All he wants to do is drink the blasted stuff—puts down so goddamn much of it he finds himself with none to sell. He wouldn't have me around for no other reason—but I suppose in his state, gin is more important than our differences. And I know he'll never admit it, but every time he comes back from the mountains, he looks more and more like an old man."

"Got any of Pa's old gin around? Batches he made?" I asked, salivating at the thought.

"There's a couple in the cellar—and while you're down there, fetch me another bottle of rotgut; we are going to have ourselves a time, young fella, one that's long overdue."

That's just about all I remember from the first day, and I couldn't tell you a blame thing about the second or the third. Actually, my recollections started at about the end of the week and considering Pa's gin was heavily involved throughout, I'm surprised I remember that much. It'd been many long years since I'd tasted that sweet ambrosia, and when I left, I did so with two quarts sewn into the lining of my coat. That being said, most of the memories I maintain from that visit were from our time at Pike's.

In the ten years since I'd been there, Pike's, too, had changed faces. For one thing, it was half the size. Table games, along with all other gambling, had been shuttered out in recent years and pool tables adorned with signs proclaiming *'No Betting'* now predominated in the formerly flouting establishment. All the real fun took place in the private back room, cordoned off from the guise in front, and unless you asked the bouncer to keep your bottle behind the old bar, liquor was no longer served. Those were tough times in hard-drinking Denver, but men like Uncle John were constantly manufacturing ways to offset the loss.

Before we set out for our first night of poker and dissolution at Pike's, Uncle John instructed me to take along more than just a bottle of my favorite liquor. As we were leaving, he slipped a roll of crisp, new bills into my hand.

"That's two grand there," he informed me with a sly grin and watched as I examined it with astonishment before he went on. "They're fresh off the presses, impossible to distinguish by eye, and all marked."

"This is counterfeit?" I asked.

"We got the press set up right in your old bedroom. Can't lose a cent this way. As long as money is exchanged, even if you lose, you come home with more than you went out with. Best racket yet."

Assured of my monetary gains for the evening, I strode into that old parlor oozing with more bona fide confidence than any two-timing, half-starved federal fugitive ever possessed before. I'd come to Denver because I'd wanted to be someplace where people recognized me; well, at Pike's, nearly the whole damn room stood up when they saw me coming. I was cleaned, combed, and slickered up with pomade in my beard and shine on my borrowed shoes. I was a gambler of repute east of the Rockies, a force to be reckoned with, and by no means had I ever been desperate or hungry even one single moment of the ten years I'd been gone. Boy, was I a liar—and how sweet I made it all sound. Fortunately, I had skill and graft enough to legitimatize all my hot air. When we finally made it back home at dawn and spilled our pockets out onto the kitchen table, I counted not only $1,200 of counterfeit bills still in my claim but an additional $2,200 of Uncle Sam originals.

After a couple more evenings of such luck, I'd amassed a $5,000 bankroll—more than twice the amount that'd passed through my hands since I escaped McAlester. Before long, the gleam of traveling dimmed some, and the appeal of remaining in Denver in relative safety amidst such a lucrative enterprise heightened tremendously. However, when I made my intentions known to Uncle John, he was quick to dissuade me.

"If you weren't on the lam, Jack, you'd be more than welcome to stay— but there're some loose ends around this whole counterfeiting business, and if we link up, they're more than sure to tie us up into a whole bushel of trouble. See, those bills are starting to get around. A gambler of taste rarely hangs around Five Points for any spell, but unfortunately, some of them fancy spending a good deal of their spoils before they move on and the bills make their way into the hands of regular people. Just last week, that old flame of yours, Katie Mae, was in the general store buying nipples for her baby's bottles, and she tried to pay with one of our five-dollar notes. That clerk has seen a lot of our work lately, and as soon as he realized the note was fake, he called the cops, and they took her down to the station to question her. Caused quite a commotion around town that day."

"Serves her right!" my undying resentment replied.

"But it ain't just Five Points cops getting wise," Uncle John went on, "Them bills have been popping up all over the state, and they've been tracing 'em back to Denver. Now, I ain't worried yet, but I don't want you around when I am, and if you've got men after you, Jack, I just can't afford you in my camp."

It didn't take much good sense to see that he was right, so I stayed on with him another week and left well-outfitted on a passenger train west at the end of it. For its brevity, it had been a propitious stop-over. Not only did I board that streamliner loaded with gin, bills, and a new suit, after some rustling around in Ma's old dresser, I did so with my birth certificate. Of course, in the eyes of the law, that wasn't very much, but to me, even a little bit of something was better than nothing.

Although I allowed myself some luxuries in the following months, I lived conservatively in the hope that my money would last. The year was 1930, and it was not often you found an honest man strolling about town with a $5,000 bankroll in his pocket. In fact, even the cons were scrimping and saving. Spendthrift gamblers bet a little more wisely, and the working man hardly bet at all. I saw my formerly limitless arena shrinking before my eyes and knew not for how long such dearth would last. So I, like every other man of reason, held on just a little tighter to what I had.

1930 had arrived as all new years do: under cover of darkness, dotted by strings of electric lights knocking against glass storefronts in the wind, dimly illuminating pinpoints of hopeless night. Despair loomed heavy over the nation, and that dull goading ache I called fear loomed heavy over me, driving me continually on. By a stroke of luck, I spent that inauspicious evening warm in the cab of a semi, nursing an extremely poor bottle of homemade Kentucky bourbon that the driver had retrieved from under his seat after he picked me up around dusk outside a soda fountain in some nameless town east of Tecumseh. After several hours of driving, we were passing through yet another indistinct town when a salvo of fireworks and shotgun blasts split the night and ushered in the new decade with confidence and conviction. Their eruptions cut through the fog and echoed fitfully before fading into the gloom—a barrage of hope followed by nothing but uncertain silence.

And that is what remained. A span of three years rarely contains enough precipitous change to produce an era that is unrecognizable. However, during my time in prison, the outside world had changed faces with such unprecedented swiftness that by the time I got out, life as I'd known it was considerably altered. The whole country was reeling in the wake of a catastrophe so sudden and shocking that it divided society entirely—and it happened pretty much overnight. The apathy and independence of the prior decade had outlived its function and appeal as men and women presently desired nothing more than to hunker down, pool their assets, and wait out the raging socio-economic storm with as much security and comfort as their means allowed. However, few could maintain that approach for long.

Hitting the rails had formerly been reserved for migrants, bums, and what was otherwise known as the dregs of society. But after the Depression hit, it suddenly became the preferred—and in some cases, only—form of transportation for millions who had lost everything in the market or become casualties of those who had. And, as the years wore on, it seemed that hungry hoboes were the most numerous class in America. Men flocked to the railyards like devotees on a pilgrimage. Whispered rumors of work afar were heard as gospel and pursued with a brand of vigor and desperation that only manifests in those fending off starvation by the skin of their teeth and who had whole long lines of children to feed before they themselves could take a sustaining bite. When all prospects at home dried up, men took to the rails in hopes that the train would carry them away from their troubles and to a bastion of opportunity that the Depression had not yet touched. But, there was no such place. The Depression had penetrated every corner, every region, and every industry and left a mournful scar across the country so grim that it was impossible to ignore.

The great exile of the hobo became the harsh reality for whole swathes of dejected, downtrodden, luckless men who didn't know whether to turn left, turn right, or just lay down dead. As the months dragged mercilessly on, I saw the railroads become increasingly populated by such denizens and my lifestyle adopted by men who, just a few years prior, would've turned me away from their doorsteps hungry on principle alone. It takes a turn of fortune for some men to learn, but you can't eat principle, and nothing humbles a man faster than going hungry. When you can stare down into your empty palm and see all that you've worked hard to own, when your empire as a man does not extend past the bindle on your back, when your last meal was the product of charity, when you're not sure where you'll lay down your head to sleep at night, and you're sick and tired of being sick and tired, that's when you know you've reached rock bottom. But, as it is, rock bottom is a misnomer; for, most often, rock bottom is made of cold steel. It's no way to live, but a couple million of us out here did. And, after the dust engulfed the Midwest, those numbers only increased twofold.

I remember traveling through the Texas Panhandle on a freighter in the early days of the Dust Bowl. The train was a doubleheader, and I was decking her in an effort to fend off the billowing clouds kicked up by her wheels. We weren't long departed before it seemed relief would soon be upon us. The sky was getting dark, and the wind was kicking up—a storm was brewing. Desiring to keep dry, I shimmed down inside an open boxcar and settled in to watch the show.

The clouds rolled in quick—all loaded down with cool, clean water in their saddle bags. It was to be the kind of rain that promised to fall hard and fast and beat back the dust, pack a wallop, and splash up all around as it struck the ground and tried to make that dust forget all about the new liberty it had found.

It didn't work, though. It couldn't hit hard enough. The rain was outmatched by the dust, and though it blew in, roaring and crashing, ready to settle its dues once and for all, it couldn't lick the dust. No matter how many sidewinders, haymakers, and humdingers it drilled into the dust, the dust just got its dander up and fought back with a vengeance. It stirred like an arched-back cat thirsty for blood and boiled up and out until it filled the sky, wrapped itself around those big, black, angry clouds, and choked them up until nothing more than mud came falling from the sky. And no matter how many men like me looked on and cheered and rooted for the storm, the hopeless battle kept on just the same until the rainclouds got fagged out, dried up, and moved on.

As a result, everything in dust country was the same damn color, and that was gray. I saw men heading west out of Texas, Oklahoma, and Kansas, and they were gray. I saw locomotives crossing the plains with their rolling stock in tow plastered clear over with the same color dust and truckers riding hard on rotten springs with nothing to breathe for four hundred miles but cigarette smoke, their windows shut up tight in the cabin to keep out the blame dust. I saw all kinds of rusty heaps piled up alongside the road, their radiators clogged shut, air breathers caked with silt, and gas tanks as dry as the unforgiving earth beneath their stilled wheels—their owners having long since abandoned them, forced instead to drag their feet across the dust-addled wastes as they headed on toward the next catastrophe that awaited them.

For most, the end of the line was California, but contrary to widespread belief, the golden state was not so richly packed with wonder and opportunity as it had been made out to be. As the farmers' contingent and all those dependent upon them surrendered their homesteads and claims to the unrelenting dust in the Midwest, necessity gave rise to a well-known faction of the hobo collective: the fruit tramp. If there was one thing that was poignantly known in those years, it was that everybody had to eat, and getting that food off the vine and one step closer to the mouth was an occupation that could ill-afford to be underemployed. Tanking market or no, in those climes that were safe from the dust, that food would keep on growing, and sheer desperation sent millions of men and their families into the fields and the orchards as pickers. And when the pickings grew slim in one locale, as best as they could, they started off toward the next. The fruit tramp has always been a mainstay of the hobo echelon, but never have they numbered so greatly as they did in those years. They were so numerous, in fact, that for six weeks in '36, you couldn't even get into California.

For as profitable a milieu as it often was, California could be somewhat treacherous for men like me who carried skeletons in their duffle bags. It appeared the government in California was determined to keep up the guise that the state was immune to the social and economic forces crippling the rest of the country and ensured that the cops did their darndest to round up just about every supposed hobo and bum they could find. Rumor is you either paid them off or were dealt your 180 days of beans and abuse on the county work farm. But despite their most valiant efforts, it was plain to see that people were suffering in all except the wealthiest neighborhoods. In such places, life went on just as it always had, and little concern was given to those of us who slept on the streets they owned. Granted, it was rare that you'd ever find hobos in the 'good neighborhoods' of any given town, mainly because we knew better.

You don't get so much as a crust of stale bread trying to bum off rich folks. They look at you like standing starving on their doorstep is some kind of personal choice. They've never known the feeling of hunger and can't imagine it too well either. If they had, they'd undoubtedly be more accommodating. It'd always been that way, but after the dust and the

Depression hit, the rich folks seemed to develop a sort of uncanny vision; they simply didn't see us. A man with enough dough in his pockets to feed every man in the breadline could stroll by whistling Sweet Adeline and not so much as bat an eye at the beggars huddled around the soup kitchens and the unemployment office.

As a result, those new to life on the road quickly learned to search elsewhere for their prospects. In the cities, you got what you could from the mission or the Salvation Army. They offered a pretty sweet deal—sleep through a sermon and get a free meal. No bum worth his weight in salt would pass up those odds, and I took advantage of their haughty generosity on many occasions. In smaller towns or neighborhoods where such relief was not so readily available, throwing your feet in the blue-collar districts was considered the best practice if you wanted a guaranteed meal. While being denied vittles even in these locales was no rarity, more often than not, no matter how many times the homeowner or his wife were called upon to extend their kindness to a soul in need, they complied in earnest—even when they had little to give themselves. Sit-downs soon became far less common than they once had been, but I've never seen a man turn his nose up at a knee-shaker or even some punk and plaster thrown together for a poke on the run. Invariably, these offerings were paired with sympathetic eyes, well-wishes of health and luck on the road, and hope for a job at its terminus.

In those days, just about everybody on the road was after a job. Not me. As long as I had cards and dice at my disposal and vinegar in my blood, unless it was unavoidable, there was no way in hell I'd be pushing a broom, swinging a hammer, or stripping a branch of its bounty. In fact, just about the only time I occupied myself with any measure of manual labor was when I was in jail. And, at times, the great preponderance of honest tramps made life for a dishonest tramp like me considerably less perilous.

It is generally regarded as quite a feat if the average bum can make it a couple of months without a run-in with the law, but apart from some small-time stints for vagrancy and trespassing on railroad property, I made it three full years. For that, I can thank the Depression. Once the economy collapsed and hopping trains became the most practical mode of transportation for whole leagues of the population, illicit ridership increased ten-fold. While the railroad companies attempted to crack down on the 'bo's, the engineers, brakemen, and conductors were generally less severe. More so than in prior years, they'd turn a blind eye to our presence, warn us against the bulls, and sometimes even go out on a limb to hide us. Even when local authorities demanded the trains be halted and searched, the operators were sometimes known to pass along word to the riders so we knew where to get off and what towns to avoid. In some measure, this was due to compassion, but moreover, there were so many of us that there was no way even the most draconian bull could hope to slough every bum he stripped off a boxcar behind bars. And, lest I forget, there were many incidents I've had concerning the law that seemed hopeless before providence intervened and changed their course.

One such incident occurred just before dawn on a coal train outside Gary, Indiana. About thirty Chicago-bound hobos were nestled amongst the gondolas, and as usual, I'd confined myself to my own car, away from the huddled masses. I was beginning to doze off, lulled to sleep by the rocking of the train and the clicking of her wheels. I knew the freight was billed to a factory siding and that I'd have to ditch her outside city limits to avoid the bulls, so I was caught off guard when the train began to slow and pulled to a shuddering halt in what seemed like the middle of nowhere. I raised my head and peered above the lip of the car, and immediately, the calm of early morning was shattered by shouting voices as the railroad bulls swarmed. Tramps and itinerants of every color, culture, and creed dropped to the ground, scattered in every direction, and ran, tripping over cinders, bedrolls, and their own feet, but there was nowhere to hide. The tracks were wide open, and more bulls were already searching the cars for stragglers who'd wrongly presumed they could catch another free ride if they stayed put. Quickly and deftly, with their clubs in hand, the bulls rounded us up like cattle at slaughter and marched us through the trees and up over a low embankment to the street where the police wagons were waiting.

"Dirty, no good tramps—always bumming," one of the more peremptory bulls chastised us, "Ain't one of you got the natural sense to pay your own fare and travel like civilized folk."

The whole cluster of hapless, disheveled, coal-dust-covered men gritted their teeth but said nothing. We had them outnumbered, but it would have taken three of us to match the strength of any one of them. It was clear that none of us had eaten a proper meal in days, and we were all hungry, exhausted, and desperate. Rather than just load us into the wagons and ship us off to the county jail with what remained of our dignity intact, these bulls decided to mock us instead.

"If you can produce the price of a ticket, you'll be escorted down to the depot where you'll buy one," one bull explained. "If you can't, you'll be detained. Now, I know the idea of a nice warm jail and three meals square sounds like heaven to good-for-nothing moochers like you, but we don't want you in our town or our jail. We know you've got the money; you just want a free ride. So, we're goin' to make sure you ain't holding out and tryin' to pull nothin' over on us. We'll start with you," the bull reached into the crowd and snatched out a wizened old hobo, plenty creased and worn but none too short of pride. "Start with yer shoes," he ordered.

The grizzly hobo did nothing of the sort, "Mister, you know I ain't got nearly enough money to pay the fare," he protested, "I ain't even got money enough to feed myself. Ain't none of us have! 'Ats why we're here!"

"Then you'll just have to stay here for sixty days," the bull replied cruelly.

The 'bo then turned to begging, hoping to be a voice of reason for all of us. "Mister, please, I need to work to feed my family. If I go to prison, we'll all rot."

The bull turned and flashed his eyes, "and that's exactly what you deserve!"

The 'bo, woefully unused to dealing with ornery bulls, did the unthinkable—he spit in his face.

Immediately, the bull yielded his club and struck the 'bo, knocking him to the ground. For as much as it should have, such an attack did not seem to satisfy the wanton bull, and as he wound up with his club to deliver the 'bo another savage blow, the entire scene erupted into a fray. The hobos jumped on the bulls, jabbing and clawing and pulling at their clothes and hair, and the bulls clubbed the hobos into a bloody, plaid pulp. I and a few other quick-thinking bums ran like hell away from the fracas and tore back down the embankment to where the coal train was just pulling out. Ostensibly stripped of its pestilence, it would pull into Chicago unmolested, and we would ride for free once more.

The next day, down the line, I learned that the instigator had been killed and four more of the men hospitalized. None of the bulls had sustained any significant injuries. The papers sensationalized it as yet another vicious attack on the railroad police by itinerant felons. As usual, the perpetrators were portrayed as innocents, while the conduct of the 'bos was grossly misconstrued. As it turns out, the 'bo that'd been killed had been born and raised there in Lake County. Before he'd been laid off, he'd spent more than half his life working at a local granary. Yet, that bull had struck him down like he was a mad dog. He left behind a wife and five hungry children.

My response to the bum who proffered this melancholy story was, "that's tough luck—but better him than me." Now that sounds callous as all hell, but death is a daily occurrence on the road. In the life I've lived, I haven't just cheated death; I've taunted it, I've mocked it, I've dangled my soul as bait before its imminence and laughed victoriously every time I landed with two feet on the cinders. As ugly as it is, death is something you get used to seeing—its sting allayed by the comfort that its scythe has culled another.

I've borne witness to a lot of death in my life, both as its source and as a bystander, but by far, the worst I ever saw was on a Q spur in Arkansas. I was riding the pilot of a heavy freight up a grade through some sparse woodland as it limped along at about eight miles an hour. In the distance, I could see another train approaching at the same languid speed. Along with it came two figures—a man and a woman. Both were clad in overalls and quite portly. I watched with mild curiosity as they shared an embrace between the tracks, and when they parted, he boarded my train, headed west, and she boarded the other, headed east. It was clear neither were strangers to such a means of transportation, and despite her size, she deftly hoisted and shimmied herself up to the deck of one of the first boxcars where she stood, waving.

"Blow me a kiss!" I heard her companion bellow from behind me as the two trains passed, and she complied in earnest. However, just as she did, the train hit a hard joint, and immediately, she disappeared from view. I heard the shock and alarm of the man riding the hog behind me, and I dismounted along with him, mainly out of curiosity. We stood along the siding and waited with bated breath for the freight to pass. Once both trains cleared, we rushed over, and I will never forget what I saw there. There was a shape on the tracks. She was lying face down in a puddle of dark red blood three feet wide and spreading. She'd fallen hard between the cars, and that train cut her clean in two, right through the middle.

I haven't stood atop a boxcar since without thinking of that woman and her perilous fate. And, while I'd be hard-pressed to remember an incident more sudden and gruesome, hers was a quicker demise than those that befall most unfortunate hobos. I've seen men mangled by trains—the ones who survived to tell about it having left various pieces of their anatomy along the tracks, the unlucky others having left their lives. I've seen shootings and stabbings in the cities and jungles—the result of personal beef or pure malice. I've seen drunk men fall into fires and burn to a crisp, and I've seen them die with a bad batch of moonshine at their lips. I've seen section hands removing the stiff bodies of long-dead hobos from where they'd frozen or starved to death in boxcars or the ice holds of reefers. I've seen death at the hands of cops and bulls, I've seen it dealt by weather, and I've seen it dealt by steel. But I think the most dreadful way to go is a combination of illness and time.

The closest I ever came to it myself was in the winter of 1933. I was snowed in at Quimby, Iowa. I had been for two weeks, and it hadn't been good for me. I was sick, and I mean sick. I'd been nursing an awful heaviness in my chest since my encounter with the Cascade Tunnel, and as the cold set in and the frost took hold over the land, it only worsened. Consumption was my main concern, and it remained a nagging afterthought, exacerbated by my incessant travels. By the time I ended up in Quimby, I could hear my lungs rattling with every painful inhalation, and not only was I struggling to breathe, but my symptoms had grown to include a raging fever and a pressure in my head so great that it felt like Joe Rollino was trying to press my ears together.

My ailing finally came to a head in a densely populated pool room downtown. Yet another blizzard had rolled into northwest Iowa that morning, and it had brought with it the sort of cold that makes you feel as if your insides are twisted up in one continual tremor. For me, so afflicted by chills already, it was too much to bear in my frigid rooming house, so I'd sought out the shelter of the pool room in hopes of a warm stove and some bootleg liquor to ease the shuddering of my innards. I got only the former, and to my dismay, I found such comfort was but momentary.

Shortly after I arrived, two men in uniform blew in out of the cold to look the place over, and their presence did little for my morale and even less for my peace of mind. They did not announce themselves or state their purpose there; instead, they immediately began canvassing the hall's patrons. When they approached me, I received them cautiously, trying to appear nonchalant and unaffected by their presence. However, I was already sweating profusely from the fever and trembling from the cold, and their interrogatories certainly did nothing to lessen these afflictions.

"What business do you have here?" the first harness cop asked gruffly.

"None, sir, just a stop along the road," I replied, mustering all the energy I had left to make myself appear as if I was not about to crumple to the floor at their feet—which was just about all I felt like doing at that moment.

"Where are you headed to?"

"California, sir," I lied.

"What business do you have in California," the second officer inquired.

"Work," I croaked out as I suppressed the overwhelming urge to cough.

"What sort of work?"

"Pickin'. "

"Pickin'?" he repeated as he narrowed his eyes and looked me over good and hard.

Before I could explain myself, the first officer drove his point home, "we don't allow no hobos or tramps in this county. Anybody who comes here lookin' for a hand-out gets thrown in jail."

"No, sir, I don't blame you, sir," I struggled to reply, "but you see, I'm travelin' respectable-like. I ain't hitchin' or bummin'. I—" my response was interrupted by a mad fit of coughing that made my eyes water and my head pound so hard it felt like it was about to explode.

"You ain't no lunger, are you?" the other asked, stepping back.

I shook my aching head no.

"Sounds like the prison scourge to me," the former replied accusatorily, "you ever spent time in jail, mister?"

"No," I wheezed in assurance, but it did me no good.

"What's your name?" they demanded, and I replied with my proper address.

"Do you have any identification?" they asked in reply.

I produced my papers, which they examined without question. Apparently satisfied, the documents were returned to me, and I was scrutinized once more before they turned and wordlessly left the hall without interviewing anyone else.

In their wake, I scanned the room to see how many patrons had been observing our exchange and then, as casually as possible, turned back to the stove. However, within me, panic began in earnest. If I looked half as bad as I felt, I knew that already made me plenty suspicious, and I had no doubt that I was a haggard, unshaven fright, even from afar. Every ounce of good, tempered sense I possessed strained toward the door, but the sickness and exhaustion were too much for me to suffer in the cold again. After much agonizing deliberation, I decided to remain where I was—for I felt if I were to flee amid the storm, I would be choosing to cheat death one too many times. Even standing in front of the stove in the pool hall, body and soul weren't entirely assured of their union, but in my state, I determined that was by far the best place for me, and I resolved to stay there for as long as I was able.

That is, until the rack boss, who'd been hovering about in my general vicinity since the two bulls came barging in through the door, finally approached me.

"I don't know who you are, but if you're wanted for anything—run," he warned me sagaciously.

My head was throbbing so intensely I could hardly open my eyes to see his face, and even as little as an hour later, I couldn't have picked him out of a line-up if my life depended on it, but there was something in his eyes— a kind of gravity and knowing concern that made his cautionary notice that much more severe. And I heeded it.

The quiet foreboding I'd tried to suppress with rationale and desperation arrested me suddenly and sequestered fear bubbled up from the depths of my soul and flooded my faculties. My weary, addled mind began scrambling like a rat in a trap, and I left with haste, angst, and phlegm heavy in my chest. The half-hour during which I'd ignored instinct may well have sealed my fate, and knowing this, I chastised myself with reproach and dread.

My ragged breath froze in my lungs as I stepped onto the street, my boots sinking into the four or five inches of fresh snow that had accumulated during my brief occupancy of the hall. If there was ever a time in my life that I was nearly willing to hand myself over to the court of justice in exchange for warmth and reprieve, it was that glacial evening in Quimby. The wind sliced through my wool suit and coat as if they were shirtsleeves, and the icy flakes stung my face like embers as they rushed by, caught in my beard, and instantly froze. My face was numb before I reached the end of the first block.

The squall served only as a catalyst to both my burgeoning paranoia and my ails. I needed to get out of town and out of the elements posthaste, but, as usual, transportation proved to be a bane. I headed due north up Main Street as fast as my frozen feet could carry me through the drifts, and as the edge of town neared, I realized I was in a bit of a bind. There was nowhere to go but on, and the snow—already up past my calves—was getting heavier.

I paused under the dim halo of the last streetlight and briefly considered my seemingly hopeless situation.

It was at this point when the large, gray barn in the distance proved irresistible. Frantically, I trudged toward it and fumbled around in the darkness until I'd cleared enough snow away from the bottom of the door to pull it partially open. When I stepped inside, it was as black as sin, but the windbreak and the inviting smell of warm, dry hay drew me in like a nest of sirens. Every withering cell in my body urged me to forsake my impending frigid journey into the unknown and curl up in the loft without another thought of fleeing. But, instead, like a mad fool, I blindly navigated the stalls until I found one that was inhabited. Its occupant grumbled at my approach but was otherwise docile. I did not have the patience or time to locate a saddle in the darkness, and I did not dare light the lantern. Luckily, I had many years' practice of riding like a wild Indian without one, and this steed was already bridled.

With the deepest breath my poor, scarred lungs could muster, I led him out of the barn into the midst of all the most inhospitable horrors the Midwestern winter could conjure. He balked at the snow and the cold but allowed me to mount him without much protest. The lights in the adjacent home were put out for the evening, but regardless I rode by slowly to avoid drawing undue attention from any late-night lingerers who might've been monitoring the storm. However, as soon as I was out of view, I smacked that nag on the rump just as hard as I could and took off like a shot. A shiver ran through my veins as he hit his stride; now, not only was I a half-frozen, half-dead fugitive, I was a horse thief—and in rural Iowa in the early 30s, according to vigilante law, that was still a hanging offense.

But, even the chilling concern of a rogue rope around my neck hardly evoked its usual fear. Consequences were no longer of any consequence to me. This had been my final last-ditch attempt at self-preservation. I was as close to surrender as I'd ever been and just about as miserable as a man could feel. The concert of pain in my skull thundered and pounded harder and faster than the horse's hooves, every breath was a shuddering challenge ravaged by a blight of cough, and the sweat produced by my feverish effort to hold on poured off me in torrents, dripping into my half-closed eyes and freezing against my quivering skin. As I rode bareback, my rigid fingers knotted in the stallion's ice-matted mane, all that kept me from screaming out into the unyielding night was the lingering faint wish of a soft cot and a red-hot stove waiting for me at the end of it all. But, for as much as I lived and breathed, I would've sworn that return to a vermin-infested cell was the only fate that awaited me.

What scores of miles must have passed as the night wore endlessly on with nothing but dread and shallow breaths to sustain it. There were no stars, no moon—nothing but perilously open prairie, farmland, and sparse woodland that did nothing to obscure or direct me. The snow cover was so thick there was no telling how far we had strayed from the road, and I traveled wherever the horse took me on sense alone, hoping only that he had not turned to spite me and was, in fact, galloping on home. If there was a sole moment at any point along the journey that I could see the horse's head for the snow, I do not recall it, and if there was a path that balky nag followed, it was blind to me. I could've been two hundred feet from an establishment or two miles away and had no way of telling the difference.

There are very few times in my life when I legitimately prayed, even in the crude way that I know how. But at about three a.m., as I rode hurtling down some treacherous wooded track, scaling knolls and skirting trees as the horse's hooves slipped in the slush, I asked God or the Devil to either deliver me or kill me quick—and it appears both requests were answered simultaneously. One moment I was mounted, nearly frozen solid as I clung to the poor beast; the next, I was flying through the air, and the moment that followed, I was in torment.

It was not immediately apparent to me what sudden shift had occurred. However, it became evident enough when I heard my charge, huffing and snorting, pick himself up out of the ditch he'd landed in and hurry away, leaving me hopelessly behind. That unwilling old stallion that I'd held down with more tenacity than any flat-wheeled freighter I'd ever ridden had come upon the lip of a gorge concealed by the snowdrifts and, having sunk in with his front foot, reared up and threw me mercilessly to the ground. Having grown up around horses, I was not altogether unused to such treatment by contrary animals, but it was the only time that I recall landing with my foot past my ear, and surely the first time I heard anything snap when I did. What snapped was my leg, and the pain was immediate and unbearable. This time, I could not stifle the scream.

If I'd thought my situation had been dire before, I was now immobile and stranded. I knew beyond a shadow of a doubt that if I spent more than an hour out there engulfed in snow, I'd freeze to death—and the chances of even a policeman finding me in that time were little to none. So, I did the only thing I could—I began to crawl, heaving myself through the drifts on my hands and one knee, dragging my useless fourth limb behind me. I felt like a wild beast, alone and gravely injured, my prospects of survival futile, fastened closer to death with every passing second—but I refused to die cold if I could help it, so I kept crawling.

The direction I crawled in was just about as arbitrary as any other I'd taken that evening, but there was one slight hope caught in the wind that influenced my course—wood smoke. Somewhere near me was the promise of life amid the silent, blizzardy wastes—if only I could find it! The low clouds and snow drove the smoke down close to the ground, but the wind swirled about me from all directions. At first, I thought I was nearing its source, but after dragging myself several agonizing yards, the wind changed course, and I found myself further away than ever. After several redirections, overcome by despair and frustration and gravely weakened by sickness and pain, I did what any man would—I screamed.

At the very top of my lungs, I cursed the snow, the wind, and the pain that crippled me. I cursed the night and its treachery. I cursed Iowa and its law officers. I cursed Bertha Steele and her loathsome father. I cursed the train and the land. I cursed McAlester and its denizens and the cell to which the chilling idea of return forced me out upon such an ill-fated journey. I cursed this wretched life of mine and my folks who'd brought it upon me. In fact, I cursed just about everything I could think of aside from myself—for, as usual, I could think of no reason to blame me for such hapless circumstances. And, right around the time I ran out of people and things to curse for my misfortune, my lungs failed me, and I dropped my burning face into the snow in a feat of total exhaustion.

How long I remained there, motionless, I do not know, but when I feebly raised my head again for a final bout in the face of demise, in the distance, I caught a glimpse of the miraculous. It was a light—a single, flickering light, illuminating hope and promise and navigating me away from the gaping maw of death that threatened me from all sides. With every last ounce of strength that remained in my broken and wizened bones, I heaved myself along that illumined course. My best estimate now is that it was about a hundred yards from the seat of my despair to that long-awaited reprieve, and I am certain I traversed every inch of it with my soul a good foot ahead of me, leading my body on. Thinking back on it, I have no idea how I, in my sorry state, was able to make it that far. I suppose it's as they say: that when the soul is set on living, it causes the body to perform remarkable feats.

But after I'd made it close enough to the house to reach out and rap upon the door, my body was all out of remarkable feats. I was so paralyzed by cold and pain that I could not raise my clenched fist out of the snow, no matter how hard I tried. What was remarkable, however, was that the proprietor of this vital refuge opened the heavy, wooden cabin door out onto that recently swept stoop just as I reached it. I remained conscious long enough to hear my savior exclaim their shock and surprise, and then I collapsed on the threshold at their feet.

III

For the next two weeks, I didn't even know my name. While I'm not entirely sure what those divine hands administered to me, I know there was not a lick of pain—which, by all measures, is somewhat of a miracle. That broken leg of mine had to be set and having observed several of my brothers go through the ordeal, I knew there was nothing pleasant about the procedure. However, during one of my brief lapses into lucidity, in which my eyes actually focused, I saw that my pant leg had been cut above the knee, and not only had it been set already, but it was lashed and bound as well. This came as a great relief to me, and without questioning why or where or by who such a favor had been done me, I just closed my eyes and drifted back out with the current.

For the first time in what felt like an eternity, I was clean, warm, and comfortable as my illness retreated and my body healed. As long as such treatment continued, what great benevolent force was behind it all did not concern me. The only thing I knew without question was that whoever my rescuer was, they were well outfitted with laudanum, paregoric, and whiskey and used none of these any too sparingly. As a result, I was kept in a constant state of dream that no unpleasantry of any kind could penetrate. For all the misery I had endured in the preceding months, the veritable peace that imbued me in that time has no equal. And, to my everlasting surprise, thanks to my caregiver, it remained long after the tinctures had worn off.

It was immediately apparent that my sweet savior was a woman, but for the first few weeks, I knew her only from her voice—and what a voice it was. Hers was a voice of gold—sweet and nurturing, tender and earnest. When she spoke, all the confusion and dissonance of life settled into order and accord. It was a voice distilled by all of her womanly depth and concern. It

166

was a voice of calm reassurance, positive notions, and unconditional compassion. Her voice could raise a man from the well of despair, quiet the raging depths of his fear, and resurrect him from certain death. After all, I was mighty peaked when I arrived on that fated doorstep and had it been a man that saved my sorry ass, I doubt I would have recovered.

Between the blur of fever and delirium, I could hardly see, so for all I knew, she could've been Carry Nation just as easily as she could've been Hedy Lamarr. But between the tenderness of her voice and the warmth of her touch, for once in my life, I didn't much care what she looked like. Or so I'd thought.

Three weeks in, as spring broke in northern Iowa and she wiped the beads of sweat from my forehead one fair April morning, my eyes fixed on hers for the first time, and for a moment, I truly believed I was still in the midst of a fever dream. Her eyes were blue, sapphire blue—bluer than virgin stones that haven't yet been cut from the rock, bluer than the clearest mountain stream—and how they shone when she saw the soul begin to stir in mine. In fact, her whole face lit up—and it is a face that I will see clearly in my mind until I lie upon my deathbed. It was bright and smooth and the color of a new copper penny, framed by a shock of deep golden hair so long and straight that it swept across the waistband of her floor-grazing skirt. Around her neck, she wore a leather band embedded with elk's teeth, and around her wrists wound strings of beads. She wasn't a day older than me. Her name—like her face—at first a mystery, was Rosalie McFall.

By the time I finally comprehended the magnitude of her stunning presence, my fever had broken, and the pain in my leg had lessened to a dull ache. This awareness was made possible by the fact that she'd finally laid off the opium and cut back on the whiskey, and it wasn't until I opened my eyes and saw her face that I realized just how close to death I'd been. Afterward, the idea that I'd spent three whole weeks in her company and hadn't made so much as a pass was inconceivable. If I wasn't hungry enough to eat the horse I'd ridden in on and desperate to have a conversation with her, I would've pretended to be sick for longer. Though I did squeeze one last coherent sponge bath out of the whole deal, and while I was basking in the residual glow of that affair, I decided that I would've endured the sum of my misery all over again just to have that sublime pleasure.

She was a modest, homespun girl, but at the same time, entirely unfazed by the fact that a stranger was struggling to cross the divide between life and death on her daybed. She didn't seem to care where I'd come from or what I'd done—she just wanted me to heal, and I kept mum about my circumstance. All I told her was that I'd been thrown from my horse during the storm, and she didn't ask for specifics. If suspicion abounded within her at all, I was ignorant to it, and if she ever felt the common fear of women when alone with strange men, she made no display of it. Rosalie was the salt of the earth: indifferent to pretense, unconcerned with propriety, and capable above all else.

She flowed through life with quiet efficiency. Every morning the cow and goats were milked and the eggs collected, every afternoon, bread was made and supper cooked; and every evening, she'd sit in a straw-stuffed rocking chair beside me, reading. She radiated strength and stoutness from every pore but retained a gentleness I'd never known in a woman. The women in Denver were rugged—the daughters of pioneers and the wives of stalwart settlers. There was no mistaking their grit and tenacity, and as sweet and tender as some of them were, a distinct aura of hardiness always surrounded them. Rosalie boasted those same qualities with parity, but she lacked entirely the rough edges had by other women of her caliber. She was compassionate without being maudlin, open without being vulnerable, and stoic without suppression. She was the kind of woman who could cut the head off a rattlesnake with a single strike from a shovel, yet do so in such a way that not only did you feel mercy for the venomous creature, but you even got the inkling that she'd somehow made it understand why such a fate had come to it.

With such a force of beauty and goodness tending to me so dutifully, it's no wonder that as I regained my strength, I felt myself to be twice the man I'd ever been. It's also no wonder that after two weeks in torpor, once I noticed with awe the stunning countenance of my caretaker, it took me another few weeks to notice anything else. However, as the weather warmed, she spent an increasing number of hours outside, which gave me little else to do besides look around.

The McFall homestead was a quaint two-room cabin, crudely but sturdily built by a man with a working knowledge of carpentry but little more than the materials at hand to exercise it. Some old rags were stuffed into the more egregious gaps between the old logs to fend off the draft, but otherwise, it was cozy, homey, and inviting. There was a potbelly stove near the door, a squat escritoire in one corner, and a sewing machine in the other. I occupied the daybed in the center of the room. The floor was earthen but covered almost entirely with hides, mostly deerskin interspersed by elk and one large buffalo that lay alongside the daybed. The walls were unadorned and windowless, except for a large bookshelf stacked high with paperback novels and leaflets, their spines creased and their pages worn and yellowed. A Remington rifle and double-barrel shotgun rested astride the doorframe, and several oil lamps dotted the dim space.

The only natural light streamed in from the kitchen, where a rather large window was situated above the sink, centered between the coal stove and pantry. A coarse wooden table was the only other furnishing besides the flame-blackened pots and pans hung upon the wall. And, seeing as she'd sacrificed her usual accommodations for my benefit, a modest quilted pallet upon which she slept lay on the floor in front of the stove.

At that point, however, all I knew of my surroundings was what I could see from the bed I'd yet to leave. Once I was well enough for my customary restlessness and curiosity to stir, the first early suggestions of spring had begun to alight the land, and broken leg or no, there wasn't any way in hell I was going to stay cooped up inside.

My first attempt to stand unaided was perilous and unsuccessful, so using the scant furniture as my crutch, I staggered and lunged my way to the door, which I opened upon the most picturesque scene any man has laid his ever-loving eyes on. As I braced myself against the frame, I noted with pleasure that the frozen plains I'd blown in on had morphed into a sloping, grassy brae of unequivocal beauty. Uninhibited by clouds, the balmy April sun bathed the warmth-deprived land with all of its springtime splendor, and a crisp breeze rustled the tender, supple leaves of the cottonwood shelterbelt that ringed the cabin. I squinted against the foreign brightness and gulped down massive lungfuls of the cleanest, most invigorating air I'd ever tasted. With each breath, I could feel myself getting stronger as the horrid recollections of crawling through the snowbank like a wretch and fighting fever in the clammy darkness blew away from me with the breeze. That air was just about the best medicine God ever put upon the earth for men to find—its powers of healing superseded only by the vision of Rosalie washed golden in the sunlight.

Down past the grove of trees, the ground all along the face of the hillside was turned over and ready to receive the seeds of the summer's bounty. It was dark and fertile and still moist from the freshly melted snow, and standing right there in the center of it was my Samaritan, resting against the handle of a plow while two horses drank from buckets she'd drawn from the nearby river. Her long hair hung loose and shrouded her shoulders like a flaxen veil, and when the sun shone upon her, it reflected the light like a halo. Her plain, homespun dress waved softly in the breeze, and her leather moccasins sunk into the rich, fresh-tilled soil as she peered out over the knoll and surveyed her progress with gentle care. Just the sight of her alone was enough to take my breath away.

After I'd stood there awhile, I felt my good leg begin to quiver with the exhaustion of disuse, and I tightened my grip on the doorframe as I attempted to remain upright. However, no matter how hard I tried to support myself, I could feel my muscles aching, straining, and failing. I struggled to turn in the doorway and readied myself to return to my sickbed, but the extent of my weakness alarmed me, and I realized there was no way I could make it back across the room without falling flat on my face. With the last rally of my strength, I started to call for her, but just as I opened my mouth, I felt a pair of narrow yet powerful shoulders buttress my rest-weary form and a smooth bronze arm wrap around my waist—as if she'd read my mind.

"What are you doing up?" she exclaimed breathlessly as she eased me back to the safety of the cot.

"I needed to feel the sun," I told her, "and boy, did it feel fine! I want to sit outside. I'm sick of lying in bed."

"Certainly not," she responded, wrapping me in a quilt like a swaddled infant, "sun feels fine, sure, but that cool breeze is a sly one—and as sick as you've been, you'll be feverish again before you know it, sitting out in that April air too long. Spring isn't spring in Iowa until the banks of the river flood."

"Please?" I entreated, gazing up into her liquid blue eyes.

Rosalie just shook her head definitively and continued tucking. Her seriousness amused me.

"You know," I told her, "this is the first time a beautiful woman has had trouble getting me into bed."

The corners of her lips rose in a smile, and she gently ran the back of her hand along the side of my whiskered face. "Of that, I have no doubt," she replied, her silken voice demure, "although, considering you have a few more weeks of rest ahead of you, I doubt it will be the last."

Her assurance was disheartening, but while I remained in bed, she did not simply leave me there to stultify. On the contrary—every day, she helped me to stand and strengthen the leg that had been so egregiously injured on that fated winter night several weeks earlier. The process was arduous and agonizing, but she met the challenge with such contagious enthusiasm I could not help but find myself eagerly awaiting each day's session.

During the second week in April, the Little Sioux River burst its banks, irrigating the entire hillside with its cool, clean, nutrient-rich floodwaters. In the wake of the flood, Rosalie kept her promise. She moved her rocking chair outside where I could sit contentedly on the bank, bathed in the spring sun like the Fisher King while she worked barefooted with her fair hair in braids, whistling and singing a selection of songs so vast they ranged from Sioux medicine hymns to *Molly Malone*. My fondness for her had grown so much that I could spend days on end merely watching her. I was so utterly taken by her that everything she did captivated me. The way in which she pressed her precious seeds into the black dirt with care, as if she was sealing the envelope of a love letter, watching her carry water in buckets on a yoke across her back with effortless ease and seeing her petite form split and haul wood with strength and execution enough to rival any man nearly hypnotized me. She took to life in a manner so calm and leisurely that observing her for any duration felt like it caused time itself to slow. There was a peace and contentment about her that was unshaken by any trifling ill. Not once did I see her become frustrated or annoyed, nor did she ever curse or exclaim. Her eyes were at all times full of concern and warmth, and the same tenderness with which she cared for me she exuded when she rubbed down the horses, kneaded her dough, and blew out the lamp for the evening. There was a richness in her soul that turned everything she touched to gold, and as doubtful as it seems, she had that very same effect on me.

She'd nursed me back to health in every way a body can be healed. She'd rehabilitated my broken leg, strengthened my weak and atrophied muscles, cut my hair, shaved my beard, dressed me in new clothes and moccasins, and nourished my weak and haggard form with home cooking and love. But even more importantly than all of that, she'd nursed my soul. In those few short months, she instilled in me a renewed sense of hope. The dread that had hung over me like a dark cloud over a lake for so many soul-rotting years dissipated like a fine mist on a summer's day. I found that all the joy and pleasure I'd been denied for so long was allotted to me all at once by her. My staunch mistrust of the world was challenged, and all those convictions that accompanied it began to waver. She was far too remarkable a force of good to be worthy of the sweeping suspicion I formerly applied to all men and women alike. She was in every way a goddess and having stumbled upon her the way I did made it hard for me to believe she was the only one.

By the time Rosalie finished her spring planting, I was up and walking independently—albeit with a limp. During my recovery, I'd come to know her intimately. As I was confined to bed with little else to do, conversing became our most frequent recreation. She was more than willing to share the story of her life with me, and I was more than willing to listen. And unsurprisingly, the more I learned about her, the more she amazed me.

She was the only child of parents she described as so devoted, gentle, and kind that they appeared to rival even her. Estranged from their families, her parents had left South Dakota, where they'd met, and settled in the quietest and most secluded place they could find. Her father had built the homestead and been the first to turn the virgin ground, growing wheat and potatoes for sustenance and sale and chopping wood for the townspeople when crop yields ran low. Her mother was the homemaker who taught her to sew, bake and preserve the food her father grew so that it may later preserve life. Theirs was a simple, peaceful, and solitary existence—exactly what all three wanted.

"I never had any family except my parents," she'd explained to me late one evening, "their marriage was condemned by their relatives, and they were ostracized. They came to Cherokee to begin anew, where they could live peacefully and love one another without entertaining anyone else's opinion on the matter. But folks in Iowa are just the same as folks everywhere. They get comfortable living a certain way and thinking a certain way, and pretty soon, anybody who comes along who looks or lives or thinks differently becomes a pariah. Pop was Irish, and Mother was Blackfoot Sioux. On their own, they already weren't anybody's favorite, and together they certainly weren't what you would call welcome. His folks hated her because she was Indian; hers hated him because he was white. But they loved one another, and they both loved me. They had many children, some before me, some after, but I'm the only one that lived. Winters here get mighty cold, and we had a lot of hard years. The first few were the hardest of all. The townspeople disapproved of them and would not buy Pop's crops or hire him for work, but they persevered. Once I was school-age, the townspeople gave our family another chance. Once they saw that I wasn't a thief or a savage, that I'd been taught manners and respect, many of them changed their opinions of us. The townspeople have always been very important to me—as I have never known anyone else. And after the death of my parents, they became even more so...."

As it turns out, Rosalie's tranquil upbringing was fated to end in tragedy. It was her father who fell ill first, and then her mother. Amid a winter even harsher than that which I had endured, she cared for both her parents alone—too afraid to leave them and make the trip into town to fetch the doctor. Her father recovered from the worst of the illness, but her mother was not so fortunate. She died just before Christmas, and, heartbroken, her father took a turn and followed her into the court of the Great Spirit no more than a week later. Rosalie had been alone ever since. And, while such an admission had been absent from her tale, it was no wonder she had been so hell-bent on keeping me alive.

For weeks, we traded stories of the occasions and experiences that'd hewn us. I regaled her with the wild tales of my travels and the reckless freedom and wanderlust of my youth—excepting any related to my misadventures in Oklahoma. She listened intently to my accounts, wide-eyed and bated-breathed as I recounted harrowing back-room swindles and narrow escapes from baton-wielding railroad agents, totally captivated by the mischief and debauchery that I'd involved myself in. And each time I ended a tale, she'd smile, amused, shake her head, and study my face with her sagacious azure eyes as she expressed gratitude for the fact that she'd not been imbued with the daring that'd lured me from the security of my childhood home.

By the time we ran out of stories and the spring rain yielded to the sailing clouds of summer, I was ripping and raring and back in my brawn with fervor. Every morning, I rose with the sun and assisted Rosalie with the daily tasks and chores she normally undertook on her own. I tended to the animals, shoveled manure, drew water, and even spent long, backbreaking hours cultivating the budding crops she'd planted. If Ma had lived to see her indolent, rebellious son doing unremunerative farm work entirely of his own volition, she would've died at the sight of it. And, if anyone had suggested the possibility of such endeavors to me at any prior time, I would've used up every vile word known to man to express to them how wrong they were. Magnanimity has never been one of my shining qualities, but I owed Rosalie my very survival, and I found I cared so deeply for her that I was willing to do almost anything if it would make her smile or ease her burdens.

That being said, anytime I could trade the hoe for a fishing pole or a goat's teat for a rifle, I did so with immediacy. The Little Sioux River was positively laden with catfish and yellow pike, and I believe I took more fish out of the river that summer than my brother Ronny did in all the time he spent on the banks of the South Platte. The fish were not the only bounty that the land produced in abundance. There were so many rabbits and deer I could've fired blind and been guaranteed to hit at least one.

Having grown up on the edge of a city, the vast open prairie was nothing less than Eden to me. For one, the valley was completely noiseless. Unless it was a bird calling or the wind running through the reeds, no other sound reached my ears. The bustle of the downtown cardroom, the persistent clink of glasses in the speakeasy, the din of city traffic, the clacking of the trucks over the rail joints, the songs and shouts of the 'bo's and brakemen—they were all absent there. Not even the sad, distant whistle of a freight train could be heard.

The cabin was so remote, in fact, that the closest road was more than a mile distant and whatever wagons and automobiles passed over it were much too far away to disturb us. Such protections eased my mind and furthered my enjoyment of such unfamiliar, pastoral surroundings.

And, of course, all of these joys were heightened immeasurably by the fact that they were accompanied by a beautiful woman. Although, the fact that she was likely the most alluring woman I'd ever laid eyes on was the least of the compliments I could give her. Her beauty wasn't just skin deep; rather, it emanated from her soul. She was goodhearted through and through, and in addition to all those tenets that made her the pinnacle of womankind, she had something else that set her far apart from any others I've ever known.

Perhaps it came from her native heritage, or perhaps it was the result of never knowing a city, but whatever its source, Rosalie possessed an inseverable link with nature so strong it seemed to substantiate her entire being. Each morning when her eyes fluttered open beside me, she immediately whispered her gratitude to the sun for rising on another new day, and when the night took its shift, she danced for the moon. She communed with the warblers and thrushes, ran and played with the horses, and spoke tenderly to the trees and crops as if they were her children. She knew how to nourish the ground and the perfect time to collect the bounty it bore. She could foretell rain, wind, or hail days before it arrived, and when it did, she left our bed and slept in the barn to allay the fear of the livestock huddled there. And, every time I came through the door with dinner in tow, she accepted my offerings with appreciation and then offered the same thanks to the animal I'd killed for the gift of its life and the nourishment it was sure to provide.

Her awareness was so sublime that it even extended to me, a man so far removed from the spiritual purity she exuded. She knew immediately when I was tired, troubled, or in pain. Likewise, she knew when I was pleased and content. She understood my desires and aversions, and she saw into my soul—no matter how much of its ugliness I tried to keep from her. And best of all, she was always no more than a stone's throw away. Rosalie only went into town once or twice a month, and each time she did, I remained behind, thankful she never questioned my reluctance to accompany her.

However, one mid-summer evening after she'd returned with a wagonload of necessities, I learned my perfect asylum had been compromised. We sat at the kitchen table, tucking into a supper so mouthwateringly grand that it was hard to believe she'd fixed it herself while heavy rain fell upon the ever-receptive crops outside. Ever cheerful, Rosalie told me in great detail about all the acquaintances she'd run into, the clothier's wife whose Dalmatian just had puppies, and her dearest friend, old Mr. Hufnagel of the general store.

"He sold me sugar at half price and traded me leather for eggs," she told me excitedly, "and he was funny; he saw I was buying more than I normally do and asked if I was planning to run away and elope," she chuckled, "of course, I told him about how you came to me and how much of a blessing you've been. They're all excited to meet you."

Her words shook me like a clap of thunder, "you told him *what?!*" I cried with unconcealable dismay.

She knew well enough she need not repeat herself and instead met my wild eyes with ones narrowed with poignant concern. She inquired about the reason for my staunch objection, but I provided her none, and supper was completed in silence.

The next few days proved incomparably troublesome. I continued to work alongside her, but I did so ravaged by the long-dormant fears that'd pursued me when I arrived, along with a mess of new ones. The fact that the people of Cherokee now knew of my residence at the McFall homestead presented a caveat that threatened its continuation. I had no knowledge of how far the news of my horse theft in Quimby had traveled, whether or not the animal had ever been recovered, and if so, how far from Rosalie's home such a discovery had been made. Moreover, I was unaware whether or not the authorities there were still pursuing me—or if they ever had been in the first place. The thought of remaining in a locale where my presence was known, even if such knowledge was seemingly benign, caused the hair on the back of my neck to stand up. After all, few classes of people are more nosy and curious of outsiders than small-town white Anglo-Saxon Protestant farmers.

Such potential gossip endangered Rosalie as well. It was her home where I had sought refuge and was now living, and such a fact could prove disastrous. I would be apprehended and escorted back to the federal pen where I'd never see the light of day again, and she would face trial for harboring a fugitive—or worse. The latter was a hazard I could not risk—although the thought of leaving her for good affected me more than the thought of losing my own freedom—or even my life.

The joy I usually took in my sporting recreations had all but escaped me, and the chores I had now grown used to undertaking with pride and duty caused me to mourn the thought of their absence. Every time I looked at Rosalie, emotion stirred in my breast, and it killed me to turn away. When she spoke to me, I hung on every note her voice produced, and when I ate her cooking, I savored every bite. I held her closer to me in the depth of night, and I could've cried each time I awoke to her shining face.

I kept up my agonizing for nearly a week, torturing myself with the unbearable consideration of either outcome, until one evening at supper, she finally asked me what was wrong.

In the plainest of terms and with a voice fringed with regret, I shared with her my most reviled intent.

"Rosalie, I cannot stay here any longer."

When she heard these words, she stiffened, and with great composure evident everywhere but in her eyes, she asked me why.

"You said the other day that you told some people in town about me and how I arrived here. Well, there's something about that night I never told you, something you know nothing about...."

I went on to tell her everything. I must've talked for an hour, weaving for her the tangled web of my life. I told her of my crimes and punishment, of my return to liberty, and all the running I'd had to do in order to retain it. I recounted every detail of that cursed night when she laid her hand across the deal of fate and took the cards for herself. I shared with her all of my fears, especially those involving her.

Rosalie received all of this very calmly and responded to me in a voice so soft and sure that every last one of my fears turned tail and ran like shadows in the sunlight, "I always supposed your circumstance was less than honest. I never asked because I knew you would never tell me, and it wasn't any of my business besides. No honest man in his right mind would have been out in the storm that night, and even if some situation had produced such urgency, your only concern afterward would have been getting to the destination you'd been trying to reach. But, you never had a concern or a destination. Yes, I've been harboring a fugitive, and I've been doing so knowingly and willingly since the night I met you."

Such an answer surprised me more than it should have; although relieved as I was to learn that she was not shocked by my past or by the fact that she could be considered criminally implicit for sheltering a murderer for the past five months, it still did not change the awful circumstance. Whether she was defiant of the law or not, if any of our neighbors in Cherokee discovered the truth behind my arrival in their county, it would result in nothing but trouble for both of us.

However, to this fact, she was unexpectedly indifferent. She assured me that as far as the law was concerned, I had little to fear. She believed that if any word of my crimes or my alleged proximity had been in the wind, she would have been made aware of it on one of her trips into town. Furthermore, her description of the sheriff's department was enough to further convince me that she was right. The sheriff himself was about fifteen years overdue for retirement, and his deputies served on a rotation basis, also fulfilling the duties of telegraph operator, postman, and grocer.

"After all," she continued, "even if there is a possibility of the law catching up to you in Cherokee, wouldn't you rather remain here where you feel safe and comfortable than go back to the same road you crawled in on?"

I agreed wholeheartedly, and as gladness rallied deep in my chest like a phoenix, I promised her I would stay.

"I want to make you a home that you'll love and treasure more than any adventure," she whispered softly, peering across the table into my soul.

At that moment, I felt something run out of me, "Rosalie," I said, "if I could spend the rest of my life with you, I would never yearn for another day on the road for as long as I live."

An unconstrained smile spread across her face and lit up the room like a stroke of lightning before slowly receding again.

"There is one thing folks in town may object to," she spoke tentatively.

"What's that?" I inquired.

"That we're not married."

I wasted no time. Immediately, I reached across the table and grasped her slender, bronze hands in mine, "Rosalie McFall," I asked her, "Will you marry me?"

"Jack," she answered in a voice thick with emotion, "there's nothing in this world that would make me happier."

One week later, Rosalie and I were married in the county courthouse by the Justice of the Peace. The ceremony took no more than fifteen minutes and was followed by no grand festivities or presentations of gifts. The rings we exchanged belonged to her parents, and the clerk waived the fee for the marriage license in exchange for a dozen jars of pickled eggplant. Congratulations were offered in abundance from her lifelong acquaintances, who received me graciously and welcomed me as one of their own. As always, I was wary of pretense but so drunk on love and good fortune that if Sheriff Steele himself had come calling on the morrow, I wouldn't have minded, just as long as I had today.

The months that followed were consummate. Rosalie and I never shared a harsh word between us. She never nagged, never complained, and was understanding right up to the hilt. Our days were filled with work, and other than during my time in prison, I do not believe I ever labored harder at anything without reward. I was never in want of a chore, but when the day's work was done, revelry presided.

In all matters of fun, Rosalie was competitive—and a worthy opponent at that. I taught her games like Euchre, Pedro, and High Low Jack, and even with my most clever sleight of hand, she still managed to find a way to foil me. I maintained my advantage at throwing dice, but she had me beat in checkers and backgammon and could shoot with an eye that rivaled that of Annie Oakley. Come harvest time, she resurrected an old copper boiler, head, and tubing from the cellar, and we distilled fine homemade whiskey the way her Pop had taught her. Of course, my penchant for gin outstripped even the finest quality hooch, and that fall, two stills thumped on the riverbank.

That pastoral paradise was a respite from the horrors of reality. Laughter filled the crisp autumn air, and amid those halcyon days of sanctuary, shrouded by the idyllic folds of copses and waving grain, could be found a soul assuaged by love; my withershin feet momentarily paused in their wandering. The isolated cabin was not only a refuge for me but a buffer from the troubles afoot in the rest of the country. All concerns over the bank holidays, Germany's new chancellor, and General Johnson's purportedly harebrained schemes could not penetrate the dense thickets of heather and greenery that shrouded our land from the ills abroad. The 3 R's of the New Deal were all but foreign to us, we had no tickets for the Irish sweepstakes, and the only time we saw the blue eagle of the NRA was on the front door of the shingle factory in town. We had no radio to carry worried talk into our home, and the strain we heard in the voices of others was hardly present in ours. We lived so simply and self-sufficiently that money was rarely necessary—and Rosalie was nothing if not prudent. The sale of the summer crops was enough for us to afford adequate winter supplies, and once our own cellar was full, she gave away the crops we couldn't sell to struggling neighbors, and whatever surplus corn and barley remained, I gladly turned into liquor. It seemed as if the Depression, even in its darkest year, was on hold.

However, one piece of news was so pervasive and intoxicating that town drunks the world over made Paul Revere-like rides through the uninformed countryside proclaiming their victory to the dries and inviting their compatriots to rekindle the merry carousing of yesteryear. At 4:32pm on December 5, 1933, the golden spike of repeal was driven into the coffin of federal Prohibition. Printers across the nation held back press times for their evening dailies in hopes that such a triumphant headline would adorn the front page. The girders of Evangelical churches in every town trembled as stampedes of the religious faithful crowded in to pray for the future of the country. Uptown and down in every city of the USA, there was dancing in the streets. In Chicago, New Orleans, and New York City, speakeasies tore off their false fronts, and saloons that'd been boarded up for years threw open their doors in a nationwide expiration of relief and excitement. Even Iowan townsfolk, who were so well assured that Prohibition was the answer to all legal and moral dilemmas that some had even sold their jails, gathered to celebrate in such numbers that the local bureaus of enforcement waived their curfews.

When the news finally came that the dread Prohibition was dead, the local potato farmers and wets of every other social echelon in Cherokee gathered that fabled evening intent on giving that town a tear unlike any other ever seen before. Rosalie had been in town that morning and returned with this revelation. Elated, I convinced her that we should attend—after all, neither of us had ever legally drank in public in our lives.

It was as cold as the Iceman's ass cheeks when dusk crept in that night and as grey and still as a painting.

"Snow's coming," Rosalie cautioned me as we saddled the horses.

"Don't worry about it," I dismissed her, "if the weather turns, we can just stay the night in town."

She warily agreed, and together we set out on that frigid trek, our saddlebags bulging with quart jars of whiskey.

When we arrived, the word of the day was very clearly 'liberty'. The misery and anxiety that had presided over the nation's mind were washed away in the tidal wave of liquor that flowed forth. Even in the middle of rural Cherokee, men and women threw away their hip flasks, bellied up to the bar, and made merry on equal terms. The feminists' dream had finally come to pass—just not in the manner in which they had so richly envisioned.

John Barleycorn was alive and well—and during those years he'd been forced underground, he seemed to acquaint himself even further with the delicacies of the human palate, for when he emerged from his exile, he did so robed in debut attire—cocktails. Despite the fourteen-year ban, while every able-bodied, whistle-wetting citizen flooded the halls and restaurants of Cherokee that jubilant night, there was no shortage of liquor to sate them. However, there was not a drop of club soda to be found anywhere in Iowa after 11 o'clock.

Considering we'd never held a formal reception for our wedding, much of the local cheer was poured upon us, and our union was the toast of the town. We dined at the favorite local eatery, were treated to dessert at yet another, and concluded with a nightcap at the town's oldest tavern, which had reopened just for the occasion. The experience was unparalleled; my only regret was that we'd decided to attend.

Rosalie had been right; it snowed that night. As far as the vagaries of weather are concerned, snow is something I most certainly could have lived my life quite comfortably without ever seeing again, but that night, as it drifted down the street in the dim orange glow emanating from swinging saloon doors, the snow was a beautiful sight to behold. It came on suddenly, and the already frigid temperature dropped like a stone in a lake, but it hardly deterred the hoards of parched imbibers eager to grasp at a pastime they'd been denied for over a dozen years.

When the grip of cold alighted, we poured ourselves another round. Rosalie's prowess in the matter was hardly a surprise to me—she was the daughter of an Irishman, after all, and she could really pound down the firewater. As drinks flowed freely around the hot coal stove in the barroom, she chatted merrily with neighbors and townsmen who showered us with drinks and well-wishes of health and prosperity. Even as the evening hours crept past midnight, that woman kept her composure and—believe it or not—loaded me spread-eagled onto my horse before leading us home through the snow. Rarely are there evenings I forget entirely, but the culmination of that most auspicious night remains to be one of the few. My only memory is crawling, half-frozen, over the threshold toward the stove as I had so many long months before—and in much better condition at that.

When I regained consciousness around noon, Rosalie was already awake, and the smell of fresh eggs frying on the stove was the first to greet me. By then, the snow had piled up to the doorstep, and the aftershocks of the evening's revelry had alighted me. Despite her own plague of chills and neuralgia, Rosalie was at my bedside. Warm compresses and a hot meal were only part of my woman's indomitable charm, and her care stirred perennial memories of the first few months I spent in her company as I fell, utterly and unexpectedly, in love.

"Pa always told me to marry a girl who could outdrink me," I told her as she pressed a hot rag to my pounding forehead.

"Mine always told me to marry a man who hated whiskey," she replied with a pained smile.

I'd married her in the fall of 1933. By 1934, she was dead. A powerful shame it was, a total waste. She was a beautiful girl, my prairie rose, with a smile so kind and bright she could make the devil feel loved. And, I reckon, that's just what she did—she up and made him feel so loved that he thought he ought to take her for himself. It certainly wasn't any act of God; God ain't that cruel. No merciful God would deprive his creation of the joy that gentle creature gave it. And yet, on December 8, 1933, Rosalie McFall succumbed to a fever so quick and fierce she wasn't two days in bed before I buried her. The doctor made it out to us about an hour before her time came; by then, there was no time left. I got what I could for the livestock and the land, though it wasn't any fortune to speak of. Back in the good old days, I'd won more in one night of poker than I left Iowa with on that snowy New Year's Day. Yessir, for the twenty acres of land she and her folks had toiled long and hard to keep and every earthly thing they'd owned with the exception of one quilt and one suit of clothes, I'd been paid two thousand ninety-one dollars and seventy-two cents.

As I stood on the platform that morning at the depot, waiting for the train which would carry me forever away from the love I once knew, it was so cold that songbirds fell dead from the treetops like clumps of snow. It was so cold that each breath froze in my hollow chest and deepened within me a shock of gelidity so pervasive that it remained even after my surroundings thawed. Few souls stirred on such a soundless, dismal morning, but those that passed by offered me their condolences and shared sorrows. Not one received a reply, for it was too cold to speak. It was too cold even to feel— for I was about as stolid and lifeless as a statue. I hardly shifted, hardly blinked; I just remained there motionless, all the while cut deep by razors of prairie wind and stung by inexorable grief. All I could do was think of what I'd had, what I'd lost, and whether or not it'd all been a dream. Through narrowed eyes, I looked up at the old grey sky with all my questions, my pleas, and my sorrow, and the cold wind and rain was the only answer I received in return. Above me, ice sickles hung from the station's eaves, glistening despite the cloud-covered sky, and when the Illinois Central came thundering in, they shattered upon the ground like the hopes and dreams of a broken-hearted man. There I was again, on that same old road, and before me, I saw nothing more than where I'd already been.

I've always had an uncanny ability to forget—and with all that legal liquor around, I certainly had all the means I needed to do so—but as it goes, I seemed to forget everything except my pain. During the intervening weeks between Rosalie's death and my exodus from Cherokee, no matter how many empty bottles rolled across that kitchen floor, no matter how many burning mouthfuls of that homespun cure-all I swallowed, the image of

Rosalie lying in her plain wooden casket, her dancing feet stilled and her sage eyes closed in sleep forevermore was all that lingered in the darkness. When I laid down in that cold bed that we once shared, the room around me swirling in great concentric undulations as my grief-stricken consciousness drowned in gin, all that alighted my ears was the morose tone of the bagpipes and the choir singing *Danny Boy*.

I could not stay in that cabin. I could not remain on that land. Its warmth and safety had departed with its maiden. Its richness and splendor had blown away with the summer leaves and her last breath. Even the life-bringing waters of the river Sioux had frozen over, its animus suspended like the blood in her veins. That bright, golden hillside as rich and pure as the soul that once resided upon it recoiled against the fierce blows of winter and, in time, relinquished its hold and was overcome by the snow.

Despite the security it had provided and the joyous memories it held, to live within those four walls without her was maddening. To step across the floor where she'd died was unnerving, and to wake each morning to the taunts of stolen love was demoralizing. I quickly decided that I'd rather stand upon the gallows with my head in a noose than live another day in that desecrated sanctuary, and, with little preparation, I left it all behind me and traveled ever deeper into the dark night of the soul.

Slowly, softly, and with great trepidation, that night moved...that endless night, with all its twists, turns, and uncertainty. Through tribulations, I stumbled and spun, at all times remembering the things I was trying to forget and forgetting everything else. A three-day drunk for a man like me, living a life like mine, is nothing to speak of, but how I spent those next few months down around South Sioux City, Nebraska, is known solely to the devil...and the bartenders. The money I'd earned from the sale of the McFall estate kept me in gin for quite a while, and it was spring by the time I ran out.

Spring in northeastern Nebraska is just the same as spring in Cherokee. The calendar says it's there, the papers say it's there, people talk about it on the street but try to find it, and you come up empty; try to grasp it, and you're left with a handful of permafrost and a mind full up with winter depression. The icy hand of snowfall season was slow to relinquish its grasp, and as a result, the streets were just about empty, all except for the outcasts who limped in from across the river: broke gamblers, jonesing hopheads, and discouraged hoboes. Even in Sioux City proper, the ghosts of prosperity drifted by without a destination while dereliction and debauchery ruled in their place. The prevailing air was that of a boomtown gone bust, and that condition persisted just about everywhere—painting for me a clearer picture of the hardships the rest of the country had been enduring while I'd been sheltered in clover. The old men and downtrodden farmers teetering on the brink of foreclosure who sat next to me in the neighborhood beerhall told stories about the way things used to be and lamented over their turn of fortune and loss of same.

It was the ultimate bummer. My wife was dead, my land sold, my money spent, and my boredom terminal—and seldom did I speak with a man who was hardly any better off than I. Such melancholy surroundings did little more than magnify my depression; however, I was further from the clutches of the law than I had been in years—which came as both a great relief and a welcome change. Despite the fact that Nebraska was still largely dry, even in the wake of federal repeal, South Sioux City shared the sentiment of its Iowan sister and openly flouted the edict. The sheriff was in for a glass of homebrew at the end of his shift every afternoon, and I got drunk with the deputy every other weekend.

All things considered, I'd had much worse stints. I had no wants for close to four months. I never had a run-in with the locals or the law, never needed to turn any coin, and the bar never closed—I didn't even have to pay room rent! That extra expense was spared me by the kindhearted proprietor who allowed me to sleep on a pallet in the stock room on the condition that I swept out in the mornings, procured a box of old vegetables from the storekeeper next door and a mess of scraps from the butcher down the block and put on each day's mulligan. I knew every face in town by the second week and was accepted as one of them by the fourth.

Although, as I'd come to learn quite poignantly as of late, nothing good lasts for long. Right about the time my money began dwindling, my five o'clock companion, the sheriff, arrived for his daily drink with a paper folded neatly in his breast pocket. Once the customary bumping of gums had subsided, he unfolded it and showed it to me. It was a wanted poster, faded and tattered by many long winters outside the express office. Yet, the face evident upon it and the name printed below appeared ominously familiar. The face was that of a boy, scant and scrappy, the expression naïve, eyes discouraged and afraid. The countenance bore little resemblance to the one I now showed the world. Still, after enough hard looking and some digging—both activities the sheriff confined himself to in the slow winter months—it wasn't too difficult to piece together my history. Being an observant man, he likely suspected me from the first, but rather, he kept mum, inserted himself into my frequent company, and before long, had a case. If there was any shred of surprise or recognition when my eyes fell upon the poster, I doubt I showed it. Regardless, the sheriff was awfully sure of himself.

"As long as you pay your way, ain't none of us gon' be comin' aft' you," the sheriff spoke that fateful evening. "If it war' up ta me, all of them prohibition dicks would be lyin' dead 'longside the legislators passin' the blame laws, so you ain't got no enemy in me."

The sigh of relief I tried to repress felt like it came from down in my toes.

"But," he continued, "If I was keen enough to catch on, different as you look now, I reckon I ain't the only one who will. I's the same as all small-town sheriffs—as soon as a new face appears, I go over my stack of posters and bulletins. You make a habit of it, and every so often, you get lucky. If I were you, Straw, I'd keep out of towns like ours if you plan on stayin' for any length of time. Them big city sheriffs have better things to do than go thumbin' through stacks of faces. You'll have better luck there."

I did not reply.

He refolded the poster carefully and returned it to his pocket, then finished his beer in silence and left without a word or a glance behind him.

I was glad for his reassurances and quite sure of his veracity, but I packed it in and left the next day anyway. After doing time, I made it my policy to remove myself from any situation which aroused even the slightest bit of suspicion, and, once again, I was relegated to the exile of the Union Pacific until I found asylum a thousand miles west of there in California.

IV

Playing In The Band

I started out on a freighter headed west. The sheriff in South Sioux City had advised me to spend my time in the big city, and that's precisely what I intended to do. In fact, I was en route to the biggest, wildest city on this side of the Mississippi—Los Angeles.

It had been over a year since I'd hit the rails, and the prevailing conditions had not been subject to any vast improvement in the interim. The train was a highball and running along at a pretty good clip, but the whole string of boxcars, including my own, were flat-wheelers—and empty. Every time we hit a rail joint, the train lurched like it was about to jump the tracks, and I bounced across the car floor like a frog mine. I certainly had no illusions of riding in comfort—and decking her was guaranteed suicide. If I started out sitting, a rough joint would bounce me to my feet, and if I started out standing, I'd be back on the floor in no time.

And, to make matters worse, it was brutally hot. The desert south of Barstow was dull and featureless, full of dry scrub, colorless sand, and arid cacti surrounded by a ring of distant mountains that obscured the horizon. The merciless noonday heat beat down on the hot steel unimpeded and baked the car and its contents. Even the breeze from the open door was breathlessly hot, and I was sweating like a guilty man standing before the bench.

As a result, I was in one bully of a bad mood. You might've stacked me up against every cantankerous hobo out sifting the cinders, and I still would've come out atop the heap. I pitied myself something awful and mourned the course my life had taken as of late. Alone in that oven of a boxcar, I raged like a madman. In fact, I was so busy cursing the sun and everything under it that I was caught uncharacteristically off-guard when a bearded, gnarled, weather-beaten old tramp swung into my car like Tarzan, loudly announcing his presence before removing his hat to wipe the sweat from his forehead.

The man was a caricature of a bum and quite easily one of the strangest fellows I've ever met—which, after forty-five years on the tramp, is quite a weighty statement. His shoulders were rounded in a permanent arthritic hump which made his blue, starched thousand-miler—about three sizes too large—hang clear down to his knees. His pants were made from stitched jute and fastened with safety pins, and his shoes were so worn and cracked that I could see a couple of toes. He was bowlegged, and his fingers were crooked and drawn up into his atrophied hands like claws. His hair was blazing red and streaked with thick bands of grey and white that had taken a stronger hold in his beard. He was missing a few digits and a few teeth, his nose was hooked like a raven's beak, his cheeks were fleshy and pale, and his eyes were icy blue and crazed. Around his neck hung a large, wooden crucifix fastened to a thick piece of twine, and pinned to his chest pocket was a shriveled rose. His voice was booming and grandiloquent.

"Which way, 'Bo?" he thundered, and his voice reverberated through the empty boxcar like a cannon blast.

As painfully curious as I was about this bizarre denizen of Hoboland, I was still in far too ugly a mood to play nice, and I returned his boisterous greeting with a sneer.

"Don't matter where I'm going; there's always going to be some bum along the road who's goin' to ask me about it like it's any of their damn business," I answered sullenly.

"Sure didn't mean to offend you, son," he replied, "Just always felt friendly conversation to be better than riding in silence. I'm Stephen." He held his misshapen hand out for me to shake.

I looked him up and down and then returned to surveying the landscape in silence.

I'd hoped my reticence would've been enough to terminate our interaction, but as is expected amongst the most objectionable class of hobos, Stephen was a talker.

Utterly undeterred by my impertinence, he hobbled across the rocking car and sat down on the opposite end of the open doorway, talking all the while. Fortunately, I had the ceaseless chatter of the wheels and clanking of suddenly shifting iron to partially drown out his caterwauling.

If this desert stretch had seemed endless before, it appeared twice-so with the addition of the loquacious Stephen. However, after some time had passed, all that talking must've made him thirsty, for he pulled a glistening thermos out of his bindle and raised it to his lips. His exclamation of pleasure after he swallowed made it clear that whatever liquid it contained was cold and refreshing, and my canteen was just about empty.

"Can I get a swig of that?" my parched tongue begrudgingly asked of him.

The picture of magnanimity, he rose unsteadily to his feet and carried it across the car to me. I snatched it from him and drank from it greedily, but after the first swallow, I recoiled in disgust. The coffee it contained was so thick you could've cut it with a knife.

"It's a bit strong," he admitted.

"A bit strong?" I gagged, thrusting the thermos back into his gnarled hand, "that shit'll make you grow hair on your tongue!"

Stephen shrugged and took another generous gulp. "Ain't a tramp alive who'd waste good coffee," he mused, "you must not be long on the road."

I scoffed, "been nearly fifteen years now. You ain't very observant, Mister."

The old man's head dropped in dismay at my mention of years, and he clicked his tongue at me like a prioress, "too long...too long...may the good Lord have mercy on your young soul."

I stared at him quizzically, "too long for me? You look like you were born in the tender of the first steam train that ever touched its wheels to a track."

Stephen jerked his head up from his mournful repose and calmly unfolded his hands, "I am not a bum," he spoke matter-of-factly, his cerulean eyes boring cold fire into mine, "I am a conductor."

"And you're right sure of that, ain't ya," I laughed derisively, "well, alright, Conductor, you asked me which way. I'm going to Los Angeles—is this blasted iron bitch going to get there before my ears burn up from yer yappin', or am I gonna bake to death on this train?"

"Man knoweth not his time," he recited coolly, "which is why I asked you which way you're going."

"I told you already, you damned old coot, I'm headed to Los Angeles."

188

Despite my abuses, Stephen maintained his sanctimonious composure, "no, son, you misunderstand me. We're all headed west. I meant, which way are you going—north or south—heaven or hell?" The nature of his question struck me off guard, and the force of his unwavering gaze only furthered his intensity. The tone of his voice suggested that my answer should have been glaringly obvious. His eyes smoldered like dry ice.

"Oh, you're a wise guy, eh?" I jokingly replied, knowing full well that he was not.

His stoic expression evidenced that Stephen was as serious as sin on the subject, and as usual, intrigue got the best of me. So, I figured to hell with it. I was stuck with the guy until the next stop either way, so rather than riding in uncomfortable existential silence for the next few hours, I decided to play along.

"I've always fancied hell myself," I responded drawlingly to his pressing question. "I heard the devil tends an open bar, and you've got to pay for your drinks in heaven."

"You'd best be advised, my son, that there ain't a freight train on earth bound for heaven," he spoke with utter solemnity.

"That's good for me then; I bet I wouldn't know a single person when I got there."

"Only a fool disparages the question of everlasting life," Stephen replied morosely.

"If I can eke a few more free years out of this one, that'll be long enough for me," I answered curtly.

With the prowess of a tennis champ, Stephen promptly changed his serve. "Don't you ever want to get off these railroads?" he queried.

For the first time, I gave a straight answer, "Was off once. Woman died. Suppose I'm just damned now. I'm on until the end of the line."

Stephen's response to my pathos was simple and human, "So did mine."

"Is that why you're here too?" I ventured.

"No, son, I am here as a conductor for Christ. When the Lord called my Rosemary home, I knelt down and asked Him how He wanted me to continue His ministry. The angel of the Lord appeared to me that night in a dream and told me to go forth as a missionary of His Will. He commanded me to be a sponsor for the poor in spirit, for the mourners, for the meek and for the hungry, for the wretched and the lowly, to inform them of the heavenly banquet that the Lord has prepared them should they abdicate their chosen life of spoils and lust, of trickery and thievery, of drunkenness and sloth. I've yet to meet a man along the road who wasn't searching for a better life, and no matter how long he searches, in this life or in the next, he will never find it. There is not a depot, barroom, gambling den, pleasure palace, or speakeasy that upholds the works of the Lord. A man whose master is the manifest rejects his heavenly Father. A man who lives by sin collects only its wages—and as the Lord said in Romans, the wages of sin is death. On the road, there is no such thing as a free lunch, but when you place your faith in Jesus and lay your fears and worries and the trespasses of your enemies along the tracks, you will have eternal life in Christ."

"I hate to break it to you, Bub, but faith don't fill your belly. It don't keep you dry and warm at night, and it certainly don't line your pockets with any extra coin," I replied to his sermon.

If the Lord had endowed Stephen with any asset beyond a good set of lungs, it was patience. "Jesus is the bread of life. When the Lord is your Savior, you want for nothing," he countered.

"Listen," I told him, "You ain't the first bible-thumper I've met along the road, and I'll tell you what; even though the likes of you don't swear or drink or lie or cheat or steal or hang around loose women, I've seen them suffer just as much as me. No matter how much they pray and preach and cast their good works upon the swine, they suffer just as much as me. And, if they are the sort who beg for alms, collect tithes from the poor, and sell absolution to sinners, they are no less cons than I am myself."

At my conclusion, Stephen fell silent. Satisfied that I had won our verbal joust, I snatched his thermos for a victory slug that I spit out the door to prove not only that I wasn't some poor lost soul wandering aimlessly across the country in search of salvation but also that I was no slouch.

Stephen permitted my insolence without comment, but once I'd unhanded his precious brick of coffee, he pulled a pocket bible bound in brown paper out of his shirt and thrust it toward me.

"Take it. Read it."

I looked at the article contemptuously, "I didn't even read that book when they gave it to me in prison."

He mournfully returned the bible to his thousand-miler, then met my eyes and lobbed me up a good one, "do you have any enemies, son?"

"Not as many as you, I'd reckon."

"And do you pray for them?"

"Well, let's see...I curse 'em every so often and damn 'em to hell once or twice a month, but I can't say I've ever prayed for 'em—nor can I fathom why I ever would."

"Jesus said on the Mount, 'love thy enemies, bless those who curse you, do good to those who hate you.' He who digs a pit will fall into it, and he who rolls a stone will see it roll back on him. You see, son—"

Stephen drew in a great breath and then continued, "At some point, every traveler boards a train for the first time. You remain on this train for a spell and then get off at a station. After a while, another train comes by, and you board that train and travel to another station where you get off again, and so on and so forth as the journey continues; it never ends. As long as you are resolved to travel, you will take trips from station to station for all eternity; there is no end of the line until you get off for good. And throughout that journey, every conductor you flout, every straw boss you cheat, every honest man you deal dirty, and every woman you lie to, you run the chance of meeting again. And so your enemies do you. Those who plow evil and sow trouble reap it. For all the squandered plenty your wrongdoing earns, for all the fleeting pleasure your wickedness brings pales in the light of the Father. For one day, this world and all you love in it will pass away, and if you do not give your life to Christ, your immortal soul will be punished with everlasting destruction and shut out from the presence of the Lord and the glory of his might!" His booming voice echoed inside the sweltering metal boxcar, and sweat poured down his wizened face as he strained with the effort of conversion—for both my soul and his pride were now at stake.

I couldn't help but scoff at his severity, with a good chuckle thrown in to address the absurdity with which I regarded his moral suggestions. "I don't know about some of the other saps you find out here, but you won't find me swearing off women and booze and gambling for the hope of future gains I ain't well assured of."

"Oh ye of little faith," he rebuked me with platitudinal wisdom.

"For once, you're right," I replied, volleying a drop shot, "I don't trust nothing but my own two eyes and my own two hands—and sometimes I can't even trust them. You turn all this talk about my 'immortal soul' and how it's so important to the old man in the sky that I don't swear lest I lose it, but all that don't do nothing for me while I'm living. If I stop swearing, confess all my sins, and refuse to commit another evil deed as long as I live, it won't make this boxcar any less hot, this ride any less long, or my throat any less dry. In my life, I've seen more often the honest man fail while the liar prospers and the innocent man take the blame while the guilty get off scot-free. It's sure easier for the losers to believe in some kind of compensation in the afterlife to make that tough pill a mite easier to swallow, but I ain't a man of pretense. I don't want pie in the sky when I die; I want it now. I'm here to have a good time. I've had a bad enough time already, and I ain't looking for more of that. Pleasure in this world is hard enough to find as it is. I sure ain't going to deprive myself of any of it willingly, and if it finds me of its own accord, I ain't gonna deny it. Whether you call that good or bad don't concern me. We're all living on borrowed time, so I'm going to take it as easy as I can—but I'm still going to take it."

Stephen shook his head mournfully at my declarations. "You, my son, are a hedonist, a pleasure seeker."

I grinned at him the way I once did my priestly brother when a stay of my wickedness was in question and produced a sack of tobacco and a book of papers from my breast pocket. Once the cigarette was rolled, I offered it to him, and he recoiled in disdain.

"He whose master is the devil's fancies is shackled by his desires. A man whose treasures are the world's sacrifices the treasures promised him in the kingdom of God."

"I'll take my chances," I assured him before flicking the burning butt into the wind as the air brakes engaged, and the train began to shift and moan as it slowed and swung into the right of way ahead of the coming town.

"Don't you think you better get off here?" he asked abruptly.

"This is Colton. I told you I'm staying with her until we hit Los Angeles."

"A smart 'bo never rides into Los Angeles unless he wants to spend the next ninety days eating cold beans in Lincoln Heights. You gotta get off here and take a bus or your thumb the rest of the way. Get yourself cleaned up in Colton before you go on, and whatever you do, don't stop in Pasadena—those rich town cops can smell a bum anywhere within city limits—even when he's wearing a new suit."

I hardly expected this bit of sage advice from the zealot, but I heeded it nonetheless. After all, I needed no further excuse to get off that sweltering hell-bound train.

"Thanks for the coffee," I smirked as I dismounted.

In response to my exodus, Stephen rose to his feet, "God bless you, my son!" his voice reverberated after me as the train carried him swiftly away, "may you walk always with the Lord!"

Another bum pounded his feet in my direction as he followed in quick pursuit of the train.

"Good ridin' in that car?" he called out as he approached.

"Oh, that car's a heap of good ridin'," I guaranteed him with a wild grin as he whizzed past, "just a little loud!"

I turned and stopped to watch as he deftly hooked his hand on the ladder and pulled himself up.

"Good luck, you poor devil!" I shouted with a laugh as he disappeared into the mouth of the departing boxcar.

Per Stephen's suggestion, I spent the next few days hitchhiking from Colton to Los Angeles. I remained there unmolested for the remainder of that month as I drifted through the skids along Fifth and Main, surveying the gambling houses and catting around the bawdy underbelly of that city of lights. Once I'd assembled a suitable bankroll, I passed out of Los Angeles in the same manner I'd entered and continued on west. A few days later, I found there was no farther west I could go, so I settled myself down in Santa Monica for a time.

Even amid the bustling piers, ballrooms, and beach clubs, the Depression had left its tawdry mark. Among the lavish padlocked hotels and towering office buildings with boards across their first-floor windows were the shops and restaurants that'd dug their toes into the promising notion that 'it'll only last one more year' and were still fighting the good fight. But, even upon these more fortunate storefronts were signs posted 'No Work.' However, as in all warm-weather locales, bums flocked regardless of opportunities. They dotted Third Street like panhandling seagulls, fished for their dinner off the end of the amusement pier, and slept on the beaches below during low tide. Glad to not have to number myself amongst them for once, I scored a fifty-cent flop in a cheap hostel on Ocean Ave, bought myself a pipe and some blended tobacco at a corner store and a bottle of white line down the road, then went tramping around to see the sights.

When I reached the pier, I unlaced my shoes, tied them together, slung them over my shoulder, and walked barefooted in the warm, dry sand along the base of the towering palisade cliffs. The beaches were bespeckled with bathers and laughing children, all worries abroad in the town above momentarily forgotten. A large family gathered on a quilt where a diapered baby crawled, a woman in a bathing suit poured cups of lemonade from a large pitcher, and a fat man sat smoking a stogie and reading a paper. Groups of sunburnt kids tore through the sand like wild Indians on the warpath, their hands clutched around the handles of buckets and prize seashells. No pensive concern could be detected in the faces of the sojourners, and they splashed about merrily as if they had no idea what it felt like to be under the gun.

The farther I walked from the pier, the less commotion there was. Some swimmers bobbed above the waves, and gulls and terns skimmed the sand, looking for delectable morsels left behind by the picnickers. A young couple walked along the tideline hand-in-hand, admiring the natural splendor as little waves bubbled into the sand around their fair ankles. They strolled lazily about in utter comfort, and as I watched them, I could not help but think of the summer anterior when Rosalie and I would amble along the South Platte just as guileless and carefree. I could feel a knot of envy tighten in my stomach. I felt like a dirty wretch lurking alone in the shadow of the cliffs with my shoulders hunched and my head drooped while they strutted along, proud of their love. I wanted to look away, but I couldn't. I wanted to curse them. I wanted to run down to the water and wrench their adoring hands apart. But as I watched the girl lean in and steal a kiss from her suitor mid-step, that raging envy turned at once to sadness— I just missed her, and I missed her something awful.

The melancholy I played host to during that time was largely a foreign element in my life. I'd traipsed through many devastating circumstances before without feeling intrinsically lost, but after Rosalie died, everything changed—even how I felt about myself. I felt like I'd been cut off at the knees and was walking around three feet tall. In the swift change of a moment, I was right back where I'd been before she'd saved me—always no more than a few dollars from broke, shifty, spiteful, and exhausted from the burden of running scared. I felt like there was some part of me that I'd left back in Cherokee, and it'd been laid in the grave with my bride. The evangelist back on the train had had his own explanation of what it was, but as with everything he'd said to me, it was laughable to consider. And, even if he was right, if knowing what he knew meant having the same look in my eyes as he did, I felt very comfortable taking my chances with ignorance.

As I trekked north, the beach eventually became vacant. A long rock jetty loomed ominously in the distance, and the remains of an old pier stuck up out of the surf like spears in a prostrate body. Once the shoreline gave way to the sea, I set my feet upon the rocks at the base of the old wharf and looked out over the endless span of blue. It was a Sunday evening, and all was quiet in man's world. A few rickety boats bobbed noiselessly along the horizon, their nets cast into the sunset surf. Long trails of clouds drifted across the sky, accompanied by the earliest suggestions of night. I could hear the loons and seabirds calling to one another up and down the coast as they circled above me. Below me, flotsam and jetsam and dead fish floated, caught between the jagged rocks, their gills gaping and necrotic, their shiny silver scales bleached white by the sun. I watched them with boredom for a while as they bobbed on the surface, lifeless and inert. A few other live ones swam around them, navigating the canals of carnage and death in search of a better life and a different fate. And there I was amongst them, very much intent on doing the same. I stood there for a long time.

When darkness came to sweep the shoreline, I left my empty bottle on the rocks and hoofed it back to the pier. As I climbed the steps from the beach, the flashing lights of passing cars strobed through the still blackness and roused me from my introspection. I could hear the boisterous voices of fishermen as they stood along the railings and the sound of their catches splashing fitfully in the surf below. As I drew nearer to the street, one voice rose above the rest—and I recognized it.

'I must be going mad,' I chastened myself as I followed the sound, and when I reached its source, I rubbed my eyes in disbelief—but there was no mistaking the mouth from which it came. At the foot of the pier was a stooped evangelist in rags standing on a soapbox, shouting and gesticulating like a mad jester with a fire of purpose burning in his eyes. A small crowd of half a dozen had gathered around him to listen while curious others walked by slowly or paused momentarily for a taste of his stem-winding sermon. I lingered at a distance in hopes that he would not notice me—but I was reasonably sure there was no chance of that; after all, I could've been a quarter-mile away and still clearly heard every word he said.

"In the early days of this century, when the Anti-Saloon League and WTCU had the ear of Congress and the president, King Alcohol trembled before the cause of Temperance!" Stephen shouted from the sidewalk, "With every state that signed a dry act into law, the devil retreated another step! We had him on the run! Back into the pith of hell was he to flee, for sober men had cast him from their hearts and homes! Our country was on the road to righteousness! It had answered the call of grace and temperance! But oh!" Stephen mourned, "Oh, how weak are man's vows when trouble comes! It is easy to uphold the will of the Lord and praise Him when times are good, but the real test of faith is to remain thankful when times are hard! When Depression struck, men got scared. They got scared and reached out for comfort—but rather than finding comfort in the Holy Spirit, they found comfort in drunkenness!"

Incensed by man's disappointments, Stephen raised his arms above his head as he shouted with uncontrollable zeal, "The Lord said in Ephesians, 'do not get drunk on wine, instead be filled with the Spirit!' For with every swallow, you invite the devil into your heart!"

"Who hath woe?" he beseeched the growing crowd, "Who hath sorrow? Who hath contentions? Who hath babbling? Who hath wounds without cause? Who hath redness of eyes? It is those that tarry long at the wine! All your hardship, all your troubles, all your sorrows will cease when you cast off drinking and give your life to Christ! And so, I entreat you, one and all—take the hand of the Lord and climb out of the whiskey bottle and toward salvation!"

A few of the crowd responded with resounding "*hallelujahs!*" but most answered only with laughter and contempt. As for myself, I'd heard enough.

As I strode away, the orator's thunderous voice followed in pursuit, "Why are you turning your back on the Word of God?" he implored me.

"You're making me thirsty," I called over my shoulder.

The nearest saloon was two blocks from the pier. It was long and narrow, with an L-shaped bar running its length dimly lit by hanging lights suspended from above. Its brass rail was well-populated.

"Did you all get a load of the fella standing on the soapbox out on the pier?" I asked as I leaned against the short end of the bar.

"You mean Saint Stephen?" a husky voice replied from down at the other end, "he's always there. He'll disappear every so often for a few days or weeks, but he always comes back."

Another man raised his head, "you remember the time when that bunch of kids started throwing stones at him until he packed up his pulpit and ran away?" the raconteur laughed raucously, "even then, he was back the very next day, determined as ever...just a little further away from the rock pile."

A couple others at the bar chuckled at this recollection.

"What's his deal?" I inquired.

The first man to speak continued, "He's been a fixture for as long as I've lived out here. As far as I know, he's some kind of reformed bum. Spent a good deal of time on the road, then some conductor took him under his wing, and he worked years as a brakeman on the S&P. Got a pension and everything. He's always been a little bughouse, but then his wife died, and his mind really went to pot."

"She was another one," a third local interjected, "Rosemary." He rolled his eyes, "we called her Ramblin' Rose. She would talk to anybody all the day long and was such a prude that she made Carry Nation look like a lush and a harlot. She was as big as Brunhilde with a voice like Billy Sunday...I can still hear it." He held his head.

"Now he preaches to the drunkards and the bums," the chortling drunk proclaimed, "like God wants *them.*"

"He used to have a beautiful Victorian on the corner of 16th and Alta. Had this big courtyard in the back where she kept a garden. She'd grow all sorts of exotic plants—flowers as big as your head and so much ivy it covered the house. After she kicked the bucket, he gave it all up—donated his pension and moved into the poorhouse...What was today's sermon?"

"The evils of drink," I replied, holding up my glass in a toast.

"Wow, he's really wound up on that, ain't he?" another mused, "That's his third temperance lecture this week."

"Cops don't hassle him none?" I asked, now teeming with curiosity about this inordinately strange fellow.

"Naw," was the answer I received, "for the town, he's sort of a free amusement—California's own Father Coughlin. Certainly draws crowds. So does his old house."

"Why's that?"

"Rumor has it, Rosemary's buried in a plot in the courtyard, and her ghost tends the grounds. And I rightly believe it too, because the garden still grows—even though she up and died five years ago."

The next day before dusk, I set out in search of this fabled estate to see if the barstool gossip was true. As I walked there, feeling like a foolish schoolboy for paying heed to ghost stories, I wondered how much those fellows were getting paid for telling tall tales to drum up tourism in the town. Jaunting along the palm-lined streets, I took in all the sights and sounds of the neighborhood—the kids playing in the road, shouting "car!" and scattering when one came purring along, the birds perched upon the high wire singing, and the muffled conversations of housewives as they chatted through open windows.

The house was easy to find and near impossible to miss. The Victorian-style mansion was painted a murky oxford blue, surrounded by a high stone wall, and covered entirely with ivy so thick it had even grown up to the tip of the weathervane. All the shutters were closed, and the city had nailed a sign upon the front gate stating, "Do Not Enter." A large red X was painted across the front door, signifying that the place was condemned. As I drew nearer to it, I noticed suddenly that it had become eerily quiet. No cars approached in either direction, all the kids had disappeared up the street, and the housewives had closed their windows. Even the birds had fallen silent. I felt the hair stand up on the back of my neck.

Shaking off the heebie-jeebies, I crept toward the back gate and saw that it was long closed, with vines as thick as my thumb wound around the door and latch—so I shimmied over the wall. The garden within was silent, as if the ivy that had grown over everything choked out the noise and kept it from entering. Apart from the vines, the rest of the garden appeared very well-kept. There were thick clumps of lavender, lilac, manzanita, and roses, and the smell of them was dizzyingly intoxicating. An old slate-roofed well stood in the center of the courtyard, and a shiny gold bell that hung from its crossbar caught my eye. I had no doubt of its authenticity and decided to take it with me when I left, as I figured old Rosemary wouldn't miss it. On the farthest side of the courtyard was a headstone. Atop it lay a fresh-cut rose. I broke out in goosebumps at the sight of it.

From where I stood beside the wall, I turned to survey the rest of the garden and immediately almost jumped out of my skin. Across the courtyard, near the opposite wall, stood Saint Stephen with a bucket, calmly and noiselessly watering the flowers. At once, I backed into the ivy to conceal myself, but he seemed undisturbed.

Suddenly, he stopped pouring from the bucket, stiffened, and turned in my direction. He crossed the garden silently. There was no crackle of dried leaves beneath his feet and no clanking of the handle against the bucket, nor did the silence cease when he paused at the well and lowered the bucket down into it on a rope. He cranked the handle for what felt like eons, but right when I began to think the bucket had dropped straight into hell itself, he reversed direction and brought it back up. When it reached the top, it hit the golden bell, and the bell rang—but it did not make a sound. A chill as cold as death ran up my spine. I wanted to haul ass right back over the wall, but I dared not leave before he did.

I waited another eternity until Saint Stephen completed his rounds and returned the bucket to the well, and once he had done so, he approached the grave. I watched as he unpinned the shriveled rose from his shirt pocket and discarded it, then tenderly reached out and picked up the fresh rose that lay upon the headstone.

"A cut rose is doomed to die," he murmured, and his voice reverberated throughout the silent courtyard as if we were inside a chamber.

At last, Saint Stephen turned his back to me and ambled across the courtyard until he passed out of sight on the opposite side of the back steps leading up to the house. I remained in my hiding place until I was certain he was gone and then darted over to where I'd last seen him, expecting to exit through the same gate as he had. But there was no gate. All there was behind the steps was another high wall covered over entirely with undisturbed ivy. There was absolutely no evidence whatsoever that anyone had passed over it. Needless to say, I scrambled up the wall in haste, leaving the golden bell and that bizarre house behind.

I ran the first few blocks, hoping to catch a glimpse of Saint Stephen to ensure that I'd actually seen him and not some freak apparition. Once Ocean Avenue came into view before me, so did the hunched figure of Stephen, carrying his soapbox. I sighed in relief and decided to follow him. Unsurprisingly, he led me back to the pier.

From a distance, I watched as Saint Stephen stepped upon his makeshift pulpit and boldly began haranguing the indifferent masses:

"Gather around, gather around one and all! I'm going to share with you a little bit about the greatest story ever told! It is the story of our Lord and Savior, Jesus Christ! Do any of you know about Moses? Moses was the son of slaves—and yet when he came to know God, he was able to part the Red Sea and free his whole race from oppression! How about Abraham? Because Abraham believed in God's will, his wife bore him a son at one hundred years old—and that son went on to become the father of all Israel! Ever heard of Gideon? Gideon was no more than a boy when God called him to defend the Chosen People, and against insurmountable odds, Gideon achieved victory in the name of the Lord! These three men—these three ordinary men—through their faith in God, were able to do extraordinary things! And so it is true with all men. Put your trust in the

Lord, and with the Lord, you can do all things! When you put your trust in the Lord, you can revoke Satan! When you put your trust in the Lord, you can move mountains! When you put your trust in the Lord, you can call fire down from the heavens like Elijah of old!"

A substantial crowd had gathered by now, and beside me, a heckler began to shout, "Hey, Mister! If your trust in the Lord is so great, I want to see *you* call fire down from the heavens! If you can do as you say, you'll get me to believe you, but until then, all your yowling and preaching ain't goin' to make me believe in nothin'!"

This wasn't the first time I'd heard Saint Stephen heckled and abused by bystanders, but it was the first time I saw him pay them any mind. Uncharacteristically, I watched as Saint Stephen paused in his oratory and addressed the mocker.

"What has been done before through faith can and will be done again!" Saint Stephen shouted with zeal, "If it will take a miracle to turn the eyes of the ungodly away from vanity and sloth and toward the glory of the Lord, then so be it! Tomorrow night, right here on the shore below us, I will call upon the name of the Lord, and the Lord will deliver a sign of his everlasting presence! If it is fire from heaven that will reclaim your hearts, then fire from heaven is what will be shown to you! Go now and repent! For the hour of oblation is near!" With haste, Saint Stephen stepped off his soapbox and hurried away. Immediately the crowd began to buzz with excitement.

The heckler beside me nudged my shoulder, "So Saint Stephen is gonna call fire down from heaven, huh?" he laughed with contempt, "All old Elijah did, I bet, is stand out in a lightnin' storm!"

Due to his local infamy, news of Saint Stephen's promised miracle took Santa Monica by siege, and by noon the next day, his name was a part of every conversation you heard on the street. To me, the whole thing was oddly fascinating. I had no vested interest in this man or his assertions, nor did I have the faintest expectation that he was to succeed. Yet, the strength of his convictions compelled me.

I had always been of the opinion that the whole world is full of people so busy looking at where they're going they forget to pay attention to where they're at. I could never understand why so many spend so much time and energy trying to figure out the meaning of life, God, and where they're headed. The way I always had it pegged, by the time they're done figuring out all the ins and outs and deeper truths of the matter, all of life has passed them by, and they've got lumbago and rheumatism and a whole bunch of cynical complaints about how life is a crock. I've always felt sorry for those men who waste their lives sitting around wondering behind closed doors in chapels, monasteries, libraries, and universities—and I certainly never took a word of theirs to heart. I've learned more on the move in a boxcar than I ever did sitting still in any stuffy institution that guaranteed me knowledge and salvation. But even still, there was something about Saint Stephen that intrigued me.

Even in all my years spent on the fringe of society, where all radical philosophies find favorable soil to root down into, I'd never met another man who believed in anything more strongly than Saint Stephen believed in his god. He slung his proselytism out to anyone with a set of working ears, and to see him nonchalantly pick up the gauntlet of challenge that had posited him a champion of the divine made me think. As hard as I tried to ignore, discourage, or discount him as bughouse, every so often, a word or two stuck and got to working on me and making me wonder—even if only out of boredom—that perhaps he was right and if so, what that would mean.

And I was far from the only one. That night just before dusk, it seemed like every man, woman, and child in the city of Santa Monica gathered on the beach beside the pier to watch Saint Stephen call fire down from the sky. According to the next day's papers, it was the grandest public gathering of the year, larger even than the Fourth of July. Families trekked down to the shore with beach chairs and picnic baskets in tow, onlookers chatted and doubted, and confused tourists caught in the trawl gawked and rubbernecked as Stephen stood in the surf and prayed. From miles around, people had come to watch him perform this impossible feat, and excitement crackled through the salt air like electricity. The sky was clear and the heavens bright when Stephen, as somber as ever, raised his arms and addressed the crowd.

"You've all been asleep in the darkness of sin!" he shouted to the agog masses, "Now, you will see the light and glory of our Lord and Savior, Jesus Christ!"

Saint Stephen commenced his supplications at once, beseeching God for the strength and power to act as an instrument of divine will and guide all of us poor lost sheep home. And he put on quite a show. Wailing and gesticulating, Stephen raved before his watery alter, calling upon the name of the Lord with every ounce of energy his haggard old form could muster.

There certainly weren't very many people who believed in him, but I think quite a few wanted to. Stephen's unshakable faith was enviable, and his trust and certainty even more so. For every mocker, I'll bet there were ten others who secretly turned their disbelieving eyes toward the sky with aching hope.

But nothing happened. There was no spinning wheel of fire, no celestial flame, not even a break in the clouds. Saint Stephen failed, as everyone knew he would. He'd started out strong and fervent, but as the hours passed and night fell, the voices of the jeerers began to grow louder and drown out Stephen's invocations.

"Maybe God ain't in the mood for fire," one detractor shouted.

"Yeah," another called out, "maybe you'd have better luck parting the Pacific!"

Laughter reigned.

In time, hecklers and hopefuls alike began to pack up and leave, but Stephen continued his vigil. His voice grew hoarse, and his legs grew weary until he was on his knees in the coral sand, begging and pleading and offering up his sins for the salvation of the dogs. When dawn came, I looked about me and realized I was the only one who remained. Exhausted, drenched, and desperate, his stentorian voice now reduced to a whisper, Saint Stephen turned his face toward the crystal morning sky in a daze, his eyes wide with fear and doubt. They were glazed over with disbelief and did not waver in their fixity as he struggled to his feet and slowly stumbled away. I remained there a while longer, gazing out at the watery grave of Saint Stephen's faith as the sun cast its brilliant rays upon the surf, and I asked myself the same question I've asked myself every morning for as long as I can remember: "now what?"

I'm sure Saint Stephen's sentiment was the same.

II

After leaving Santa Monica, I continued down the coast in much the same fashion as I had been. But as the months wore on and wore harder, men began holding on tighter to their dollars, and I soon realized that I needed to find another meal ticket—and fast! Fortunately, that opportunity seemed to find me well before I recognized it for what it was.

I made it as far as San Diego before I went broke, and as is the cruel nature of fate, a man never goes broke on a beautiful day. It was raining so hard that the sewer grates overflowed, and I'd ducked into the nearest downtown bar to escape the weather. I exchanged my last dime for a beer and shortly thereafter was thrown out when the bartender realized I had nothing left to spend.

I departed the bar disheartened and hurried to the end of the block, where there was a rail crossing. I stopped momentarily on the tracks in hopes I'd see a slow engine approaching, but the alley was as dark and dreary as everywhere else in town. The closest establishment that offered shelter from the deluge was an old vaudeville theatre on 4th Avenue. The announcement for the evening's showing was plastered upon the marquee, but the entertainment had yet to take the stage, so while the ticket vendor had his vested back turned, I slipped under the velvet rope and out of the rain.

I crawled into that theatre soaked to the skin and three days empty. I was after a cushioned seat and solitude, for once without a thought in my mind of any quick gains. I was one of the first faces in the joint, and stagehands were still setting up. I eased myself into a seat in the last row under the shadow of the balcony, pulled my hickory stripe cap down over my eyes, and drifted off into no man's land for the first time in weeks with some lumbar support and no chance of being awakened by an angry brakeman.

—But, nonetheless, I was awakened. No more than a few minutes after I settled in, something jostled my leg and roused me from my slumber. I was expecting an usher or some similarly recruited high-tone tart bent on expelling me, but when I pried open my sleep-laden eyes, I found myself staring up at Gypsy Rose Lee.

Her skirt was the first thing I saw. It was as red as a bullfighter's muleta and grazed the tops of her gold-laced sandals. Over it, she donned a linen blouse and more beads, chains, and talismans than Cleopatra. She wore a ring on every slender finger, wrapped around her dark hair was a silken headdress, and from her ears dangled a pair of gold hoops that nearly rested on her shoulders. Her eyes were purple.

She greeted me with a mystic's smile and a voice from another world. "Hey, Rube," she spoke softly, reaching out to run her glittering fingers along my wet pant leg, "I have a job for you."

To my randy amazement, she asked me to be her partner for the evening for four bits and a feed. My job was to sit in the audience as a shillaber, follow her prompts, and come to her when called. She handed me a drumstick, outfitted me in a dry suit that almost fit, and instructed me to stand at the bar in the foyer until about half the seats were taken.

Once the ticket collector lowered his velvet rope, the theatre filled up rapidly. Warm from a couple drinks provided by the house, I took my seat and waited for the lights to dim. The act was a mélange of a circus troop, pared down to accommodate the restrictions of an auditorium as opposed to the big top.

The ringmaster-turned-MC was about five-foot flush with white Irish curls that boiled out from the sides of his head like smoke from a pipe. He wore a gold-trimmed suit with tails and had all sorts of ribbons and adornments pinned to his meager breast. A watch chain with links nearly half an inch thick was draped across his chest, and his alligator shoes shined so brightly that their pattern could be seen from the stage. His voice was shrill and strident, and he talked quicker than an auctioneer. The prolific signage identified him as Charlie of Cosmic Charlie's Varieties and Thurmaturge.

His face was a shrunken caricature with valleys running horizontally along his forehead and vertically around his whiskerless mouth. A crooked stogie bent in the middle at a 45-degree angle was clenched precariously between his lips. He had a bulbous nose and a cleft chin, and his eyes were as big as half dollars. They spun in two different directions at all times and hardly ever blinked. As the calliope that'd been playing puffed its final few notes and was rolled offstage, he greeted the audience with a resounding, "How do you do?!" and then proceeded to introduce the acts with unparalleled enthusiasm.

The strongman was the first to follow him, in stark contrast. The fellow was considerably above six feet tall, with muscles that rippled under his leotard. He bent pipes into loops with pride and ease, supported a covey of acrobats that hung from his arms and balanced on his head, and lifted the engine of a 1934 Packard with his teeth as a finale. The crowd exclaimed and applauded.

The strongman was bookended by a barefoot Negro kid with a monkey who scampered and cartwheeled about the stage as he danced and sang. He was followed by more than half a dozen other acts, including jugglers, tumbling clowns, ukulele players, soft-shoe dancers, singing children, and minstrels with faces painted black with burnt cork—but I saw no more of the mystery woman from earlier until the end of the performance. Her act came second to last, and she was the star of the show. She sauntered onto the stage with an air of grace and command as the lights above dimmed and a spotlight shone down to encircle her alone. She spoke clearly and with purpose, explaining the mesmerizing act that was to come. The MC, in his spiel, had already introduced her as a hypnotist, but even with her vague instructions, I knew not what to expect.

Volunteers were called for, and I raised my hand. After appearing indecisive for a moment as she surveyed the crowd, I was ultimately selected, and she beckoned me. I strode through the darkened aisles to the stage, where I was greeted by the gypsy woman.

"Please tell the crowd your name, sir," she requested after I'd kissed her warm, slender hand.

"Mr. Jones," I replied, rather diffident.

"And, Mr. Jones, have you ever been hypnotized before?"

I replied with a truthful "No."

Her purple eyes flashed through the darkness like the blade of a knife as she slowly circled me several times before pausing before me and pulling a large gold coin from within the folds of her clothes. She then held it out in front of my eyes, so I had no other recourse but to stare fixedly at it.

The coin dazzled in the spotlight as she spoke grandly, preparing her induction.

"When I touch your forehead," she announced with all the fervor and mock confidence of a shill, "you will be asleep."

Long conditioned to masquerading in my dealings with the law and in my chosen profession, I believe I turned out to be an even better plant than she expected. When at once she tapped my forehead, my eyes wilted shut, my knees buckled, and I crumpled to the floor where I lay prostrate and inert.

"Ladies and gentlemen," she orated, her alluring voice lilting over the audience like rolling fog, "you will now witness the power of animal magnetism. The state of this hypnotic trance is so deep that a century ago, before the aid of modern anesthesia, European physics used this very method to perform surgeries without any pain, fear, or recollection for the patient. You will see the same technique demonstrated here today."

"Saw 'im in 'alf!" a heckler cried from the audience, and I could sense her eyes flash in his direction.

While, thankfully, none of her experiments were quite that extreme, our combined effort did very well to convince the awestruck audience that I was suspended in a kind of dreamlike trance in which she had complete control over my body and mind. When she 'awakened' me from my feigned slumber, she had me bark like a dog, scratch for fleas, and—enraged by mange—chase my tail. The audience was in stitches. Following this apparent feat, she had me play an imaginary game of tennis, kiss an imaginary girl, and then flee her imaginary father. And, to satisfy all those in the crowd who doubted the authenticity of the act, she encouraged the heckler who'd shouted earlier to come upon the stage and stick a pin into any part of my anatomy he pleased. Being in want of a pin, he asked the woman seated beside him. She granted his request, and he strolled upon the stage sporting a sinister grin. He held up the glistening pin to prove it was genuine and then turned and drove it straight into my outstretched hand. A horrified shriek rose up from the audience in response to my assumed pain. But in reality, no such pain existed. The pin he stuck me with was sharp enough at its point to produce a bead of blood; however, when pressure was applied to it, the pin telescoped. The heckler's name was Calvin, and he traveled with us to every show. When he reclaimed his seat and returned the real pin to its owner, she turned white and fainted.

Beaming with pride, the gypsy rendered me catatonic once more and demanded I awaken from my somnambulistic state. I arose from the stage in a contrived daze, clutching my stricken paw, and after a hasty farewell, hurried toward the theatre door. The roar of the crowd followed me.

"Ladies and gentlemen, the Mystick Althea!" the mosquito-like voice of Cosmic Charlie announced as the calliope was wheeled back out accompanied by amateur aerialists who swung from trapezes fixed to the catwalk. The audience began to pack the aisles. As the curtain closed and the applause waned, Charlie retook the stage, bowed, and told the crowd, "time to go on home now; I hear your mamas calling you!"

The Mystick Althea came and found me after the show, invited me backstage, and proposed an offer. Apparently, my prowess for the job exceeded that of her usual shillaber, who'd been nabbed for picking pockets that afternoon. In turn, she asked me to join the troop for seven dollars a week, clothes and board, and whatever else I managed to scrounge up on the side. I signed on.

Late that night, after all the trunks and props had been loaded into a convoy of decommissioned liberty trucks, I piled in with the rest of the performers. There being no further south we could travel, we headed east, stopping some thirty miles away in the town of Alpine, where we played three shows a day to a paltry crowd at a playhouse no bigger than a chapel.

By 1934, Cosmic Charlie was likely the only variety show manager who had not yet heard the death knell of vaudeville. Though, in time, I found this to be far from surprising, as I learned that Charlie rarely heard any sound or found favor with any idea that originated outside his own mind. As a result, we were underpaid, underfed, and traveled like gypsies in a band of lurid canvas trucks in which we often camped on the outskirts of town to save the price of a room. For most of us, living such a trite, nomadic lifestyle was no deviation from the norm. Many of the performers were castoffs from the Barnum and Bailey/Ringling merger, vaudeville stars who'd found no fortune in radio or pictures, or like me, were simply denizens of the road who turned whatever tricks were necessary in order to make a buck.

Soon after joining them, I learned that Cosmic Charlie's Varieties and Thurmaturge rarely played theatres at all. Instead, he favored carnivals, piers, state fairs, and even sideshow work. Such environs are ripe with the prospect of easy money, and Charlie took quick hold of every opportunity that presented itself. He was clearly multitalented—as were all the entertainers in his employ—and while he made a rather convincing master of ceremonies, I soon realized that his real skill was in graft. Our little troop was populated by just about every sort of grassroots con there is. The spielers doubled as short-change artists, the magicians as kings of the shell game, the acrobats as pickpockets, the children as beggars, and myself and some assorted others as card and dice sharks who kept the money flowing when we weren't performing. At minimum, we played two shows a day. Sometimes we played up to ten. Cal and I changed our clothes and donned wigs in between each performance and, at times, even traded jobs. While I was off the clock, throwing monte for the patrons and carnies, he had them mystified at the pool tables with his trick shots and loaded cue. In the midst of all this, Cosmic Charlie would flit about the fairgrounds or front of house, overseeing the various ruses with a larcenous grin so wide the corners of his mouth just about met in the back of his neck.

I'd thought Saint Stephen was batty, but he had absolutely nothing on Cosmic Charlie, whose name was perfectly befitting. Charlie was, as they say, 'crazy as a bedbug,' and I'd be none too surprised if it was bedbugs that'd made him so. In all the various despicable digs I'd found myself occupying throughout my life, I never encountered such a menagerie of vermin as I did traveling with them. However, considering some of his more prominent features, it is quite possible that some degree of inbreeding was also responsible—and I'm sure his boiling penchant for cocaine didn't help much, either.

The man was evidently born cross-eyed, and his habits only seemed to intensify his condition. He was continually dead set on some trajectory and babbled incessantly to himself. The only time he ever spoke and made any degree of coherent sense was when he addressed an audience. I don't believe I ever had a single intelligible conversation with him in all the time I traveled with the show, and come to think of it, I'm not sure I would've wanted to.

Cocaine, stogies, and boating seemed to be the only affairs he evidenced any concern for besides money. There was, at all times, a velvet sack of white powder hanging from a button inside his shirt and a kinked cigar protruding from his mouth. Aside from his great fondness for stimulants, Charlie's passion for the water was unlike any obsession I've ever encountered. Every spare moment he found, he spent on the water—and when he couldn't find water, he actually had a canoe built out of thick cardboard and nailed to a dolly that Jimmy would push him around in.

Jimmy was the errand boy of the outfit and Cosmic Charlie's personal lackey. He was a wisp of a boy and black as night with a thick accent straight out of Southside Chicago. Being about twelve years old and growing like a weed, every suit of clothes he owned had sleeves that were halfway to his elbows and pant legs that were halfway to his knees. He was nearly always barefoot. His appearance was profitable for both his stage act and the begging he did around town; therefore, Charlie forbade him from buying new clothes.

Other than when he was out battering the townies for alms, Jimmy and his capuchin, Julian, were inseparable. Julian was a mischievous, sheisty little thing, on par with the rest of us. Most often, he could be found riding on Jimmy's shoulder, except at mealtimes, when he would sneak around and snatch whatever morsels he could from the plates of unsuspecting diners.

As Cal told it, Jimmy had run away from home with the show several years earlier and found fast friends in the monkey, who was already in Cosmic Charlie's charge. To Charlie, he quickly became indispensable, and as they had shared close quarters for several seasons, some of the crazy appeared to have rubbed off. After the show closed for the evening, while Charlie nabbed his three hours of daily respite, Jimmy outfitted himself with a shotgun loaded with rock salt and proceeded to goose-step around the circle of trucks to ensure no prowlers or traitorous performers made off with the money box.

And, while none of us trusted Jimmy with that gun, Charlie's decision to appoint a guard was understandable, as the players were part-time show-offs and full-time crooks. We lived a gristly, lawless existence and had little cause to trust one another. We were supposed to turn over all our extraneous earnings to Charlie, which he would lock away for safekeeping and then equally distribute on payday, but not one of us fully complied with such demands. Even with little to no privacy, we all managed to stash away a grouch bag of varying but considerable worth.

Most of us traveled together, which made for awfully crowded quarters. Fortunately, there were few long journeys, as we generally just puddle-jumped between towns, which minimized the cramped living conditions we had to endure. But even still, it was a far cry from a Pullman. When I joined the troop, I was given a trunk and a cot, both of which had seen previous use. I was told that my cot used to belong to a juggling midget named Tiny Jim—and for the six months I traveled with them, I slept with everything from the knees down hovering over the dirty floorboards.

There was only one facet of the whole spectacle that was appealing, and that was Althea. From the sparse particulars she shared, I gathered that she'd been born to a family of ambulators, and her childhood had been that of a road kid. From her progenitors, she'd learned how to con, beg, lie, and mooch—and once she'd received a suitable education, she set out on her own. She'd joined a smalltime circus and remained with them for many years before ending up in Cosmic Charlie's camp. She was at least midway through her thirties, and while she never explicitly told of a husband or any children, she did mention 'the people she'd left behind.' Looking into her sibylline eyes, it was clear that she'd lived many lives in her years.

Born a gypsy, Althea embodied every ounce of her heritage both on and off the stage. She performed as an all-purpose mystic—hypnotist, palm reader, and oracle—and while the strength of her actual abilities in any of those disciplines was questionable at best, she was undoubtedly alluring. No woman has ever made better and more compelling use of her feminine assets than the Mystick Althea. Her act was successful mainly because nobody really cared if she was truly hypnotizing me or not—as long as they got to watch her saunter across the stage batting her eyes, swinging her hips, tossing her hair, and making a man cater to her every whim. She practically oozed sex appeal and certainly wasn't stingy when it came to flaunting it. She was as sultry as an August afternoon and as seductive as a hot meal. She moved with slinky mystique and spoke in a sensuous, breathy tone that drove any listener half-mad with desire. Even when asleep, the whimpers and moans she produced as she dug her toes into the cot were enough to prompt any man within earshot to rise early and find a cold shower. She flirted with every man who looked in her direction and teased any foolish enough to follow her.

I—along with every other man alive—found her beguiling, but although she stroked my ego often enough, she never seemed to respond to my genuine advances, which confused and irked me. She attracted me more out of curiosity than lust, and as it had so many times before, that curiosity compelled me. Forever aroused by the thrill of the chase, I could frequently be found in her presence, most often tripping over my own tongue.

One pastoral evening in a field south of Modesto where we'd spent the day masquerading as second-rate sideshow artists, Althea and I sat around a crackling fire, chatting mildly as we watched the moths dance, the two of us being the only souls besides Jimmy inclined to wakefulness at that advanced hour. The fare that evening had been frankfurters and beans, and we dined as long as the cookfire continued to burn.

As was consistent with her seductive character, Althea didn't roast her frankfurters with the skewer stuck into it perpendicular—no, on the contrary, she inserted her skewer vertically and ate it the same way as she reclined back on a straw-stuffed mattress. I sat across the fire from her and watched wordlessly. I believe that frank received more extensive loving than most men do in a lifetime.

"Why do you have to be like that?" I demanded, frustrated.

Sensually, she glanced up from her dinner, "what would I be if I did things the way you men do them?" she responded.

I turned away and didn't reply.

"—wouldn't you like a woman who's a little more like me than like you?"

I flopped down on my bedroll. "I'm swearing off women," I professed bitterly, "they're no good for men."

"Hmmm, and why is that?" she asked, rising to her knees with a pout.

"The bad ones land you in prison, and the good ones up and die."

I could hear the straw crunching as she settled into a more comfortable and suggestive position, "that's not always the case."

"Well, it has been for me. Good night."

Althea was quiet a moment before abruptly asking, "Don't you ever take those things off? Every bum I ever met uses 'em as a pillow." She was referring to my boots.

I rolled over with a sigh, "Ever since I started wearin' shoes, I always slept with my boots on...never know when I'm gonna have to move."

"I have no doubt you're well used to that," she replied wryly.

I sat up, "and what makes you assume so?" I bitingly responded.

"You forget my abilities," she spoke omnisciently.

"Oh, you're no more than a fraud," I discounted her, "a fraud and a coquette."

Her lips pursed as she concealed a smile, "Men. Always so sure of themselves. Always the last to suppose there may exist fields beyond those of their own understanding."

My narrowed eyes met hers with a challenge, "then tell me what you know."

Her smile broke free of its restraints, and she stepped over to me, "Give me your hand."

I complied, and she cupped it in hers as she studied it for a time in the light from the fire.

"This is your life line," she whispered, tracing her nimble fingers in a semi-circle around my thumb. Their tips felt like they contained tiny electrodes that made every hair on my body stand up when she touched me. A titillating chill ran down my spine.

"You will live to be an old man," she told me, "and you will have a legacy."

"Oh, go on!" I snorted sarcastically.

My scathing disbelief was lost on her. "This is called your wisdom line," she continued languidly, running her electric fingers across the broad palm of my hand, "It tells me all about how you think and the kinds of things you think about."

"Is it shorter than most?" I snorted jokingly.

She held out her deeply-creased palm beside mine, "No," she replied in earnest, "But it is considerably more shallow."

She spent a few more moments considering her interpretation. "You're scared," she replied finally, "of everything. You feel there is nothing you can trust. Treachery has dismembered you time and time again as of late...treachery dealt out from friends, from lovers, from the law, even from perfect strangers."

I nodded heartily in agreement, even before realizing just how right she was.

"You need sanctuary, a sense of security, peace of mind..." she trailed off as her fingers wandered to the center of my palm.

"This is your love line," she spoke in a voice so saccharine my whole lower body felt as if it was reduced to a liquid, "and it is *very* interesting."

"I'll never love another woman again," I professed, cutting her off, "never again, no matter what."

"What you think you want and what you're bound to get differ most considerably," she responded, her eyes flashing. "A man like you needs a woman, as much as you think you don't...but I understand your frustration...." Her fingers wandered from my hand up my arm, tracing lines that lust had drawn.

"You just lost a woman," she stated suddenly with conviction.

The expression on my face gave her all the confirmation she needed.

"Yes, I see here that the woman you love the most will be the only one who walks away from you—not because she wants to leave, but because she feels she has no choice."

"Yeah," I told her dejectedly, "except she didn't walk; she died."

Althea met my eyes with an indecipherable expression, then turned back to my open hand and continued her reading. "This vertical line through the center of your palm is called your luck line, or line of fate."

I sneered at such a suggestion, "I don't need you to tell me my luck's been shit my whole life through," I interjected before she could continue, "I must've been born under a bad sign or something."

Althea appeared amused by my conviction. "Your luck won't change, Jack, until you are no longer the man who committed that terrible crime."

Her words and her certainty blindsided me. I tried to deny it, but my surprise was evident.

"Well, I can't exactly crawl out of my skin," I admitted, finally.

A sly smile crept onto Althea's face, and her purple eyes flashed in the firelight. "It's not all of your skin that you need to leave behind you," she breathed, running her sultry fingertips across my own, "just your fingerprints."

"And how do you suggest I part with those?" I asked sarcastically.

Her eyes tracked toward the fire. The flat rock in the center where we'd heated the can of beans glowed ominously red amongst the embers.

"No way," I dismissed her, "not a chance."

"I'll hypnotize you," she offered with the magnanimity of a saint, "you will feel no pain."

Peals of laughter escaped my incredulous lips, "Yeah, right! You ain't no real hypnotist! You're nothing but a charlatan. If you were the real McCoy, I would be out of a job. Who are you trying to play the fool, you jezebel?"

Her eyes flashed again, but she did not submit an explanation. "What do you have to lose?" she whispered as her fingers once more commenced their journey up my arm, now dappled with gooseflesh, "Even if I am a fraud, as you call me, what are a few moments of total agony when set against an eternity of the same? Surely a couple minutes of pain now do not equal that of a lifetime in prison."

Her point was indubitably taken.

From behind us, Jimmy emerged from amongst the trucks where he'd evidently been listening with rapt attention. "Mistah Charlie tole' me ta shoot any of you's if you's wakes 'im," he threatened with his shotgun.

"Oh, go row your boat," Althea callously called over her silk-clad shoulder.

He lingered a few moments more and then slinked away with Julian in tow. The monkey, appearing as curious as his handler, emitted a worried-sounding murmur and then scampered along behind him.

Once we were assuredly alone, Althea turned back toward me and looked me dead in the eye. "Switch places with me," she instructed, and I left my bedroll for the paillasse that she'd vacated.

"Close your eyes and get comfortable now," she directed me as she leaned over to loosen my shirt collar. I felt her hands run along the length of my arms to roll up my sleeves and then down to my waist to unbuckle my belt—at which point she promptly pulled away. "You're going to breathe now—deep breaths—and with every word I speak, you will become more and more relaxed and slip further and further into a deep, deep sleep."

Some time passed before she spoke again, this time from further away.

"There's an energy about you now, a channel of peace. You can feel it in your toes...wiggle them, relax them, and it will travel...first into your feet...and then your ankles...up to your calves...and each part of you it passes through will relax in turn...." The sensation she described, I felt, and her instruction accompanied it throughout my whole body. By the time she reached my head, I felt as if I was suspended bodily and enveloped by her voice. "I want you to imagine that you are standing beneath a waterfall, and you can feel the water running over your entire body. It is a serene, comfortable feeling, and you are in a state of complete and utter peace...but the water is cool...a little too cool for your liking. A shiver runs up your spine." —And it did— "But you are not alone in the wash...there is a woman with you, and she is warm. You reach out to touch her. You run your fingertips along her waist, and it sends a rush from your head to your toes. You run your fingers slowly along her body...up her back...over her breasts...up her neck...into her hair...and as you do, you are filled with a sensation of deep and penetrating warmth...."

The next thing I remember was opening my eyes to her on top of me, her sensuous, alluring lips pressed against mine. I moved beneath her, and her lips parted. "Welcome back," she breathed in my ear before dismounting.

I'd awakened in bliss, but it was fleeting, as all bliss remains to be. After she'd withdrawn her lips from mine, the first sensation I felt was intense, burning pain. I looked down at my hands; my fingers were seared, blackened, and bubbled up to the second knuckle. Horrified, I stared back at Althea, my heart pounding as she calmly examined her work.

"Those'll heal up in a few weeks," she assured me and then disappeared at once.

When she returned, it was with arnica and gauze. She wrapped each throbbing digit tenderly and deftly, with every ounce of care and concern Rosalie had shown when she'd nursed me back to health on my sickbed— but she never kissed me again.

Due to the visual nature of my malady, I spent far more time practicing my chicanery on the locals than acting as Althea's shillaber. The gains were fair to middling throughout most of the ranch towns in central California and cause for some degree of concern, but what was utmost in my thoughts was of an entirely disparate order. Having known the splendor of Althea's embrace, my mind could be filled with little else. I inserted myself ever more frequently into her company and shamelessly pursued her in a manner not unlike that of Julian after Jimmy. She never yielded. Any mercy for men that she may have at one time evidenced was not once directed toward me, and she remained ever the tease. I shaved, I groomed, I bought myself new duds, I brought her meals and decanted her poison, but all to no avail—I couldn't catch her affections with a butterfly net.

One brisk autumn evening in Visalia, my frustration finally hit the ceiling. I'd been strolling through the convoy in search of her when I spotted her emerging from Cosmic Charlie's truck. Ever curious, I ducked behind a drum and remained unseen. I watched as she paused to return a ribald goodnight and then surreptitiously glanced to either side as she departed, adjusting her cloak as she went. Disgusted by both the prospect and reality of women, I left my empty bedroll beside the fire and started walking. A couple of midnight miles later, I found myself in the center of town where a proper degree of mind-erasing debauchery could be had. I never returned.

III

There's no place like a full bar to help a man forget his troubles. For me, this sanctuary was found in a rowdy joint downtown plastered from wall to wall with payday men getting plastered. The sublime absurdity of such surroundings is enough to warrant an uptick in the mood of even the most morose man. Once the liquor begins flowing, it is often not long before the formerly disheartened subject finds himself guffawing and caterwauling along with his drunken compatriots, no matter how terminal he previously considered his misfortune to be. Such a man was I that night.

I dragged my feet over the threshold like they were two lead bricks affixed to my limbs and plunked myself down on the barstool like a water bag from the shoulder of Gunga Din. I ordered a double, neat, and the bartender returned with a heavy pour. I slid two bits across the bar top in exchange. He just looked at it.

"Yer short a dime, bud," he informed me.

"Thirty-five cents for gin?" I exclaimed.

"Thirty-five cents for a double if you want it. It's forty-five across the street."

I begrudgingly dug into my pocket and rolled a dime in his direction, which he snatched up before moving down the bar to wait on the ceaseless line of thirsty customers.

"Two-bit piece ain't enough to buy some lousy California gin," I muttered to myself as I hefted the glass.

The chap beside me heard my griping and chimed in, "This whole blame world is going to hell in a handbasket faster than the money's leaving the bank. Pretty soon, your surname's gonna need to be Rockefeller or Carnegie if you want to drink at a bar. They repealed prohibition, but all I can afford is homebrew anyhow."

As is proclaimed so often, 'misery loves company,' and I was pleased to have found a companion as unsatisfied and disenchanted as I was.

"My Pa used to make the best gin in the whole damn country," I bragged, "every time you took a drink, it tasted like coming home. He sold it for two dollars a quart—a small price for a sip of heaven. Ain't none of this two-bit, four-bit rotgut that can compare."

My companion drained his glass and nodded, "Can't find none of that good shit around anymore—and we thought we were drinking the dregs in those days...little did we know..."

"Little do we ever," I grumbled, "I never had half of what I thought I did."

"Amen to that, brother," he raised a fresh pint and knocked back half in one slug.

I chased my first double with another, and the clean, crisp dollar bill I laid on the bar top ordered me a third. After I poured that glass down my gullet, that most agreeable familiar feeling began spreading from my innards to my extremities, warming my toes and distilling my mind. Before long, my disappointment ceased to be recognized, and my frustration failed to find a befitting seat for itself. The conversation soon turned to politics and technocracy and the ever-pressing matter of man versus machine that was being hashed out up and down every bar in the country as the eagle flew that Friday night and left all parties wondering why those men in government couldn't come up with the same great resolutions themselves.

Like most barflies, my companion turned out to be quite loquacious and had no trouble climbing up on his soapbox and so generously demystifying all matters of national importance for me. After a couple more stout glasses of cheap brewskis, he was really on a roll, bawling out Hugh Johnson, condemning the new taxes, and excoriating Roosevelt's farm policies. Where foreign relations were concerned, he did more than put in his two cents—in fact, he pretty near emptied his billfold expounding upon the looming apocalyptic catastrophe he was sure would arrive before the end of the decade. He'd pushed back his barstool and was standing, flush and wobbly, as he continued his blistering commentary on the state of the union with boot stamping, spit-flying, arms gesticulating, and his cigarette waving madly around, the red glow of the embers on its tip burning trails into my drunken mind.

While we were fervently solving all the world's problems, the door behind us blew open, and a skeleton in a dark grey suit stepped in carrying a case. He nary looked up as he joined the writhing mass of drunkards and hastened to the far corner. I lost sight of him when my next drink appeared and regained it when he pulled out a guitar.

"No wonder the drinks are expensive," I remarked, cutting off my companion amid his soliloquy on the unfitness of the League of Nations, "we must be paying a cover on behalf of the entertainment." I gestured to the man in the corner.

"Ah, he's been here every night the last week," my barstool political analyst explained, momentarily abandoning his roast of foreign despots. "Ever since one brawling bastard put some poor fool's head through the jukebox, he's been on the regular payroll."

My ossified curiosity piqued, I watched as the troubadour alighted a stool of his own and, seemingly oblivious to the entire audience, strummed the opening chords to *Stagger Lee*. He played as if he were in a room alone, not surrounded by several dozen shouting drunks. My curiosity quickly intensified.

"Imagine killing a man over a five-dollar hat?" the fellow beside me mused after realizing I was no longer listening to his diatribe.

"I'm sure he had good reason," I muttered.

"Wouldn't still be singing about it unless he did," was his reply.

I did not offer a response. Instead, I listened and listened hard to how much those townspeople had reveled in hanging Stagger Lee—that mean old man, the terror of the town, who'd had his property struck and stolen. There weren't any lyrics about his little babies or his darling loving wife, and I found myself wondering what the words would've been if Billy de Lyon had been the last man standing in that infamous fight.

I've never been one to find myself captivated by saloon singers of any sort, but this particular folk slinger wasn't half bad. Above the noise of roaring voices and clinking glasses, his guitar's full, rich melody filled the windowless barroom and turned most men's heads toward his space in the corner. His voice was something of a paregoric; whereupon hearing it, all the shouting, stamping, and cackling reduced considerably to a far more tolerable din. Evidently, I was not the only man who noticed his prowess and was grateful for the music and song. Though, he certainly didn't look like all that much—in fact, I'd seen men three days dead that looked healthier. He was tall, thin, and lanky, with greasy black hair full of so much pomade that it didn't move so much as an inch as he bowed his head and plucked away at the strings. His thick, woolen suit hung heavier from his fleshless bones than on a storefront mannequin. He had dark, sunken eyes with bags around them so pronounced it appeared that he had not slept a wink in the last two lifetimes. His cheeks were colorless and sallow, his fingers were long and bony, and his skin was pale grey and the same color as an apparition. If alcoholism ever had a face, it was his.

"What's his name?" I asked my neighbor.

"That over yonder is Black Peter," he answered, drunkenly wiping foam from his mustache onto his shirtsleeve.

"Black Peter?" I repeated, "I know there ain't much light in here, but ain't he white?"

"Oh, well, sure he is," the reply came, "that isn't why they call him Black Peter."

"Why's that, then?"

"Black Peter's been dying since the day he was born."

I paused, confused, "Ain't that mainly the case with just about all of us?"

"Trust me," he answered, "there ain't nobody that's been dying longer than Peter."

I figured I wasn't about to get much more clarity out of the lush, so I let the subject lie for a time.

As the night progressed, Black Peter's choice of songs grew to include some tramp classics, and halfway through *Hallelujah! I'm a Bum*, some of the men in the fray began calling for the addition of a harmonica. A lifetime ago, when tramps would swing off the freights in Five Points and impart their parcels of wisdom to us boys, how to play the harmonica was one of the first things I learned. Soap, a razor, and a harp were staples in the pockets of most traveling men, and I learned how to carry a decent tune early in life. I'd put it down for a time, as the sound had haunted me like the warden's boot steps when I was behind bars, but I picked it up again during my stint with Cosmic Charlie and just so happened to have my harp with me at the time. I appeared to be the only one, so I stepped up beside him and fell into tune. When that song was over, I blew the best goldarned train whistle I could muster and Black Peter, in turn, laid down a whole lot of blues. Everywhere in America—no matter what part of the country you may be in—when somebody pulls out a mouth harp or banjo, every man within earshot begins tapping his foot. That Visalia bar was no exception. A couple of the men began dancing, and several others started tossing change into Black Peter's open case. For an evening that had begun so intensely maudlin, I sure had one hell of a good time.

The two of us kept it up until last call, at which time Black Peter rose shakily from his stool, laid his guitar back in its case, and shuffled over to the bar, where we shared a long drink while the bartender wiped down the bottles and rolled the last few remaining drunks out onto the street. Peter was far from being a socialite, but for a grey-skinned migratory saloon singer, he sure dressed well. His suit was more expensive than any I'd owned in years, and he donned adornments seldom seen in those days of dearth and scarcity. A handsome ring, platinum gold watch, and matching cuff links were amongst them.

"The Lord must smile down on you," I told him as I sipped away at yet another thirty-five cent gin, "there ain't many men making much more than a living doing what you do."

His reply was painfully serious, "isn't the Lord that's the cause of it," he stated matter-of-factly, "I'm a Satanist, a devil worshipper."

"Is that so?" I asked him, my Anglo-Saxon Protestant eyes widening, "I ain't never met one of your kind before."

Peter scoffed, "Sure you have. There isn't a man alive who hasn't made a deal with the Devil at one time or another."

"I'll agree with you there," I told him, "the devil and I are on a first-name basis, but I never got down on my knees and prayed for the lug."

Peter shrugged and emptied his third tumbler of Goslings. "I've never had any taste for religion," he explained, "Folks have always been saying that the Devil was gonna come for me one day, so I figured I'd save him a trip and meet him halfway."

"Well, I can't say it appears to have hurt you none," I pointed to his watch and cuff links, "you certainly didn't get them things off of no brass peddler."

Peter looked vacantly down at his trimmings, "These old things don't mean nothing to me," he replied, void of the pride evident in most men's voices when boasting of their fortune, "I only wear them out of necessity."

"Necessity?" I repeated.

His colorless, unfocused eyes gazed emptily into mine, "If I die in a strange town, these things will be enough to get me a decent burial...." He paused and turned back to his glass, "but I hardly reckon now that I'm going to need them. I'm leaving on the seven a.m. freight to San Francisco and, from there, back to Chicago. I was born there, and I want to see it once more before I die."

"You're dying?" I inquired, remembering what the man from earlier had told me about him.

"Yes, boy, I'm dying," he mourned. "Sold my soul before, and now the rest of me is going with it."

"Real shame," I responded absently, my attention averted by the handfuls of change that Black Peter scooped up out of his guitar case and deposited on the bar top.

I watched curiously as the dying man divvied up his profits. "Four and a quarter," he muttered, pushing one of the piles in my direction.

As I collected my take and felt the weight of the silver drop into my pocket, my trajectory instantly shifted. I suddenly decided I'd had my fill of Cosmic Charlie's Varieties and Thurmaturge. In addition to the profits from my other varied talents, four dollars a night was a vast improvement over seven dollars a week paired with vermin, madness, and unyielding temptation.

"I'm heading east myself," I commented, peering down at my smooth, red fingertips, "I've done just about all I can here."

Peter, continuing to mourn his ill fate, said nothing.

"That harp of mine sounds mighty good next to your guitar..." I propositioned him.

"I'm not opposed to having company," he snapped before returning to his lament, "but I don't know how many more times I can so much as lift this old guitar with how these hands of mine tremble. I can feel the breath of that Leviathan on my face and the cold hand of Death closing around my heart." He raised his fresh glass and gazed intently at its contents, "if it wasn't for this medicine to straighten me out, I'd hardly be able to speak..."

Unfortunately for me, trouble speaking was the one affliction Peter never experienced. By his estimation, it was because he never missed a dose of his most effective linctus: rum—or whiskey, or dago red, or canned heat, in a pinch. From the outset, I knew that Black Peter would not be the most cheerful companion, but seeing as I was of the opinion that God never had any mercy on me in my life, I figured it was due time to try his counterpart.

And so I went cross-country in a side-door Pullman, as I had so many times before. One-hundred thousand tons of steel barreled through crisp night air into the sparkling dawn dew over rails I knew as well as Rosalie's smile. We hit every hub from San Francisco to Chicago—Salt Lake City, Denver, Kansas City—and Peter was no stranger to the route. He stalked through the railyards and avenues like a ghost—fading in and out of the shadows of boxcars and boarding houses, his change-filled guitar case—and me—in tow. Despite Peter's low estimation of his abilities, in order to keep the blood out of his alcohol stream, we played in what felt like every smoke-choked bar in the west. When he wasn't strumming sad ballads for the drunk and generous on the seedy side of town, he was propped up on Main Street stumbling over chords he knew as well as his beggar's spiel—never without a mickey within quick reach.

Black Peter fell into just about every category of bum that can be named. In the saloons with his guitar, he was a tip canary, beaten down by life and years, toting a talent that'd been tempered by his sorrows. On the streets, he was a moocher, his con cleverly disguised by cunning as he shamelessly extracted sympathy and coin from passersby. In the yards and the jungles, he was a sponger, moaning and wailing about his hunger and hardships until the other 'bos took mercy upon his ravaged form. In the vestibules of churches and the back porches of private homes, he was an unregenerate tramp, one of a luckless class of unfortunates so hard-worn and godforsaken that most sensible folks were inclined to offer whatever food or funds were necessary to expel him from their vicinity. In all the time we traveled together, I never ate a meal that wasn't begged, as there was rarely an occasion Black Peter limped away from a mark without a poke. He had a better eye for opportunity than any other bum I'd ever met, and his doom-ridden appearance only aided his intent. Even the most cheeseparing locals tend to reconsider withholding a meal from a hungry man when it looks like it may be his last one. Of course, in these moments, his riches were concealed in his pockets, and his face and form made to appear even more forlorn than they were naturally—although this feat required little aid; daylight alone did that for him.

Throughout history, the dead man walking has always been the recipient of pity and kindness, regardless of his caste. In this world where the dead cast long shadows over the living, Black Peter had found his niche—and purposeful or not, it seemed to matter little, for he was all-consumed by his malady. For him, it became an obsession, the matter of death. Its dark mystique outstripped the valor of living and replaced it with a cruel inevitability from which he could not be distracted. Black Peter had been dying so long that he had forgotten how to live. Every other week, he was stricken with another affliction. When I met him in Visalia, he assured me it was consumption, and when I finally departed his company about a year later in El Paso, it was smallpox. He was constantly dying, and when he wasn't dying, he was seeing all sorts of weird things like snakes and St. Elmo's fire. He was sick alright, but his illness was not borne of fever or infection, cancer or age. No, his illness was purely self-administered. Sure, he evidenced the symptoms of his claims—but those tremors and chills, sweats, anemia, and emaciation were the direct results of a constant affair between his blue lips and a bottle of ninety-proof bug juice. Besides his raging hypochondria, there was not a thing wrong with him other than the fact that he was a stone-cold alcoholic. There was not a single time when I saw Black Peter sober; in fact, if there was one thing that could've killed him, it'd be the hangover that he'd had coming for the last twenty years or so.

Black Peter insisted that he couldn't work because of his condition, so he struggled along the best he could with his guitar and gained an ounce of esteem that would not have been otherwise accorded to him under any circumstances. When you saw him dragging himself along the street, shambling and wheezing pitifully, you would hardly be inclined to question his honesty; however, I'd seen him take off after a departing train in a yard full of cinder dicks with more stamina than even a healthy bum could muster on most days. If there was any deviation between Peter's perception of himself and the face of pain that he showed the world, it wasn't conscious. He simply recognized the most auspicious times to play up his hard luck—and he knew that most men reserve little compassion for drunks. And as in the case of Robert Johnson, Black Peter's pact with the devil had bestowed upon him considerable musical talent. The guy couldn't even crawl along a straight line, but boy, could he play. If it had a string on it, he could make it sing. It didn't matter if he had a guitar, a banjo, or a goldarned washtub bass in his hands; he could make it cry.

Together, we made a strange but appropriate pair—as we were both awfully sick. I was afflicted by a terminal case of 'won't-work-itis' just as crippling and genuine as Peter's TB. During the Depression, when even those men who were more than willing to work couldn't find a job, it put a goldbrick like me in a tight spot. In the past, I would've sought out some

222

lucrative graft and thought little about the consequences, but even with my fingerprints eliminated, a persistent concern loomed.

Nineteen thirty-four was the year the outlaw died. In quick succession, Bonnie Parker, Clyde Barrow, John Dillinger, Pretty Boy Floyd, and Baby Face Nelson all fell in a mortal shower of g-men's bullets. As much as I preferred a life of luxury to hitting the skids, if my options consisted of petty cons or prison, the choice was obvious. However, despite the objectionable nature of his company, Black Peter turned the life and practices of the common tramp into something of an art. We still bummed it the vast majority of the time, but the money was easy coming and supplemented by the losses of whatever late-night suckers I could reel in at the bars where we played.

Unfortunately for our bankroll, the closer we got to Chicago, the weaker, lamer and more pitiful Black Peter became. He did not even pull his guitar from its case in the final few towns where we stopped. All he did was drink; drink away our every last penny until he had to hock his handsome ruby ring reserved expressly for funeral funds to keep him sated. I was able to produce enough coin to get us over the last leg and right on time, too—as Black Peter was looking mighty peaked.

Accounting for all the stops, it took us about two weeks to hit Chicago, and as soon as we arrived, Black Peter's demeanor changed. His haggard walk became jauntier, his bony shoulders straightened, and his vague, coal-black eyes glittered with focus. His manner was that of a man with a job at hand. We rolled into the yards south of the Loop after riding a cattle train up the easternmost stretch of the Santa Fe out of Kansas City. Chicago was the closest I ever got to New York, and even with all the years I'd been on the tramp, nothing could've prepared me for the magnitude of dereliction I saw there. Every train that pulled into the yards was so heavily laden with hobos that when it finally shuddered to a stop and they got off, it looked like a flock of starlings all flying out of a tree at once. So numerous were they that the bulls had no choice but to remain motionless and watch the floating fraternity shamble into town. All throughout the city, homeless, jobless, shiftless, penniless men outnumbered respectable citizens two to one, and establishments catering to their needs flourished. One particular block of Madison Street boasted ten employment agencies, eight flops, six saloons, four barbers, two gambling halls, and a mission. It's no wonder

Peter did not attempt to draw attention to himself—there were about fifty thousand men worse off than him already there.

The first establishment Peter visited in Chicago was that of a druggist. I waited outside, and when he returned with pockets bulging, he hastily led me to a cheap, second-story hovel on Clark Street offering one-night flops for the same price I'd paid for a single tumbler of gin back in Visalia. I followed Peter up the steps to a long, grimy, dimly lit hall smelling strongly of tobacco and unwashed men, where he stopped and called out in a wretched, trembling voice, "Annie, Annie Bonneau—where are you?"

Instantly, a short, squat, tawny-headed woman in a flour sack dress poked her head out from one of the rooms, eyes bulging, and exclaimed excitedly before hurrying over to Black Peter and throwing her arms around him. His wizened body sagged and crumpled under her weight. The whole encounter surprised me considerably, as Black Peter was not the sort of man who seemed like he'd have friends anywhere.

"Peter! You're alive!" she cried out as she flung herself at him.

"Not for long, I fear," he lamented, cradling her face, "lead me to my deathbed, angel Annie; I'm dying for sure this time."

Her expression somber, Annie took him by the hand and led him to an empty room about half the size of a matchbox. It contained a bed and nothing else. There were no windows and little air. A switch beside the doorway controlled a single bare bulb fixed in the ceiling. While Annie fetched fresh blankets and attended to Peter like a wet nurse tends to a bairn, after an uncomfortable spell in the doorway, I turned to leave and was immediately recalled.

"Please don't leave a wretch alone to die," he beseeched me pathetically, "Devil's got his thumb hard on me now. There's no telling how long he'll be, that master of fate, Death. All I can ask for, all I could want, is the company of a few friends to be beside me at my grim end—"

Annie sobbed uncontrollably as he continued his dirge.

"—I won't trouble you long, for my eyes won't look upon this world another day. Into the depths of perdition is my soul to be commanded— into torment eternal!" His faltering voice cracked, "I can feel the fever rising inside me, and if I can close my eyes at last upon the faces of true friends, I will have a moment's peace ahead of damnation!"

I'd known the man nigh on two weeks and yet was being hailed as one of his closest friends. Granted, considering the frequency and intensity of these episodes, I was hardly surprised. And so, to shut him up, I pledged my company until he croaked and heartily expressed my hope that it did not take too long.

Seemingly assuaged for a moment, Peter settled into the threadbare mattress and, armed with a glass in his left hand, a 12-oz bottle of druggist's alcohol in the other, and a pitcher valiantly beside him, proceeded to drink himself far closer to death than he ever would have come otherwise. The vile concoction was offered repeatedly to me. I refused. Instead, I extracted a bottle of my own taste from my coat and nursed upon it, languidly throwing cards against the wall until Peter lapsed into unconsciousness and I could slip out onto the street without having to endure his ceaseless lamentations on the way out the door. Annie, however, accepted his offer and, being no stranger to alki herself, consumed a considerable quantity of the dreck before continuing her appointed rounds. I learned from brief conversations with her that the two of them had known one another for years. After meeting in Los Angeles, they had traveled together for a time— but not even she could shed any light on Black Peter's history, character, or inscrutable actions.

During the next two days, whenever his consciousness rallied against the stupor he imposed upon it, he mixed up the alki and raised it to his lips. All other food and comforts were vehemently refused, and when the alki ran out, Annie was sent to procure more. It appeared as if the cycle showed no signs of stopping until he really did die, but on the evening of the third day, something utterly incomprehensible happened; Black Peter asked Annie to fetch a priest. From a dying man, such a request is reasonable, if not expected, but from a self-proclaimed Satanist, even on his deathbed, the presence of an agent from the opposite camp is hardly an anticipated demand—especially from one so ardent about the matter as Black Peter. So, when a young cleric fresh out of the seminary arrived in that den of sin and squalor to administer last rites, I remained quietly in the corner to observe what precipitated—and what I saw, I will never forget.

Even upon stepping into the Stygian room, it was readily apparent that this clergyman was new to his calling. He approached as tentatively as a spooked stallion, wet behind the ears and woefully unprepared for the task at hand—his gold ordination ring still some years short of making its time-worn indent on the finger that bore it. And, I am sure that being greeted by Black Peter writhing and howling hysterically at the very top of his lungs, bewailing his fears of death and the devil and the flames he saw engulfing the walls of his room didn't cause his confidence to surge any. Gulping, he readied himself to his spiritual charge and likely uttered a silent, urgent prayer that he would not be outmatched. Peter, by contrast, was raving. Whenever the cleric reached out to touch him, Peter recoiled as if in pain, and his voice rose an octave. Thrashing and clawing at his clothing and bedding, eyes rolling back in his head as he screamed, Peter's reception to his last rites appeared to me as more of an exorcism than a sacrament. As expected, such a performance drew a motley crowd of onlookers ranging from curious to panicked as Black Peter's ungodly wails echoed down the dingy halls of the Alaska House.

Eventually, the priest was able to calm him, and by the time he completed his blessing and hurried away, wide-eyed and visibly shaken through the throng in the hall, Peter was out cold—granted, whether or not this was due to exhaustion, alki, or the hand of God one could not be certain. Once Annie and her satisfactorily fogged mirror had examined Black Peter's catatonic form, I stepped over to his side. His twisted face of horror had relaxed into its natural furrows of age and time, and his labored breath passed evenly and peacefully from between his lips. Such a calm appearance entirely belied the turmoil of mere minutes earlier. Only the hair still bristling on the back of my neck remained as a clue to what had transpired, and as I continued to gaze upon him, all the rest of the hair on my body rose along with it. For, as he thrashed about so wildly, the priest's shiny new gold ring had slipped off...and right onto Peter's pallid hand.

The next day, while I was still reeling from what I had witnessed, amidst all the empty bottles of alki scattered around the cot like hulled nuts around an insatiable primate, Peter threw off the covers and rose from his deathbed. Seemingly restored, he picked up his guitar, kissed Annie goodbye, and led me down to Madison Street, where we procured a feed from the Salvation Army and played a late-night selection of cowboy blues to an eclectic array of Wobblies, artists, tramps, and bohemians at an indescribably strange joint known as the Dil Pickle. At no point did Black Peter say a word about what happened back at the Alaska House. Though as the days went on, I did find that his consumption had been miraculously cured. His malady now was advanced stage rheumatism which caused the tendons in his fingers to curl up into talons when he reached out to shake the hands of those who posited a few cents into his guitar case—but, curiously, in no way inhibited his ability to play.

All madness duly considered, Chicago was a profitable town for us, as Peter knew all the best haunts along the Near North and Lower West Side to busk and beg and flop for cheap or free. We remained there until New Year's Day when a reefer freight—likely packed with the meat of the stock we'd rode in with—facilitated our journey back west.

Nineteen thirty-five began with a thunderstorm. Rain as cold as a witch's tit poured out of that Chicago sky like bullets piercing the flesh of the defeated and downtrodden who shambled along the avenues as numerous and impervious as rats. The rain kissed the dirty, week-old snow piled on street corners and melted the ice that crowded around storm drains. Ladies and businessmen wrapped snug in their long coats and scarves cleared the streets in a minute flat as they sought cover with alarming urgency; as if they feared they'd melt if a drop so much as touched their skin. I watched them with fascination from a window in a saloon on Canal Street as they scurried toward the nearest cover like ants after you lift a log. As a traveling man used to the lack of shelter and the harshest reality of the elements, their sheer panic amused me. In droves, they flocked through the door of that humble saloon and crowded around the windows to watch the deluge stream down the glass.

As the weather had driven a far more significant crowd than usual into that bar, at the prompting of the owner, Peter and I started to play right away in an effort to keep them there. Holiday drunks are the best kind. Not only is their generosity heightened, but they are so focused on drowning their sorrows and enjoying themselves that they tend to forget they already contributed once and do so several more times before the end of the night. This particular evening was no exception. The bar remained a revolving door of semi-soaked patrons who parted so readily with their nickels that it was as if they had each been given an allowance to spend by the night's end. When we packed it in after the most melancholic version of Auld Lang Syne ever played on this side of the Pond, we found that Peter's guitar case was at least five pounds heavier.

Once the stroke of midnight passed, the storm subsided, and the partiers fagged themselves out, the saloon owner closed up shop with full pockets. Having nowhere to stay, nowhere to be, and everywhere to go, we swiped a bottle of Dewar's from behind the bar and went staggering down the slick Chicago streets amid the fading echoes of firecrackers and shotgun blasts offered up to welcome in a new year that, come the hush of dawn, felt woefully indistinguishable from the last. We stumbled down the dark alleys, clammy in our boots on the wet sidewalks, pulling our coat collars up around our ears and taking hard swallows of cheap sipping whiskey to fight off the frigid night. We chased the wind down to the docks, where it fought itself tooth and nail and ran screaming through the sails of the schooners like a woman wailing lamentations in the throes of hysteria. It wrapped itself up in knots around the mast poles and bowsprits, howling like an alley cat with its tail caught in a trap. It ducked and sucker-punched, feinted and double-backed, and gave itself a proper thrashing out before rushing over the lake and into the mists shrieking like a banshee and hollering like a war party of Injuns all at the same time.

"The Hawk sure is out tonight," Peter barked over the gale, "there's nothing in this world that cuts through a man like the Chicago wind. Makes my bones ache something awful." He withdrew another mouthful of whiskey from the bottle and, grunting in approval at its effect, tucked it under his arm.

"I'm ready to head back west myself," I remarked, shivering in a vain attempt to shake off the dampness that had taken hold.

"If these tired old legs can make it to dawn still standing, I'll catch the first west-bounder after daybreak. I can't even beat a sided train in the dark anymore... You coming?"

I mumbled my agreement and received the half-empty bottle which was proffered to me.

Despite his incessant beefing and rallying against the ills of the world, Black Peter did have a certain mysterious intrigue about him, and it is that intrigue that kept me in his company. For all of his swindling ways amongst strangers, toward me, Peter was consistently generous. My cut was always half, and in turn, I allowed myself to be led pell-mell around the country by this exceedingly strange testament to the sheer depths of man's pessimism and ability to torment oneself when given license and half a burden. He spoke little of his former life—if he'd had one—and primarily confined his discourse to bewailing the plight of existence, lock, stock, and barrel. While this griping was undoubtedly repetitive, it was no more so than the oft-repeated, blatantly embellished tales of most wanderers, all of whom insisted equally that their version was the irrefutable truth.

Furthermore, his behavior in Chicago clearly evidenced that he was no more possessed than the lush who crawls through the gutter searching for cigar snipes and prematurely discarded bottles with a little something left in them to sate him. The unholy force which had commandeered Black Peter's soul was not Satan but John Barleycorn. Granted, some of the more ardently religious would argue that both are one and the same.

One evening shortly after we had returned to more hospitable climes, as Peter and I ambled drunkenly along yet another city block toting guitar case and bottle, we passed before a towering stone church, and these very thoughts befell me. Curious as to what his reaction would be, I paused and confronted him. Leaning against the front steps, I crossed my arms and denounced his claims.

"I don't believe that you really sold your soul to the devil," I declared. "If you did, how can you stand before this church without going mad or wear that priest's ring without your finger burning off? It sure sounds good around a fire in the jungle or drunk in a dive, but admit it, there ain't any more of the Devil in you than there is in me."

In response to my accusations, Black Peter actually smiled. It was the first time I'd seen him do so, and it remains one of the most disturbing sights I have ever witnessed. His top lip curled back, quivering as if in a snarl, revealing a set of blackened, decaying teeth—every other one of them missing—and a gum line replete with abscesses.

If I'd thought that was horrific, it paled in comparison to what he did next. Without replying, Black Peter reached past me to one of several rose bushes that lined the steps and, with his long right thumbnail, removed one of the brightest flowers from its stem and held it in the palm of his outstretched hand.

"The Devil loves a skeptic," he spoke in a hollow tone, lifting his colorless eyes from the rose to meet mine, "for he holds no stock in faith and has no qualms about showing off. But he hardly appears as you suppose—he's no red monster with horns and a tail carrying a pitchfork any more than his adversary is some old man in the sky. In fact, they both wear all the same clothes. He doesn't show himself to a man as a pit of burning hellfire but as a cold canteen amidst endless desert. He doesn't appear as evil but as a miracle—the key to a cell door, a means of escape. He makes you believe that this is hell and makes himself out to be a savior. But do not be deceived; this is not hell, and for those of us who were foolish enough to believe that it is, we are the ones who are destined for the real McCoy. You are mistaken, Jack; the Devil and his powers are very real— but there's one thing you do have right, there ain't any more of the Devil in you than there is in me."

At that moment, he retracted his blank stare from my eyes of contempt and looked down at the rose in his hand. Still unconvinced by his mad theatrics, my gaze followed his, and when I looked back at the rose, with a shudder so intense it chilled me to my core, I saw that it lay shriveled, dry, and dead in Black Peter's gnarled hand.

The subject never arose again. From then on, I never questioned his verity or demanded proof of his claims. Our travels continued in much the same manner, with the addition of a certain degree of humility on my part. Every few months, when Black Peter's paranoid hypochondria hit critical mass, he'd pack in the last remaining vestiges of his sanity and head back to the Alaska House and Annie Bonneau, where he'd receive another dose of alki, sanctity, and good loving before he spun off into the next tail of his downward spiral.

Peter's last trip to Chicago on account of Munchausen's by the Devil was in late summer, after which we spent seven torrid weeks roasting in New Mexico as we followed a town-hopping circus down the Rio Grande to its American terminus in El Paso. By that time, Black Peter was well on his way to hysteria over the case of smallpox he swore now ailed him—this lethality being occasionally outstripped by insufferable prickly heat, which I, too, was a victim of. The circus we trailed after bore little resemblance to the utter madness I encountered while traveling with Cosmic Charlie, and in time, a number of the players grew fond of Peter and I and would frequent the saloons where we sang and strummed away our evenings.

One such evening, three of these protean performers tumbled into a large, semi-respectable saloon in the shadow of the city's water tower, one carrying a fiddle, another a horn, and the third toting a set of bongos. I don't believe any of us would have ever formerly described ourselves as musicians if asked, but that night, all five of us were so enraptured by the sounds we found we could make together and so bolstered by the cheering and square-dancing of the crowd that we declared ourselves to be just as proficient as the Benny Goodmans and Artie Shaws of the world. In fact, we were having such a bang-up time that we stepped to our instruments shortly before nightfall and did not put them down again until after the moon had set. Between the free drinks and fistfuls of change being cast in our direction, we saw no reason why we should. Even after the proprietor approached us saying it was nigh-on midnight and that we had to cease and desist as per the town's noise ordinance, we refused to stop playing.

That is, of course, until a band of unamused policemen stepped through the door. As none of us wished to spend the night in the hoosegow, we allowed ourselves to be led reluctantly out to the street, where we were given a warning and some very fine advice to go home and stay there for the remainder of the evening. As soon as they were out of sight, we scurried back into the bar, procured a bottle, and went on parade. This parade soon ended at the foot of the water tower, which was encircled by a wire fence that had already partially fallen to the ministrations of local trespassers. It was at this point when one of the men voiced his grand idea of climbing to the top of it.

Rip-roaring drunk and high on the excitement of the evening, none of us dissented, even Peter, for whom such a feat would have been considered Herculean. Having not quite overcome my imbued childhood propensity for competition, I volunteered to go first. One more mouthful of courage down the gullet, and I was set to climb. The ladder was caged, but at no less than 50 feet, there was nothing but a tight grip to keep me from falling straight down. Fortunately, it was dark, and I did not look.

The other four topped the tower in sequence. Upon ascension, instruments were removed from belt loops, and another round of shots was underway to ease the trembling nerves of those who decided—after looking down at the pinpoints of light that defined the town below—that he was not a fan of heights.

Standing up there on my perch atop the tower, I felt invincible—and more like a man than I had felt in many a year. From that vantage point, I could see the four corners of the world spread before me and all the ills and breaks they had offered me at will. In the west, I could see the fair face of my mother and the home I had abandoned, untouched by time and death. In the north, I could see the chains of McAlester in which I had so arduously slaved and would have languished if opportunity and ingenuity had not combined in my favor. In the east, I saw the arms of my blonde-haired woman, gone now for so long, and in the south...in the south, I saw nothing but darkness—prospects, gains, and riches that my eyes had yet to behold. I pulled my harp from my pocket with a rush and, gathering them all in a cacophony of triumphant hoots, shouts, trills, and laughter, played until my lips nearly bled. It was not until the bell in the tower of the mission rang six times and the new day broke over the land that our concert of rebellion ended.

As the mission bell ceased tolling, Black Peter abruptly dropped his guitar and, in horror, pointed a trembling finger in the direction of the looming Franklin Mountains, which were bathed crimson as the rays of dawn streamed over the sand and stone and wildflowers of El Paso.

"Do you see that?" he implored us, his voice rising in terror, "do you see what's coming?"

"That's the sun, you insufferable dolt," one of the three explained gently.

"It's a dragon!" Black Peter cried, fueled by panic, "it's setting the whole mountain on fire!"

"Sure it is," another of our companions laughed, completely unaware of the hysteria his wisecrack would soon unleash, "an' it's comin' right for you!"

As if in cognizance of this, Peter's eyes widened further yet. "The Leviathan!" he howled, "at long last, he has come for me! His eyes will pull my soul from its very seat; his breath will set my body ablaze! The hour of judgment is at hand; all my sins are due to be reckoned, my soul to be cast down!" He began digging his nails into his face and tearing away at the flesh until streams of blood trickled down his sallow neck.

The three carnies, now duly alarmed, began to back away as Black Peter raved. They had nowhere to go but down, and when we looked in that direction, to our dismay, we saw that several flashing orbs of red and blue now swelled the ranks of neighborhood lights that were turning on in quick succession.

I grabbed the wailing Peter by his shirt collar, cuffed him about the head, and begged him to be quiet, but akin to his alki-fueled paroxysms in Chicago, he was inconsolable. As the sun touched the horizon and a blanket of light spread over the town, Peter decided that he was no longer content in waiting for the devil to come for him and now intended to issue Satan his soul on his own time. With the strength of two men, Black Peter tore his garments away from me and strode toward the tower's edge. I caught him again by the fabric of his coat and pulled him back on his heels, but he would not step away. Two of the three carnies who had already begun to descend the tower into the waiting hands of the law rushed back to help me. They were immediately followed by two coppers who, along with the carnies, helped me subdue Black Peter and lower him down the ladder to the ground below. Even after he'd been lashed and bound and stuffed into the back of the wagon, his frantic cries did not cease.

Needless to say, that fated morning in El Paso marked the end of my short-lived musical career. The three carnies and I were arrested for trespassing—in addition to drunk and disorderly, resisting arrest, and disturbing the peace. Black Peter was committed. To the best of my knowledge, he was never seen again.

V

The Other One

I spent the next ninety days on my back as a guest in El Paso's greystone hotel. All grievances considered in their turn, El Paso was easy time. The hardest labor I did during that stint was fight off the flies and vermin, although they were present in such vast quantities that I'd be a liar if I didn't admit there wasn't a moment or two that I regretted not having a pick or hammer thrust into my hands as an alternative. Unlike the omnipresent bugs, my human company was subject to continual change, and by the end of my stay, I was likely more well-informed of the conditions out on the Road than I'd been when I was out on it myself.

My cellmates were predominately gamblers of every echelon, from pikes to high rollers. They were in for petty offenses, and most had enough coin to bail themselves out in the morning. In the meantime, I had the privilege of listening to the accounts of their arrests, every detail of the events that precipitated it, and, if I was lucky, the harrowing tale of their luckless attempt to flee. When enough of these unfortunates had amassed, I and a few other short-timers took the liberty of holding Kangaroo Court for the benefit of those awaiting trial and subsequently relieved them of their holdings—for the benefit of ourselves.

Otherwise, there wasn't much doing. The meals were three square, albeit course, and there was usually a ragged newspaper or two making the rounds, which occupied the rest of the time otherwise spent loafing or swatting at roaches—or, worst of all, thinking. Introspection has never been the hobo's preferred method of mental recreation, but when all other avenues have been exhausted, it is undertaken as a regrettable necessity.

If there's one thing that confinement stirs in a man, it is the inclination to think. Even at that time, after the frequent and prolonged confinement that I'd endured, it was still hardly an occupation I subjected myself to without considerable persuasion. However, during that stint, I began to wonder if it all meant anything: Saint Stephen and the ice he had planted, Black Peter and the wind he had harvested, Althea and her eyes that saw the world...Was there anything to this most recent series of mad dogs I'd encountered other than poor luck and strange coincidence?

Perhaps, if I had been the spiritual type, I would've read more into it and made something out of it, but that not being the case, by the time I was free, I had long since come to the conclusion that it all meant nothing, nothing at all. My mind was occupied by much more important prospects, such as my drunken epiphany atop the water tower. And, in staying true to such, I irrevocably decided that my trajectory was due south, come hell or high water.

This resolve was further strengthened by a conversation I had with one of my transitory cellmates. He was one of the few who wasn't a gambler or a drunk—or at least that isn't what he was in for. He was a big son of a gun—well over six feet tall and probably three hundred pounds, the skin of his face scorched by the southern sun and the rest obscured by lurid and ribald tattoos. His crime was murder, and the idea of his looming punishment was enough to bring that mountain of a man to his knees.

"Tomorrow, they're shipping me back down to Mexico. The day after that, I'll be dancing the hempen jig at the Mexicali gallows matinee. I'll tell you—if you got even half a mind of jumpin' the border like some of the gay cats I've met in here, you can consider me a fine picture of what you've got comin'. You steer clear of Mexico like you'd steer clear of Jeff Carr in Cheyenne or a flophouse full of typhoid. The only thing Mexico will do for a man is make him see roses, then be the ruin of his life."

As with most men whose days are numbered, it didn't take much convincing to get him to elaborate.

"Ran up one hell of a tab in Reno...kept shootin' off my big mouth but had no money to pay. Borrowed a sum from the wrong fellow. I should've known better, but in the end, I was smart—I hauled hide out of there before I lost more'n half. Knew my luck waren't gon' change—not when I needed it to, so, in the interest of keeping my tongue in my mouth and my thumbs where I like them, I paid for a cushioned ride to Bakersfield and from there, beat it across the border in a possum belly. Rode for two days with only hunger pangs and the hum of those razor wheels on the track to keep me company. When I got into Mexicali, I was broker than a dog. Couple days doin' my best impression of a dirt stiff on a gradin' gang got me outta hock real quick—and in Mexico, tequila costs only twenty *centavos.* I found me a little cantina right on the main *calle*—quiet in the afternoons and busier than the devil in the evenings with dancing girls, Mariachi bands, and cockfights out back. The cantina seldom closed, so I didn't even need a flop if I didn't want one. There was a veranda that faced the street, and I could sit in the shade at the bar each *mañana* eating *machaca* and eggs, sipping *cerveza*, and watching the heat waves roll down the sidewalks....

They were somethin', them jamborees. I'd pull into Mexicali, go on a tear for a fortnight, then ride back out on the gang and turn dirt for more *dinero*. It was the perfect arrangement. Should've known the devil wouldn't let me keep it up for long. One day, I rolled into town with a stake and headed down to my cantina. I was taking in that sweet tequila and buying rounds for the *primos* when Felina walked in; she turned every head in the room like they were on turrets. Her hair was as straight as an arrow, thick, shiny, and black, and hung loose down to her *culo*. She was tall for an Indian, broad-faced, and beautiful...wore one of them ruffled-up dresses the flamenco dancers wear. It was red...red all the way through.... Ain't a man in creation who could resist that."

He paused to give such a treasured recollection the veneration it deserved. "And as the gods would have it, she only had eyes for me. I ain't exactly Don Juan, but I've had my share, and I ain't never asked for any sweeter pootang than that little lady gave me. Waren't more than two nights went by, and I was already in love. And that's where the trouble started—it always starts with love. Suppose I'll never know why, but Felina loved me too. I never had a woman so devoted, a woman so pure...'cept I didn't know quite how pure she was.

It waren't too long before a man stormed in, brewing with all kinds of fever. Indian. Rode in from outta town on a burro, still had the dirt from the asparagus fields on his hands. He spoke in real broken English, but his intentions were as clear as soup in any language. She didn't want to go, but he was going to take her away from me anyway, and I had no say. But that poor bastard was sorely mistaken. I did have a say. I said '*bang-bang*' and fired away. That gink hit the barroom floor with two holes in his chest before he even had the chance to draw. Turns out he was her father...and she was just fourteen.

I ran like a highball behind the hounds. I was hoppin' the border 'fore he was even cold. Should've forgotten it all, left that evil, foul deed behind me—but I couldn't leave Felina. So, back to Mexicali I went, tangled up in all sorts of blues. But it was all in vain. Them *Federales* ain't nothing to mess with. Warned the border guards agin' me. Took a bullet in the flank tryin' to escape 'em. And now I pay. Ain't no help on the way for me; I'll be dead 'fore the week's end. Felina's flown and gone, and all Mexico's got to offer me now is a slipknot around my neck and a plot in potter's field.

I'm warning you, mister, Mexico ain't no place for a man weakened by spoils and pleasures. She'll show you women like you've never seen—the most beautiful women in creation...willing, doting, gentle—every bit as sweet as the lies they tell—and then she'll cut out your tongue. She'll give you tequila, mezcal, and pulque that'll make you feel like you're the king of the world and then drive an arrow into your side. She'll give you wonders, vistas, and sights no American can rightly dream of and then render you blind. She'll make you fall in love like no rightful man ought to ever, and then she'll carve out your heart and offer your blood to the sun."

My condemned cellmate did not remain in my company long. The following day, he was collected by a cordon of armed, badged khaki-clad Federales with faces so expressionless and severe they appeared to be carved from stone. He rose from his cot and commanded himself to them with his jaw set firm and his sunburnt head held high. His deportment was that of one practicing for the gallows. As my eyes leveled upon this exchange, I shivered as I viscerally remembered a time when I feared that I occupied his shoes myself. I looked away. When the heavy door at the end of the corridor slammed shut behind them, the echo that resounded through the cellblock sounded eerily like a rope snapping taut.

When my stint was finally up, and they turned me loose out onto the dusty streets of El Paso, I had nothing to my name other than the clothes on my back and a small sack of smoking in my pocket, all funds having gone to fines or otherwise evaporating the way a man's money always seems to when he is serving a jolt in the stir. However, what I did have was direction. Never having been one to believe much of what I heard if what was expounded wasn't to my liking, I decided rather than head north into impending winter, I would immediately head south to a land of mystery, enchantment, and, most importantly, a thermometer that never dipped below 60°.

Despite the grave warnings of my tattooed cellmate, all that stuck in my libertine mind were the images he'd conjured of star routes, exotic women, and good hooch. So, promptly following my release, against all better judgment, I found myself crouched behind a clump of ocotillo atop one of the southernmost hills in El Paso, waiting for a Mexican Central freight. When, toward nightfall, one came groaning and puffing up the grade, I waited until a good dozen cars passed before I sprung from my hiding place and rushed toward a passing boxcar. I concealed myself on the deathwoods between cars until we'd crossed the murky Rio Grande, then climbed atop the deck of the train and settled in for the long ride to anywhere.

I'm sure many would consider my haphazard resolve after enduring so many hardships of every nature imaginable the decisions of an incorrigible restive somewhat crippled under the hat, but for those similarly guided, my trajectory would be considered perfectly natural. From the first instant that I swung upon a freight train at the age of fifteen after a childhood replete with tales of adventure on the road, I became terminally affected by a condition far more damaging to a man's prospects in this world than my congenital won't-work-itis—wanderlust.

To those affected by wanderlust, it's known as the Tramp Plan. The same lust I found in women, I found in adventure—in grabbing the world by the stones and making good use of every opportunity well-afforded me. I went to Mexico not because I was looking for more trouble than I'd already had but because I'd gotten into so many snares north of the border that I figured I was due for a fresh start. Denver Jack was the moniker I went by, and unless they were on the Tramp Plan themselves, most of those I encountered didn't even know where Denver was. The anonymity was appealing, as were the novelty and freedom. At no time did I have a destination—although I did make sure to steer clear of Mexicali; after all, not all good advice is lost on me.

After several months of drifting from cantina to cantina and fonda to fonda on rusty, grinding freights, sleeping under the stars, and reciting my mendicant yarns at the backdoors of *casas* and *haciendas,* I found myself on the coast. I hadn't been there long when a port city on the Gulf of California called Guaymas temporarily suspended my vagabondage. I'd fallen asleep atop the cargo in a lumber car billed to Empalme and awoke ditched on a siding. In the interest of a feed and some coin, I'd crawled out of the car in the middle of the night and, finding myself alone, followed the dim glow of the signal lights through the fog over a nearby railroad bridge toward what I hoped was a town. After a long moonlit night of shuffling along the shimmering rails, unsure of my terminus, dawn broke in all its crimson splendor, and the sun rose over the city of Guaymas. Little did I know then, trudging through the cinders in dew-soaked shoes, how many more mornings I would witness such a magnificent sight after I'd been persuaded to stay.

Famished, I found breakfast by following the smell of frying eggs. Such provisions were procured a few blocks from the tracks in an unassuming adobe shack with a sign out front advertising *chilaquiles*. I threw monte for the cook with my meal as the wager and waddled out of there sometime later after gorging myself with every sort of Mexican trimming he had in the kitchen. My next objective was cantina or bust. Fortunately, after the fall of Montezuma, cantinas were no rarity. I found one along a sleepy avenue in full view of the surf. At the time of my arrival, the old, mustached innkeeper was scrubbing pots in the slop sink. I ordered mezcal, neat. He grumbled something about the drinking habits of *gringos* and then served it to me in a cracked mug before returning to his chore. Nothing tastes more like the heart and soul of Mexico than good mezcal. It tastes like the very earth itself—and it ain't good unless it numbs your tongue. This particular batch left me speechless for an hour.

Sated and content, I reclined back on my stool against the wall and peered out the open window at the street where the local urchins chased after cigar snipes and cigarillo butts and pestered tourists to buy lottery tickets and shoelaces. Industrious little kids, those Mexicans. One even stuck me for five *centavos* before the day was out.

As I soon came to find, Guaymas was a sort of tropical Elysium—a paradise for any man with a healthy appreciation of beauty and recreation. For a tramp like me, there was no shortage of leisure. If you walked far enough outside Guaymas proper and west of the little village of Chino, it was easy to forget that civilization existed. Under the broad leaves of tropical palms, you could hear the breakers crashing on the rocks below, their cadence interrupted only by the calls of gulls and the bellows of bull seals reveling in the ecstasy of the warm waves. There were no railroad tracks, no cars, and no telephone poles—just enough shade, breeze, and grass to tempt an American expatriate into enjoying a mid-morning siesta.

And that's not the only thing the coastline of Guaymas was good for; on the beach below the brand new Playa de Cortes Hotel, leagues of American sporting men cast their lines into the surf and reeled in marlin and sailfish by the dozens.

Being a port in addition to a tourist stop, about one out of every ten marks in Guaymas spoke English, and the vast majority of boatswains, fishermen, and locals played a fair hand of poker. And fortunately for me, the locals were almost unanimously unfamiliar with the mechanics of Rocky Mountain Euchre, which made my stay—extended as it was—quite lucrative.

But, once more, I am getting ahead of myself. The reason I stayed wasn't on account of the scenery or the dough or even the mezcal—which, I soon discovered in Guaymas is the best in the world. No, just like in Tulsa, my anchor in Guaymas strode innocently by me the first day I arrived.

As I was walking around Grosvenor Square in the center of Chino on my way back into town, I was suddenly blindsided by a vision so distinct that the memory has been like a tattoo on my brain ever since. A woman was strolling in the opposite direction across the square, well-dressed and proud, carrying packages wrapped in brown paper.

Now, I've been all around this world, and I've seen more beautiful women across every caste than any man who lives life on all one shift could claim to be acquainted with, but I never saw a woman more beautiful than her. She stood as straight and tall as a desert candle. Her hair was the color of a black dahlia and cascaded down over her shoulders in tumbling curls like strands of ivy. Her mestizo skin was the color of sun-scorched wheat, and the embroidered Puebla dress that enveloped her buxom figure like petals on a tulip was stunning scarlet. Tucked behind her ear was a cluster of begonias carefully chosen to match.

In an instant, the residual heartbreak that had smoldered like a lump of coal in my chest since Rosalie died took leave of my senses, and I was immediately consumed by the presence of the woman before me. It wasn't even the way she looked as much as it was the way she moved. As she walked, she almost seemed to glide over the ground like a wraith, leaving the dirt beneath her shoes virtually undisturbed. Her steps were smooth and seamless, her hips rolling, the very picture of ease and comfort, poise and confidence. Someone could have lit a stick of dynamite next to my head, and it would not have garnered my attention. As soon as my eyes set upon her, I became rooted to the spot like a man turned to stone in the court of medusa. I felt like my head was an electrical outlet, and someone had just stuck a metal tine into my ear. At first blush, I was blown away. Doubtlessly and without contest, I knew at that moment I had never encountered a woman quite like her before.

I watched her until she rounded the nearest corner and disappeared from sight, my presence—let alone the impression she had made upon it—utterly unbeknownst to her. She remained the sole occupant of my mind for the rest of the day.

That evening, a short walk up the hill from the harbor brought me to a large saloon densely populated by sailors and merchants. Come nightfall, the ranks were swelled by a four-piece band and dancing girls in vibrant costumes that whirled through the crowd. A game of conquian soon erupted in the back corner. The mezcal had done little to dull the image of the woman from earlier, so I sat down at the game in an attempt to clear my head. The other men at the table were all in good humor, grateful to be ashore at the week's end. Rounds of drinks were bought and flowed as quickly and freely as the hands. The pot grew rapidly, and my winnings along with it. Fistfuls of pesos were extracted from jute pockets and swiftly deposited in mine.

The crowd continued to swell as the night moved, and before long, the bargirls could hardly keep up. A fellow American and grafter like me sat down in a vacated chair and began a run of his own. Familiar with his tricks, I folded and let him have his share of the shearing. Drunk and largely satisfied, I returned to the bar. Enveloped by the din, I watched the women spin and sway around the platform where the band played, accompanied by men of all stations in various stages of lechery and inebriation. Naturally, echoes of the enchantress from earlier began to resurface, and I sighed as I turned away to face the massif of bottles, the disappointment of missed opportunity fresh and raw. Aphrodite had passed me by, and despite the great preponderance of Athenas, none of them seemed to compare.

A ripple of exclamation arose from the poker table, and I glanced up from my drink. In the shiny aluminum of the beer tap, I caught sight of a woman standing behind me. A familiar woman. The flowers in her hair were still red, but they had changed to roses. Her dress was fuller, brighter, sexier. Her face was every bit the same. Our eyes met in the reflection, and she did not look away.

Half-stunned into speechlessness, I turned toward her. On her face, a mysterious and intriguing little half-smile spread. She reached into her hair, picked one of the roses, and held it out to me.

"Dance?" she propositioned me in a voice as sweet as nectar.

We danced through three whole numbers before I could even catch my breath, let alone find my voice. She moved like a song. Between her skirt fanning out around her as she twirled and the smile of ecstasy she wore as she sambaed, I was rendered helpless. I knew there was something special about her the moment I looked into her eyes. They overflowed with the vibrancy and passion of a life unencumbered by the hardships I knew so well. They were the eyes of one who lilted across the surface of reality and danced nimbly through the minefields. For the second time in my life, I burned with overwhelming desire—to be one with her, second only to talking with her.

But, to my dismay, our dalliance ended all too soon when a staggering drunk shouldered into me and knocked her clean out of my arms. Before I was even back on my feet, a vulture of a man swept her away into the gyrating crowd. My customary response would have been to beat this offender into a bloody pulp, but, heeding my dead cellmate's dire warning against falling in love with Mexican maidens, I returned to the poker table, crestfallen. Granted, after half a bottle of mezcal and countless cervezas, my skills were significantly diminished. The compelling distraction of her hardly helped either. After every bet I laid, my eyes left the game and scanned the crowd. I couldn't help myself; the pull was too great. On one occasion, when I could not find her, the hand came all the way back around to me before I realized I was still looking for her. Disheartened, I sunk into my chair and folded. Beside me, the stool pulled back, and a voice as sweet as nectar addressed the croupier, "deal me in."

I was broke shortly thereafter. As it turns out, this most mystifying maiden was also one hell of a poker player. She was incredibly perceptive and so fluent in reading body language that all I needed to do was pick up my cards, and she knew instantly what her chances were of winning. She could sense a trick the moment it entered my mind and played so defensively that I never saw her lose more than her ante to the pot. The rest of the players hardly fared better than me. The sight of her leaning casually back, observing the laying of bets while her ringed fingers fondled the pesos stacked before her was enough to throw any man off his game. Most men object to the presence of a woman in such environs, but her intrigue and prowess seemed to negate that opinion entirely. She was distilled in confidence, as shrewd as the day is long, and had no problem sitting down with men at their most sacred ritual and beating them at their own game.

As the evening began to wane, the dealer packed up and left, and a floating crap game docked itself in our corner. Many patrons had already dispersed, but the band evidenced no signs of fatigue. The men that remained around the table tucked away what remained of their holdings and retreated with the tide until the following night. The woman beside me stretched and rose alongside them. I could not let her go. By then, the mezcal had tightened its hold upon me most intensely. I struggled to stand without swaying and speak intelligibly, but I managed to stammer out a magnanimous offer to buy her a drink. She politely declined, so I ordered another for myself and asked her to dance. A glint of excitement appeared in her wide, brown eyes, and she eagerly accepted. The last thing I remember was the tinkling of the silver bells sewn onto the leather straps of her huaraches as she swirled dizzyingly about me, my eyes paralytically caught in her contagious smile.

The next morning, I awoke in a jail cell. I was just about as dirty and disheveled as a body could be, with absolutely no recollection of how I'd gotten there and a hangover that would have killed a lesser man. Seated alone on a bare cot with my pounding head in my hands and one eye open, I begrudgingly surveyed the worn gray brick of a holding cell, the mounting concern I felt regarding my presence there swimming upstream against my current misery. I hadn't the slightest idea of what behavior was responsible, but I couldn't shake the thought that the last time my infatuation with a woman had been followed by incarceration, it had been in the form of a life sentence. I tried like the devil to recall the full course of my evening, but with every attempt, I came up empty. It was as if the tinkling of those silver bells had wiped my memory clean, and even when I heard them ring again, they did nothing to bring it back.

At first, I thought I had only imagined the sound, as my ears were already ringing, but after the Herculean effort required to lift my aching head and focus my bloodshot eyes, I realized incredulously that I hadn't. Beyond the iron bars that confined me was the ethereal image of a woman. The same woman. At first, I thought I was hallucinating on top of it all, but as I persuaded my disbelieving eyes to widen, the image only sharpened.

She was standing before my cell, holding a tray with a dishcloth draped over it. When she saw that I was alive enough to notice her, she set the tray on the wicket and leaned back on her heels, wordlessly contemplating me. My first inkling had been that she'd put me there, so the fact that she was proffering me breakfast—despite the inscrutable circumstance—was something of a relief.

In addition to the sight of her, the smell of fried meat and coffee emanating from the tray invigorated me, and I rose with a stifled groan and shuffled over to the cell door.

"If they'd told me I'd be getting this kind of service, I would have made a citizen's arrest on myself," I said, trying to sound as cheery as possible as I ran my hand through my tousled hair and straightened up my ragged suit. "Why am I in here anyway? Who'd I kill?"

"Nobody," she replied, her melodic voice echoing strangely inside the harsh stone walls, "You were arrested for drunkenness and disorderly conduct."

"Drunk and disorderly? In *Mexico*?!" I exclaimed incredulously.

"Well, you did drink a whole bottle of mezcal—and when you didn't have enough money to pay, you bet one of the regulars fifty pesos that you could swim across the Sea of Cortez."

"That's it? A friendly little bet is all it takes to get a man thrown in the stir around these parts?"

"Hardly," she scoffed good-naturedly. "They put you in jail because you actually tried."

"No kidding! Did I make it?"

At this, she actually laughed. "Of course not! You were in the middle of the *malecon*!"

I've never been easily embarrassed, but at this particular moment, I could feel the tips of my ears turning bright red. Now it all made sense: the torn clothes, the scrapes in places scrapes should never be, and the fact that I had more dust in my hair after one night out drinking than I did after weeks of straight traveling across every kind of desert. It wasn't a brawl at all; I—in all my drunken wisdom—had just decided it was a good idea to swim across a dry pier.

I scratched my dirty head sheepishly. "Your mezcal ain't nothing to mess with."

She smiled knowingly. "You Americans have the stomach for it but not the head. If you think the mezcal will do you in, you'd better not try pulque."

"I don't remember all that much, but I seem to recall your telling me that you don't drink."

"I don't," she replied soberly, "I've seen too much of what it does."

"Yet you spend your time enticing men in bars, and then when they've gone and made raging fools of themselves, you bring them breakfast behind bars just to tease them more?"

Now it was her turn to blush. "You misunderstand. Such temptation is not my intention at all. You see, my mother left me on the step of a mission when I was an infant. I was raised my whole life by the friars—and received far better treatment as a little girl of mixed blood than I would have otherwise. I was well-educated, protected, and cared for—but there was little tolerance for fun, and I've always loved to dance—a love that was always strongly discouraged. So, when I turned fifteen and left the mission, the first place I sought out was one where I could dance."

"—and you found yourself in a cantina, eh?" I interrupted.

That mysterious little smile flitted across her face once more. "No, a cabaret—as a burlesque vedette."

I could feel my ears turning red again. "Figures," was the only reply I could manage.

"Again, you get the wrong idea," she insisted. "It does not make me a bad person."

"What do the brothers think of your chosen profession?"

She chuckled, "understandably, they would have preferred if I had become a nun."

"They are undoubtedly the only ones," I assured her.

Her smile returned. "To answer your question," she segued, entirely derailing my attempt at flirtation, "since I chose not to serve God in my work, I try to help the less fortunate in my free time."

"Your decision is admirable," I told her, "but make no mistake about it, I'm hardly less fortunate."

"Oh?" she replied, glib and curious, "how did you come to figure that? You are locked in a jail cell, after all."

"Yes, but I get to talk to you."

She returned to examining my face, and her little smile remained.

"Did the brothers happen to give you a name?"

"Of course," she answered, "Bonifacia Leocrita Rodríguez y Castro Santa Rosalía de Mulegé. But everybody calls me Bonnie Lee. What's yours?"

"Jack," I answered.

"Just Jack?" she mused.

"Just Jack," I replied wittily, "unless you are interested in adding my surname to the rest of yours."

Her little smile crept further up her face. "Finish your breakfast," she admonished me, "it's getting cold."

I needed little invitation to clear the tray. "So, Bonnie Lee," I asked, "When are they going to let me out of here so I can treat you to breakfast?"

"Don't worry," she assured me as she departed, "you're only in here for twenty-four hours. The constable will let you out tomorrow morning."

And so, he did. But while I was confined there, all I could think of was Bonnie Lee and the love I felt for her. Now, I've loved many women. In fact, if you gathered them all together in the same place, I bet they'd amount to near about the female population of Denver. I don't deny that I've fallen in love every other week for most of my life, but to truly love rather than be in love was something I'd only felt once before. Rosalie was the first. Bonnie Lee was the other one. I'd love another yet, but that is another part of this story. From the first moment I saw her, I knew I wanted to marry her. And, while I'm not usually the marrying type, for her, I would have done anything...and that's very nearly what it took.

Bright and early the next morning, a sombreroed and bewhiskered constable stuck a key into the cell door and released me without the generous serving of vittles and badinage I had been permitted the day before. Unshaven, unkempt, and dead broke, I hit the streets—my eagerness and enthusiasm joined with one objective. Many years of experience had proven that there was merely a short con and a little fabric separating me from the coin in the pockets of any other man I encountered. Preferring to stoop to begging only when more cunning methods had already been exhausted, I plied upon the easiest target in Guaymas—the enterprising and industrious kids.

I only needed to traverse a few short blocks before I was accosted by the first of them, offering to sell me shoelaces. Noting to the gullible young fellow that my footwear was already suitably laced, I offered to gift him the ten centavos they would have cost if he could correctly guess the queen amongst the three dissimilarly ranked cards I laid face down upon the sidewalk. Of course, after he easily disposed of the first hand, before I produced the money, he wanted to try his luck again. In this, the same manner that Uncle John had first introduced me to the wily methods of monte, I not only recouped my debt of thirty centavos from the young urchin but swindled from him a few pesos besides.

By the time I made it to the shore-lined street I had attempted to swim across, I had enough silver clinking in my pockets to secure a handsome midday meal. The remainder I took to the gambling house and, over the course of that afternoon, procured a sum great enough to cancel my debt at the cantina and outfit me in new duds worthy of Bonnie Lee's notice. As the sun set over the harbor, satisfied with my day's work, I retired to the same cantina, hopeful of that matchless maiden's return. I expected to be obliged to pay my dues before I was served, but with surprise, I found that it had already been taken care of. The author of such generosity was revealed to me as none other than Bonnie Lee herself.

I remained at the cantina for several long hours, awaiting her return with excitement and giddiness comparable to that of a love-struck schoolboy. Every time the door swung open, my head turned expectantly toward it, and the weight of disappointment when each newcomer proved to be a stranger did not lessen as the evening progressed. As my heart sunk slowly back down to its rightful place in my chest after each instance, I turned to the bar and relieved my glass of another sip of mezcal. Granted, I did so with uncharacteristic mindfulness, not wishing to make a fool of myself as I had the first time.

When she finally stepped through the door, I was assured of her stunning presence well before I even turned around. Her face flooded my whole body with such a sensation of warmth it was as if my heart exploded in my chest. And when my eyes took leave of her angelic face and saw what she was wearing, my brain might as well have leaked clean out of my ears for all the good it was doing me. She was dressed in a satin burlesque costume, her hair tied up in a black velvet chignon framed by a bouquet of fresh flowers. Draped over her shoulders was a blue satin cape that she wrapped modestly around her curvaceous figure as she stepped into the company of so many lecherous drunks. I watched, practically open-mouthed in desirous awe, as she spoke briefly to the few persons who greeted her, and by the time she came to notice me seated at the bar and drifted over in my direction, I was honestly quite dizzy.

Any comment on her divine appearance would have occasioned a complete eclipse of my mental faculties, so instead, I stammered out my thanks at the unnecessary kindness she had displayed in paying my bill— and as I came to find, my fine as well.

"The money was all yours anyhow," she shrugged with a grin, "you handed me your purse more readily than an old widow when passed the collection plate."

Sobered by her playful jibe, I returned the crack. "I'll play you again— anywhere, any time."

"How does right now suit you?" she asked, her sparkling brown eyes peering into mine.

"If you're feeling froggy, leap," I told her.

Bonnie Lee's smile broke free from its restraints and spread across her face like a sunrise. She ordered us a hightop, where we sat hardly two feet across from one another with a candle between us. I produced my well-creased deck of cards and the remainder of that afternoon's take. She produced a box of matches and told me to put away my money.

"I don't want anyone to think I'm trying to make a beggar out of you," she quipped.

"I haven't bet with matches since I've been a kid!" I protested, stifling a laugh.

"Well, I've seen you bet with real coin, and I'm inclined to think that matches are more on your level."

My laugh could no longer be stifled. "Alright, hustler, I'll play your game. But if I win, you serve me breakfast tomorrow."

"You intend on getting yourself arrested again just for that?"

"*Not* behind bars," I clarified.

"Coffee? Huevos? Chorizo?" she offered.

"And you have to wear that same outfit."

Her eyes narrowed playfully, "deal," she agreed.

My eyes dropped to the cards, "deal," I instructed.

She beat the hide off me. At the close of the game, as she neatly slid her surplus matches back into the box and rose from the table, Bonnie Lee thanked me earnestly for my company and asked if I had a place to stay. Being in want of a match, I lit my cigarette off the candle and leaned calmly back in my chair, but inside, my heart raced to palpitations. I confirmed the negative, as the only bed I'd laid upon since my arrival in Guaymas had been furnished by the jailhouse. Upon learning this, to my complete and utter amazement, she invited me to come with her. I immediately jumped up from the table and followed her out, attempting with every ounce of my strength to maintain my composure as six kinds of passion all began looking for an exit. Alone, the sight of her hips rolling was enough to send a man to the madhouse—and when paired with the rest of her, I wasn't sure I'd ever recover—and she was a Catholic girl at that! I couldn't believe my luck.

—And I shouldn't have. When we stopped a block from the cantina in front of a two-story lodging house, I realized that my randy mind had gotten the best of me. She bid me cordially *adios* and carried on in the direction of home, and I watched her, very nearly in pain. The following day, she met me for *desayuno* at a nearby café. She was not wearing her burlesque costume.

Nevertheless, that breakfast marked the beginning of a brief and intense courtship. She did not yield to me quickly, but once she did, our fate was well-assured. She was as sharp as a thorny rose and as passionate as a final kiss. She had a capacity for clean fun that was unlike any I have ever encountered, and she found joy and excitement in such simple things that it was contagious. Good food and music were all she ever craved, and casual repartee was her specialty. She commanded her intelligence and wit with a sense of confidence and self-respect that rivaled any woman I'd ever met. She spoke better English than most Americans, and her intellect, if properly nurtured, could have won her acclaim from the world over and wrought some degree of profound change. When she performed, she was the belle of the cabaret and the muse of any man fortunate enough to behold her. The advances she received were continuous and unrelenting, but Bonnie Lee was seemingly uninterested in men other than as fandango partners, and she dismissed all of them affably. All of them—except me.

I never understood what she saw in me. I was just another booze-soaked bum who'd blown in with the wind. I'll admit that I was quick with the cards and as charming as Satan's snake, but she was smart enough to see through all that. Still, for some reason, she sought me out. I never questioned it, wary of poisoning my turn of good fortune. We swapped stories of life over strong Colombian coffee and horseback rides along the beach, and I shared with her the sum of my adventures—at least the ones that were not incriminating. While Bonnie Lee had some stirring stories of her own, I did not doubt that my chances with her would be wholly diminished if she learned I was an escaped federal prisoner. Therefore, I kept mum on any subjects relating to crime and punishment—which significantly condensed my repertoire. Fortunately, I was also endowed with a fertile imagination.

It wasn't long before I was recognized as her regular companion. Bonnie Lee was ubiquitously well-liked and respected despite the fact that her occupation and haunts were usually affiliated with the most unsavory sort of woman. But, Bonnie Lee flew in the face of those casts; she skirted around the edges of all debauchery, never got into trouble, and took her place upon the long wooden pews at the cathedral every Sunday. Therefore, by proxy, my association with her afforded me considerable trust and esteem that I could never have earned myself. And, for the first time, I endeavored to remain worthy of the accord granted me.

Not long after I had settled into my Mexican digs, I was offered a job at the gambling hall as a faro dealer. It was one of the few legitimate jobs I ever held, and the pay was unobjectionable. The gambling house itself was not particularly crooked, nor was the dealing box gaffed, but I was still able to garner some 'supplemental income' whenever necessary. Due to the nature and inclinations of the sea-weary merchants and deckhands that moored themselves to my table, I needn't turn all the tricks in the book to make a substantial profit; these individuals usually made lousy enough bets on their own.

All in all, I had no complaints. I had a steady income, a roof over my head, food in my belly, and a beautiful woman who enjoyed my company. Since our crepuscular working hours aligned, I did everything possible to be near her in my free time. Once, I even swept out the jail while she brought provender and prayers to a hapless fugitive who'd been caught stowed away in a U.S.-bound banana crate. I wanted her more desperately than the Duke of Windsor wanted Wallis Simpson, and in the worst way. But, as badly as I wanted her, her presence alone was enough to sate me, and I was uncharacteristically patient, hoping that she'd come around in due time.

Given her station, Bonnie Lee was a woman of statutes. Being raised in the manner she had been, one would expect no different. However, despite our moral disparity, our attraction to one another was immediate and enduring and had but one conceivable end. The memory of the evening it was reached is one I will doubtlessly recall until the moment of my last breath and invariably dances through my mind at least once a day.

There was music that evening at the cantina; one lone troubadour and his guitar—an instrument that sounded like it had crossed more lonely roads than I would in my lifetime. His songs were stories, and those stories warmed my soul. Some I remembered and some I'd never heard before, but I've heard them all now. And when I think of them, I think of Bonnie Lee—the folds of her dress cascading over her savagely tan legs, the crimson ribbons streaming through her long, black hair, her quivering knee pressed into the back of mine, and the quips and badinage that sustained an evening in flux.

She was closer to me that night than any before. She drew nearer in her chair, reached out to run her bronze fingers through my hair, and pressed her hip into the side of mine. With every move of hers, I melted more and more. By the time the troubadour packed up his instrument and the cantina locked its swinging doors, there was not enough willpower in the world to keep me from endeavoring to spend the rest of my waking hours locked in her passionate arms. Fortunately, she made the first move.

As we stepped out onto the street and I grappled for the words that would entice her to linger longer, she turned to me and asked, "how about a cup of coffee?"

All the cafés were long closed, and when I inquired where we would procure such libations, she just motioned for me to follow her. The walk was not far, and we trekked in relative silence, listening to the distant crashing of waves and the calls of wild animals as anticipation ravaged me.

Bonnie Lee lived in a little adobe shack in central Chino, a small residential neighborhood east of Guaymas proper. The exterior was almost entirely grown over with the thickest bunch of climbing roses I've seen to this day. They wound their way around the frames of the windows and over the smooth clay walls until they reached the roof. The smell of them was intoxicating. She picked one, tucked it behind her ear with the others, and invited me inside.

Upon entry, the first thing I noticed was a corner bar just left of the door and rows and rows of sweet potations that lined the shelves behind. Three high-backed barstools hung their steel legs over the rail and rested gently against the mesquite bar top. When I inquired after this most peculiar facet of a teetotaler's home, Bonnie Lee just shrugged. She was under the impression that its former tenant was one hell of a *fiestero*, but I retained the lingering suspicion that the place was a decommissioned brothel. I stepped over to the bar and picked up one of the bottles. It was covered in dust about a quarter inch thick, but the liquor it contained was just as sweet as that served at the cantina. It was Spanish rum, and I took it with me.

The rest of the establishment was in considerably better repair. Bonnie Lee had an enclave of a kitchen, cupboards full of clayware, and a Formica table that was well-worn but clean. There I sat for what felt like hours while she served me coffee, black and modesty, neat. Finally, at about three a.m., when the conversation had faded into repetition and longing glances could not be shorn away, I was granted entry to the vault. Her bedroom envied the quarters of a courtesan, with silk and lace adorning every corner and a strong aroma of roses that clung tenaciously to everything. There were no windows.

I sat on the edge of the bed and looked wonderingly and wantingly up at her. She sat down beside me and laid her hand atop mine. As her star-specked eyes wandered across my countenance, I reached out, cupped her face in my hands, and kissed her. My life has never been the same since.

Of course, the change would have been even more consummate if she had allowed the whole affair to continue to its natural end, but to my balking dismay, when the opportunity for such sublime pleasure arose, so did Bonnie Lee. As we lay together, partially clothed and still wrapped in one another's arms, she breathlessly explained that, unlike other aspects of her faith, one that she upheld most strongly was that of the sanctity of marriage.

"I was hoping that had gone with the dancing and gambling," I groaned.

She apologized and kissed me sweetly.

I knew all attempts to sway her would be futile as well as resented, so I didn't try. However, since she'd broached the subject, I decided to pose a question that had been weighing heavily on my mind, but that I'd kept to myself out of fear that she'd laugh at me when I asked.

"Bonnie Lee," I began, "By now, you are no stranger to the way I've lived my life. I ain't the most moral man or the most honest man. I ain't got family or friends to share. I ain't got a bank account or a home or a car or a business. Wandering and womanizing are some of the greatest pleasures I have ever known. At any other time in my life, I wouldn't have given them up for the world. But, Bonnie Lee, since the moment I first laid eyes on you, I haven't so much as looked at another woman. Now, if I had the whole world to give, I'd give it all to you. I love you, Bonnie Lee. Now that I know you, I don't think I could live without you, and I don't particularly want to try. I'm tired of living the way I always have. I've spent my whole life looking for the next best thing. I've finally found it, and it's you. I want to marry you, Bonnie Lee. I want you to be my wife."

She didn't laugh, but she didn't accept either. Instead, she plucked my proffered soul from where it hung in limbo between us and fed it back to me as gently as she could.

"Oh Jack..." she kissed me again, her voice raw with disappointment, "Jack...I wish I could. I truly wish I could. I want to believe that your intentions are good and honest, but I've been propositioned this way far more times than I even care to count. You've been good to me, and I've had more fun with you than I've had in a long time. I could love you too, Jack, but as a woman, I need to look out for my best interests. I am sure you understand and do not fault me for it...."

As if the whole evening had not become bittersweet enough, she kissed me again. There was nothing much I could really say. She was right on every count. But I was not so easily dissuaded. Never in my life had I begged anyone for anything, but that night I was so overcome with love and desire, so full of passion and lust, and so intoxicated by her overwhelming presence that I veritably begged her to marry me. To this day, I do not know what spurned its intensity. I think it must have been the roses.

I continued to profess my undying love to her without reservation and to no avail until, amid some romantic adjure, I told her that I wanted her to wear my mother's wedding ring. I'm not entirely sure if I had simply worn down her resistance or if such a statement truly did strike a changing chord within her, but to this request and this request alone, she responded—in typical Bonnie Lee fashion—telling me that if I produced the genuine article, she would very happily don it—and then she relegated me to the couch.

Thus began my search for the perfect ring to give to the woman who had unwittingly turned me into a home guard. I was well assured that if I were to procure an inauthentic version from anywhere on this side of the Mexican border, Bonnie Lee would undoubtedly find out about it, and all would be lost. Therefore, I decided to go out on a limb and hunt up Uncle John to see if I might be able to get the real McCoy.

The last contact I'd had with him was when I'd stopped by my old homestead shortly after I left McAlester. As a man whose habits were not unlike mine, I knew the chances of one of my letters reaching his hands were slim to none. Nevertheless, I made a valiant attempt. I wrote to

Leadville, Denver, Boulder, and just about every other city I could think of. All were returned unopened, their addressee unknown. Finally, after months of attempts and subsequent disappointment, I received a letter posted from Pagosa Springs, Colorado, addressed to John Sampson Jones Jr. It had been over ten years since I'd received a letter and longer yet since anyone had referred to me by my full Christian name. It read something like this:

Howdy Kid,

I figured you were still on the green side of the grass. Gave me one hell of a good laugh when I got your letter. As soon as I saw the Mexican postmark, I knew it had to be from you. Granted, I expected a confession when I opened it...that you had gone and held up a bank or a train and landed yourself in a whole heap of trouble. I surely didn't expect to hear that you'd landed yourself a woman...which is all well and good, but just about amounts to the same in the end. I expected you to ask for your Uncle John's help to get yourself out of Dutch...and here you go asking me to help you get yourself into a parcel of it. But that's Jack Jones for you, always doing the blame opposite of what anybody figures. I've never been such a fool myself, but I'll give you a hand in getting yourself hitched if that's what you want. You ain't gonna be using Delilah's marrying ring, though. That thing's been digging a notch in Billy's wife's finger for so many years the only way I'd be getting it is if I cut her finger plumb off. However, I can get a rock from a fence who owes me a favor. I'll send it along with a letter to show your little Spanish bride it's bona fide, seeing as you've winged yourself a smart one. And, now that you're settling down to family life, don't forget to write your old Uncle every so often. After all, you're going to need somebody to complain to. I'd close by telling you to keep out of trouble, but it'd be a waste of good ink.

Fare Thee Well,
John Cassidy

Uncle John kept his word. The goods were delivered as promised about a week later. He never elaborated on the nature of the favor owed him, but it must've been a whopper—for the stone was a whole carat set in a twenty-four-karat gold band. I presented it to Bonnie Lee in the same manner that every lovesick gentleman in history has offered up the fruit of his toil to receive his shackles—bent on one knee with my heart beating clear out of my chest and my upturned face simply pleading with inconcealable desperation. To my complete and utter shock, the inimitable Bonnie Lee, that most coveted pinnacle of womanhood, agreed to be this scoundrel's ever-loving wife. The rush I felt at the moment of her acceptance was only surpassed one other time. I was in seventh heaven. I was sitting on top of the world. I was as happy as a man could ever claim to be. I suggested we be married immediately, and that's when my elation plummeted. Apparently, I had grossly underestimated the depth of Bonnie Lee's moral obligations. Courthouse nuptials may have been sufficient for Rosalie McFall, but that was hardly the case for Bonnie. She insisted that we be married in the Catholic Church—which would not only require me to feign some degree of virtue, but I would also need to be baptized, communicated, and confirmed.

Bonnie Lee's vetting process for potential suitors was nothing if not effective. At no other time in my life would I have waited around the several months it took to jump through all the various hoops she presented; however, the power of love—or at least the idea of it—can compel a man to commit follies of character previously inconceivable. Needless to say, I went through with the whole ordeal. After spending nearly a year in the company of a self-proclaimed Satanist, lying to a priest was no trouble for me. Although, when I pledged to reject Satan, his works, and empty promises, I didn't actually feel like I was lying. Despite all the misdeeds of my earlier life, I had no intentions of conning or deceiving Bonnie Lee. The desires I had professed to her that evening in her bedroom were some of the purest truths that had ever left my tongue, and they ran deep.

Throughout the long and exhausting months of catechumen, rituals, prayers, and masses, I only needed to think of my sweet reward for this superfluity, and suddenly all was admissible. I couldn't help but remember the reformation my brother Robbie had undergone and how he'd beseeched me to abandon my devilish lot and embrace a pious life. I laughed heartily when I thought of him seeing his miscreant brother reciting holy incantations and going in for Sunday mass—and as a Catholic, no less!

I figured Uncle John would also enjoy envisaging such irony, so I wrote him a letter detailing the conversion process my undying love for Bonnie Lee had subjected me to. In his reply, he told me he'd nearly had to send for a doctor after he'd read my letter. Apparently, the idea of a dyed-in-the-wool sinner like me who had broken every one of the Ten

Commandments more times than could be counted sitting in a little wooden pew and beseeching olden day saints for salvation had caused him to laugh so hard that he hadn't been able to catch his breath for twenty minutes. We kept in close contact from then on.

Most of our communication consisted of catching up on the years since the last time we'd broken bread together. I remembered Rosalie to him, in addition to bits and pieces of my wanderings and the various kooks and oddities I had encountered along the road. He wrote back enthusiastically and often.

After a series of missives containing a general retelling of his last half-decade of mischief and debauchery, he finally got around to mentioning that Pa had died. I was hardly surprised. According to Uncle John, his alcoholic spiral had begun quick and fast after the death of my mother, but in 1930, when his back gave out and the union laid him off, he'd taken up moonshining full-time. He'd lasted out less than a year and then gone off west peaceably one Indian summer day. The patrimony had been willed to the eldest born. Phil didn't want it, Mick had settled in Connecticut, and Robbie had no use for it, so it fell to Billy—who sold off the land and distributed the profits amongst the four of them. Having been presumed long dead and otherwise undeserving, I saw no part of it.

Of the four, Billy was the only one who still remained in touch with Uncle John, although begrudgingly, it seemed. As far as the Jones progeny were concerned, all were living full and prosperous lives as productive members of society—all except me, living in Mexico, still on the lam, and hopelessly in love.

Uncle John seemed to have gotten into some degree of Dutch himself. He'd been run out of Leadville and was now 'on a retreat' along the San Juan River somewhere south of Pagosa Springs—which, in criminal argot, basically meant that he'd pissed off somebody dangerous and was laying low for a while. He informed me that his camp was so replete with fish and game that it could keep a man sated for a lifetime, but there wasn't a poker game or a beautiful woman for fifty miles. Although he was a terminal bachelor, Uncle John was quite jealous of the fortune I had found in Mexico. I didn't blame him. I'd be jealous of me too. Not only was I living in a tropical paradise unrivaled by any other locale I'd ever seen, I had Bonnie Lee by my side, and she did not disappoint.

As the months progressed and my devotion to her became increasingly apparent, her affections only grew. If she'd thought my intentions were ambiguous before, by the time we were finally married, there was not an earthquake in creation that could have shaken her convictions that I was totally and irrevocably earnest. And, after I'd gone through all the prerequisite motions to the satisfaction of the local *monseñor* and my bride-to-be, taken a dip in the baptismal font, washed down the wafers with a generous swig of sacramental wine and promised that I wouldn't be a bad boy anymore, we were finally allowed to tie the knot.

The wedding was an all-out, town-wide, days-long affair. The ceremony was held at the oldest and most revered cathedral in Guaymas. Seeing as Bonnie Lee's talent and charisma had made her something of a local celebrity, every last seat in the pews was taken. In addition to her friends from Chino, men from all over Sonora came to weep as one of the brothers who raised Bonnie Lee gave her away to me. I would've never thought I could have loved her any more than I already did, but as I stood before the altar and saw her coming down the aisle in her hand-sewn wedding dress and floor-grazing lace mantilla, I very nearly fell over. This was the woman I had sweated and studied for almost a year to have and hold, yet awe and disbelief were the prevailing emotions that day. I felt like I was truly dreaming—as if, at any moment, an ornery brakeman was going to throw a bucket of cold water on me and bring me back to my senses.

I recited the prayers I had memorized, uttered a very real and thankful one for my apparent run of good luck, donned the *lazos*, and knelt before the altar—all in strict accordance with time-honored tradition. In fact, I was a perfect gentleman at every stage. I needed to be, lest I be humiliated or usurped on my wedding day. I imagined the massive turnout was due partly to local curiosity as to what free-wheeling ruffian Bonnie Lee had gotten herself mixed up with, but if any of them were opposed to her choice of husband, they did not make it known. On the contrary, they showered us with rice and rose petals as we marched with the *callejoneada* to the banquet, where we were serenaded by a mariachi band and danced the night away. I danced more that night than I had in all my life—although this was mainly because all the women who wanted to dance with me pinned pesos on my *guayabera*. By the end of the evening, Bonnie Lee herself was so covered in notes that you could hardly see her wedding dress beneath them.

The fiesta went on for days, and at the end of it all, I got my woman. The night of our wedding was the very best of my entire life. For it was proven to me once and for all that some things are worth waiting for—and perhaps better for having done so. Bonnie Lee was not a stingy lover. In fact, she was, by all counts, skillful, generous, and endowed with such a desire to please that it shook me to my core.

Unlike most marriages that, once consummated, disintegrate shortly after, ours continued to carry on strong. That first year was unrivaled, and I have never known such love and contentment before or after. Immediately following our wedding, I moved out of the boarding house in Guaymas to Bonnie Lee's abode in Chino, and from that moment on, we were nearly inseparable. Chino became the center of my world, and in all truthfulness, there was nowhere else I would've rather been. It was a small, quiet, modest neighborhood bordered on one side by the bay and on the other by a nature preserve. Looking across the water, you could see the marina and port in the distance, punctuated by white sand beaches and crags of massive antediluvian rocks. It was populated mainly by native Mexicans, few of whom spoke fluent English, which was so common in the municipality as a whole, but they were a close-knit bunch and exceedingly friendly. There wasn't a week that went by that we didn't come home and find that one of our neighbors had left a tray of tamales or enchiladas on our kitchen counter for no reason other than that they were feeling generous.

Generosity was a fairly ubiquitous trait amongst the natives, and so was easy living. In the mornings, Bonnie Lee would bring meals to those detained in the calaboose, and I'd sleep until noon. When the sun was high, we'd go on walks through the shade of the palms, pick mangos and bananas right off the trees, and eat them then and there. We'd amble along the shoreline and wade in the surf, swimming and sunning ourselves to our heart's delight. I even bought a 16-foot river skiff in which we'd go on excursions around the peninsula and fish in the bay on days when the waves were calm. Come siesta time, Bonnie Lee could nearly always be found napping in the sun on the bow as I puttered around the harbor, casting my line for snappers and yellowtail. When the light of day began to wane and *Sol* commenced setting over the craggy hills of Guaymas, I'd bring the skiff to rest at its mooring. Hand-in-hand, we'd mingle with the merchants in port or venture into town to laugh away *hora feliz* in the cantinas and gamble in the halls until the six o'clock bell tolled in the spire of the old cathedral, and it was time for us to part ways for the evening.

The best part of all was that neither of us had to work. We both had jobs but got paid to do what we loved. I'd run the tables until closing time while she danced three shows a night. Around daybreak, we'd meet at the cantina and walk home in the morning dew that came to rest upon every inch of the land and set it all to sparkling in the new dawn's light like a transitive nightfall of diamonds. Most mornings, we stepped across the threshold just as that old bell tolled to signify the resurrection of the sun and the birth of a new and better day in paradise.

II

Those months ran along quick and endless. They were days that seemed as though they would last forever, but they have long since been memories to me now. That first year was heaven—but as I've come to learn so many times throughout my wretched life, heaven never lasts.

Shortly after our anniversary, Bonnie Lee—though just as sweet and gay as always—began to rag on me some. Novel phrases appeared in her vocabulary, and not-so-subtle suggestions were increasingly made—all of which revolved around me procuring a more respectable job.

I balked at the suggestion like a stallion at the mouth of the Grand Canyon. Seeing as this was the first time in my life that I'd held down a legitimate job for more than a week, I saw no reason why I should go about changing in any way. After all, the status quo greatly favored both of us. We'd never had to worry about a lack of funds, and our life together was nothing if not enjoyable. As far as I was concerned, we were thriving—but as inscrutable as it was to me at the time, whatever bug had crawled into Bonnie Lee's ear showed no signs of making a quiet exit anytime soon. Her reasoning revolved solely around the idea of children and what preparations should be made hitherto having them. She was never harsh or argumentative on the subject. Still, I scathingly objected, utterly buffaloed by the idea that one so practical, clear-thinking, and intelligent would rock the boat of what I had previously thought both of us considered to be a perfect life.

"Nobody is going to want to watch me dance when I'm the size of a hippopotamus," Bonnie Lee gently explained on one of our beach walks one otherwise idyllic afternoon. "And I can't keep my job and care for a child. I just want to ensure that we never end up living above our means. Besides, it's improper for a family man to work in a gambling hall."

"Bonnie Lee," I responded to her nudge with just about as much waning patience as I could muster, "My Ma had eight kids and never worked a job in her life. We never wanted for anything more than any other family did, and even all those years ago, living in Denver was still more costly than living in Chino could ever be. Right now, I can buy you anything you need and most of anything you don't with the commission I get from the faro layout. I'm not sure why you are dead set on spoiling an arrangement that could easily support a whole parcel of kids, let alone one."

My explanation left her undeterred. "If I'm going to have to rely on you to support me while I raise our family, it would make me far more comfortable if your earnings were just a little more consistent and honorable."

"Make no mistake about it; I can make my earnings as consistent as you want, but my methods sure ain't goin' to be honorable," I assured her.

Her piqued eyes glanced up at my exasperated ones, "Jack, I'm not asking you to cheat or steal; I just need you to cover my ante. I'm not asking you to quit cards and go into business or do something you hate. You could tend bar at the cantina, you could run a charter boat for the *turistas—*"

"Bonnie Lee," I cut her off abruptly, "if there is one thing I will never do in this life, it's waste my time making some other bastard rich."

"Just change how you think about it, Jack," she urged me, "Don't think about work as making *jefe* rich; think about it as taking care of your family."

"Bonnie Lee," I told her matter-of-factly, "if you want to see change in me, I'm going to have to swallow a handful of *centavos.*"

When she looked up at me, I turned away, so I did not have to see the disappointment I'd spurned dim her sparkling brown eyes.

In order to avoid this conversation or otherwise dull my annoyance when it inevitably arose, I began going down to the marina in the mornings while Bonnie Lee was busy with her appointed rounds at the jailhouse. More and more, I'd go out fishing with the fellows rather than lay about the beach with her, and come Sunday, when she was in church praying for my soul, I'd be drinking mezcal for breakfast at the cantina. And, as time went on, I became increasingly restive. After all, I didn't want to be mulling about the marina, fishing with the fellows, or getting sloshed on the

Sabbath—I wanted to be in my woman's arms, but my woman was being a nag.

Eventually, I managed to assuage her by agreeing to look for an inoffensive job opportunity, but I never lifted a finger to fulfill my promise. Instead, the time I told her I was out 'looking,' I spent drinking on the pier with the cooks and cabin boys of ships in quay and writing Uncle John to tell him about my troubles. The letters I received in response contained a fair deal of amusement concerning my predicament, which I had expected, and a proposition that came as a surprise.

"I told you you'd need a body to complain to," Uncle John wrote, *"You would've been better off robbing a bank. The old ball and chain are starting to chafe, huh? Should've listened to your uncle. Women ain't even worth their weight in salt once you put a ring on 'em. Marriage had to've been invented by a woman...there ain't never been a man born fool enough to think up the idea on his own...we're just stupid enough to let them convince us to go through with it. Women are only good for one thing, and marrying ain't it. Luckily for you, I know just how you can hustle up enough coin that your little woman will never utter another peep about your getting a job ever again. This one is a sure bet. Last week, this old scissorbill in town was flashing around a whole head of lettuce, and I persuaded him to tell me just where he got it. Cost me a whole afternoon and about a dozen drinks, but that'll amount to no more than a jit with how rich that conversation is gonna make me. You see, down in the Chihuahuan Desert along the Pecos River, there's a whole parcel of silver mines...and a few of them have turned out more gold than Sutter's Mill. According to this cat, about a century ago, they were some of the highest-producing silver mines in the southwest, but when the Mexican war broke out, their production was halted, and their location secreted. Years passed, men died, land changed hands, and some of the mines got 'lost.' Well, one of these mines has just been found. And I know where to find it. This old scissorbill said he's been prospecting forty blame years and ain't never seen the likes of this mine...said he rustled up more pay dirt in less than a year than he had in the forty before, then sold it off to a smelter for a small fortune. I'm telling you, Kid, it'll be the biggest payoff of our lives, and it won't even take that long. All you've got to do is come with me, and it's all yours for the taking. What do you say?"*

At first blush, all I said was 'no.' After all, the whole reason I didn't listen to Bonnie Lee's incessant pleading and get a more respectable job was because I was perfectly happy living the way I was. Even Uncle John's promise of the sun, moon, and stars wasn't enough for me to give up the riches I'd found in Chino—especially when Bonnie Lee was acting like the woman I'd married and not like the harpy that came and shanghaied her personality at least once a day. Besides, for a man who'd spent his whole life chasing rainbows, Uncle John was awfully confident about striking it rich on the touting of a drunk stranger.

However, as time went on and neither he nor Bonnie Lee let up, his offer got to working on me. For the first time since I'd laid eyes on my bride, I felt something crawl back into me. When I wrote Uncle John, telling him I was on my way, my decision was met with unprecedented excitement. The same could not be said for Bonnie Lee.

"Prospecting?" she repeated, very nearly aghast, "Sometimes I just don't understand you, Jack. I only suggested you find a day job to earn a little extra when I can't work, not travel hundreds of miles and break your back prospecting in the desert.

"Bonnie Lee," I replied, "If I'm going to work, I'm going to do so for a worthy reward. Nothing less. This way, we'll never have to worry about money again."

She was far from convinced. "I don't know about this uncle of yours. Why do you have to travel all the way up to Colorado just to turn right around and come back down south again? And how can you be sure he even knows where to find this mine if it's been lost for almost a hundred years? It just doesn't make sense."

"Oh, don't fret over it, Bonnie Lee," I assured her, "it's all part of the plan. Uncle John knows what he's doing; he's been at this game a long time."

"Game? What game?" she asked sullenly.

"Prospecting."

"I don't see why he'd still be at it if he was any good," she replied.

"Why, Uncle John's been rich at least four or five times—which is more than I can say for you or me."

"How can a man get rich four or five times if he doesn't get poor all those in-between times?" she countered, the look in her eyes evidence enough that she was already fully abreast of the answer.

"Uncle John's hit his fair share of hard luck and trouble, but who hasn't," I explained. "By golly, Bonnie Lee, this is the opportunity of a lifetime; it's far too good for me to pass up."

"Well, I sure hope it's that and not too good to be true. It's a long way from here to Colorado and back. That's a lot of time and a lot of places where you can get yourself in a whole lot of trouble, and I know you well enough, Jack, that even before you get the chance to go looking for trouble, it finds you."

"Trust me, Bonnie Lee, I ain't gonna be getting myself in no trouble. As soon as I've got that payoff in my pocket, I'm coming straight back down here to make you a life more beautiful than any you could ever dream of."

Bonnie Lee just crossed herself and held me tight.

A few days later, I arose at daybreak after spending the evening at home with my Love. Together, we walked into Guaymas, where I would catch the six o'clock bus to Chihuahua, the first leg of my journey north. By the time we reached the stop, our clothes were damp from the morning dew that rolled in like thick fog over the bay, and we huddled together in silence amidst a small, sleepy crowd of travelers waiting for the bus.

"I'll miss you," she whispered.

"I'll miss you too," I told her.

"How long will you be gone for?" she asked, a hint of nervousness in her voice.

"Baby, I promise you I'll be right back here before Christmas—and the next time you see me, you'll be married to a rich man."

"Jack," she murmured as she wrapped her bronze arms around my neck, "I don't care if you had not a peso to your name; I'd still love you just the same."

The bell in the cathedral struck a low, droning knoll to announce the time, and a flash of headlights illuminated the street as the large, hulking outline of a puttering omnibus emerged from over the crest of the hill.

"I love you too, Bonnie Lee," I replied, "don't miss me too much; I'll be back before you can say Jack Robinson."

She slid her hands into my hair and kissed me for a minute straight. If that kiss hadn't convinced me to stay, there was not a force in creation that could've.

As I turned to board, she cupped a Miraculous medal into my hand and told me "goodbye" and "fare thee well" in a voice that sounded more like she was pleading with me not to go.

I waved and waited until the bus pulled out of sight before letting the grin of raw excitement I'd been fighting for days crawl across my face.
As the bus bounced on its rotten shocks down winding clay roads that cross-cut the mountains of Guaymas, past fields of dew-dressed gladiolas that shimmered like a rainbow in the dawn's early light, after the last two years of idleness and predictability, I felt the thrill of wanderlust once more.

VI

Me & My Uncle

Traveling is a funny thing. I've never talked to a man bedding down in a freight car, stuffed into the ice hold of a reefer, bumming along the tracks, or waiting near a grade who told me he liked traveling this way. I don't reckon there's a fully sane man who rightly does, but I have talked to many men in freight cars and reefer holds and along the tracks who've stopped traveling—settled down—given it up. And if you ask them if that's so, how come they're there, they'll tell you they don't rightly know. For those on the Tramp Plan, the allure of the road has few bounds. However, I'll wager a significant sum that of those men who cannot resist the siren song of the road, few have ever traveled very far on a Mexican bus.

If there's anything besides Bonnie Lee's kiss that could've gotten me to turn tail and head back to Chino straight away, it was spending twenty-three hours on that godforsaken bus. First off, the driver was a complete and utter madman. He spent the entirety of the trip yammering away at the passengers in what sounded like one long sentence—not to mention the fact that he would avert his eyes from the road and turn around every so often to ensure that his fares were still interested in what he was saying. Moreover, most of the windows were stuck shut, which made the average temperature inside that bucking tin can on wheels no less than a hundred degrees with no breeze. The roads—if I am generous enough to call them that—were narrow, winding, and by no means in good driving condition. We careened around one-way mountain passes as we navigated what felt like every hair-raising peak and plunge in the Sierra Madres. If that death trap of a bus did have working brakes, we made it the 700 kilometers to our final destination without ever using them. Even when trails of smoke began seeping out from under the rusty hood, the driver remained absolutely unfazed and continued to plow down vertical inclines and through villages without any regard for signs, directionals, or oncoming traffic.

When I arrived in Chihuahua, the first thing I did was locate the freight yards of the Mexican Northwestern Railway and climb aboard an empty boxcar—entirely content to never lay eyes upon any other form of transportation again. It took twice as long as passenger rail, but in the interest of crossing the border unmolested, I remained in my side-door Pullman.

I arrived back on American soil in El Paso on July 3, 1938—just over two and a half years since I'd left in search of a new lease on my bastard life. The whole town was gearing up for the next day's patriotic celebrations as buntings and banners were hung across storefronts, and flags were draped over balcony railings, hoisted to full mast in all of their Old Glory. Busy sections of parade routes were cordoned off, and as night fell, you could hear crackling explosions courtesy of impatient children who had broken into the holiday supply of fireworks.

After a well-deserved evening's rest upon a down mattress in the plushest hotel I could find, I left under the guise of a dignified gentleman in a coach of the Rio Grande, El Paso, & Santa Fe amid the festivities. As the train chugged past, it felt like a grand reception, welcoming me back to the country of my nativity and a lurid fanfare sending me off upon the trail of all the wealth and fortune that would befall me during my brief return.

When I landed in Santa Fe later that day, I got off at the station and walked into the trackside Harvey House. After I'd ordered a cup of coffee and a sandwich, I asked the Harvey Girl for a newspaper, and she handed me a read and refolded copy from under the counter that had been left by a former traveler. Ironically, it was an Oklahoma paper, and I chuckled as I turned it open and read the headlines—most of which were just as dull and uninteresting as if I'd been sitting there with nothing to read. However, when I finally reached the front page, I just about spit my mouthful of coffee clean over the counter. Printed in big, bold letters across the banner were the following words:

LONGTIME TULSA COUNTY SHERRIFF DEAD AT 70

A photo of Sherriff Steele in all his pompous, paunched glory was featured below. I remembered the promise I'd made to that wretched rube from behind the iron bars of the Tulsa County Jail the night before my sentencing, and immediately, all my well-laid plans evaporated. I left the restaurant, made a beeline to the ticket office, and bought a fare on the Detroit Lightning to the crime scene of my former life.

I didn't much like the idea of traveling through Oklahoma, but I figured since nearly fifteen years had passed and I was well-dressed and unassuming, arriving by way of regular Pullman instead of the side-door variety, I should be safe. After all, my mortal enemy was pushing up daisies in the cemetery and, therefore, considerably less of a threat.

The express stopped in Tulsa at about ten o'clock on a clear and mild Tuesday morning. I got off at the depot, ran my hand through my sandy hair, and pulled my cap down over my eyes like in days of old. I walked the mile and a half to the cemetery where the newspaper had said he was interred and entered through the gates a vindicated man. With a clenched jaw and veins in my teeth, I bore forward, wishing to taste the blood of the man whose testimony against my character had sentenced me to a life of misery and horror.

The grave was not hard to find. It was covered by fresh earth, ornamented by flowers of every color, and marked by a wooden cross—the headstone yet to be carved. I stood upon it victorious, my free, Mexican leather-clad heels digging into the same dirt I had so hastily cast over the body of Shannon Todd on the bank of the Arkansas River all those long years ago.

Satisfied by how circumstances had turned in my favor, I gloated and cursed the man buried there, each utterance fouler than the one that preceded it, waiting and hoping to feel him turn in his grave. Once some time had passed and I'd yet to feel any tremor beneath my feet, I decided to make doubly sure that Sherriff Steele would not rest in peace until I, too, was dead.

"See you in hell, you rat bastard," I promised him.

As I was zipping up my fly, I looked over my shoulder and saw the tall, frail figure of a wisp-haired old coot heading toward me over the crest of the hill above. I immediately tensed up, nervous that he had witnessed my contribution to the offerings of grief and sympathy piled on the ground at my feet, but as he neared and I studied his furrowed countenance, a glimmer of familiarity struck me. He approached in silence, and together we stood facing the grave, neither providing any indication that we had met before.

"Shame, ain't it," I spoke, puncturing the eerie silence of the graveyard.

"Sure is, mighty powerful shame," Joe McDunlop agreed.

"He was a good man," I testified.

"Sure was," he replied.

"I heard he put a lot of bootleggers behind bars," I mused.

"Lot of killers, too."

We shared a glance and then went our separate ways.

"A killer and a lawman have the same number of enemies," Uncle John sagely observed as I recounted the episode to him after strolling self-satisfied into his camp on the banks of the San Juan River three days later. "You should consider yourself mighty lucky, Boy, for that could've been Bertha Steele walking down to the grave."

"You ain't wrong," I told him. "According to the paper, he was survived by his daughter, a son-in-law, and twelve grandchildren. Any suffering bastard who'd marry Bertha would have to be dumber than a bowl of wax fruit. Some legacy Steele ended up with—no wonder he kicked off."

"I'll bet you made it for that outbound train faster than a bloodhound after an escaped con," he mused with a humorous expression on his scruffy, whiskey-numbed face.

"Damn right. And I would've been here a whole day sooner if you'd picked me up in town like you said you would in your letter. These dogs weren't planning on a thirty-mile walk today," I remarked snidely as I rubbed my aching feet near the fire on that crisp mountain evening.

"I waited as long as I could," he explained, hardly apologetic, "but them town folk ain't exactly right fond of me. As soon as I start showing my face around longer than it takes to load up a truck full of provisions and get a haircut, the constable insists on escorting me back out again. Besides—thirty miles of ankleing it in this good mountain air ain't gon' hurt you none. I can see that tropical miasma you've been breathing's been anything but good for you. If you didn't have that yellow mop on your head, I'd say you're red enough to pass for an Indian."

"It sure don't bother me none," I replied to his disparaging remarks. "For a man who once almost froze to death in a snowdrift, I ain't got no qualms living anywhere the mercury never dips below seventy degrees. Hell, I ain't been this cold in years!" I griped, wrapping myself in the old, moth-eaten quilt he'd provided me.

"Boy, living the good life has certainly made you soft," he quipped. "You complain just as much as that old broad of yours."

"Ah, Bonnie Lee ain't all that bad," I rejoined, feeling yet another of those sharp pangs of loneliness that had become ever more frequent since I'd departed her company nigh on a week ago. "I don't know what's gotten into her lately, but she's the most easy-going and fun-loving girl I've ever met. If it wasn't for all that religion she's got, she'd be the perfect specimen of womanhood."

"Bah! There ain't no such thing," Uncle John assured me, "but at least you know she'll be true to ya. That's the only good religion ever does for a woman—keeps 'er faithful. There ain't gonna be no other mule kicking in your stall while you're out bucking the tiger."

"You're sure right on that account," I agreed, "and when I come walking home with more riches than she can wrap her pretty little head around, there ain't never going to be a disagreement betwixt us again."

"Here! Here!" Uncle John resounded, raising a glass of the worst rotgut whiskey ever shared between two men of taste.

I toasted with him and knocked it back. "As soon as we've got our gold, I gotta get you down to Mexico so I can show you what good drinking really is. I wouldn't even use this shit to clean the deck of my boat—as strong as it is, it'd likely eat clean through the hull and sink the blasted thing."

"Ah, I tole' you that you was gettin' soft," he replied, casting away his glass and upturning the unmarked bottle between his lips. I watched his grizzly Adam's apple dance as the unholy liquid poured down his throat and that mad glimmer of momentary satiety appeared in his coal-dark eyes.

He let out a long, satisfied sigh and then proffered me the bottle. I sighed with significantly less satisfaction and took it from his hand. "I've never missed Pa's gin more," I confessed. "I'd give my left nut for a supply of that elixir. This fortyrod ain't even half a step above dehorn—turn you into an alki-stiff real quick."

Uncle John snatched the bottle from me, drank his fill, and then emitted another satisfied grunt. "That's only true for home guards who can't handle the firewater of the road. You surprise me, Jack—I'm beginning to suspect both your nuts are back in Mexico—in the top drawer of Bonnie Lee's wardrobe!"

I scrambled to my knees and rehanded the bottle as it decanted its foul contents into his mouth, spilling some and consuming the rest. "Keep riding me, old man, and I'm going to come over there and put the screws and trimmings to you—ain't gonna be no question then who's more fit for fucking," I grumbled, throwing the empty bottle into the blaze that licked at the star-specked indigo sky.

Rather than return with an equally threatening remark, Uncle John slapped me across the back and guffawed so loudly that snow slid off the nearest mountain peak. "There's that good old mile-high Denver blood! A little anemic, but that woman ain't drained you yet! Now it's time to talk business—go get us another bottle!"

Reluctantly, I rose and retrieved another square-face from inside the rotting lean-to that Uncle John called home. After it was ceremonially opened and blessed, in a booming voice full of all the whitewashed grandeur of a shill, Uncle John hashed out for me the half-cocked plan by which we might acquire the payoff of a lifetime.

"They call the mine Beggar's Tomb," he declared, "and wrapped up all snug and warm in ten thousand years of lead and quartz is more gold and silver than we could find if we robbed one of these stinking holiday banks— and it's all ours. We'll rest up here for another few days, then drive down to Santa Fe. There, we'll sell the old Packard and get ourselves outfitted with a team of horses and drills and dynamite and ride on out south of Pecos. I know just what to look for. That old gab described the front yard of that mine with such detail I can see it now just like I was looking at a photograph. In just six months, I reckon we'll have more gold between us than we'll be able to carry back. I can just about pretty near taste it."

"You're fixing to go on horseback?" I asked with surprise.

"Well, certainly," Uncle John replied, "there ain't no passable roads out in that desert—there ain't a town around for nearly a hundred miles in some places. We'll just follow the Pecos River south from its headwaters below Santa Fe until we find our mine. Knowin' all I do about it, any man with both his eyes and half his brain wouldn't be able to miss it."

"How far south of Pecos do we have to travel?"

"The man said a two-days ride...so no further than thirty or fifty miles, I suppose."

"Thirty or fifty miles?" I repeated, stunned by how casually such magnitudes rolled off his silver tongue, "On horseback, in the middle of the desert, in the middle of summer? He didn't give you no landmarks a little more precise than that?"

"A horse ain't got no odometer, Kid!" he snapped, "Besides, all the good claims left in this country are out in the middle of nowhere. Everywhere else, the treasure's already been found, counted, and spent. Gold ain't just gonna jump up outta the ground at you already pressed into coins! You gotta put in some degree of work—but then you'll never have to work again."

I ruefully raised the square-face of caramel-colored liver poison and sourly toasted to never working again.

Uncle John joined in. "Chin up, Kid—it'll be the adventure of a lifetime! Can you imagine the excitement the first glittering gold dust will send pumping through you? If you need proper motivation to hoist that pick, dig that shovel, and sift that pan—that there'll do it. I remember the Klondike—when we struck the motherlode, men three days dead from hypothermia took up their tools and joined in the rush. The gold is as good as ours, Jack—there's just one thing—"

With Uncle John, there was always just one thing.

"He didn't tell me if Beggar's Tomb was two days south of Pecos, New Mexico, or Pecos, Texas."

"Oh, that insignificant triviality!" I replied dismissively, so drunk now that his negligence was nothing if not a laughing matter. "What's the difference between thirty and fifty miles and thirty and three hundred anyway!"

"That's the spirit!" Uncle John rallied, clapping me deafeningly across the back once more. "Makes no difference at all to men fixing to be millionaires! T'ain't no difference at all—thirty, fifty, three hun'red, five hun'red, three thousand, five thousand miles! Makes no difference! Hand over that bottle now, Kid—I can hear the Sandman ordering up last call."

I awoke the next day well after noon and so hungover I could do little more than lay in the lean-to and moan pitifully like a sick dog—the Panglossian glory of drunkenness faded to the retched recoils and aftershocks that men of our customs know all too well. The dappled sunshine that patterned the underbrush of the Colorado pines and leaked in through the sides of the lean-to appeared to me so bright it was as if I was standing on the cowcatcher and staring straight into the headlamp of a locomotive. The gentle trickle of the San Juan—a good twenty yards away— sounded no softer than if I'd been standing beneath Niagara Falls after a solid week of rain. And, the smell of the trout that Uncle John was frying up did little more to rouse my appetite than offering me a tall glass of dumpster juice in the middle of July.

"Rise and shine, Kid, or pretty soon, the moon'll be up before you are!" Uncle John bellowed.

He had clearly made a full recovery, and his reply to my mumbled retort that he and his whiskey should go to hell was that my only problem was that I had too much blood in my alcohol stream, and I'd feel fit as a fiddle as soon as I had some hair of the dog under my belt. I repeated my previous suggestion, and as soon as I was fit enough to drag myself to his old flivver and drive into town, the very first thing I bought was a sufficient supply of drinkable liquor.

That night, as we tucked into a supper of bacon and beans and cracked open that ever-ready elixir, our plans were rehashed and streamlined—sans the needling I'd been subjected to upon my arrival. The seriousness of our impending endeavor seemed to have sobered him some—as did the gin I'd brought back to camp. While his thirst may've grown over the years, his fondness for the Jones family favorite had not.

"To hell with going to blazes after blind leads and all the picking and shoveling and fire assays that come with ordinary prospecting—the hardest work has already been done!" His voice was wild with anticipation, "all the access shafts and adits were already carved by a mess of poor devils decades ago. All we gotta do is blast away where they left off and collect our bounty. Hell, even just sifting the tailings in the riverbed will bring us riches no man can resist! The processes in use before the war weren't nearly as thorough as they are today, and there's a great deal of gold-rich ore that's been cast back into the waters of fortune by miners too impatient to assure they'd squeezed each rock for all it was worth."

Uncle John's aspirations were indeed lofty—that was plain enough to see. However, owing mainly to stories of the vast profits he'd reaped during the Klondike years that I'd heard told throughout my childhood, in addition to his present confidence, I resigned myself to the assurance that ours would not be an entirely fruitless trip.

As we wiled away the evening and the contents of the bottle, Uncle John described to me in the minutest detail the precise location of the secreted mine. From his recitation, it appeared as if the old coot Uncle John befriended had not failed to recount the exact size, shape, and orientation of every boulder, clump of sagebrush, and blade of arid grass within a 100-

foot radius of the tunnel's mouth. Yet, even in the face of such sureness, a degree of suspicion lingered.

"Ain't there other veins in the area?" I finally asked, just about exhausting my knowledge of mining practices, "ain't it uncommon to find a blind lead all by itself?"

"Oh, it's a wildcat, alright, but she's already coming in solid," Uncle John assured me. "That old prospector told me right and well that he'd taken more out of it than he could carry on horseback."

I met his excitement with doubt. "Then why isn't he hurrying back down there himself to unearth some more of the riches he claims to have found?"

Uncle John met my narrowed eyes and smiled sinisterly, "What? And split the pot with us?"

The next day, we loaded all our remaining provisions into the trunk of the Packard, waved a hasty goodbye to the mountains of home, and aimed the car south toward the desert, our heads hot with gold fever. The drive took most of the day and was largely uneventful, aside from a flat tire. Uncle John suggested we hole up at a cheap adobe hotel for the night and rest up for the following day's excitement; however, in keeping with his uncanny ability to sniff out men with money to lose with greater accuracy than any gold digger alive, we soon found ourselves in the back room of the La Fonda Inn shooting dice with a couple of trail-weary cowpunchers.

It wasn't long before I discovered the real reason Uncle John had so doggedly insisted upon my accompanying him—money. In short, I had it, and he didn't—and whether I liked it or not, it appeared our resources had been pooled for the duration of our journey. I fronted him a c-note to buy into the crap game, and while he made good initially, as the lateness of the hour progressed, and drinks continued to flow, so did all of his winnings— right back into the pockets of the suckers he'd extracted them from. Once his funds were exhausted, mine were the next to go. I could see the writing on the wall and secreted about four hundred dollars about me, but even that did not last very long.

The next morning, I dipped into my reserves once more to pay for the room and a small collection of mining tools, whiskey, and sundries. Uncle John's contribution was the Packard, which went to a set of three old plugs he'd found advertised for sale in the classified section of a local farm journal. In reality, they were good for little more than glue, but looking at the glimmer of greed in Uncle John's expression when he learned the price he could get them for, you'd've thought he was beholding the finest thoroughbred horseflesh he'd ever laid his larcenous eyes upon.

Eager to get underway, we rigged up our three steeds and plodded twenty miles south to Pecos, New Mexico, and the banks of the river that held our fortune. We reached it just before sundown, and at my request, we camped that night just outside city limits. I knew that if I wanted to keep from going broke, I needed to keep Uncle John out of town, and while I anticipated some degree of protest, he was so transfixed by the idea of gold so near to our grasp that he didn't kick. And, while he would rather die than admit it, I could tell that twenty miles on horseback had sent quite a shock into his old bones.

As dawn broke the following day, we fought off the stiffness that had set in overnight, boiled up coffee and grits, roused our reluctant horses, and set out searching. It was immediately apparent that we were not the only souls on the gold trail in that vicinity. We never ran across any other prospectors, but their leavings were evidence enough. All throughout the hills of the Pecos could be found man-sized burrows a few feet deep where hopeful diggings had ceased shortly after they'd begun as the granite and limestone refused to yield anything of mineral worth. Along the wash, too, the remnants of gold fever lingered. Mesh-lined pans were discarded amidst heaps of tailings, ash piles littered with blackened cans and empty bottles dotted the banks, and bone-dry sluice boxes stood idly upon the shore—the fingerprints of speculation were everywhere.

We rode past these sites confidently, without little more than a second glance. For, the treasure trove we sought was far older, far better concealed, and far less likely to be so quickly abandoned. However, after three days of painstakingly combing over every outcrop, crevice, spur, hollow, bend, ledge, and grove for well over fifty miles, we grudgingly reached the unpleasant conclusion that our mine was south of Pecos, Texas—three hundred miles away.

Wearied by the thought of the trek ahead, with drawn faces and set jaws, we mounted our tired plugs and hobbled on. The days were hellish—you could fry an egg in the shade—but the evenings were positively glorious. I'd found myself out along some lonely tracts before, but never anywhere quite as far beyond the black stump as I did during that tour of west Texas on the back of a hack. About an hour after dusk, there was nothing to be seen except the inky black shadows of scrub hills and a wash of stars overhead. There were so many stars, in fact, that even on a moonless night, you could see nearly well enough to travel. Of course, Uncle John and I had our fill of that during the daylight hours and spent the evenings camped around a crackling fire made from scrounged scrub pine and pork fat. Akin to every old bum I ever shared a jug with in the jungles of days gone by, Uncle John's favorite pastime proved to be rehearsing lurid tales of his life from the moment he dismounted his horse and caught his breath until he slipped into whiskey slumber. Therefore, as well expected, Uncle John relayed a veritable chorus of his life throughout our journey—and I daresay his was even more dastardly than my own.

"I've swindled men in every manner a sucker has ever been taken," Uncle John boasted proudly one night. "Some of the rackets I pulled were just pure genius. I've sold snake oil wholesale, dealt marked cards from gaffed boxes, hawked fabricated tips at fixed races at just about every course in the country, borrowed dirty money from honest men under false pretenses, and played the shell game in every city from Seattle to St. Augustine and on north to Dawson City. I ain't never been the type of man who counts his winnings once they've been spent, but I wouldn't be a bit surprised if I've had over one million dollars to my name during my life."

"Of course, I ain't got that now," he admitted in a rare bout of modesty, "but then again, I ain't never thought highly of the man who collects a bounty only for his widow to toss about with her new beau after he's dead and buried. I'll be damned if I remember every dollar I stole and spent, but I can tell you the whole lump sum of 'em together made for one hell of a ride...." He reached out and roused the dying coals of the fire with a stick, "Lately, I've been thinking, Jack, that it's about time for me to retire. That's why I just couldn't resist this lead. It's about time I land me a fortune I can take the rest of my time spending."

I spat a mouthful of whiskey into the fire and scoffed, "What's an old man like you gonna do with a fortune, anyway?"

"If I'm lucky, spend all I can and still die rich," he replied.

We reached Carlsbad the next day by sunset. Food stores were replenished, the horses were stabled, real beds were slept in, and more dissipation was had. I wrote Bonnie Lee and told her about the grueling journey we'd endured, but reassured her that we were safe and well and near to our objective. To allay her natural suspicion, I took special care to describe the route we traversed and all the wonders we saw. I depicted the banks of the Pecos as being so rich with silver that the rocks along the banks shone—and told her how we passed these riches so selflessly surrendered by Mother Earth as if they were no more than worthless mica. I couldn't resist embellishing just a bit, but it was for good reason. I didn't want her to worry for even a moment that there was a possibility I would return home without the fabulous riches I'd promised her. And, needless to say, it was my every intention to deliver—but you know what they say about good intentions...

We crossed into Texas in the middle of a heatwave. Temperatures were well above 90° by eight in the morning, and by high noon it felt like we were subject to hell's sneak preview. The horses waded in the water most of the time, and the hotter it got, the more frequently Uncle John called for us to stop and rest. Shade cover was scarce, so whenever a suitable tree was reached, it was not bypassed. I suggested resting during the day and traveling by night, but Uncle John refused, citing the rocky bank as reason enough to keep the horses parked until morning. As a result, it took us three endless, sweltering days to reach Pecos.

When we finally arrived, we stowed our half-dead horses underneath a low bridge and trudged up the embankment to stand upon the steaming pavement. About a quarter mile in the distance was a lone roadside establishment. Hot, hungry, and most of all, parched, we hobbled, stiff-legged and sore, in its direction. I believe God's final act of charity toward me was making it a saloon.

It wasn't very large, and there were no windows, which did little for the temperature inside, but there was a back room where we could wash up, and the beer was ice cold—therefore making it just about as close to an oasis as we could hope to find. The bar was a walk-up manned by a teenage kid who wore a bolero hat and was likely a relation of the owner. Scattered around the rest of the small space were low, round tables—two of which were occupied by imbibers. Once we'd soaked ourselves in cool, clean water and tied our damp bandanas back around our necks, we ordered a round of beers and sat down at a table in the furthest corner of the room.

The table nearest us was full of half a dozen happy-hour ranch hands. They'd scared up a card game between them but stopped before they could get a deal going to speak to the pair of cowboys at the adjacent table. Any subject that could steal the attention of six tired, sweaty, dust-caked men away from drinking and losing their hard-earned money to one another had to be worthy of our interest, so Uncle John and I quaffed our first two beers and then sallied back up to the bar in order to hear their conversation.

The object of the ranchers' fascination was not the cowboys themselves but the things they carried. The two of them were young, no more than a few years older than the bartender himself. They dressed just as ruggedly as the rest of us, but their hair was meticulously combed, and their clothes showed no sign of recent work. The older of the two was twenty-five at most, dark-haired and quiet. His air was pensive and observant, and he had a visible uneasiness about him that suggested suspicion.

Meanwhile, his younger, tow-headed counterpart did all the talking—and with such a devil-may-care attitude that it made the greasy hearts of swindlers like us do somersaults at the sound of it. They shared enough features for me to automatically assume they were brothers. This point was near-immediately proven correct when the loquacious one extended his hand out to the neighboring table and explained to his curious listeners where he had procured the twenty-dollar gold piece it contained.

"Our grandfather willed 'em to Pop," he spoke casually. "He worked in the mint during the war between the states when most gold coins were melted down or sent to Europe. They're 1862 double eagles—uncirculated and mighty rare. He saved all he could. Pop got 'em when our grandfather passed, buried 'em when Roosevelt woulda confiscated 'em, and now Pop left 'em to us. My brother Pauly found a collector in Pasadena who said he'd pay two thousand dollars per coin; that's how rare these babies are! We've been working as drovers since we've been knee-high to a grasshopper—seldom home—and Ma is getting up in years. We're gonna take the money, buy a ranch and a few hundred head, and make something of ourselves."

Among the oohs and ahhs of congratulatory amazement that escaped the open mouths of the ranchhands came the booming voice of Uncle John.

"So you've given up the saddle and the lasso for the back porch and the Harvest Dance, eh? Bet'cher grandpappy would'a never'a thought he shoulda' done struck two more zeros on them there coins before he shoveled the earth over 'em for seventy-odd years, eh boys? Golly, that's a mighty lucky break!" he exclaimed in a Texan drawl so convincing that I needed to turn around to ensure it was actually my uncle doing the talking.

As usual, he was, and everybody in the room commenced listening. "Do you mind lettin' me have a closer look at that there, Sonny?" Uncle John asked with just about as much cloying politeness as I could stomach.

The young yokel dropped the shiny gold coin into Uncle John's grubby hand without a second thought.

"Why! Ain't that a pearl button bangled billy!" he exclaimed, holding it up to the light. "I thank ye kindly, Boy," he went on, fingering the piece with admiration, "It ain't too often I get to see somethin' older than me! You say you've got a number of these coins, ain't you?"

"Why sure, Mister," he cheerfully replied, "we've got lots of 'em. Why I'd reckon we ain't got less than—"

"Luca!" his brother snapped, slamming his empty pint onto the table, *"Parli troppo. Bevi e statti zitto!"*

The former ducked his head and collected his precious coin from Uncle John's palm.

The conversation immediately dropped from the subject of inherited wealth and turned instead to manufactured wealth. The ranchers returned to their game, and Uncle John asked if they'd deal us in. They consented, and Uncle John turned to the loaded drovers and invited them to join— citing the well-known fact that it's far more fun to win money than simply watch others do so. Luca, the younger of the two, eagerly joined, while Pauly, his elder, did so reluctantly.

The game of choice was Pitch—or High Low Jack, as it was known to us in the mountains. We were all familiar with it, and every man played for himself. We each put up a buck a round and played until ten points were reached—winner take all. There was never a pot over $100, and Uncle John and I played a square game—other than forfeiting points to one or another of the cowboys when they were markedly ahead.

Uncle John and I needed only to share a glance to agree upon a proper method of sheering these two. We knew they were out-of-towners planning on spending the night in Pecos—and just so long as we could keep them there, we had pretty good odds of coming into some of their patrimony. With Luca's unbridled enthusiasm and his brother's cautious frugality, it was no challenge to maintain their rapt attention—and as the lack of other patrons suggested, there were few men searching for thrills that night in Pecos. Their gold—or at least a portion of it—was as good as ours.

An hour or so into the game, the ranchers began filtering out. After the final lingerer's wife phoned the bar at half past eight, the two cowboys, Uncle John and myself were the only players that remained at the table. It was at this point that the rules of the game changed. Uncle John called for a round of shots to be brought out to us and suggested that we play doubles now that there were only four of us left. I choked down the whiskey and applauded his suggestion. Our darling Luca voiced his agreement, and Pauly was overruled with a moue.

The ante was gradually raised from a buck to five and ten and finally to twenty. The brothers, who had been winning right along, put up their money without kicking. Even the ever-vigilant Pauly got comfortable sliding his big bills across the table as the drinks continued to rack up on Uncle John's tab and the dangerous combination of luck and a good time got to working on him. Luca won the first game at $20 ante, and then the worm turned. From that point onward, neither brother won another cent. Some of the games were nail-biting close, but the revolving queue of trump aces, jacks, and twos in my and Uncle John's sleeves ensured that we remained the victors. In little more than an hour after the ranchers had departed, the cowboys had not only lost all that they'd won but emptied their purses as well. Uncle John and I were ahead by about twenty-two hundred dollars.

An amateur swindler would have sunk his teeth into Luca alone and swept Pauly aside as a lost cause. However, men like Uncle John and I, who'd been around enough blocks to see what parsimony can do to an otherwise rational individual, knew well enough to grant Pauly the dubious honor of being the unfortunate subject of our finest hour. Luca was far too high on whiskey and visions of grandeur to be any too concerned with the loss at hand. But, the nervous gulp and expression of shock that accompanied Pauly's final shuffle of greenbacks across the table were evidence enough to Uncle John and me that we had him—hook, line, and sinker.

In fact, when Uncle John magnanimously offered to put up the whole twenty-two hundred dollars the boys had lost if they put up just one of their prized $20 gold pieces, Pauly was the first to reach into his pocket. He was also the first to glower when I swept it across the table along with the game point. And, after the hopes spurned by the first two rounds of 'double or nothing' were met and dashed, both boys began to panic.

"Not to worry," Uncle John responded calmly after the boys had lost their fifth and final double eagle, "don't even bother puttin' up this next round—we know y'all are good for it. After all, it's about time Lady Luck smiles upon you again."

Uncle John's willingness to allow the boys a chance to win back their precious grubstake had its intended effect. They played as astutely as they had been, but as Uncle John and I knew well, Lady Luck had left the building. They missed their bid of four and lost by two points—as the trump jack had failed to make the deal. Unbeknownst to them, that was because it had spent that last round nestled snugly under Uncle John's cuff with the other three.

As soon as the points were counted, the tensions that had begun to build between the brothers during the last few hours boiled over entirely. In a fit of rage, Pauly stood up, knocked over his chair, and began berating his brother, who'd overbid, with a series of unintelligible but stinging foreign insults. Luca cringed in embarrassment and then issued back a few of his own digs in order to salvage a degree of his pride.

Uncle John—in his suavest wolf-in-sheep's-clothing manner—played peacemaker. Cooly, he wrote out an IOU on the scoresheet and offered to put up for another game with no ante if the brothers agreed to bet more moderately.

Beet red and trembling as he attempted to regain his composure, Pauly refused and, as he righted his chair, sent his brother out to their car to fetch enough gold double eagles to see our bet.

With the excuse of getting some air, I followed Luca outside into the hazy dusk and watched as honor led an honest man into the court of fools once more.

Sweating, Luca reached into the backseat, rooted around for a minute or two, then slipped the objects he had been searching for into his pants pocket. However, even in the darkness and with his attempt at concealment, I could clearly see that he'd retrieved something that made for a heavier bet than any number of his gold coins. Flustered, he hurried back to the door, which I held open for him with a smile—and before I walked back in myself, I pulled up my pant leg, unholstered my pistol, and tucked it into my belt.

When I reached the table, the gold double-eagles were produced from Luca's pocket and placed gravely beside our standing bet. Uncle John ordered another round of shots to break the tension and soothe everyone's nerves, but by that time, we were all far too whiskey-soaked to exhibit any degree of calm.

Glasses were emptied, cards were cut, and Uncle John dealt the first round. Save for both brothers' ragged and heavy breathing, the game was played in complete silence. And it was a close one. As points were tallied for the last round, which proved victorious for our camp once more, Uncle

John got sloppy, and the suspicious Pauly caught a glimpse of an unused hole card peeking out from Uncle John's cuff.

"He's cheating!" Pauly roared, knocking glasses and cards from table to floor as he pinned down Uncle John's arm with one hand and reached for his pistol with the other.

Uncle John began to protest, but it was all over. Acting on instinct alone, I drew my gun from my belt, aimed at Pauly, and fired blind. With a yell, he released Uncle John and dropped to the floor. Wild-eyed and horrified, Luca shakily drew the pistol he had retrieved from the car—his worst play of the night. He never had a chance. Another blast of gunfire met him, and he followed the same route to the floor as his older brother.

I spun around and met the haggard eyes of Uncle John—who seemed to realize immediately how close he'd come to sharing their fate—and then both of us turned to face the bar. The young bartender, who up until that point had proved to be little more than an apparition flitting around and tidying up as he whistled quietly to himself, threw up his hands in horror and backed away in the direction of the wall phone, his eyes so wide they could've passed as saucers.

This time, Uncle John unholstered his gun, leveled it, and fired point blank. The bartender crumpled atop the sink.

For a shock-laden moment that felt like eternity, Uncle John and I stood in silence and surveyed the carnage, surrounded by blood and gold. He roused himself before I did, swept the contents of the table into his pockets, and then reached down toward the dead men on the floor, intent on emptying theirs.

"Wait. Don't touch them." I commanded.

Uncle John stopped and glared at me in protest.

"Let me do it," I explained tersely, "I have no fingerprints."

Hurriedly, I fished through their trousers and transferred all the gold pieces into my own. I then took Uncle John's pistol, wiped it clean, and placed it near Pauly's outstretched hand. I retrieved Pauly's gun from where it had landed under the table and handed it to Uncle John. I traded my own gun for Luca's and placed it on the floor beside the bartender. Once I ensured that we hadn't stepped in any blood and left nothing else behind, we rushed toward the back door and down the hill to the cowboys' car.

Upon glancing through the back window, I could see a collection of canvas pokes in disarray, all bulging full of rare and valuable coins. Amidst the raging panic, a flash of greedy excitement coursed through me. I climbed into the car and jammed the key into the ignition.

"Get in!" I hissed to Uncle John, who had pulled open the back door and hoisted the heavy bags into his arms.

"What the hell are you talking about, Kid!?" He spat, "Grab that goddamn gold and get back to your horse!"

"Are you bughouse?" I countered, dumbfounded, "Fuck the horses; get in the car!"

"Jack, you half-witted numbskull—I ain't gonna be caught dead in a dead man's car! Now grab those bags and follow me!"

I could've pulled away and left him standing there in the dust with half the gold, but in the interest of getting out clean, I exited the car, hefted the heavy satchels upon my shoulders, and struggled down the ravine to the banks of the Pecos where our horses snuffed and pawed, blissfully unaware of the burden they would shortly bear.

If you surveyed every criminal in history, they'd all agree on one point. When under the weight of unbearable pressure, the human form simply reacts for the sake of preservation and preservation alone—no matter the cost. We couldn't afford to spend another second arguing on the roadside, so I followed him. I knew better, but I followed him.

The horses protested as we stowed our plunder in our saddlebags, clumsily mounted them, and drove our spur-shod heels into their sides. They were off with a start through the shallow water and up the bank where, once they got on solid ground, we made them run west out of town for all they were worth. The sky was cloudless and we had half a moon, which made for surer horses and better time—but at that moment, we had absolutely no plan beyond getting as far as we could from Pecos as fast as possible.

We finally stopped a few hours before dawn. I would've kept pushing until my horse collapsed beneath me, but the pace was far too great for Uncle John, whose pitiful pleas to rest droned on for at least an hour before I finally halted. I watched stoically as he eased his horse to a stop, then emitted a chorus of grunts and groans as he heaved his rheumatic leg over the horse's sweaty back and slowly dismounted.

"Don't ever get old, Jack; you'll never forgive yourself," he cautioned me as he tottered knock-kneed over to a fence, which he leaned upon.

"Ain't got no intention of getting as old as you, old fool," I informed him. "But I do have every intention of staying out of prison. If we'd taken that car, we'd be out of Texas already," I lamented.

"Ah, quit yer damn bellyaching about that car," Uncle John growled in reply. "Ain't no filling stations open this time of night."

"No, there ain't, but they had nearly a full tank. We would've made it a hell of a lot farther than we're at now, and there would've been no way of knowing which way we went. As it is, we've been leaving a trail clear enough for a blind man to follow!"

Uncle John put the kibosh on my paranoia. "Oh, there ain't a detective alive who'll think to go down to that riverbank! It's obvious what happened—those two boys lost all their money playing cards and couldn't pay their tab. The bartender was a mite ornery—guns were flashed about—then one or another pulled the trigger. They shot each other—that's plenty clear from the way you left it."

"A smart dick ain't gonna leave it at that, believe me. Maybe we don't get the rap for murder, but as soon as John Law has a conversation with the mother of those boys and finds out about the four sacks of gold coins they left home with that have now disappeared, they're going to be looking for somebody—and those ranchers can place both us and those coins at the scene. We've got to get these things to a buyer or a fence as fast as possible— or stash 'em in a safe deposit box and wait until the trail goes cold."

"All the more reason to stay on horseback," Uncle John insisted, "sure ain't as comfortable as a Cadillac, but far safer—nobody'd look for us out here."

"Unless one of those ranchers happened to be a little more observant and remembers that we didn't arrive by car—that we walked to the bar in riding clothes and washed up before we sat down."

"Boy, Kid, are you one nervous Nellie," he berated me, "I know a fence in San Francisco who'll pay at least a G-note each for these coins. We'll have them off our hands soon enough."

"In San Francisco?" I echoed indignantly, "I suppose you plan on riding these miserable nags all the way up the pacific coast?"

"Of course not," he bit back, "only until we cross the border into California. The way things are, I ain't driving through no checkpoints with out-of-state plates."

"Do you know how many miles it is from here to California? What kind of country we have to go through? How many towns we'll need to stop in?

We'd be better off melting them coins down, whacking 'em into bars, and selling 'em off down here in Texas."

If looks could kill, I would've dropped dead right there. "You want to melt them down?! Two-thousand dollar-a-piece uncirculated mint-condition pre-war double eagles?! By god, Jack, I'd melt you down before I destroyed one of them!"

I turned my back on him in disgust, "I can tell you right now you're going to love prison."

"If you ain't got the balls to come with me, I suggest you hand over your half and leave now. I'll meet you in Reno."

"Oh, I've got 'em alright, and they're big and brass," I retorted. "I've also got brains—brains enough to know what you're saying is just plain daft!"

"Brains?!" Uncle John exclaimed, "Brains?! Need I remind you, Kid, which one of us has a prison cell all nicely done up and waiting for him in Oklahoma?"

"You'd never make it all the way to California alone. Hell, I ain't even sure you're gonna make it another hundred miles the way you wheeze and cough and carry on. I'll be damned if you think I'm gonna leave you to die out here and let some rancher get rich off your corpse. *I* killed those two cowboys—you would've been lying dead instead of them if it wasn't for me. By rights, all that gold is mine."

Uncle John stood up from the fence and stepped into me until his potbelly alone closed the distance between us. "You'll have to kill me too if you want my share," he snarled.

My hand started for my gun, then I stopped and stared at him through narrowed eyes until the rage subsided. "You'd best get back on your mount," I cautioned him, "or I'm leaving you here."

"If I were you," Uncle John answered in a voice so cool, calm, and serious it was like the smooth edge of a steel blade, "I'd think twice before turning your back to me."

I froze.

His point firmly made, Uncle John stepped away and pulled a sack of smoking and a book of papers from his pocket. While my blood still pounded in my ears, I watched as he slowly and deliberately extracted a paper, filled it with tobacco, rolled with precision, and licked it up. He handed it to me, then began rolling his own.

"Take a load off, Jack. Have a smoke. Quit your worrying for a while."

I remained motionless and stared at him, quite uncertain of his next move.

"Only a few hours have passed. It was near to closing when we left that bar. Odds are, nobody has discovered the bodies yet. And, when they do, by the time the initial hue and cry is up and over, it'll likely be days before anybody finds out about the gold. By then, we'll already have a head start." He paused to take a long drag on his cigarette. "Now, can I guarantee beyond a shadow of a doubt that nobody saw us, that nobody came into the bar just a few minutes after we left and is following us right now? No, I can't. But, if they are, we have guns and bullets, and we'll go down fighting—" he was interrupted by a coughing fit and another draw, "But you know what I can guarantee, Jack? Look at that horse over there. If you keep pushing him the way you did tonight, he's going to go lame—or his heart will explode. And when it does, what are you going to do? It's mighty hard, Jack, to run carrying the weight of gold."

I looked down at the red orb that glowed on the end of my cigarette, "It ain't that easy with a chest full of lead, neither," I muttered under my breath, too low for him to hear.

"Now, I'm an old man," he continued, stating the obvious, "and I didn't make it this far through good clean livin'. I've taken my chances many a time—far more than I can recall—far more than you ever have. And pretty near every time, I got away clean; and when I didn't, they never hit me with anything that stuck. I've been around, Jack, and I know how to play this out. We ain't got no other options—no other good ones, that is—and if you're in this for the whole haul, you're gonna call every bet I lay down— understood?"

I listened to the horses snort beside me and remained silent.

"At the very least, we've got to cut that pack horse loose," I finally replied, "Ain't no need to be lugging around all those tools and materials—and guiding him slows us down."

"See, now you're thinking," Uncle John lauded me. "After all, we've already got our gold mine."

The first few days were agonizing. I wanted to crawl out of my skin at every turn, terrified whenever a town materialized on the horizon that news of the crime had traveled faster than we had. I was no longer afraid of returning to prison for the murder I'd been convicted of—now, I was afraid of frying in the electric chair for the killing of two more. And, with Uncle

John leading our charge, I felt all but helpless. We no longer had the Pecos or a definite route to follow—not a highway, tracks, or even a herd trail. At the mad insistence of Uncle John, we just looked down at our compasses and headed dead west.

We reached the outskirts of El Paso three days later. We were nearly out of food and needed ammunition that matched the caliber of the cowboys' pistols. Considering how nervy I was already, I regarded El Paso as anything but a good omen—as the part of the city I knew most thoroughly was its jail—but Uncle John wanted no part of my misgivings. Rather, he made me hand over my share of the gold and sent me into town while he spent the day circumventing it and met me in New Mexico.

As a halfway rational individual, this move—like all that preceded it—was utterly unintelligible to me. I would've gladly taken my chances crossing the border into Mexico rather than remaining on American soil with our plunder. But citing fears of the Federales and general unfamiliarity with the terrain, Uncle John immediately refused this suggestion.

I relaxed some once we were out of Texas, but at no point did the hair on the back of my neck cease standing on end, nor was I able to sleep for more than fifteen minutes at a clip. As any worried man faced with seemingly endless uncertainty knows well, such a combination of time and fear gets to working on you and working on you fast. I did everything but flat-out beg Uncle John to turn his horse south and head to Mexico. I cursed, I threatened, I yelled—but he remained unfazed.

"If you ain't got nothing new to say, don't waste your breath!" Uncle John bellowed as he trailed behind me. "You're worse than the sun, the heat, and the dust all rolled into one!"

I kept it up for a few more days and then quit talking entirely, having gone silent with resentment.

Upon crossing the Rio Grande, the landscape was more of the same flat, featureless wasteland we'd been traversing for the last week, but one day into New Mexico, we began to hit some hills—at which point our pace dropped substantially. By the time we reached the town of Hachita—over one hundred miles from El Paso—we had slowed to a crawl.

Hachita consisted of little more than a water tower and a general store; therefore, we did not feel compelled to avoid it entirely—as there was no law beyond the common, and we appeared to outnumber the citizens present at any given time. Once we'd considerably lessened the store's inventory of beans, jerky, coffee, whiskey, and salt licks, we rode out of town and made camp about a half hour west, just over a rise that hid us from the nearest road. Contrary to my every exhortation, we remained there a whole day. There was reasonable shade, a muddy rivulet that gurgled through the rocks, and enough scrub and greenery to refuel the horses for another push west.

Uncle John took the opportunity to sleep well, eat hardy, boil up his clothes, and empty the satchels to count the coins. In total, we had 135 polished gold coins—all of them refugees from FDR and the smelter. At face value alone, we had $2,700—but if what the boys had told us was true, their actual worth was nearly one hundred times that.

"Dirty money is always dirty money," Uncle John mused as he poured handfuls of the coins back into their pokes. "Take those two cowboys— their grandfather weaseled these coins away from Uncle Sam, and we weaseled the coins away from them. Gold makes men crazy. Don't matter how young or old, civilized or not. They weren't particularly dumb kids— at least one of 'em wasn't. They likely would've made it to their destination and bought that ranch if we hadn't come along. They should've cut their losses early, packed up, and gone back to their hotel, but they were too green to know better. They didn't know when to say die—made us say it for 'em." He leaned back on his calloused elbows in the sand and examined one last coin a long time before adding it back with the rest. "All of life is loaded, Jack. All our cards are marked from the start. You can't win always playing a straight game—gotta use every advantage you have. And, if some blame good opportunity falls into your hands, you're a blame fool not to take it."

"Plato speaks," I grumbled, rightly agreeing with him but wishing to hear no more on the subject.

Uncle John reached for his bottle, and I stood restlessly and went to scout the area. The sun was quickly setting, and from where I stood atop the ridge, looking back toward the east, I could see the dark figure of a horse and rider vaguely outlined against the sky, about five miles distant. Uneasily, I watched him pick his way across the horizon. After he dropped into a valley and disappeared from sight, I returned to camp.

Uncle John was asleep when I got back. I dug my boot into his gut.

"Wake up," I spoke ominously, "we've got company."

"This whole country is crawling with drovers and ranchers and cowhands," he replied after I explained what I'd seen, "Better pull down your hat, Kid, you've been out in the sun too long—I think you're starting to develop a leak in your attic."

Despite his flippant dismissal, he consented to packing up and moving on before morning, at which time we found ourselves about ten miles west of Animas on the Arizona border. While Uncle John stopped to catch his breath for the dozenth time since our departure, I hiked to the peak of a spindly scrub hill and looked east. My eyes instantly froze as I scanned the horizon, and my blood ran colder than the Kenai River. In the distance, just about as far away as I'd last seen him, was that horse and rider. I nearly tumbled down the rocky slope in panic.

"He's still out there," I gravely informed my uncle, "you'd better shake your tail." —Then I rode on without waiting for him.

As we continued our grueling trek through the plains and canyons of Arizona, despite my all-consuming fear, Uncle John demanded we stop and rest no less frequently. Whenever we did, I found a nearby ridge or escarpment and kept a sharp lookout for our pursuer. To my increasing dismay, he was nearly always there.

"He's got to be a Texas Ranger," I told Uncle John apprehensively, "he's been with us for days now."

"I suppose you can see his badge from here," he replied dryly as he adjusted the straps on his saddlebags.

By the time we passed Benson, Arizona, sleep eluded me entirely. I spent our stops camped out at the highest point I could find and was allowed no respite from my dread. My dissent continued to be unwelcome, and I was often reminded which of the two of us had been awarded a life sentence for the sum of his errors.

We reached the border of Pima County two mornings later. The horses were running on fumes, and so were we, subsisting solely on cigarettes and coffee. It was at this point that I gave Uncle John an ultimatum. Either we stopped in Tucson and stashed the gold or pushed straight on to Mexico as hard and fast as possible.

At long last, he yielded to my urgency and chose the latter. However, hard and fast lasted only until nightfall.

"I can't, Kid. Gotta rest the night," he called in a series of haggard gasps from behind me.

I rallied the sum of my humanity and relented. We were a few yards from a desolate road in a canyon just south of Tucson, the heart of cattle country.

As the sun set, while the horses rooted around the saguaros and Uncle John boiled up our coffee over a fire, I smoked the last of our cigarettes and worried. Before we'd descended from the top of the ridge, I'd caught a glimpse of a man and his mount no more than four miles distant. If he kept his pace, he'd be upon us by first light.

I laid upon my bedroll that night, staring up at the indigo sky with eyes so wide they ached. My heart pounded so hard I could just about hear it echoing off the canyon walls like a jackhammer—and I had no doubt that our pursuer—whoever he was—would hear it too. Assuming, of course, it was audible at that distance over the sound of Uncle John's incessant snoring.

Preparing for battle and unable to rest, by the dim glow of the dying fire, I broke down the pistol I'd retrieved from the body of the man I'd killed and cleaned it meticulously and repeatedly. The evening was balmy and warm, pleasant even without a shirt on, and Uncle John slept soundly. I, however, was quaking—my whole body engulfed in an interminable series of tremors that lasted throughout that miserable night. My mind was consumed by the events of that Texas barroom, and I remembered something my uncle told me when I was just a boy. I could hear his voice just as audibly as if he was sitting up next to me, just as clearly as I had the first time.

"Jackie-boy," he'd cautioned me, "don't you ever look a dying man in the eye, especially if your bullet is the cause of it. You see, a dying man has got more power in 'em than a regular ol' man. A dying man will do just about anything to keep on living, including sell his soul."

"That's right," he'd assured my wide-eyed, attentive, twelve-year-old self, "once the devil's got his due, a dying man can steal the soul of a living man right out through his eyes. Oh, he'll die yet, but he won't go alone. The man who met his eyes will be the next to go—his luck will run out first, then his life."

I'd always respected my uncle more than I'd ever respected any other man, and I'll be goldarned if I didn't take his advice. It was mighty good advice, too—in fact, my Uncle John was just about the only earthly man that I ever listened to at all, and there isn't one thing that he ever said to me that I didn't take to heart. In the case of the three men I'd sent shuffling off to the docks of Charon's ferry, my eyes had never so much as glanced upon their faces, let alone peered into the windows of their souls. In such a way, I felt that I'd perhaps evaded the grasp of what some men might call fate.

Dead men had no claim on my soul. It was those still living who were keen to bury me.

The first weak strains of morning light seeped through cracks in the clouds at about five o'clock. Uncle John roused himself with a wheeze and a snort, then commenced groaning about the sorry state of his aching bones. I glanced up silently from where I was sliding the clip back into the gun and listened to him grouse.

"We have to go. Now." I spoke.

Uncle John huffed and puffed himself to his feet, stretched some, then slowly eased himself back down to his bedroll.

"Can't, Kid," he answered. "Get a fire going. Boil some coffee. This old body ain't ready to move quite yet."

Obediently, I laid the pistol down on a rock, rose from the blankets where I'd conducted my evening vigil, and took hold of the coffee pot. I decanted its contents into an empty can and handed it to Uncle John.

"Cold coffee?" he remarked with surprise. "Ah, well. Been good enough for every bum before; it'll be good enough for me now."

I returned to my blankets and wrapped them up as tightly as possible, then proceeded to fasten them to the saddle of my horse, which shifted uncomfortably under the weight of the gold in her saddlebags. I untied my uncle's horse from the willow tree that had been his stable for the night and then returned to Uncle John. He was still sprawled upon his bedroll, sipping cold coffee with his back to me.

I leaned down to retrieve the dead cowboy's pistol, then cocked, aimed, and fired one shot. Spooked, his horse ran for the hills, and mine struggled against the branches of the willow that held her captive. As it turns out, in the end, that old man did die rich—with one bag of gold in his disbelieving hand and one sitting beside him in the dust. I stood there a moment and watched in silence as all his good mile-high Denver blood pooled in the dry desert silt, then grabbed those two bags of gold, mounted my nag, and took off up the canyon at full gallop. I never looked back.

Uncle John had been right, though. I whipped and goaded that horse for all she had in her, and she only lasted out one more day. I stopped only for water and made it nearly fifty miles by the following dawn. By that time, however, my horse had folded up completely and could barely hobble at a steady pace. I'd created significant distance between myself and Tucson, but with a lame horse, I was about as good as dead.

I followed the fence line until I came to a small, decrepit barn, outside of which was a pig pen occupied by a few filthy hogs. The barn door was ajar, but whoever was responsible for its condition was not inside. However, a fresh horse was. A second thought never entered my mind. I led my own sweat-soaked, dirt-caked animal into the stall, threw my saddle on the docile chestnut mare that originally occupied it, and was out of there within minutes. By noon, I'd reached Nogales, Sonora, and finally exhaled.

The horse I rode was unbranded, which came to me as a welcome relief, as I'd neglected to check when I first found her. This made her easy to dispose of. I bought a large, plain-looking suitcase into which I carefully laid the four bags of gold coins, wrapped in the blankets from my bedroll, then paid two pesos to board the mare at the railroad station where she would remain until she was auctioned off or somebody else stole her.

I spent the rest of that day dragging that burdensome suitcase along with me while I got a bath, a shave, and a haircut and bought myself a new set of duds—the most expensive and luxurious that any clothier in Nogales had to offer. My boots alone set me back a hundred American dollars. The suit was gray seersucker, with a vest, watchpocket, and double-breasted waistcoat. In keeping with my love of Mexico, I abandoned the traditional tie and chose the bolo variety, fastened with a jade clasp.

Outfitted thus, I boarded the night train west to Mexicali. I arrived there the next day, at which point I crossed back into the states and continued north to Pasadena unmolested. My late uncle had flatly refused to even consider the idea of looking up the collector that the cowboys had promised to sell the coins to, but I was able to find him with little trouble, introduced myself as the same Paul with whom he had corresponded, and took the chance. Such a gambit was well-rewarded, and I departed his stately villa with $270,000 in thousand-dollar bills.

The notion of such wealth was unfathomable to me, but before I had a chance to spend it on anything else, the first thing I did when I left my buyer's home was find the nearest saloon. There, I ordered myself a double shot of the best whiskey they had and, with the most respectful deference I've ever mustered, tapped my glass on the bar in honor of my beloved uncle, whose consummate selfishness had made me rich beyond my wildest dreams.

VII

Big Boss Man

The interregnum that followed my unexpected windfall was characterized predominantly by a state of lotus-eating excess that most men cannot even fathom. The degree of reckless hedonism I enjoyed was legendary. Goaded on by the gambler's maxim that 'money comes to money' as well as a desire to make up for the years of suffering and privation that I'd endured, I splurged with the same unabashed ease as John D. Rockefeller himself. Of course, there is another gambler's maxim of equal veracity—'easy come, easy go'—but that one seems to have escaped my mind entirely during those purple passages. More than anything, I wanted to turn tail and head back down to Chino, but Bonnie Lee was no slouch. There was no honest way I could have acquired even a fraction of the nest egg I was sitting on in just one month, so I decided to go off on a full-blown jamboree until enough time had passed to allow me to return home without any accompanying suspicion. And, when Bonnie Lee wrote to tell me that she was pregnant, that only further reinforced my decision to indulge in a shameless tear. After all, I doubted I'd be able to retain the full range of my current freedom with a brand-new baby around. However, if one thing was certain, neither Bonnie Lee nor I would need to work anymore.

After drifting about the west coast for a time while I recovered from the events of the last month, I decided to hang around Reno for a while. To ensure that Bonnie Lee remained ignorant of my lies, I had my mail forwarded from Saragosa, TX—about thirty miles south of Pecos, near to where Beggar's Tomb supposedly was—and had a special postmarking outfit made that replicated the mark from Saragosa on all of my letters, no matter where I mailed them from. As for my boodle, a portion was designated to a standing reservation of the most luxurious suite in the Ames Hotel, which also served as the quarters of the Monte Carlo Cocktail Lounge—home of blackjack, craps, and roulette. Whatever wasn't being carelessly wagered or squandered on glut was tucked away in a safe deposit box in the First National Bank of Reno and dipped into whenever the need arose—and the need arose quite often.

Down the street from the Monte Carlo was another casino called the Fennario. The Fennario was what real gamblers call hell; I suppose that's where it came from and where anyone who patronized it was destined to go. In 1938, Reno was nothing like the little Vegas of the north that it is today. The first gamblers to come and play and win and lose were there at the same time I was, and along with them came the same element that has always accompanied my infamous race throughout the ages: pretty women and predatory men.

The Monte Carlo and Fennario, as well as the numerous other small casinos that dotted the city, were about as straight as the Snake River. Even the bingo parlors maintained a house advantage far too great to be considered bettors' fortune alone. Needless to say, men who set upon the town intent on cleaning up had about the same luck as those who'd fallen into the clutches of faro operators throughout the west in days of old—they lost and lost heavily. And when they did, that's when the Wolves began to circle. This particular pack of grafters was by far the most cutthroat criminal syndicate I have ever had the misfortune of associating with. They operated with the same ruthless confidence as the gangs of Chicago and subsisted entirely upon dirty martinis and the misery of their marks. While I took my share of swigs from the cup of cozen myself, stacked up against this collective, I was about as wicked as the Pope in Rome. I never learned precisely what circle of hell the Wolves ascended from, but I have a few educated guesses.

Worst of all was their ringleader, a certain John Thomas Banjo. He can only be described as larger than life, and that holds true in all regards. Two of me could have stood in each leg of his britches, and they still would've required a belt to keep from falling down. He was so massive that he created his own magnetic field, and those drawn into it were divided proportionally between fellow criminals and suffering bastards. He was as smooth as a river of whiskey running downhill, and even those most discerning faced a formidable challenge when pitted against him. His company of cronies was equal parts minion and enforcer, and what they lacked in criminal intelligence, they more than made up for in brutality. The crux of their organization was loansharking, but I have no doubt they had a hand in every form of palm-greasing from soda to hock.

I'd always considered myself slightly above average when it came to profitably navigating this wild world, but Tom Banjo was on another level. Through one method of wheedling or another, he managed to put himself in such a position that both the casino and its patrons were simultaneously indebted to him. He could almost invariably be found seated at the corner of the Fennario bar wearing a black silk suit and a 10-gallon hat. It was impossible to miss him; his head was the size of West Texas.

Tom Banjo was what you would call a bad man. I'm not making any excuses for myself; I'm a liar, a cheater, and a crook, and I'm not ashamed to admit it, but most often, my crimes are merely forms of retribution. I lie to liars, cheat cheaters, and steal from those who have already stolen—and when an innocent mark does get caught in the shuffle, he went in with his eyes open and deserves entirely the loss he suffers. I'm a gambler; anyone who sits down to a game with me should rightfully know that they stand a chance to lose, and if they don't, then they are indebted to me for teaching them a very valuable life lesson. Am I a scoundrel? A bastard? Most certainly. But am I a bad man, through and through? Perhaps, but I've met worse. You see, the really bad men, the ones any man ought to worry about, will rarely give you the impression that they are, in fact, what they are.

The night I discovered the Fennario was in the middle of August, and uncharacteristically for northern Nevada, it was raining like a bitch in heat. I'd gone for a romp down by the Truckee, and rather than walk the rest of the way to the Monte Carlo and get soaked, I ducked inside, mainly just to keep dry. As was to be expected, my plans changed immediately when I got a glimpse of the facilities. I ended up rolling the bones against this little chink with more money than God until nearly daybreak. I successfully misappropriated about $16,000 of his pocket change through the skillful handling of a set of loaded dice, and when I left him, he had more tears in his glass than saké, and I had more than money in my hand. After all, what is it for a man to live a life of such an exciting and voracious nature without a woman beside him?

Annemarie was a table girl at the Fennario and worked all the layouts in rotation, bringing the players and the dealers anything and everything they needed. That fortuitous evening, she was working the craps circuit, and the shine we took to one another was immediate. Her red skirt was short, and her confidence was high. Her hair was dark, her cheeks were dimpled, and her eyes flashed like heat lightning in the inky-black desert night. As her position necessitated, she flirted with every man who lingered about the game. Still, whenever she wasn't running after a drink or a cigar, I found her standing next to me. She watched my shots with a keen eye, keen enough even to catch onto the hijinks that the croupier missed. Once all the men at the table had gotten their fill, I caught her by the arm and asked if she cared to accompany me to the bar for a nightcap. She whirled around and smiled—then declined. "Unless," she suggestively offered as an alternative, "you've got a bar in your room."

Fortunately, I did. However, even if I didn't, I would've had the cocktail lounge of the Monte Carlo moved upstairs to my suite before I denied such enthusiasm. We arrived at quarter to five, and drinks were poured immediately. She had a face like Claudette Colbert, legs like Betty Grable, and moves like Ginger Rogers. She was sweeter than a June peach and redder than a September rose. I was agog. I pulled down the shades at dawn and didn't raise them again until the dawn that followed. Such ecstasies were punctuated by breathless conversation, and I soon learned that her life was as withershin as my own. She'd been born in a sod house on the prairie, ran away at the age of eight, and took no straight path to her current home. There wasn't the slightest semblance of direction in her world; she rode on the wind like a rogue leaf in a hurricane, her life subject to all the vagaries that the fates could draw. She was an angel in flux with a license to kill issued by the devil himself.

The following evening, I took her and her friends out for cocktails at a lavish restaurant and threw around hundred-dollar bills like they were confetti on New Year's Eve. This became at least a weekly occurrence, and the Fennario became my new regular haunt. When I wasn't watching her flit around the casino in her tight little outfit, I was buying her jewelry and lingerie and planning excursions to Lake Tahoe. Curiously, even though I was the one who was married, she was oddly particular about where and when we met. She never drank with me at the Fennario and, when at work, rarely bestowed upon me any greater affection than she accorded to the rest of the men who gambled there. This professionalism was surprising to me, but I hardly questioned it, and at least once every few days, she found her way back into my arms.

As the months passed, I continued to write my ever-more-pregnant wife as often as I deemed appropriate, relating to her all the riches that Uncle John and I were finding and assuring her of the ease and comfort in which our little family would live upon my return. I never told Annemarie that I was married. As much as I enjoyed her presence, it was just an affair—void and meaningless, skin and body when I had nothing other than my own for 3,000 miles. She took up the space between Bonnie Lee and me, and there was not a moment when Annemarie had my mind or my attention entirely to herself. Our affair was sublime and endearing, though, after it'd run its course, I found myself of the opinion that I could've lived quite comfortably without it.

My stint in Reno, while eminently enjoyable, was also fairly homogenous. My days were an endless cycle of frivolity and excess, each more grand and sumptuous than the one that preceded it. I lived the life of Riley, deported myself like a Hollywood agent, dressed like Clark Gable, and behaved like Monty Brewster. My rendezvous with Annemarie remained steadfast throughout and were the only thing that took the sting out of all the money I lost.

I may've come into town toting an impressive bankroll, but as far as the skills for accumulating more are concerned, that's something of another matter. Crooked gambling is not nearly as lucrative in a casino as it is in a back room or bar. Every advantage tool that E.M. Grandine or any of his successors invented for the advancement of the crafty gambler had its match in an equally ingenious object designed for the dealer. However, while both sides enjoyed a marked edge, it accomplished little in making the game any fairer. If a player was caught employing any one of these devices at the table, he'd be taken around back to have his head busted in by the Wolves. And, if a player felt unjustly served by the dealer and kicked about the game being below the level, he'd be treated to the same fate. Therefore, I abandoned the more elaborate and easily-detected shiners and sleeve hold-outs that I would've normally put to use and relied only upon a diamond ring with a gold setting that I'd had specially fitted with a tiny stylus I could use to mark the backs of cards already in play. Of course, I could've purchased such a contrivance for just a few dollars, and it would have been just as effective, but staying true to my newfound penchant for high living, I went all out. That being said, the results it produced were far less striking than the instrument itself. Casino cards are subject to near-constant turnover, and every time a pack was thrown on the floor by an irate player, I had to start all over again, literally, from scratch.

I knew I was getting beat, that was never a question in my mind, but even while thousands upon thousands continued to blow away as if they were caught up in the Washoe Zephyr, I refused to bow out. I considered myself a master trickster, and having nothing else to do, I decided to defend my professional honor and find a way to outfox that gang of wolves. Unfortunately, my pride and tenacity held out longer than my bankroll, and due to this combination of influences, I managed to blow through a quarter of a million dollars in just under five months.

I wasn't completely broke by a long shot, but right about the time I had to retrieve the last $10,000 from my safe deposit box, I seemed to remember the anticipation with which Bonnie Lee was waiting for me—and all that I had promised her. To make good on my promise and ease her mind, I decided to send her $5,000. That left me with the same amount and a tall order to somehow turn it back into the fortune I'd lost.

Of course, I put forth that tall order, not Bonnie Lee. As far as she was concerned, ten thousand dollars was more of a fortune than she'd ever seen—and likely far more than she ever expected me to make. If I'd been smart, I would've tucked those five g's into my ivory-tipped, hand-carved calfskin boots, kissed my mistress goodbye, and headed back to Mexico, but as one can well imagine, that's not the way it all went down. Instead, I signed myself up for a $50,000 buy-in poker tournament at the Fennario and went to see Tom Banjo, the 'Dire Wolf.'

Naturally, I found him seated at the corner of the bar, shadily conducting business with a plainly-dressed man in a brown cotton suit who appeared dwarfed by the hulking, bulbous figure of Banjo. He was visibly trembling as he begged the Dire Wolf for an extension on the repayment of a loan, as he had yet to receive the interest due him from certain investments, and the rest had gone the usual way—across the table. Upon hearing this, Tom Banjo broke into a rafter-shaking bout of near hysterics and then began lambasting the hapless fellow for his rank negligence. The poor bastard turned about as pale as a bled pig and quietly asked if there was anything he could do to get another week. The Dire Wolf repeated this meek request at the top of his lungs, accompanied by some additional derision.

Finally, after he'd gotten his fill of the man's ignominy, the Dire Wolf announced that if the man got on his knees and issued a public apology for his delinquency, he would consider granting him an extension. Immediately, the fellow threw himself on the barroom floor and spread himself prostrate before Banjo, bewailing his cursed dalliance with the fickle goddess of fortune and begging for mercy for the sake of his wife and children.

After an unbearable interval, the man was ordered up off the floor, and Banjo, acting the Samaritan, agreed to a small extension of the man's loan. Dizzy with relief, the man copiously thanked the Dire Wolf for his compassion and humanity and was led away by two lesser Wolves to the office where the amended contract would be written. A few days later, the man's wife received a plain brown package containing her husband's right hand, ominously holding a full house—aces over eights. Along with the hand was a letter warning her not to contact the authorities and to immediately sign over all of his assets—or else suffer dire consequences. The terrified woman did exactly as prompted. The same day her home was conveyed, she received a second package. This one contained his head. No legal action was ever brought against the Wolves. The man's loan had been in the amount of $22,000.

Now, had I been aware of the conclusion of this saga, I would've shot my foolish pride dead in the face and disappeared without a second thought, but as it had yet to transpire, I stepped up to the mammoth man and asked for a loan. The Dire Wolf smiled genially, told me he'd seen me around the last few months and had taken note of my skill, then inquired about the amount I was interested in borrowing. I told him about my entering the $50,000 contest, and then, like the biggest jackass in the history of creation, I began to brag. At the end of my spiel, I asked him for $100,000, sure beyond a shadow of a doubt that I'd be able to escape the humiliation of the man who'd asked before me.

Upon hearing my request, Tom Banjo simply smiled again and agreed as if I'd asked him for a dime to buy a cup of coffee. His next words inquired after my address, where he could meet with me privately to discuss the terms of the loan. I gave him my room number at the Monte Carlo, then departed.

Arrogantly self-assured, I hung around my room until the Dire Wolf arrived. When he did, he knocked hard enough to just about blow the door right off its hinges. I peered through the peephole to ensure he was indeed my only caller, but his body was so massive it filled the whole hall. I took the gamble and stepped away from the door.

"Come!" I called. He was alone.

"Nice room, Jones," he observed as he stepped inside, "you must entertain plenty of women here."

This struck me as an odd comment, but I responded accordingly, "Yes, as many as I can."

"As many as you can, eh?" he repeated, "Falling on mighty hard times then, aren't you, sport?" He clapped me across the back and nearly sent me sailing across the room. "Now, about that loan...shall we have a seat?"

"Of course," I spoke up, still struck by his strange introduction, "Would you like a drink?"

"Does a bear shit in the woods?" was his reply.

"Fancy anything in particular?" I asked.

"Whatever you're having," he answered.

I picked up the bottle of sloe gin that I'd been nursing and poured a generous portion into two clean crystal tumblers.

"So you want to play in the tournament with the big boys," he affirmed after he'd taken a gulp.

"It'd be a detriment to the quality of the competition if I didn't," I responded, as cocksure as ever. "I can draw an ace faster than I can draw a gun—and if dead men could talk, they'd tell you I'm mighty quick with a gun. Fifty-thousand-dollar buy-in and seven other men already on the roster—I can pay you back with one good hand."

Tom Banjo chuckled, "Alright, Sport, you talk a big game. Let's see you put your life where your mouth is. What sort of terms are you expecting for this $100,000?"

"Oh, just your usual will be well enough for me," I replied haughtily, "There won't be any trouble paying you back. You see, I don't generally like to stay liquid. As soon as I come into money, I buy up assets—big assets—and I don't want to start selling just to buy into a little old poker game."

The Dire Wolf considered this for a moment while he drained the glass of gin. "I like how you operate," he told me. "You operate the way I do. And, because I like how you operate, I am prepared to offer you my very best terms for this loan—with just a few minor stipulations as far as the game is concerned."

"Shoot," I replied.

"This loan will be interest-free," he began casually, "and payable within twenty-four hours of the end of the game. And, in terms of the game, you'll play fair—no tricks, no tools, no advantage...no jewelry," his eyes glanced down to my two-carat shill. "And, you'll play sober—" In an instant, he reached across the table, took hold of the nearly full bottle of gin, and violently threw it against the far wall. The bottle exploded in all directions, and the red liquid trickled down from the point of impact like streams of blood.

"And, if you don't," he continued, his voice severe, "you'll be up against the same consequence as you'll be if you don't pay me back on time."

"And that is?" I inquired hesitantly, a couple of hairs on the back of my neck beginning to stand on end.

The Dire Wolf leaned his fleshy mass across the table until he was about half an inch from my face, "Did you happen to notice how many pieces that bottle shattered into?" he growled.

I gulped, "Too many to count, I'd reckon."

"You'll wish you were that bottle."

Without retracting his eyes from mine, he rose with a shift and a grunt, reached into his vest pocket, and extracted a banded stack of thousand-dollar bills, which he dropped onto the table with force.

"Good luck." He sneered and started toward the door.

"Don't you want me to write out an IOU?" I called back to him, trying with all my might to maintain my composure.

"I know where to find you," he replied ominously, "and I know where you've been, too."

He slammed the door behind him so hard that the wooden frame splintered. I picked up the hundred grand and stared at it warily, unsure whether or not I had just signed my own death warrant.

Once I'd stashed the money and cracked open another bottle to calm my nerves, I grabbed my coat and hurried down to the Fennario. Annemarie was working the blackjack table when I arrived, so I watched a few rounds and then joined when a seat opened up. She made her way over to me promptly, as she always did.

"I need to talk to you after your shift," I explained as she leaned in to hear my order, "I'll meet you at the Monte Carlo bar at two."

"I really can't tonight, Jack," she explained nervously, "I have someplace to be."

"It's important, Annie, please?"

She shifted uncomfortably and glanced up at another player who was beckoning her over. "Ok, but only for a minute. No funny business."

I regarded her actions as somewhat odd but dismissed them. After all, Annemarie was odd, and she had so many different personalities I was never entirely sure which one I was addressing at any given moment.

She showed up at the bar about a quarter after two, still in her pin-up uniform with a fur-lined, velvet cloak draped over top.

For a minute, I forgot my dire predicament and gazed desirously at her. "Are you sure you don't want to go back to the room? I think the only place that cape would look better than over your pretty little shoulders is on my bedroom floor."

"Jack," she insisted, concerningly serious, "What do you want?"

"Alright—you're working the tournament, aren't you?"

"Of course," she responded, "Why?"

"I need you to bring me the box of new decks they'll be using that day."

"What?!" she exclaimed, and then lowering her voice, said, "Jack, I can't do that! If I get caught meddling in the tournament, do you know what the Wolves will do to me?"

"Annemarie, if I lose this tournament, do you know what Banjo will do to *me*?"

She met my eyes, confused, "If you lose? Why?"

"I borrowed $100,000 from him this afternoon."

Every drop of blood drained from her rosy cheeks, and her eyes grew until I thought they were due to drop clear out of her head. "You did *what*!?" she shouted so loudly that a couple of the nearest imbibers turned to look at us.

I lowered my voice, "All my money is tied up. I needed a couple extra bucks to get into the game."

"Jack..." she spoke gravely, "this is bad. Really, really bad. Banjo...Tom... he's suspicious about us."

"So what?" I retorted, "The table girls ain't allowed to mingle with the customers?"

"No, Jack, you don't understand," her voice rose in panic despite her attempts to remain calm. "We kind of... I'm his..." she pulled at her collar and then met my eyes defeated, "his paramour."

My stomach dropped so hard it felt like it landed in my left foot. I was too stunned to respond. In an instant, all the mist rose from over her strange habits. Everything made sense now, and the fate it alleged was too terrifying to give air to.

"I'll get you those cards, Jack," she spoke in a hollow whisper, then she turned slowly and headed for the door.

I sunk onto a barstool in a daze and, in a hoarse voice, asked the bartender to bring me a bottle of sloe gin, no glass. I remained there, frozen, until the bar closed, not knowing whether to turn left or right, climb the walls, fall to the floor, go down to the police station, or just up and die. I long suspected my untimely end would come as the result of a knife or a bullet in my back, courtesy of some beautiful woman's husband or lover. Still, I hardly imagined that I'd volunteer to help the process along by unknowingly indebting myself to the bastard who already had a veritable reason to kill me.

It was clear that I had troubles, and in a gesture of pure sympathy, the bartender shuttered it up at closing time but told me I was free to remain there as long as I wanted, just so long as I locked the door behind me. The expression on his face was indication enough that he understood the ravages of my dilemma. After all, at one time or another, just about every man sits alone at a bar with his head in his hands, wondering what the hell he's done with his life.

Annemarie brought over the cards the following evening. The box was sealed and untampered with, and she was visibly anxious, afraid that she'd been followed. She thrust them into my hands, warned me of the hazard I knew would befall both of us if I screwed up, and departed.

I labored over those cards for the next two days, employing every method I had perfected to mark cards so convincingly that I could read them just as clearly from the back as I could from the front. Each deck of 52 was made to appear identical to the unwary eye while bestowing upon me a pure advantage. Once I was finished, each deck was restacked, repackaged, and the whole box was resealed with a wax stamp. The only facet that allowed for possible detection was the stamp, as I was unable to reproduce the precise design used by the manufacturer. However, such was a gamble that I had no choice but to take.

The night before the tournament, Annemarie showed up outside my room to retrieve the cards bearing a somber expression.

"Are you sure you want to go through with this?" she asked me. "You'd be much better off cutting your losses, returning the loan, and skipping town. I'm not all that sure that Banjo won't come after you just because of me, without factoring in the money at all."

"Why didn't you tell me?" I implored her.

"I thought it was better for everyone involved," she insisted. "I don't know how, but he must've gotten wind—he's been on high alert lately. We can't see each other alone anymore. It's too dangerous. I'm getting out of Reno tomorrow night after the tournament. For your good and mine, I truly hope I do not see you there."

"I'm playing in the tournament, Annie," I stated resolutely.

She shook her head gravely. "When they come for you, whatever you do, please forget everything that happened between us. You cannot divulge a word. They'll kill both of us for sure...and will most likely do far worse than that. I've seen what they're capable of. Your best bet is to get away now...far, far away."

I dismissed her pleading. "Just make sure those cards are in play tomorrow, and everything will be just fine."

Her final reply was hollow and trembling, "I sure hope you're right, Jack Jones, I sure hope you're right."

The tournament began at two o'clock the next day. I sat down at the table with six other men, including one of Tom Banjo's Wolves. Both dealer and players were thoroughly searched for any tools that would increase our confidence, and all the men were determined to be free of any such influence. Chips were ceremoniously distributed then, as a crowd of rubberneckers and pan-fish gathered like wide-mouthed gawkers attending a public hanging.

I watched cooly with bated breath as the box of playing cards was retrieved and broken into, but I was too far from this operation to see whether or not the seal was mine. The inaugural deck was opened and put into service, and relief flooded me immediately. Annemarie had come through, and I shot her a glance across the table, where she was dutifully taking drink orders from the players and the audience, her customary ebullience unaffected by the stark panic that could be seen in her eyes.

The first round of bets opened at $2,000 and steadily increased throughout the afternoon until, one by one, three of the men were forced to drop out and sullenly buttress the ranks of onlookers. That left three high rollers—myself, the lesser Wolf, and one other fellow. I played conservatively, maintaining a slight edge throughout the game but still allowing myself some generous losses. Decks were exchanged every so often as players kicked that all the luck in the one in play had run out, and each time, they were replaced by another one of my doctored articles.

After about five hours of play, Lady Luck settled down definitively in my court. I won three rich pots in a row, and at that point, it was clear that the game was approaching its terminus. My opponents continued to bet more and more aggressively, and I continued to rake in the profits. Before the last hand was dealt, the lesser Wolf, whose cold cash was swiftly gathering in piles of colorful chips before me, called for the introduction of another deck. The dealer obliged him, and all eyes turned to Annemarie. Annemarie's eyes turned to meet mine, and I need not be a psychic to recognize the fear-based urgency I found there. I was, at that moment, very far ahead of the pack, and the way the bets were being laid, I knew that both the lesser Wolf and my other opponent would most likely go all-in on this hand. It was, as they say, the moment of do or die.

The cold deck was presented to the dealer, and fifteen cards were dealt. My hand was a looloo—A, K, J, 10, 4—all spades. All I needed was the queen—and I had her in my sleeve from the previous deck. I could taste every dollar of that $250,000 coming back to me.

My opponents also appeared to have favorable hands because they both went all in before the draw. However, from looking at the cards they were holding, both were bluffing. One had a small pair, and the other held nothing more than a king high. I saw their bet. Deadwood was discarded, and new cards were dealt. I drew the six of clubs. With bated breath, I surveyed the hands held by the other two. Neither had drawn the queen of spades. My heart was hammering away in my chest like a pile driver. Rather than lose to the Wolf with the small pair, I decided to take the gambit. Surreptitiously, I slipped the queen of spades out of my sleeve and exchanged it for the club I'd been dealt.

I called, and all three hands were laid on the table. Immediately, every voice in the room rose in exclamation. However, to my mind-numbing dismay, I discovered their commotion was not due to my crushing victory.

It was due to the fact that the lesser Wolf and I had both laid down the queen of spades.

I had about a quarter of a second to react. I sprung from my chair and flipped over the table. Chips and cards scattered in all directions, and I ran out of there like the devil, escaping the clutches of the lunging Wolves by a hair's breadth. I was instantly pursued by a mob of about two dozen men, and only through the combination of swift feet and a well-timed freight was I able to keep the skin on my back—and that's just about all I was left with. Every possession that had not accompanied me on one of my frequent trips to the hock shop was back in my room in Reno, and if I ever set foot in Reno again, I knew I would lose it. Of the $270,000 I arrived with and the $100,000 I'd borrowed from the Dire Wolf, I was left with a single twenty-dollar bill in my pocket. I was busted, broke, all-in—shattin' on my uppers and down the creek without a paddle. And, worst of all, I was on the run—again.

It didn't take me long to figure out what had gone wrong. The plan was simple yet brilliantly contrived and proof that the Wolves were masters of the skin game. Banjo had known that I wasn't going to play straight—not with both a fortune and my life resting on the line. Whether he'd pried the truth out of Annemarie or not, he'd discovered the substitution of my special cards, and himself being an expert in the field, was able to compare my deck to an unmarked one and duplicate my markings—on different cards. I'd been outfoxed by a Wolf, and now the hunt was on.

The fortuitous freight I'd boarded was primarily composed of gondolas full of old ties headed east in no great hurry. I secreted myself atop a pile of them and tried to stay below the lip of the car and not freeze to death. In my haste, I'd fled without my overcoat, and the December wind whipped, stung, and tore at my thin clothes and bare head. I'd been on the plush for so long that I'd forgotten the misery of such climes and desperation, but the interminable evening did well to remind me. Sleep was all but impossible, as I was uncertain whether anyone had witnessed me board the train and whether or not I could expect the cars to be searched when we stopped to take on water. Therefore, I remained awake and watched the sun rise over the Great Salt Lake Desert—the vast emptiness of which did little to impart any degree of hope into my ravaged soul.

Such pessimism was not misplaced, for I never made it past Salt Lake City. The car I was in—along with a good forty or fifty others—was unhitched from the engine and abandoned on a siding in the railyard. I had no choice but to disembark and head into town. I got as far as the section house when an off-duty brakeman apprehended me and hooted and hollered until two railroad dicks arrived to cart me off to the stir. It wasn't long before I was identified, the sheriff's office in Reno was phoned, and I was on my way to Nevada in the back of a Black Maria.

II

At first, I was almost relieved that the law caught up with me and not the Wolves. Even with the horrors of my past, I still would have rather served a few months in prison than risk Bonnie Lee receiving any of my anatomy via parcel post. However, Tom Banjo certainly did not spare any resources when it came to taking me down. Since he couldn't get me from the outside and none of his cronies were fool enough to subject themselves to arrest and discovery in order to get to me from within, he pulled some recently bought judicial strings and had the Washoe County Superior Court throw the book and its appendices at me. Not only was I convicted of cheating and swindling, but also evading an officer, resisting arrest, trespassing on railroad property, and a handful of other misdemeanors that all together added up to a whopping five years and three months in Nevada State Prison.

I was crushed, heartbroken, and suffering from an acute case of emotional whiplash. A few months or even a year, I could've written off and explained away, but five years and a Nevada postmark did not stand a chance at being put past Bonnie Lee, no matter how much shit I shoveled over the circumstance. Therefore, I had no choice but to write her and tell her the truth—or at least some euphemistic version of it.

After writing several drafts over the course of a few weeks, the letter I finally sent her read something like this:

My Dearest Bonnie Lee,

Words cannot express how much I regret that I have to write this and, moreover, that it is true. I will not be returning later this month as I had planned. By the close of this letter, I hope you will understand how terrible I feel about this most unfortunate turn of events and how much I miss you. Three weeks ago yesterday, Uncle John and I packed up our operations at the mine with four full bags of gold, worth more pesos than you can carry.

We left our camp late, and when we got into town, we were told there was no vacancy at the hotel. He decided we should camp the night. It was the worst decision he ever made. We were just past city limits, expecting no one, and sleeping sounder than we should have been. A cowboy rode up in the middle of the night. He wore a bandana over his face and carried the biggest pistol I'd ever seen. We were awakened and searched, but finding nothing of value on our persons, he started for our saddle bags. Uncle John moved to stop him, and the cowboy shot him dead. I threw up my hands and bargained for my life. He robbed us bare and rode away with six months' worth of sweat and toil.

I was ashamed to come home to you with nothing to show for my efforts. I was ashamed I couldn't save my uncle or our gold. I thought if I took a chance in a high-stakes game of my specialty, I'd have an opportunity to win back what I lost. However, my methods were not appreciated. They stuck me with a five-year sentence here in Nevada. I hope to get out sooner, but I cannot guarantee it.

Bonnie Lee, my heart aches for you. I know you would've welcomed me back regardless of whether I brought home a pocketful of pennies or the whole U.S. mint. I was wrong, and now we both must suffer. I cannot believe I will not be there with you when our baby comes. I cannot believe I will be away for the first five years of his life. But, Bonnie Lee, if I can shorten my sentence and come home to you even a minute sooner, I want you to know that I will do whatever it takes. Being in your arms is worth more than all the gold in the world. I wish I had never left.

Your Loving Husband,
Jack

I waited ten days for a reply and spent them pacing my cell with a chill in my heart colder than the stone walls themselves. Though I strongly believed in the integrity of our marriage and Bonnie Lee's faithfulness, I was no sight short of terrified that I'd never hear from her again. I knew the sincerity with which she had taken her vows, but I also knew that desperation has a curious way of making people act out of accordance with their general character. And being a woman nine months pregnant whose husband was imprisoned in another country certainly qualified as a situation that had the potential to spurn some considerable desperation.

Fortunately for me, I'd married a rose. Her response was full of more compassion than I could have expected to receive from old Jerusalem Slim himself. She did not admonish or question me, nor did her letter contain pity or sorrow for herself. Within, she reminded me of our commitment to one another, informed me that she was well aware of who she married and that her expectations for my success had never been high, even with my reassurances. Despite her grave disappointment, she seemed to have made peace with my extended absence long before I divulged the circumstance to her.

Bonnie Lee's letter immeasurably improved my state of mind, although it did nothing to diminish my longing for her; rather, that was only compounded by what was contained in the second half of her missive. After she'd gotten through assuring me that she did not fault me for the events that had transpired, she informed me of the healthy birth of our son, who was yet to be named. She also included a photograph of the child. He was dark complected with a head full of black hair, and although the picture was not in color, it was plain to see that he did not share my blue eyes either.

While he did not look like me in the slightest, just knowing that he was my son was enough to spurn a flood of emotions that I'd never before experienced or even imagined. I'd never really paid any attention to kids before and had spent hardly any time in their presence since I'd been one myself; however, as soon as I laid eyes on his face, I was overcome with the desire to protect and provide for him—him, and his mother who he so closely resembled. The fact that I was stuck in prison while Bonnie Lee was forced to make do without me in raising him infuriated me even more than I was already. I cursed the Wolves and how they'd outwitted me and vowed that I would not allow their savage greed to keep me away from my new family. I wrote Bonnie Lee, telling her to name our boy Cassidy—in homage to my late uncle—and that I would see her soon.

I'd escaped from prison with no ramifications once before; therefore, I was confident that with proper precaution, I'd have no trouble doing so again. Besides, not all of Nevada State Prison was high-security like McAlester—and this time around, my crimes deemed me a low-risk inmate.

All things considered, the facilities in Nevada were far more conducive to sustaining human life than they were in Oklahoma. Despite the fact that it was located in the desert just east of Carson City—which is far from being the most habitable of climes—it was overall less offensive than federal prison had been. The fare bordered on edible, the cells were larger, and the inmates were forced to keep them cleaner. Regarding inmates, Nevada did not have issues with overcrowding as McAlester did. I didn't have to sleep on the floor, and the cots provided were unobjectionable compared to most of the sleeping arrangements I'd spent my life enduring. The guards were considerably less cruel, and in all my time there, I could count on my fingers the number of instances they cracked an inmate without reasonable provocation. The place was far from being a retreat, but conditions were undoubtedly more lax than most institutions I'd spent time in.

However, prison labor was the one area in which Nevada did not exhibit a progressive policy. There were a number of easy assignments that all the trustys and 'good behavior' sect aspired to be assigned to—commissary duty, shoemaking, dairy farm work, hog butchering, and most favorable of all—a position within the prisoner casino, which operated on site. Had I been fortunate enough to score a job as a dealer, banker, or even a floor man in the prison casino, the pangs of homesickness that characterized my time there would have been considerably lessened. However, after an incident closely resembling my trouble in Reno, I was prohibited from entering the establishment—though cards and dice did find their way into my possession fairly regularly throughout my stay.

Unfortunately, my first assignment was not a desirable one. My capacity for penal labor was extracted at the Nevada License Plate Academy, where I performed the tedious task of stamping car tags for the first three months of my bid. This got old quickly, and after a few months of careful observation, when I was afforded half the chance, I decided to fulfill my promise to Bonnie Lee and take French leave from NSP. However, in this endeavor, I did not share the same success that I had enjoyed in my exodus from McAlester; in fact, I never even made it off of prison grounds before I was apprehended and brought to the warden's office.

The windows in the rear corridor of the factory were some of the few that were not barred or too high to be accessible. However, they were narrow—about six feet tall but only about ten inches wide. From them, I could see over the prison walls to the sandstone buildings of Carson City. Over time, an idea began to take form—though I acted before I'd thought it all the way through.

The approach I thought best was to cut away at the putty that held the window pane in place until it was so loose that one good gust of wind would blow it right in. With a wooden shiv that I'd worked at and sharpened, I carved away a few inches whenever I walked by unaccompanied, and finally, one morning, when we went to work in the factory, we saw that the glass was shattered upon the floor. This caused a bit of a stir amongst the guards, but as all of us prisoners had been present and accounted for at the time of the morning count, and the building had been locked all night, the wind was determined as the sole cause of the incident.

After a few hours into another inane shift, a trusty had swept up the broken glass, and the missing window was all but forgotten about—by everyone but me. The next time I walked by on some errand, I stuck my head out. We worked on the second floor, but a single-story roof was directly below the open window. In a rush of adrenaline, all rational thought sizzled up like a match in a cyclone. I tried to squeeze myself through the space, as I had envisioned so many times before, but my clothes bound and restricted me. I tried repeatedly, but my concurrent lack of success and the elevated voice of a guard back in the factory prompted my slackened return.

The following day, the window had yet to be replaced, and I arrived at my post better prepared. I'd made use of some favors owed me in the dining hall the previous evening and been outfitted with a pound of butter, which had been liberally applied before I dressed that morning. Without the resistance of my prison denim, I was able to slide through the space with only minor scrapes, hop down to the flat roof below, put all my clothes back on, and light out toward the far wall like my life depended on it. However, once I got there, I was set upon by guards before I even got the chance to scale the outer fence.

I never admitted to attempted escape, but as I had no reason to be snooping around the prison wall when I should have been helping two other guys retrieve a new roll of tin from the materials shed, I was punished accordingly. After a week in the hole, I was yanked from my comparatively plush job in front of the plate presses, handed a fifteen-pound maul, and led kicking and screaming down into the sandstone quarry where I spent twelve hours a day, six days a week, making big rocks into little rocks to be used as railroad ballast. By the end of my first day, I could hardly drag my poor broken body from the quarry back to the cellblock, nor could I raise my arms above my waist without them throbbing so severely it felt like they were going to detach from my body.

The morning of the second day, I lay in my cot as stiff as a petrified board and as sore as a boxer after twelve rounds of pummelling. That didn't matter to the straw boss; I could've woken up paralyzed from the neck down, and the same amount of work would've been expected from me.

If there was any one official within Nevada State Prison who had a particular streak of brutality about him, it was the straw boss of the quarry. His name was Daniels, and he was what you'd call a real rawhider. His enthusiasm for watching half-dead men work themselves the rest of the way there was sadistic, and unlicensed breaks were considered by him to be more of a crime than the charges that I or any of the other inmates were doing time for. Goldbricking was an entirely useless tactic when performed on Daniels, and any whining, complaining, or displays of weakness were heavily penalized. This is something I learned immediately and tired of nearly as quick. I was in the quarry for hardly a week before I decided to try my luck again and get back to Mexico.

My first successful prison escape had been purely on account of balls and opportunity. I knew that forcing the issue was not going to prove positive for me, so I waited. The guards made it clear that I was being closely watched, and I knew my options were limited. I didn't have the patience or the connections to plan anything elaborate, so I just held out until I thought I had a chance and then leapt at it.

Once we convicts chipped up enough gravel, it was loaded into gondolas and hauled to the maintenance yard thirty miles north in Sparks. The train was thoroughly combed before it came through the prison gates as well as before departure to ensure that none of the more innovative inmates decided to ship themselves up to Sparks with the product of their labor. Despite the obvious danger, I found this opportunity tantalizing, and after several weeks of continued observation, I saw my chance. One nook of the train was often overlooked—the caboose. It was constantly manned; therefore, the odds of even the slyest tramp—convict or otherwise—hitching a ride there were considerably low. However, the surest but most uncomfortable spot for a desperate man to conceal himself was in the toolbox—or possum belly—underneath the caboose. Though surreptitious, it was, at best, cramped and, at worst, totally full and inaccessible.

One particularly dreary and auspicious morning, after the cars had been loaded and an engine had backed in to retrieve them, we convicts were ordered to return to our posts, and the guards commenced checking the train. While they were at the front, I slipped away to the rear and climbed into the possum belly. It was unlocked and half full of iron wedges, rams, and chisels, which dug into my flesh as I contorted myself into a pretzel, pulled the lid down as tight as I possibly could, and waited to exhale. The guards passed by and banged on the iron lid as they completed their rounds, but the lock nor the contents of the toolbox were ever examined, and that train began its slow drag out of NSP moments later. When the whistle blew at the first rail crossing in Carson City, my heart trembled, and pure exhilaration flooded me—I was free again.

There have been few freight rides in my life as dire and agonizing as that thirty-mile hop over to Sparks, and when the line of cars pulled to a shuttering halt in the yard, I knew that the worst was yet to come. I made no move for quite some time, my whole body aching and throbbing from the unnatural position I had formed myself into. Remaining with the train was risky, but trying to sneak through the railyard dressed in prison blues was no less than suicide, so I stayed put, my heart pounding in my head, nerves taut, ears straining...waiting.

I remained in that hellish iron box for about eight hours. Every so often, in periods of relative quiet, I'd raise the lid ever so slightly, peer across the yard, and then ease it back down. I did not dare risk exposure before nightfall. I may've been able to make it into town, but as a gambler, I was not keen on the odds.

Shortly after sunset, once the crews had changed and most workers had gone home for the evening, right around the time I began contemplating getting out of Dodge, the unmistakable sound of a posse reached my panicked ears—and they were accompanied by the fugitive's worst nightmare—dogs. All of a sudden, my plans of holing up in Sparks until a southbound freight departed were waylaid, and my chances of escape were severely reduced. My cramped reprieve now lost every ounce of its security. I knew only one method of throwing off dogs—wading in the water. For me, that meant crossing the Truckee River, about a mile south as the crow flies.

I knew whether I ran or not, I was in for a bad time, and it has never been a bane of my character to roll over without a gun to my head. So, I crawled out of the possum belly, pleaded with my blood to re-engorge my numb extremities, and began lurching and stumbling toward the southern edge of the railyard.

Once my legs began working as God had intended, I ran harder and faster than ever before, but as my life of late had well proved, luck was not on my side. I'd hardly made it out of the yard before the sound of howling instantly made all the hair on my body stand on end. They had my scent, and they were on my heels.

I'm sure it was quite a spectacle for the guards and Reno-Sparks police officers to watch me lighting off across the desert dazed, half-frozen, and desperate with a whole train of baying, drooling bloodhounds behind me. I'm not entirely sure if I ever truly believed I'd make it to the Truckee River, and if so, where I'd go from there, but what is certain is that I never even got close. There was no grand and valiant showdown. The prison dicks simply waited until the dogs overtook me, tearing half my skin and most of my clothes off in the process; then they came and collected me, packed me onto one of the horses, and trotted back to Carson City.

I spent the next ten days in the infirmary, and as soon as most of my more egregious wounds had healed, the warden chucked me into the hole for the next two weeks. The day after I was released from solitary confinement, I was unceremoniously sent back to the quarry. That night, before I was allowed to return to my cell, no more than a specter of the man I'd been a month earlier, I was marched to the warden's office, anticipating the worst—and the worst is undoubtedly what I got.

He informed me that escape charges would be brought against me in superior court and that I faced an extended sentence of up to ten years. I was also informed that regardless of the judge's decision, I would lose all of my privileges and be treated as a flight risk. This included visits, phone calls, and even the writing and receiving of letters. His final words were a dire warning against any and all retaliation and the threat that another attempt at escape would more than likely prove fatal.

They had me over a barrel with my hands tied. My choices were surrender or die, and I refused to die defeated. I wrote Bonnie Lee one last somber letter, expressing as emphatically as I could how much I missed her and regretted the turn of events that had led me to become the victim of such a sad state of affairs. Her reply was eminently emotional, and I remember it word for word to this day. She vowed and swore that she would be waiting patiently for my return, that she and Cassidy would manage just fine on their own until then, and that she would continue to pray unceasingly for me until I arrived back at our door. She promised she could not live without me and missed me more than words could tell, but that I must not try to escape again. She begged me to obey the guards, if not for my own sake, for hers, so that one day we could be together again.

She closed by telling me how much she loved me and included a photograph of herself and our son.

I read that letter and looked at that photograph every night from the day I received it until I was released from Nevada State Prison. And, each and every time I did, the effect it had on me was the same. Whenever my gaze rested upon the sight of her, in all her salient beauty, and upon the eyes of our son, the wave of loneliness, heartbreak, anger, and disappointment that crashed over me never lessened—even after fourteen years, eight months, and five days.

The only other instance in which I experienced hope of reprieve was in 1941. After December 7th, inmates in every prison across the country began orgiastic appeals to their governors, higher courts, and congressmen to be released on parole and join the fight in Europe. Patriotism burned so brightly in the eyes of most every man that on a clear night in Nevada, a faint glow emanating from NSP could be observed in downtown Carson City. They were insatiable—every cent held in the commissary or accrued through work was set aside to purchase war bonds, and petitions to institute basic military training amongst non-violent, short-term offenders were in order.

While I was not eligible for parole, based on the nature of my crimes, I was eligible for training. Other than during my short-lived boyhood desire to be a soldier after my brothers went to war, I never paid much attention to the vagaries of international affairs and politics. The idea of actually being packed off to war had me quaking in my brogans, but if impersonating a flag-waving nationalist could get me out of breaking rocks and potentially shorten my sentence, I would be Uncle Sam with bells on.

As conditions worsened in Europe, more and more talk circulated around the cellblock about the possible development of prisoner platoons and squads of volunteer lifers to be sent on suicide missions. I selfishly hoped the war would go south fast and requirements would slacken so that I would have a chance at being recruited—and then desert from there. All the men who were interested in receiving training were screened. But, while I passed the physical examination with flying colors, the time remaining on my sentence deemed me unfit for such an exclusive and esteemed commission, and I was denied both the privilege and the hope.

In my entire life, the longest period during which I had a permanent residence was the time I spent in Nevada State Prison. Thinking back upon that span now, it is largely an unpleasant blur. For over a decade, I was subject to nothing more than the ardor and banality of poor food, poor souls, and work. I had no contact whatsoever with the outside world. Even if I attempted to write a letter to my wife and have a fellow inmate mail it, I would land in the hole—for every incoming and outgoing letter was read before it reached its intended address, and if the guards had a particular reason to torment you, you could bet your ass that they remembered full well what those letters contained.

For five years, I worked in the prison quarry. For five years, from dawn until dusk, I pounded rocks. The incentive and reward were the same: I got to keep my hide. I never received a word of praise or encouragement, only the raucous bellows of, "Hey there, you fellow! Take hold of that hammer!" followed by a chorus of cusses and obscenities generally reserved for beasts of burden and other dumb animals. To this day, whenever I am riding in a freight car or walking along the tracks and see the millions of stones that line those great steel highways, I always wonder how long of a stretch I am personally responsible for.

Though eminently against my will, I quickly learned to submit. Daniels was about 6'5" and stalwart. I didn't stand a snowball's chance in hell against him unless I was armed with a bazooka, and moreover, I'd seen what punishment he inflicted upon agitators. His favorite method of discipline involved soaking a long leather strap in a pail of water, dragging it through the dirt, and then putting it to use on some poor unfortunate's bare back. I often shudder to think what greater horrors would have been dealt me if Daniels had been a part of the prison posse in Sparks.

While I conducted myself with greater deportment on my work detail, by no means did I weather the rest of my sentence without some degree of trouble finding me—as is well to be expected. The source of this trouble—which should also come as no surprise—was moonshine.

I was a man born in John Barleycorn's bunkhouse. I'd been nursed on his sweetest nectar, and every one of my childhood maladies had been treated by his most potent anodyne. I'd been raised in his shadow and culled by his apparent wisdom. I'd lived the whole of my life by his direction, and to be denied his company for those long and unremitting years was unbearable. For some, such forced abstinence may've spurned conversion, but I abhorred every dry day of my life. I regarded John

Barleycorn's absence as wholly unnatural, intolerable, and beyond the pale in every regard. Therefore, with nothing else to occupy my restless mental faculties, I set about changing that.

I could hardly call myself my father's son if I did not make use of my boyhood education. The foils and fancies of John Barleycorn had gotten me into prison, and I'll be goddamned if I didn't seek to conjure him while I was detained there. Of course, I knew full well that the more I behaved and the further below the radar I flew, the greater chance I had of getting out sooner, but my desire to lessen the unpleasantries of the moment won out over good judgment and sensible logic.

I sought out the company of one of the cooks—an individual generally regarded with as much affability as a louse—and after several squarely dealt games of poker, we were road dogs. Once I'd determined that he was not a stool pigeon nor a prison jocker, I introduced him to my plan. The cook provided me with the makings—sugar, tomatoes, yeast, and the occasional batch of fruit—and I took care of the rest—by lining a pair of trousers with sheets of tarpaulin and leaving them folded in my foot locker for a few days. What resulted tasted like a denatured version of old chock. It got you drunk, sure, but it also dissolved the lining of your stomach. I wasn't sure if I ought to sell the first few batches I made to the prisoners to drink or the guards to use as corporal punishment.

It took a few months before I successfully produced a mixture that made John Barleycorn proud and could be choked down without any great deal of suffering. Once I did, I immediately began trading the stuff for all the amenities I could not purchase from the commissary. Only a privilege-denied convict understands the sublime effect that a Snickers bar or a can of pomade has on a man after being subjected to nothing but privation and toil for weeks at a time. The same goes for foul-tasting liquor. Before long, my old chock—or prison 'wine' as they euphemistically coined it—was in such high demand that I could not make it fast enough to sate the savage thirst that persisted amongst the inmates of NSP. After a while of failing to meet the demand, I was strong-armed into sharing my recipe—and profits— with other enterprising convicts. Of course, as it always goes in such circumstances, not all of the makers of such libations were as careful as I was, and many of these epigone operations were discovered and disbanded, their perpetrators chastised accordingly.

It was at this point that I decided to get creative. The prison wine did the job for the most part, but what I really wanted was Rocky Mountain gin. I knew sure and well that was a pipe dream, but if I could find a way to distill my 'wine' into something stronger, my prison days would pass with much greater ease and accord. Thus began an uncanny series of scrapes, pulls, tears, and other assorted minor but painful injuries sustained in the quarry that landed me quite reliably on temporary duty in the kitchen with my pal, the cook. There, I had all the pots, basins, coils, and fuel I needed to make a small but effective still. It took me about a month of sporadic work to assemble the prototype and cook off the first batch of what I humorously called Washoe White Line. The taste was fit to kill you, but if you could keep it down, the kick was as good as Rocky Mountain gin itself.

The greatest obstacle to my entrepreneurial endeavor was that many of the regular denizens of the prison kitchen were trustys—and it is an irrefutable fact that trustys are stool pigeons. However, it required little more than a snort for me to win the allegiance of two of them. The deal was that they had unlimited access to as much white line as they pleased, just so long as they distracted the other prisoners while it was producing and maintained my immunity with the guards. There were other trustys who would've ratted me out in the time it took to bat an eye, but I did not entrust them with my secret. Only those who were regular consumers of my 'wine' were let in on the deal. After all, even the dumbest cons know not to kill the goose that lays the golden eggs.

The whole endeavor was surprisingly successful. On the whole, contraband in NSP was far more common than in McAlester. Cigarettes and newspapers regularly made the rounds along with morphine, heroin, cocaine, and marijuana—and on occasion, bottles of legitimate liquor. How much of this was smuggled in by crooked guards themselves is uncertain, but without a doubt, quite a number of them did spend most of their time looking the other way. The still, in its various incarnations, went unnoticed for years. The natural smell of the prison kitchen disguised the noxious fumes that were released when the wine was distilled, and the resulting concoction was discreetly dispensed to those awaiting it in the serving line.

But, as with all things, nothing lasts. Eventually, one of the more attentive guards realized that every time I got injured in the quarry and temporarily assigned to KP, a few days later, half of the cellblock got drunk. This strange correlation was thereafter investigated, and our little moonshining ring was uncovered, broken up, and severely punished.

There wasn't all that much they could do to me that they hadn't done already. I'd been stripped of my privileges, condemned to solitary, worked into the ground, and marked as a flight risk in black and white stripes. As a result of the moonshining ordeal, I lost whatever 'good time' that I had made, got dealt a two-week stint in the hole, and, when I was finally let back up for air—reassigned.

No work detail on premise at NSP was as grueling and terrible as quarry work, but many prisoners were assigned to road crews, some of which were incredibly tough draws. Not all road crew work was worse, but the food and treatment certainly were—and the exasperated warden knew exactly what he was doing when he sent me out with a gang, my ankles chained to the floor of a dusty van bound for a lead mine in Humboldt County, just south of Winnemucca.

Normally, I would not have been eligible for road crew labor, as I had a history of escape and poor conduct. However, because it was mining work and heavily guarded, I did not have the same opportunities to slip away as those who worked on the chain gang or in farm or conservation work. In the mine, there was only one way in and one way out—through the same hole—and there was a goliath officer with a submachine gun blocking the entrance at all times. The whole crew was shackled together before we marched out of the mine at the end of the workday, and we were made to sleep on the floor of the van in the same condition.

The treatment wasn't overall subhuman—although spending the greater part of a decade chained to two other convicts does nothing to boost a man's ego. Fortunately, the guards who ensured that we stayed put were not bloodthirsty. In fact, as they were subjected to the same lowly conditions we were, they were somewhat empathetic. The work was filthy, foul, and unrewarding—but it was at the very least less monotonous than pounding rocks back in Carson City—and for every week that we worked free of disciplinary incident, one day was lobbed off our sentences. We labored twelve hours a day, six days a week. On Saturday evenings, we were loaded sweaty, soiled, and exhausted into the prison van, shackled down, and carted the three hours back to NSP, where we were allowed to enjoy a hot shower and a day of rest. On Monday morning, three hours before the sun rose, we were shackled together again and hauled back to Humboldt County, where we would be subjected to another week of picking, shoveling, and dynamiting in the sunless, airless, hopeless Cumberland Mine.

This strict, unwavering schedule all but defined my life for the next ten years. With the exception of Thanksgiving, Christmas, and Sundays, I ate nothing but cornbread, salt pork, and biscuits and drank nothing except cold water, milk, and the occasional soda pop. World War II and the Korean Conflict began and ended, countries and regimes rose and fell, alliances shifted, amendments were passed, and televisions had invaded nearly half the homes in the country while I worked and slaved until my feet slowly turned into the same heavy lead that we hoisted into mine carts and sent down the track.

On March 2, 1955—just about two months before my fiftieth birthday—I finally stepped through the impassible iron gates of NSP as a free man. I was fifteen years older and not a penny richer. My hair was well on its way from blonde to white, and the lines in my face looked like a well-worn roadmap of all the places I'd been and horrors I'd seen. I was time-scarred, work-worn and pain-aged, and worst of all, my mind was given over entirely to the habits of prison life. They hadn't broken me, but they'd come within a hair's breadth.

VIII

Me & Bobbie McGee

When the gates of Nevada State Prison closed behind me, all I had to show for my time was five dollars and a new suit. However, as the rest of my life has so colorfully evidenced, I've never been one to just take what Fate handed me, and I was determined to make that into a fortune.

As soon as I was released, I wielded a pen and sat down to share the jubilant news with Bonnie Lee but stopped and crumpled up my missive halfway through. After nearly sixteen years away, I could not bear going back to Mexico dead broke. I could not embrace my loving and faithful wife and welcome into my arms the teenage son I'd yet to meet with nothing to my name other than a bad reputation, so I decided to make myself a little money first. I wasn't striving for riches; I wasn't aiming to get involved in any business like I had with Uncle John or that which followed in Reno. I just wanted to make enough to show good faith and perhaps convince my wife that she hadn't married a bum all those years ago. Besides, once I went home, I was going home for good—and I'd been stuck in one place for far too long to immediately return to a life of sedentation and predictability. I needed time to relearn how to go about my day without order or schedule, without command or oppression, and without suffering or toil.

Therefore, my first act as a free man was to tuck my $5 bill into my shoe and board a freighter bound east. In all of my rambling life, I'd never traveled further east than Chicago. By now, I figured that the west and I knew one another well enough for me to comfortably move on to less-trodden pastures, so I continued hitchhiking and train-hopping until I found myself accidentally ditched on a siding somewhere in the backwoods of Harlan County in southeastern Kentucky.

I climbed out of the boxcar I'd sprung into and hiked the track spur through the budding spring forest until I came upon a coal mine where a short string of cars waiting to be loaded sat idly at the end of the line. Seeing as I was nearly as ragged and dirty from traveling as the miners were from working, I was unafraid of being molested and picked my way through the camp until I encountered a man forthcoming enough to tell me the name of the nearest town and what direction it could be found in. When I asked, his eyebrows raised, and his face twisted into a kind of humored and toothless expression, but he provided me with the information I sought. The name of the town half a mile distant was Deep Elem, and when I expressed my intent to go there, the man I was talking to simply chuckled and told me to watch myself. I knew little of what to expect, but I had a feeling I'd ended up in one of the poorest coal mining towns in Kentucky—and judging by the smell of the man, there was a bar nearby.

I soon came to find that I was hardly mistaken in my initial assessment of the place. The 'town'—as I will so generously refer to it—consisted of five blocks of rotting, canted wooden buildings. They were all in an equally poor state of repair; not a single one was painted, and only a few were whitewashed. The streets were quiet and empty, with the exception of a couple barefoot kids, mangy strays, and one or two beat-up old cars. Most establishments appeared to be general stores or restaurants. The only bank I saw was boarded up, and if there was a sheriff's office anywhere, it had to be down near the mine because there was not a single building designated to that purpose anywhere along the street. Nor did it appear that any micron of law and order had ever been dispensed in the immediate vicinity. There was one dentist in the whole town, and from the look of the residents, he did the most business by far. I had just spent the last fifteen years in state prison, yet compared to the population of Deep Elem, I might as well have just come from an extended stay at the Beverly Hills Hotel.

There are a few poor souls I've met in my time that I won't ever forget—a goodly number of them in Deep Elem—but the saddest, sorriest, poorest soul of them all belonged to Bobbie McGee. Bobbie McGee was a wiry street kid, a dirty little tramp with a face streaked with black soot and coal dust. She looked as if she'd been born in a gutter and raised in a back alleyway. She had the face of a pubescent boy—plump and round in the cheeks but sullen and gaunt in every other way. The rest of her body wasn't far from matching—she was as thin as a matchstick and lacked all those pleasant lumps and bumps that other women's bodies naturally shape into by her age. She had short-sheered, mousy brown hair that came down just past her ears and fell into her eyes—eyes that were best kept hidden. They were dark and colorless, keen and suspicious, interested yet disenchanted, innocent yet jaded.

I first saw her on my way into town that same afternoon. My main objective revolved solely around the necessity of locating a suitable establishment in which I could quench my thirst and conduct all business required in the course of building up a new bankroll. However, my single-minded focus was promptly derailed by a scrawny waif that scurried across my path two blocks from the mine.

When my head turned, it was not out of attraction or interest; rather, it was morbid curiosity that fueled the action. At first, I had absolutely no idea what I had just seen. Whether the figure was a boy, a woman, or a dog was not immediately apparent. It wore clothes, but they were the color of soot and so ragged that any accentuation of its form was imperceptible. It was short in stature, with a twisted spine, knees that bent in toward one another, and a body that consisted of little more than flesh and bones. Its face was dark and dirty and turned down out of the wind. It walked briskly as if in pursuit of some distant object or fleeing a bed of unpleasantries. I watched it with mild intrigue until it rounded the corner out of sight and then carried on along the course I had set for myself.

Three doors down from the corner where I'd stopped, I found myself staring into the threshold of the most derelict dive I've ever set foot in—and considering I've spent the vast majority of my free days in bars, that's really quite a distinction to bestow. The front door to the place was off its hinges and leaned against the wall next to it. The bar consisted of a few unstained planks stretched across empty whiskey barrels and was so short that if two men my size were to lay across it, the second man's feet would hang off the edge. The barstools were rag-tag handmade items most likely constructed by some local carpenter who was drunk when he assembled them—which would explain why at least one of the legs on every stool was a good two inches shorter than the others. The only light in the place came from the open doorway, and the layer of sawdust on the floor was so thick and soggy it was like walking across a bed of moss. It was called the Elem Grill, but I hardly believe that any solid food had been served there since it opened.

As soon as I stepped inside, it was clear what sort of patronage I could expect to find. Only one man was seated at the bar, and he looked like he'd been there so long he'd rooted to the stool. He had about a four-day beard, his hands, face, and boots were blackened by coal, and his clothes were so soiled there was no way to tell what color they were originally or would be if he ever decided to wash them. I could smell him from the doorway.

The descriptions of the other three occupants differed only slightly. Two other coal miners were doubled up against the wall in the far corner, both of them unconscious. The fourth and final occupant was the proprietor, and while he was certainly more alert than his customers, there wasn't much to be said for his sobriety. He stumbled around behind the bar, his steps rolling like he was crossing the deck of a schooner in a 30-knot storm, and every time he pulled a beer off the tap or filled a glass, he made sure to pair it with one for himself. Even for me, the place was sordid, but considering my living situation over the last fifteen years, even the seediest bar in the Midwest was an oasis for a man as parched and tired as I was then.

Later that evening, as I nursed a bottle of sloe gin, the town's sleaze began to ooze over the railroad tracks and settle themselves in for a night of life's most tawdry pleasures. Port wine and bourbon seemed to be the locals' poisons of choice; however, just before sundown, the waif from earlier stepped through the doorway toting two empty gallon buckets, one in each hand. In closer proximity, I could see that she was indeed a woman, albeit barely. I glanced up curiously from my gin as she entered and watched with piqued interest as the bartender wordlessly took the buckets from her, drew off enough beer to fill them to the brim, and handed them back across the bar. Scrawny though she was, she hoisted them up as the foam pouring over the rim soaked into the sawdust and carried them deftly to the door before crossing the street and continuing on in the direction of the mine.

"That all for her?" I asked the bartender as he filled my glass shortly after she'd departed.

His eyes settled, half-mast and unfocused, upon my face, and he took a slug straight from the bottle before answering my question. "Naw!" he responded, wiping the trickle of red liquid from his beard, "She's employed by the mine. Ain't no grogg time bell that rings in this town, but eleven o'clock every mornin' and four o'clock every afternoon, she's down there givin' 'em their second wind. Joe Brown, the straw boss, pays her eight bits for her trouble, and she comes straight back here to spend it."

He was right; she reappeared just after sunset amid the throngs of soiled miners and stepped to the bar, dollar in hand. She was so short the planks of the bar came up to her chest, and she needed to stand on the rail in order to reach across it. When the bartender—who, as a result of the spike in business, was completely blottoed—finally made his way over to her, she ordered a scotch with one ice cube. I watched as she strained to retrieve it, and once she had it in her hand, she hefted it up to the dim light over the bar that reflected off the dusty mirror. She trained her gaze upon it with a gentle intensity so warm and grateful in its expression that if I had not known any better, I would've thought she was looking into the eyes of her lover. Little did I know at the time that she was.

Considering that she was the most curious person I'd encountered in years and the first woman I'd seen in a bar in longer yet, I largely ignored the crap game that a small group had conjured up in the back corner and kept my eyes on her, trying to determine from clues alone exactly what her story was. She seemed to be an inhabitant of her own little world, consumed by thought and chiefly unaware of all the other men in the room, and in turn, they paid her just about the same notice as you would a hat rack. She spoke to no one, hardly changed position, and did not protest when the men around her would knock into her or jostle her drink. She stared unceasingly forward with a look on her face that was almost pained, an expression that suggested a struggle—either to attain some desperate reprieve or escape some dreadful imminence.

Finally, long into the night, after most of the other patrons had dispersed or passed out, the drunken bartender disappeared into the back room and never returned, leaving her and me as the only two still standing. She'd yet to give any indication that she was aware the bar's population had dwindled and had not so much as acknowledged my existence at any point in the night. However, after the bartender vacated his post, she did seem significantly vexed concerning the condition of her empty glass.

Never one to let a woman go in want of something I could provide, I eased myself up on the bar, swung my legs over the top, and proceeded to dispense a drink from the same bottle she'd requested earlier that evening.

Clearly surprised, she retracted her transfixed stare from the mirror and examined me with an air of something like suspicion.

"What's this drink going to cost me?" she asked in a dry, raspy voice as she raised her eyes to meet mine.

"Your name, if you're willing to give it," I responded as I filled my own glass with her drink of choice.

Still doubtful, she raised the glass to her lips and took a sip, never letting her eyes leave my face. "I need an ice cube," she said.

I located the icebox under the bar and retrieved one for her.

She did not thank me, rather, she attended solely to her whiskey and gradually returned to her stare.

Silence ensued. I finished my drink first and deposited the glass in the trough beneath the tap. I took another long look at her, but she was Elsewhere. Just as I was about to climb back over the bar, she spoke.

"Bobbie," was the only word she said.

I stepped down off the pail I had alighted and turned to face her.

"You got a surname, or is it just 'Bobbie'?"

"They tell me my daddy had the name of McGee, but I wouldn't know."

"'They?'"

She met my eyes again and did so with force. To this day, she remains the only woman who could ever make me step back with so much as a glance. "The people of this darling town here—ain't she a beaut?" She raised her arm and waved it over the carnage inside the bar before letting it fall limply at her side. "They've raised me if anyone has; surely they've taught me all I know."

"Ain't never had no Ma?"

"None that I can rightly speak of."

"How'd you get by?" I asked her, but my question went unanswered. Instead, she finished the drink I'd poured her and left without another word.

The next day I spent exploring the town. Unsurprisingly, there was nothing of interest to be found. After having spent the last decade and a half imprisoned in the middle of the Nevada desert, you'd think that being reinstated as a fully functioning member of a rapidly progressing society would be shocking to me, but in this town, there was little perceptible change. Deep Elem was a relic of the Depression. If it couldn't make it into Deep Elem by rail, odds are it wasn't getting there, and if it couldn't make it out by rail, it was more or less doomed to stay. A few locals had cars, but most used them mainly as portable engines rather than as a means of transportation. Everything you needed in that town could be found within a half-mile radius, and I don't suppose many residents had much reason for venturing any farther. After all, when you're dirt-floor poor, window-shopping at the Bloomingdale's in the next town over doesn't really have the same appeal as procuring a meal.

When I strolled in, the population of Deep Elem—as declared by the decaying hand-painted sign at the edge of town—was something like 3,002. I hardly think they'd bothered to count recently, but still, I doubt it was far off. People tend to be born and die at roughly the same rate, and there was certainly no abundance of newcomers. There was not a single reason under the sun for any sane person to willingly take up living in Deep Elem, and I reckon most—if not all—of its inhabitants lacked the means to leave.

Every man in Deep Elem was a coal miner, except for the very young, very old, and those who had lost their share in that sordid privilege due to some physical defect. Those men were the shopkeepers, bartenders, sustenance farmers, and handymen who kept the rest of the town limping along. The mayor was also the grocer. He was about seventy-five, had a club foot, and no teeth. Despite its profound lack of opportunities, Deep Elem did avail me of one thing: concern for the law. For the first time in over a decade, I had no governance whatsoever. Deep Elem was as lawless as Dodge City, Kansas during the frontier days and had just about the same amount of dust.

Needless to say, as there was little else to do, it wasn't long before I found myself in that decrepit bar once again. The lush from the day before had been removed from his barstool and deposited against the back wall with the rest of his kind, making me the only patron at the bar. The proprietor was noticeably more attentive than the previous day, albeit crankier. He was quick to bring me my gin and did not forget to serve himself while he was in the business of pouring. Apart from my request, not a word was spoken within the confines of the establishment, nor did a radio play or a clock tick. I could not help but imagine that had I sought out a drink at the mortuary instead, I would have had a far livelier time. However, just like clockwork, as my watch struck four, the object of my curiosity dragged herself through the door, making my boredom all the more worth it.

I supposed the previous evening's interaction would have incited a greeting or at least a familiar glance, but Bobbie McGee did not so much as look at me. She took up her burdens as she had the day before and struggled across the spongy, sunken floor as she made her way down to the mine. I watched her go and remained there until she inevitably returned. The cantankerous bartender was slow to serve her, as he was otherwise detained by the thirsty miners on the other side of the bar who had come in just before her. She waited reposed without kicking up a fuss, as if she'd spent most of her life in the practice of waiting and was no stranger to its banality.

After watching her for a few minutes, I caught the bartender's attention and ordered a scotch with one ice cube, which I slid down the bar to her. She regarded it disconcertedly as it came to rest beside her hand, then slowly raised her eyes from the glass to meet mine. Her expression was blank and dazed. Again, she did not thank me. Instead, after a few cautious moments, she lifted the tumbler in her hand, examined it thoroughly, and took a drink.

"Why one ice cube?" I asked her. I did not expect a response.

To my surprise, this time, I got one. "I like to taste my whiskey, but without it, everything in this godforsaken bar is as hot as piss."

Normally, such a statement would have made me laugh, or at the very least crack a smile, but she delivered her comment with such offish directness that to laugh seemed almost irreverent. A brush with silence followed, as there was no fitting reply I could think of.

Finally, I decided I'd had enough of her frigid pretenses and tried the avenue of simple forthrightness instead. "Bobbie, my name is Jack," I said and reached out my hand to shake hers.

She retracted her gaze from the wall and met my eyes with the strangest expression I have ever encountered to this day. She looked at me like I was a complete stranger, as if she had never seen the likes of me before in her life, let alone spoken to me. It made me want to look behind me for the man I had been a moment ago. It made me want to scour my face in the mirror to ensure myself that I was who I told her I was, but the force of her gaze, dreadful and terrifying, did not allow me to wrench my eyes from hers. I expected her to look away as she had before, but this time, her eyes lingered, if only for a moment longer, and across the blankness of her stare flashed a hint of recognition. It was only for an instant, but in that instant, as in the fraction of a second when a crack of lightning illuminates a spectral forest, something within her came alive—and once it passed, it was as if it had never been there at all.

It sounds hokey to assert, but that look in her eyes haunted me. It made me unsure of a notion that had no grounds. It ignited a fear that had no cause. In that single moment when she looked at me, she made me question whether or not I was really alive.

The next day was payday at the mine, and that weekend I continued to frequent the bar and scared up a couple low-stakes crap games to keep me fed and in gin over the week to come, but I did not attempt to speak with her again. She came in as usual at four o'clock but unaccompanied by her buckets. She stood in her customary spot, ordered her scotch, and assumed her stare. When I moved over to the bar to order a fresh one and glance in her direction, she did not give any indication that she noticed me. In some ways, I was glad—for I was afraid of those eyes.

You may think I'm just an old, dried-up con who's been away from women for too long. You may think that I was reading her wrong or that I am putting you on, but I assure you that I am not. Simply to recall that gaze can draw the truth out of a man more effectively than any lie detector ever invented. For what they suggested was doom, and what they expressed was horror, more raw and paralyzing than pulling back the devil's trapdoor and staring headlong into the gaping maw of hell.

That Monday morning, having amassed a satisfactory bankroll courtesy of the injudicious miners, I made up my mind to leave Deep Elem and its most mysterious urchin behind. There was a southbound freight coming through just after five o'clock, and rather than find an old jungle camp in which to pass the time, my curiosity got the better of me, and I beat it back down to the Elem Grill and ordered the same warm gin in the same unwashed glass and settled in for the same long wait into evening. I threw monte for the bartender for a short while, as he had grown accustomed to my presence there, and made a couple bucks off a few other day drinkers, but as I said, it was Monday morning, and most of the town was still in traction.

When four o'clock finally rolled around, Bobbie arrived as expected; however, there was something changed about her. Several large, round bruises further darkened her sooty face, and she favored her left leg as she walked, causing her to limp heavily. Her condition did not seem to be any source of concern for the bartender, and he filled her buckets just as callously as he had every other time. Bubbling foam, he slid them across the bar to her, and, wincing, she lifted them up and hobbled away.

I've never been one to provide a service for another unless there was some very real and attainable reward at hand as a result of my efforts; however, at that moment, in an uncharacteristic rush of altruism, I rose from my barstool and strode out into the street in pursuit of her. She had not made it very far when I came upon her and attempted to relieve her of her burden. I had not so much as grasped the handles of the buckets when she wrenched them away from me at once and began hollering and scrambling off in the other direction. Her eyes were wild, her stance predatory. I threw my hands up faster than I ever did when directed by a law officer or a cocked weapon in the hand of a killer.

"Get away from me!" she screamed shrilly, "This is mine! Mine!"

Bewildered, I blurted out my intent in an attempt to mollify her and avert the eyes that had turned toward our struggle in the middle of the dusty street.

"Calm down, Bobbie; I was only trying to help you!"

At once, the look in her eyes changed from anger and aggression to confusion and fear, like the eyes of a doe caught in the crosshairs of a hunter's rifle.

"Help me?" she repeated almost incredulously and then, after a moment, resumed her former emotionless reticence.

"I don't need your help." She spat, turning away, "I don't need you at all...."

With an expression of utter pain, she took up her buckets again and set out toward the mine, limping mournfully. I watched her until she was out of sight, then turned back to the bar, slated by confusion. Was she raving mad? Or subject to so much sorrow that mistrust entered her mind before all else? I considered asking the bartender about her, but he had about as much personality as a dead minnow. I spent the next few drinks thinking about our interaction but could glean no clarity from it. Finally, I decided to abandon the southbound freight and left instead in search of something to smoke. When I returned just after dark, she was standing at the bar with her foot on the rail. Beside her was an untouched tumbler full of sloe gin, and before her sat a glass of cheap whiskey with one ice cube.

When I arrived at the bar and picked up the glass, she did not say a word, but before I took a sip, I raised the tumbler in her direction and thanked her.

A nod was her only reply, but this time, she did not turn away.

From that night onward, mainly by drips and drabs, I was able to fashion a portrait of her life—and what a bleak picture it was. She told me the story of her father, a coal miner, hophead, and troublemaker who was killed in a mining accident before she was born. He'd caused it, and it had claimed his life, along with the lives of several others. She told me the story of her mother, a whore and drunkard who'd spent half of her life on her back and the other half crawling after her next jolt. She told me the story of her own life, in many ways more tragic than her parents'—how she'd lived on the street and on the infrequent charity of the townspeople. She told me her mother died of syphilis when she was six years old and assured me that if the V.D. hadn't gotten her, she would've drank herself to death before long anyway.

Already shunned by the town due to her parentage and the fact that generosity from hopeless people who can barely keep themselves alive is slim, she told me how she had to depend solely on herself to keep fed. I discovered the reason she was always so filthy was because of her manner of work. Due to her petite frame, she was taken in by the local chimney sweep, who recruited her to climb chimneys, dislodge dead animals, and drag the bags of ash and soot back to his work shed, where he permitted her to sleep. This—in addition to a few other odd jobs around Deep Elem— kept her from starvation. However, she explained, the wages he paid her were so trifling that most times, she could only afford to eat every other day. Of course, her emaciated form only proved positive for her benefactor, allowing her to fit into even the narrowest chimney in Harlan County.

She said the townspeople resented her as they would a rat they'd caught rifling through their garbage bin—and the other street children were afforded no happier fate. They were mistreated and cast off, forced to rely only on small tokens of kindness extended by the few who recognized their plight, and these, they found, in time, were expected to be paid back—with interest. From her earliest years, she'd found herself in the saloon near the mine in hopes of acquiring a small meal, and along with the slumgullion they'd serve her, the bartender would give her liquor for free. Pretty soon, she was coming back for the liquor alone.

As she grew older, the men in town began paying attention to her, although only late at night in a nearly empty bar or while walking down a vacant street. Her beneficent employer himself was not exempt from this newfound attention, and she explained that he would come into the shed some nights, drunk and ugly, and do whatever he wanted—at all times reminding her of the selfless charity he'd extended throughout the years and all she owed him for. This 'attention,' she told me, provided another source of income when she found herself in dire straits, as some of the men in Deep Elem would pay her for their filthy pleasures.

She spoke of these things with the same raw, emotionless sobriety as she did any other subject, each sentence broaching new realms of hurt and horror. She stared way off into the dregs of her haunted memories each time she started in. Her voice was as intense and unwavering as a thirty-mile-an-hour headwind. Her eyes were like broken windows.

"There have been nights some winters when it was so cold that I would go out and seek a man just to keep warm," she told me. "The miners have gone so far as to post a schedule for me on the board with the work orders...I learned a long time ago not to fight it—though there are times I suppose they wish that I would—at least that would give them an excuse to beat me...."

There had never before been a point in my life where I could rightly be categorized as the benevolent type, but there was something about her, about the nature of her story and the manner in which she told it, that made my heart hurt. There was something about her pitiful appearance and the sorrow that poured out from her tearless eyes unimpeded that got me thinking and made me want to do something for her—the terribly unfortunate creature that she was—something that could make her smile.

"Finish your drink," I instructed her one evening as she concluded that day's lament.

She regarded me strangely but obeyed.

I laid my tender on the bar and shoved my stool to the side. "Come on," I said, "You're coming with me."

She recoiled instantly. "Where?" she inquired without attempting to mask the trepidation that crept into her voice.

"The hotel on the corner," I replied, reaching out my hand.

She did not take it. Instead, she inhaled sharply, sighed resignedly, and muttered something under her breath about how she'd known it was only a matter of time. Nevertheless, she followed me down to the hotel, her head hung so low that her forehead nearly dragged on the ground. The place was in no better state of repair than the bar where I'd spent so much time those past few weeks, and the clientele was equally shady. When I arrived with Bobbie, I reserved a room on the second floor and was met with a humorous expression of contempt from the clerk.

"Enjoy your stay," he sneered.

I reached over the counter and snatched the key from him as he retrieved it from the pegboard, then marched the reluctant Bobbie up the stairs, unlocked the door, led her inside, and dropped the key into her hand.

"Lock this door behind you, and do not open it for anybody," I instructed her.

I did not linger to catch a glimpse of her expression; rather, I went out into the vacant midnight town and to the nearest clothing store I could find. I picked the lock on the back door and slipped inside. I couldn't imagine her in women's attire, so I stole a set of boy's overalls, a flannel work shirt, a flat cap, and shoes in what appeared to be a suitable size and left the rest of the store untouched. I did not so much as eye up the cash register.

When I arrived back at her room and knocked, announcing myself, she opened the door immediately, as if she was still standing in the same place I had left her an hour before. I presented the clothes to her and told her to take a bath, put them on, and throw her old ones away. I told her that the room was hers, that she was free to do as she wished, and that I'd had enough of that squalid, fortuneless town. I told her I was leaving the following afternoon—and that I wanted her to come with me. She took the bundle of clothes from me wordlessly and raised her eyes to meet mine. Even in the dim light of the hall, I could see they were as wild as they had been on the street that day when I'd attempted to take the buckets of beer from her. She scanned my face, her gaze brimming with suspicion, and then softly shut the door.

About noon the next day, I checked out of my own room down the hall, then went and called on her, but she was nowhere to be seen. She was not in the hotel, and according to the clerk, she had left without a word quite a few hours before. After scouring the town, I found her where I should have guessed—standing pat at the bar with a glass in her hand. This time when I walked in, she raised her head and acknowledged me.

"There's a freight train full of coal leaving here in two hours. I'll be on it. Will you?"

Bobbie shook her head bitterly. "Why?" she asked.

"I want to help you," I told her, "if you'd only trust me."

Bobbie scoffed cruelly, "Men—you're all the same; there ain't a good one amongst you. You're always full of lust and empty promises. No, I will stay here. I'll live and die here. If you want me, you'll have to get your fill right here in Deep Elem. I don't need to tramp around all over the country just so you can get your jollies on the run. I don't have much, but I have everything I need right here. I have jobs that pay me enough to live. I have a place to sleep at night. I know where I can get a drink, a meal, or a few dollars any time I need to, and when the time comes that I can't, there's a train trestle right on the edge of town that I can throw myself off of. There's nothing I want from you, and there's nothing you can give me, for you have nothing yourself."

"I can take you away from here," I insisted.

"I ain't never been far from here, but I've been far enough to know that it's all the same. It don't matter if I'm one town over or in California; I'll always be what I am, I'll always be from here. It don't matter how much I wash or how hard I scrub; I can't remove this place from me. It's in me, it's under my skin, it's on my hands...."

As she said this, she held her hands out in front of her. They were red and blistered and scrubbed nearly raw, as if she'd spent the whole night running them over with sandpaper—but when she looked down at them, I knew that's not what she saw. She saw upon them all the filth she'd encountered during the years she'd been a captive of Deep Elem. Her hands and her world were both tainted with the film of bad memories that flashed through her mind every waking moment and kept her scared and frozen.

In this hopeless gesture of hers, I saw my chance. Before she could pull away, I grasped her hands and looked deep into her eyes, trying to peer past the layers of trauma and find the woman that existed beneath the pain. If you had asked me at that moment, I would have told you there was no more to be seen, for the whole of her life had been pain, either taken straight or diluted by slight hopes followed by egregious disappointments. Reaching her was as maddeningly impossible as swimming to the bottom of the ocean or shooting a rocket to the moon. Still, something within did not allow me to abandon my efforts. And, if I am to be brutally honest, I knew I would not be able to leave her behind.

At first, she struggled against my grip, but only for a second. So many emotions flashed through her eyes in those few moments—anger, resentment, hesitation, mistrust, yearning, fear, pain—even hatred—but I did not look away.

"No one is going to hurt you while you are with me," I promised her.

"Even you?" she whispered.

"Especially me," I spoke in earnest, releasing her hands.

Bobbie turned away then, raised her eyes to the rotting ceiling, and sighed. She remained that way for a moment and then, defeated, dropped onto the barstool. "Kirby," she called the bartender, "bring me the bottle."

Kirby did, and over the next few hours, she drained it of every drop—for that woman could consume more liquor than any other person I have ever known. As it is, there are times when the mind is consumed by such pain and sorrow that the body finds it simply impossible to get drunk.

About twenty minutes before the train was due to depart, I eased myself up off the barstool and turned toward her. She looked at me with eyes that were changed, decided, and ever so slightly brighter.

"Wait here," was all she told me.

She returned promptly, carrying a small, battered satchel and the two empty beer buckets. Kirby, the bartender, filled them without asking any questions, and after taking them from him, she turned and held one out to me.

"I've never ridden a freighter before. I may get thirsty," she explained.

Pressed for time and unsure of the condition in which we would find the train, we double-timed down to the railyard, toting our buckets of beer with us. Luckily, the freight did not consist solely of open coal cars, and a whole line of boxcars was strung along behind them. I located a suitable stake in a pile of scrap metal beside the tracks and expertly sprung into one of the boxcars, loaded up Bobbie and the buckets of beer, and then crawled in behind them. It had been over a decade since I regularly practiced such a maneuver, and I certainly wasn't particularly quick about it, but if there were railroad bulls around Deep Elem, they gave the bums a wide berth.

Our car was billed to Columbus, Ohio, about three hundred miles from Harlan County, and I knew we were in for at least an eight-hour ride. I peeled off my coat and folded it into a pillow before stretching out my weary bones on the steel floor of the car. Just about then, the engine awoke from her slumber and called out her shrill greeting. The engineer released the brakes, the train shuddered and jerked, and we were on our way. I glanced up at Bobbie, but she was as stock-still as a statue.

"I recommend you get comfortable," I suggested to her from where I lay about ten feet from the end of the car, "we're going to be here for a while."

I dropped my head onto my coat and watched her curiously with one eye open as she digested her decision. I'm not even sure if she blinked for the first hour, and the only reason she ever leaned back against the end of the car was because the train had to climb a grade.

I'd be lying if I said I didn't begin to question what I had done. Me, Jack Jones, the man who had never in my life put the well-being of another person before my own, had taken it upon myself to adopt a half-starved, half-deformed, and at least half-crazy orphan and take her over the road with me. In all my time as a traveler, it was infrequent that I saw a woman riding the freights. Women have their own challenges, customs, rituals, and needs, which are all but foreign to men, and to introduce them into a man's world seems far from right or fair. Those women I had encountered were mostly the wives of migrant workers, themselves in search of work and feed. The rest were the consorts of gamblers and cons alike who turned tricks in each new town they reached in order to earn their keep. All in all, they were rugged, dependable, and above all, capable. Bobbie, on the other hand, was frail, scared, and unpredictable.

Additionally, after my stint in the Nevada state pen, my last few stops made it clear that I had a lot to learn. The world of barroom gambling had evolved considerably in the preceding decade, and if I wanted to keep myself and Bobbie fed, I was going to need to catch up right quick. That would take time, and there was no telling what we might encounter—for even life on the road had changed faces since I'd last had the fetid pleasure of riding the rails.

The fact that I was now responsible for Bobbie and had promised I'd keep her out of harm's way presented me with a considerable challenge. After all, if I could not send her out on the town to work over the locals while I scrounged up some spending money, what was I going to do with her?

To my overwhelming and pleasant surprise, that question seemed to answer itself.

The night I boarded that northbound freight with Bobbie, sleep eluded me entirely. It was not as if I suspected she was about to stab me in the back and steal my shoes, but she unsettled a man, and I acted in accord. That first ride, I lay on my pallet with one eye open, and it passed without advent or conversation. However, maybe fifty miles from Columbus, I was roused by a sound I hadn't heard in fifteen years. It was a woman's voice rich with song, the name of which I do not know to this day. I sat up like someone had given me the hotfoot—and there was Bobbie, mournful, morose, and melancholy, sitting against one of the barrels we were riding with, eyes closed, singing the blues like her soul was on fire. The sound of it bubbled up out of the depths of every feeling man could ever hope and fear to call his own. She sang like an angel in the midst of torment, like a siren before a flotilla.

There are a few moments in the average man's life when he sees the future spread out before him like a gilded hall ornamented with crimson carpet and stained glass, some neatly attainable reward looming assuredly at its terminus. I have had moments like this more often than most men would readily confess; however, the future promised in this particular instance delivered more practically than any other. It was at that moment when I realized not only what I was going to do with Bobbie but what she was going to do for me.

I scrambled to my feet, every hair on my arms and the back of my neck standing on end. "Bobbie, you can sing!" I blurted out.

Of course, the force of my reaction startled her, and she clammed up immediately. Her soul retreated back into her sequestered breast, and she did not answer me. In this particular instance, however, I will give her the benefit of the doubt because, judging by the condition of the beer buckets, she had to be plenty drunk.

"Bobbie," I repeated myself, kneeling down a few feet from her, "Who in Deep Elem knows you can sing like that?"

She eyed me skittishly and shook her head.

"Nobody's ever heard you sing before?"

Another confirmed negative. "It's just something...something that I do."

"Bobbie, any woman would kill for a voice like yours—a voice like that will make you rich!"

She stared blankly back at me without reply.

"Bobbie, what if I told you that you could travel to any city you want, stay in a warm room every night, eat and drink to your heart's delight, and never touch another chimney or another man ever again if you didn't want to—and all you'd have to do is sing?"

"I wouldn't believe you," she scathingly replied.

"Yeah? Well, I'm going to prove it to you," I promised.

The first thing I did when we arrived in Columbus was locate a bar in need of entertainment. Of course, this wasn't all that difficult, but finding a bar that would agree to stick Bobbie on stage after laying eyes on her was a considerably greater feat. However, once I asked Bobbie to demonstrate her talent, about half the time, the bewildered manager would take a chance on her.

Bobbie had a lot of problems, but stage fright wasn't one of them. I don't even think she knew any better. She wasn't a performer by any means, and she sure as hell did nothing for a man's eyes, but Lord, could she sing.

Like most bums that made it to my age, I could sing the old workhouse blues, I could sing the traveling blues, I could sing the I-ain't-got-where-I've-been-a'goin' blues, I could sing the I-ain't-seen-my-woman-in-so-long blues, I could even sing the I-killed-a-man-and-they-put-me-in-jail-for-it blues, but Bobbie could sing the blues for the whole world. There wasn't a time in her life that she wasn't sad and blue, and you could hear it in her voice; you could see it in her eyes—they were as blue as her soul. And, when she sang, boy, it sure made you feel good.

Surprising as it may sound, I never saw Bobbie cry. Not once in all the time we traveled together did I ever see a teardrop stain her face. Her default expression was harsh reticence ingrained by years of hopeless sorrow. The pain and despair she felt for all she'd endured must've been agonizing, but she never shed a tear. Rather, her voice cried in place of her eyes. She could sing the blues better than any of the Muddy Waters, Lead Bellys, and Bessie Smiths of the world. She knew the blues as well as any of them and better than most. Her voice was that of a bird born caged and freed from oppression after years of anguish, only to find that her wings were broken.

I don't know if Bobbie derived joy from her talent. At best, I believe it was a form of essential catharsis, an expression of her most profound pain. I suppose every person has theirs, but hers was transduced into a medium that brought solace to men's souls. She had no comprehension of her power and little knowledge of her strength. She bore every resemblance to an automaton built for the sole purpose of expressing misery. She knew nothing of herself other than that she was shame and guilt incarnate; she was misfortune in the flesh—for even the devil refused to claim the day she was born as his own.

However, for all my misgivings, Bobbie proved to be far from the average traveling companion. One would imagine that a woman would demand more stops, a slower pace, a real bed, running water, and all those luxuries rarely found along the steel highways—but not Bobbie. She weathered bumming it better than any man I've ever traveled with, and when we did land in a town, her voice carried us. By the time a week rolled around, I'd mastered the backroom conversation with the club boss. "I know she looks like one of last century's oddities," I'd tell them, "but just listen to her sing one song. I guarantee it will not be a waste of your time."

Unfortunately, that was one thing that remained constant even after the last of the coal stains wore off. No matter how many blue-light hotels we stayed in and how many new sets of clothes and makeup I bought her, it still didn't help—for dressing Bobbie up was like putting an evening gown on a rag doll. But, that set of pipes she had sure didn't quit—and so much the better because I needed to regain my touch in my own profession. Fortunately, her talent allowed me the time. Where Bobbie was concerned, there was never a shortage of time. No matter how tedious our travels and no matter how dull our destinations, she never complained.

She never talked, either. If she retained any curiosity about me in the same way I did her, she never made it known. The vast majority of her time was spent in rumination. It was a state she would slip into whenever she was not otherwise occupied and one she could not be shaken from unless she decided to emerge.

Bobbie reminded me of a painted mirror. She couldn't reflect light, and in most cases, she was far too paranoid and suspicious to absorb it. She shied away from human interaction like it was a disease and avoided eye contact at all costs. She was like a dog that had been kicked too much. I never kicked her, but she regarded me just the same as if I had. Her mistrust was rampant and seeped through every level of defense she'd erected to protect herself. Even after we'd been traveling together for months, she'd dog-eye me every time she saw me looking in her direction. She radiated suspicion so intensely you could feel it twenty feet away. Every time I posed a suggestion or told her my plan for our next journey, she'd flinch. I tried to give her as much space as possible, but getting her to trust me was like trying to get a wild coyote to eat giblets from the palm of my hand. However, despite its seeming futility, I was determined. She was human—or at least she'd been born that way—and by the time I made her my most magnanimous offer, I had more or less decided that if I did nothing else of good or consequence in my life, the least I could do was treat her like one.

After all that we experienced together, I hate reducing her to this example. Still, it is the most relatable and accurate comparison I can draw:

gaining Bobbie's trust was like taming an animal. Even once I'd captured her intrigue and curiosity, I couldn't reach out—I couldn't get close—because if I did, she'd scurry away, and I'd have to start all over again. It was nearly a month before I was able to sit within arm's reach of her, and it was another month before I could lean in and tell her anything without her shying away. We'd puddle-jumped halfway across the country before she didn't jump when my knee accidentally drifted over to hers on a barstool. I tried to convince her to leave her troubled past behind, make a new start, and forget the horrors she'd endured—let them be covered up by conditions bright and fresh, like tracks under new snow—but to Bobbie, that just didn't seem possible.

There were many months of uncertainty. We rarely decided in advance upon a route; most of the time, we just drifted from city to city and stayed until profits dwindled or my marks began to get wise. When we hit the town come evening, Bobbie would sing for a few hours and then make use of her comps. I busied myself with poker, craps, or bunco, and we hardly ever interacted. Occasionally, she'd venture off on her own and explore, but more often than not, she parked herself at the bar and proceeded to drink it dry. Generally speaking, we'd leave after last call and walk back to our room in silence, but whether or not she stayed there was a crap shoot.

Bobbie was a raging insomniac. She took sleep deprivation and somnambulism to another whole level. No matter how late we arrived back at the room, she'd nearly always rise after an hour or two and leave for a walk through the deadened town. There were many times I awoke at nine or ten in the morning and thought she was gone for good, but eventually, she always came back.

Bobbie never bit the hand that fed her. She may have slapped it down a time or two, or flat-out refused to eat, but she did respond to kindness, even if it took her a near eternity to do so. In fact, it always seemed to be at the last possible moment before I gave up entirely that she responded. I even started to think that she was treating it as a game, but I quickly abandoned this suspicion. Human decency was simply too foreign to her for her to take it for granted. Besides, there was no way she could have known what I was thinking. If she had, her trust in me would have been implicit, and none of my extraneous efforts would have been necessary. There has never been a time in my life—neither before nor after—that I wished anyone could read my mind, but in her case, that hope sprung eternal because, for the first time in my life, I had nothing to hide. In fact, the exact opposite was true—I have never been as earnest and honest with another human being as I was with Bobbie McGee. Whenever I had a chance to gain her trust, it affected me in a way nothing else had before.

My Ma used to tell me that virtue was its own reward, but I never believed nor understood that until Bobbie limped her way into my life. Never before in my dealings with men, women, or God did I enjoy such simple pleasures. Treating her good made me feel good. There was no ulterior motive, no scheme, no graft. I didn't want her; I just wanted her to be happy. She'd been born and lived in eternal night—and I just wanted to be a little light, nothing but just a little light.

After a while, I suppose this became clear to her because her approach to me gradually softened. It took nearly a year, but once she started to come around, everything improved. After about six months, she looked me in the eye. After seven months, she reached out and held my hand while we were picking our way through a crowded bar. Eight months in, stranded in a strange small town courtesy of a freight siding, cold, hungry, and nearly broke, she finally surrendered the last of her defenses and acquiesced to sleep in the same bed as me. Of course, for as much contact as we had that night, we might as well have been sleeping in two different time zones—but just the knowledge that she was beside me made me feel sort of warm inside.

As the months ambled on and the first traces of winter began to settle over the northern climes, I noticed that as her trust in me grew, Bobbie herself began to change. Her gaze began lingering longer, and it was filled with less fear. It flitted around behind her eyes as more of a cautious secondhand concern rather than an all-consuming notion that drove her every thought. A look of mild curiosity began to take the place of her stare. She never asked questions, but her eyes wondered. They wandered around my face instinctively and with purpose as a blind man gropes at a foreign object in order to ascertain its form.

Once snow started falling in Chicago, we left on the 400 and took the big river route down the Mississippi. We traveled from St. Paul to Davenport and then on to St. Louis, Memphis, Baton Rouge, and finally, New Orleans—where most of our winter was spent. We'd arrived in St. Louis in the middle of the night via blind baggage and were nearly frozen solid. We checked into the first hotel we could afford, and I paid for a week to get a discounted rate—on a single bed in a room hardly large enough to contain it. The room did have a window; however, which in this case was quite unfortunate—as it was exceedingly drafty and the central heat had gone out. Even the extra blankets we piled on the bed had not chased the chill from our bones, and we were freezing.

As usual, Bobbie was on one side of the bed—practically hanging off the edge—and I was on the other. I was cold, but she was shivering so intensely that the whole bed shook. I knew that kind of cold—I knew it well. To understand how much she was suffering and not attempt to remedy it—even if I knew my attempt was in vain—was something I simply could not do.

"Bobbie, it'd be a whole lot warmer if we got closer together," I spoke, already aware of what her response would be.

"I'm not cold," she snapped.

I scoffed, "Everybody on this floor can probably hear your teeth chattering. You're freezing. I'm freezing."

"I'm fine," she responded flatly.

I rolled my eyes, unsurprised, then turned onto my side, away from her. "Okay. Good night, Bobbie," I said.

No reply was uttered.

I lay there for a good while, listening to her teeth chatter. Even if I could've ignored her and gone to sleep, her trembling would've kept me awake. I've never met anyone besides myself as stubborn as Bobbie. When she dug in, she was a force. A force that, at times, I had no idea how to contend with. I wished more than anything that she'd give up and give in for her own good—but I also knew that it was her defenses that had kept her alive through all her storms. Frustrated, I sighed audibly and settled in for a long, frigid, restless night.

And then, when I least expected it, I felt something. It was a foot. Bobbie's foot.

Slowly and tentatively, she had reached her foot across the bed and touched my ankle. Shocked, I remained perfectly still; I didn't dare move an inch. A few minutes passed, and once my pulse returned to its normal rhythm, I felt another foot—followed by some gentle scooting. Half an inch at a time, she began moving closer and closer to me. I think I held my breath the whole time. It felt like hours had gone by—that dawn should've come and faded into day by the time she got comfortable with the idea of being physically close to me and safe at the same time. When dawn did come, she was curled up against my back—her violent tremors reduced to mild and infrequent spasms.

"Can I put my arm around you?" I whispered.

She nodded, and very slowly, I turned and reached out my arm, wrapping it around her middle and holding her close. Mere moments later, she knocked out entirely. For the first time since I'd known her, Bobbie, who, as a rule, did not sleep but a few nights a week, was spooned up against me, comfortably asleep in my arms. I, meanwhile, was wide awake with mind racing. The sheer supply of dopamine that her actions had dumped into my bloodstream was mind-numbing—and I was having these...feelings. They weren't carnal feelings by any stretch of the imagination—instead, I was...tingly...and filled with a warmth that came from a place in my soul that was usually as drafty as that hotel window. I was so happy I was almost giddy—and treated to a cocktail of contentment and incredulity that lasted well into the next day. I didn't sleep a wink the entire night—but to date, it remains one of the most satisfying evenings I've spent in bed with a woman in my life.

The following afternoon, we rose, as usual, to seek out a suitable club in which to conduct our evening affairs, and not a word was uttered about the previous night. There was no evidence in Bobbie's behavior to indicate that the evening's closeness had ever transpired, for the day yielded no greater proximity. She was as cold and distant as the ice on the Mississippi.

That night, after we returned from the club we'd selected with a fair to middling take, the heat in the hotel was still out. I wondered if the events of the previous evening would repeat themselves, but I didn't say anything like I had the night before. We started out on opposite sides of the bed— just about as far as we could get from one another in the same room—and I waited. Time passed, and the night wore on, and then, without warning, the same sequence commenced again—but this time, it happened quicker.

The third night rolled around, and the heat was still out. To my complete surprise, Bobbie snuggled up next to me as soon as we got into bed and fell asleep. At any other time in my life, if a woman displayed such forwardness, I'd be dying to cop a feel and practically drooling over the sensation of her butt pressed up against my hips—but with Bobbie, there was none of that. The satisfaction I derived from her touch resulted from knowing she was safe and comfortable. That warmth was all I needed in return.

The next night, the heat came back on, and the hotel was warm again. However, when we got into bed, Bobbie snuggled up close to me right away, just like the night before. I was bowled over. If I thought I'd been happy the night before, its intensity paled in comparison to how I felt at that moment. She wasn't just getting close to me because she needed to— she was getting close to me because she *wanted* to. We never slept apart again.

New Year's Day, 1956, blew in like a black-throated wind over the tangled web of interstate outside Baton Rouge. We'd boarded a short reefer freight there but were dispatched by a brakeman just a few miles from the city center and forced to wait for someone to pick us up on the highway. It was well after dark, and we stood underneath a streetlamp with our thumbs out but hardly expected reprieve. Baton Rouge had been good to us, but the high living and heavy drinking of the past evening had done us in, and we were busted just as flat as the soles of our shoes. A rainstorm was brewing, and the thought of it breaking upon us filled me with dread. I'd been through Louisiana rain before—and that shit comes down sideways. I'd gone down into a gulley to see if I could find any excrement that would serve as adequate cover when the storm arrived, and suddenly I heard Bobbie's voice calling out to me. I poked my head over the top of the ridge, and she was standing beside a big, red semi, its headlights illuminating the heavy, gray clouds above. I ran over, and we both climbed inside. The driver was headed straight through to New Orleans—and in turn, that became our destination as well.

As soon as we got on the road, that rain came pouring down, and I was right—it came in sideways. Those windshield wipers couldn't hardly work any faster, and to Bobbie, I bet they sounded just like a beat.

"Rainy day, rainy day—you oughta hear my baby sing the blues....." Bobbie began to croon.

I reached into my bindle and extracted my harmonica—a pastime that I'd rekindled as of late—and began to play along. That driver was a good ol' boy, and he got quite a kick out of us. He seemed to have nearly as extensive a musical knowledge as Bobbie herself, and by the time we arrived in the Big Easy, she had just about exhausted his education. He left us off on Canal Street, close to the French Quarter—and all we did from there was follow the sound of jazz.

Outside of Guaymas, I've never met a city I loved more than New Orleans. For one, there are so many bars that if you set out to drink at one a day, I bet it would take you well over three years to enjoy them all. As far as I could tell, there are two things New Orleanians love—God and rum. There was a church of some denomination on just about every corner and a bar on either side—on Sunday mornings, you could get your sacramental wine with a gin chaser.

For Bobbie and I, such a preponderance of music-loving establishments was eminently advantageous, and we remained there well into spring. New Orleans was a boon for both of our respective professions, and we were in clover before very long. Most of the time, we stayed at a fancy French hotel on St. Louis street with a balcony lined by ferns and wrought iron. In the interest of making good with the Catholic proprietors, who retained curiously high ideals despite their questionable recreations, I registered us as Mr. and Mrs. Jack Jones.

After 11 months of traveling together, Bobbie's confidence and morale had grown significantly. She was still very much the same broken and terrified woman I had squeezed into a boxcar back in rural Kentucky, but her ease of expression was much greater. Her shoulders weren't permanently bunched up against her ears, and at least once every hour, she'd exhale. She'd put some meat on her gnarled bones and plumped up enough to become distinguishable as a woman, but that was about as far as she'd come in the beauty department. She was pale and spindly, and where she wasn't, she was plain, but she wasn't ugly by a long shot. The only ugly thing about Bobbie was what she'd endured. Because of this, she seemed to defy every conventional standard relied upon by men to quantify her inherent worth. Some saw her and immediately looked away, but to others, like myself, she was intriguing.

About a week before the Mardi Gras festivities began, we stumbled across an establishment on Bourbon Street whose patronage was so fond of Bobbie that the house band asked her to sing with them. They also had a card room in the back, which served to bolster my steadily growing bankroll. On weekends, the place drew such a crowd that it became standing room only, and of the men who drank, about half gambled. It made for some very plush times—the finest I had enjoyed in over fifteen years and the finest that Bobbie had experienced in her life.

One particular Friday evening, while I stiffed the regulars at blackjack and Bobbie belted out hits alongside a jazz quartet, a peculiar set of events unfolded. To this day, I can hardly believe how they culminated. Shortly after midnight, the band left the stage and dispersed amongst the crowd. Bobbie walked outside at the set's conclusion and did not return for some time. I played a few more hands, then laid my cards down and ventured after her to get some air.

Bobbie wasn't in front of the club when I stepped out, so I lit a cigarette and headed down the sidewalk to the alley. Therein, I heard voices, so I followed them until two shadowy figures came into view under a gas lamp. They were of Bobbie and the trumpet player from the band she'd accompanied. She had her back up against the wall, and from her stance, I could tell she was highly uncomfortable. He was leaning drunkenly against the building with one arm across her, aggressively sweet-talking. It was painfully clear that Bobbie wanted no part of his advances, and he was as guilty as sin. He ran his fingers through the fabric of her dress, touched her face, and grabbed at her—all while she loudly protested. She looked like a deer in headlights—panicked and ready to run in an instant—but frozen in fear of what would happen if he caught her.

"Turn around," he ordered her.

Uncharacteristically, she stood her ground, and her firm "No!" echoed through the alley.

When she refused, the man drew back, raised his hand, and brought it down hard across her face. Bobbie immediately shut down.

"You're going to do what I tell you to do," he growled, "and you're going to do it now. Now turn the fuck around!"

Bobbie turned.

In an instant, her face was pressed up against the brick wall. With one hand, he held her arms above her head, and with the other, he began messing with his belt.

I saw red. I rushed down the alley and grabbed the man. He was caught off guard and went down easy. As soon as he hit the ground, I kicked him as violently as I could until my whole boot was covered with his blood. Blood poured in streams from his face and ears and soaked into his clothes and the ground. I hit him with every ounce of strength I could muster, but this bastard refused to go cold. I wanted to dig my fingers into his eyes, rip him limb from limb, and drag what was left intact through the streets—but the fact that he managed to scramble to his feet and stagger away likely saved me a trip to the gallows.

I stood there with my head rushing and heart pounding for a moment, then I turned to Bobbie.

"I'm getting too old for this shit," I breathed, panting hard. "Are you okay?"

Bobbie didn't reply. She remained where she stood against the wall, still frozen. Slowly, she turned to face me and met my wild eyes with her incredulous ones. Her expression was unlike any I'd ever seen before; it was as if, for the first time, she'd been shaken from a waking sleep into a state of real awareness. The blinders were off, my intentions were clear, and the result of her trust was plain to see. She stared back at me, blindsided, and met my strained, bloodshot gaze as pure gratitude swept across her face.

The emotion in her expression jarred me. Usually, Bobbie was emotionally DOA, but at that moment, the warmth and thanks just oozed out of her. Wordlessly, she stepped forward, ran her trembling fingers along my face, studied my eyes, and kissed me. Now, it was my turn to freeze. I did not react—first of all because I was bewildered, and secondly because I didn't know how. The last thing I wanted to do was kiss her back and make her think I'd only chased off her attacker so I could get a chance at the action myself, so I just let her kiss me. I was under the impression that it was no more than a sincere gesture of gratitude, but once she pulled away, her eyes found mine again, and after a moment, she kissed me a second time. Not in thanks, but because she *wanted* to. For the first time in her life of mistreatment, she expressed intimacy, not because it was forced upon her, but because she desired it. For the first time, she felt like something more to a man than just a place for him to put his cock. This time, I kissed her back.

In one of life's moments that feel like little more than a dream, we rushed back to our hotel and made love. Of all the women I've been with, Bobbie ranks head and shoulders above the rest—including both of my wives. The first time we kissed, I felt like we were standing on a fault line—that's how much the earth moved—and we held onto one another with such a depth of tenacity it leaves me breathless to recall. More even than we wanted each other, we needed each other. We consumed each other with a passion that had built up over the span of nearly a year and countless miles of relying upon one another. Without even realizing that I'd done so, I'd shown her how to trust; I'd shown her how to feel. And, that moment of bliss—though fleeting as they all are—for me will last a lifetime, for it is as imbued in my memory as the recollection of life itself.

When we made love, there came into existence a gem of experience so surreal, so elusive, and so ephemeral that, as a betting man, I wager less than one million men have, in all their lives, been lucky enough to partake in the bliss that Bobbie and I shared. In those moments, she gave me all her pain, neatly packaged in a scream. She gave me all her misery in a grasp—and when she finally let go, she'd sigh, and her lips moved. It wasn't quite a smile, but it was the closest I ever got.

The love we made that night in New Orleans was not a one-off occurrence—yet it remained an entirely unspoken part of our relationship. Generally, over the course of the day, a man finds himself lured by fantasies of his woman, her body, and their union—but such thoughts didn't overcome me the way they assail most men. At any other time in my life, they had—and still did when I thought of my wife—but when I thought of Bobbie, those thoughts were of an entirely different nature. What was so profoundly treasured between us was the trust we shared, and our love was the most consummate expression of that trust. My sole desire was to protect her. She knew she was safe with me, and she made me feel safe. I desired her presence more than I desired her body. I desired her love more than I desired her assurance that she was mine and mine alone— because I knew she wasn't, nor was I hers.

I know they say *"any port in a storm,"* and I'd docked the night in unfamiliar ports more times than I could count—but with Bobbie, it was something different, unlike anything I'd ever felt before. It was love, no doubt, but of the strangest varietal and the least clarity. I loved Bonnie Lee, don't get me wrong, and at times missed her so severely that my body and soul ached and yearned for her touch, yet I loved Bobbie at the same time.

Some men beat upon the drum of morals like it is the breath of life. I was never one of them. I loved who I loved, whether I wanted to or not. That is one thing a man cannot control—for the mind can merely comment upon the ministrations of the heart. I hadn't seen Bonnie Lee in almost seventeen years, and my love for Bobbie knew no bounds. What was I supposed to do? Remain faithful to an ideal? To a memory? To some faraway concept of love when there was a body so warm, so real, and so willing laying down beside me each and every evening? I think not. I hardly suppose it bothered Bobbie that I was a married man, and for better or worse, it surely didn't bother me.

Returning to life in Mexico—to Bonnie Lee and the son I'd never met, to the mezcal bars and siestas, to settling down and hanging around, waiting to scalp the drifters—seemed like a far cry from what I really wanted: the freedom I had been denied for so long. And even if I wanted to—despite my love for her—I could not return to Bonnie Lee without bringing something back to her other than white hair and wrinkles.

At the time, there was not a single moment when I stopped and considered that I had a wife and child in Mexico and yet chose to carpetbag around the country with a girl nearly thirty years my junior. Nor was there a moment when I stopped to consider why I found this homeless waif so alluring. She did not embody any conventional standards of beauty. Her voice did not tinkle like gentle bells; it cried like the wind and punctured your soul like a burst of hail. Her skin was not as soft as Mulberry silk; it was as dry and rough as that of any other bum on the road. Her eyes didn't reflect starlight and glow with radiance—no, her eyes were dark, sallow, and sad. Yet, I loved her. There is no telling why.

Me and Bobbie McGee remained in New Orleans until late spring. Winter in the Big Easy had yielded quite a substantial bankroll, and when we left to escape the humidity of southern summer, we kept off the freights, often hitchhiking or catching the bus instead. We traveled back up the Mississippi, hitting the same profitable haunts as we had on the way down, and after we reached Minnesota once more, we headed out west. However, we made a pact that if we were ever somehow separated on the road, we'd meet one another in New Orleans.

By the summer of 1956, Bobbie was a very different woman than she had been the year before, but some things never changed. Even after all the time we traveled together and all the clubs she performed in, Bobbie never learned how to speak sweetly, bat her eyes, giggle, or flirt—and humor was entirely outside her ken—but perhaps that was for the best. She was painfully honest at all times, and there was never any question about how she felt.

And, though it appeared more infrequently than it had in the past, Bobbie's Fear remained boundless—and it always caught me off-guard. Sometimes she'd turn away in the midst of a kiss or an embrace and stare—just stare out into nothing, out into the silence and uncertainty, and she'd greet it there. The Fear made itself at home in her eyes, and horror was the reward of any man who interrupted her rumination. For, she'd look at you with the semblance of a woman shaken from a dream, wrenched away just moments from bliss, and though she'd meet my inquisitive eyes with her haunted ones, she'd look straight through me as if I wasn't even there.

She still drank, too, and had her bouts with sleepless nights—and there was one thing she always used to tell me, which did not subside, even after the nature of our relationship changed. When it was real late and quiet, after she'd put down enough liquor to make her drowsy, Bobbie would look at me and say, "Jack, all I want outta life before I die is one good man."

I never used to pay her lament very much mind, as her former life had given her more than enough cause to wish for such a seemingly unattainable object, but, eventually, it began to wear on me.

"Haven't I been a good man to you, Bobbie?" I asked her one night as she sat upright on the edge of our bed, gently swaying with the addition of copious bourbon.

She answered promptly but did not turn to look at me. "You've been a fugitive half your life and spent the other half a prisoner—either by chains or rings—and one of those prisons still holds you captive. You find yourself drawn back to it willingly, and one day you'll be going."

"Bonnie Lee is my wife," I explained to her, surprised that she'd interpreted my question in that way, "but that doesn't mean I'm going to leave you alone. I love her, I want her, I miss her—but I've loved her, wanted her, and missed her for a long time, almost as long as you've been alive. I—"

Bobbie cut me off, "Jack, look at me. I'm an orphan, a whore, a broken down, used up excuse for a woman...shaken, battered, afraid...."

"Some might say that would make us perfect for each other," I cut her off this time.

Bobbie scoffed, "I'll wait for that one good man."

I went for it. "What if that man is me?"

Bobbie stopped swaying, slowly turned, and stared back at me, fear and sadness flitting about behind her eyes. She did not say a word.

Time moved along—as it always seems to—and for the first time in many years, all was well and remained so. Bars and poker games, comfortable digs, the beauty of the American West, and blues songs that could heal all ills filled our days. Most of our summer was spent around Utah, Colorado, and California, and Bobbie and I were going strong. The only matter that unsettled me was Bobbie's drunken insistence on finding one good man. The longer we remained in one another's company, the more often she'd say it, and before long, her comment became vacuous. Even though she'd get drunk and traipse around on sleepless nights, she always returned to my arms, and eventually, I began to pay her near-nightly lament hardly any notice—until one night when she didn't come back.

It was toward the end of September, as beautiful a time as any to spend in California. We were in a little town called Santa Rita, just outside Salinas. The club where we'd spent the evening had shuttered up shortly after midnight, and we'd returned to our room straightaway. As usual, Bobbie had brought a bottle with her and drank it down until it contained nothing but her breath—and when sleep still refused to avail her, she took to the streets. I awoke at three and found her gone. There was nothing unusual about such a circumstance, but for some imperceptible reason, I felt very uneasy, and no matter how much I twisted and turned, I could not fall back to sleep. I chastised myself for such unwarranted anxiety and, as I did so, dressed and set out to look for her.

I walked the streets of Santa Rita for hours and never encountered another soul. I had to be utterly mad, I thought, to be searching for this withershins woman at such an ungodly time of night. But regardless of how customary her absence was, something was different about that day—I just knew it.

At daybreak, I finally found her. She was standing at the depot, seemingly alone. A few other red-eye travelers were milling about, but she stood trackside by herself.

"Hey, Rider," I called out tentatively, "I didn't know we had a train to catch tonight."

Bobbie turned toward the sound of my voice just as slowly and dazedly as she always did. Her eyes were hollow, her voice cold and emotionless, "We don't. I do."

Some emotion, nameless, icy, and akin to dread, flooded me. "Where are you going?" I asked.

"I found that one good man," she answered, her voice stoic and unwavering.

I looked around the platform at the rest of those waiting for the train and then back at the woman I loved.

"What?" I blurted out, utterly blindsided.

Bobbie did not repeat herself.

I could feel my blood pressure skyrocket as it had in that back alley in New Orleans—but I did not react. Our eyes locked across the platform, and the dealer stood pat. I knew in an instant that Bobbie hadn't been coerced. This was her own decision, and whoever that good man was, he had won.

We remained that way for a long while, unmoving. The track lights began flashing at dawn, and I heard the inbound whistle blow. I knew that she was going to leave. My heart felt like it had imploded—but I didn't put up a fight. When the train pulled in and the doors opened, my lips said, "I love you," and my eyes said, "Don't go." Her lips were still and silent, and her eyes were full of pain. I watched her board, but I could not bear to see the others who followed. By the time '*all aboard*' rang out and the train pulled away, I was halfway down the empty street.

I walked back to our room in a daze. I was numb. Hollow. Empty. You could've shot me dead in the chest, and it would've gone straight through. I had never been more devastated in all my life. In my younger days, I would've fought an army of what she deemed 'good men' to remain by her side—but when she looked at me—the way she looked at me—all the fight fled from my bones. As a result, I did something I'd never done before in my entire life; I let her go. I'd removed her from a place that would've swallowed her alive and rotted her soul from the outside in. I'd shown her that she had wings, that she had a choice in the matter of living or dying, and for the first time in her life, she'd decided to fly. Who was I to stop her now?

I checked out of that hotel the next day and set out to follow her. Right off, I'd vowed that I wouldn't, but I couldn't help myself. By the end of that first evening, I was ready to climb out of my skin. I couldn't sit still for trying, let alone eat or even think about sleeping. I headed east on the first passenger train out of Salinas, knowing I'd never find her. And, there was a part of me—slight though it was—that didn't want to. All I'd ever wanted for Bobbie was for her to be happy. If she thought she had a chance at that, I couldn't be selfish enough to tear away from her all I'd given—no matter how much losing her killed me. And it was not knowing whether or not she was okay that killed me most of all.

As if by instinct, I found myself back out along that black, muddy river, scouring every town that we'd stayed in for the slightest suggestion of her presence—but in the months that followed, I found not a single clue to her whereabouts. I lit out across California, scoured Texas and Utah, and poked my head into every joint along the banks of the Mississippi—to no avail. I called every club whose name I remembered, poured out my soul to every telephone operator from Portland to Baton Rouge, but she'd faded into the mist.

Knowing I was a fool for trying didn't stop me either. Many years have passed since that terrible night, and I've long since resigned myself to the fact that I will likely spend forever running down that endless line. I'll never know where she went, where she ended up, or if that man really was good to her—but if there's one thing I know for sure, it's that I'll never be the same.

Once I made it to the mouth of the Mississippi, exhausted from searching and from life itself, I remembered our pact. I decided to remain in New Orleans for a time, still eminently hopeful that she'd change her mind and come looking for me as I so fervently did her. But it was in vain; she never came looking, and I doubt she ever will.

I've been married twice, imprisoned twice, and fettered by every kind of madness in between, yet by her influence, I am a changed man. There ain't no crying over what was or could've been, but if there is any circumstance that has made me feel like draining my soul, it is the former. I haven't walked through a crowd since then without searching or read a paper or listened to a news broadcast without hoping to hear her name. All told, there are days when I find myself in the clutches of my own thousand-yard stare, and at the very recesses of it is the memory of Bobbie McGee.

IX

Johnny B. Goode

The Indian summer rain fell like teardrops; there was something of relief about them and something of pain. The floods and storms brought in by the gulf had blown themselves out for the remainder of the year, but their scars and aftershocks were visible across Louisiana. While the residents of the cities, swamps, and bayous whitewashed their damaged homes and rebuilt their fences and docks, so did I lick my wounds. Bobbie McGee had sure done a number on me. She was stuck on my mind like white on rice. As a gambler, that put me in sorry shape. My concentration was shot to hell, and my execution fumbled and lacked like a drunk man trying to put on pants. Disgusted, I threw my cards and dice into the river and determined to find some new graft to keep me sated for a while.

Hanging around idly only exacerbated my poor condition. I would have rather been the headlight on a cross-country locomotive than in a plush penthouse all on my own. When you're riding in a coach or a side-door Pullman across the Mississippi Delta as the sun sets and darkness closes in around you, those southern nights just soak you in. You aren't you anymore; you disappear, and along with you, so do your troubles for a time.

Moving was the only thing that settled me, so I sent out some feelers along the tramp underground and got myself in touch with a member of the Johnson family. For a fee, he was not only able to get me a clean identity—J. Sampson, the unconvicted—but also a job in the mail car on the Southern Railway's Crescent, sorting mail between Meridian, Mississippi, and New Orleans, where I spent my days off wandering the streets and scanning the faces of the tourists.

Normally, with a rap like mine, I would have never been a contender for such a position, and illegitimate paperwork would have never passed the scrutiny of the government workers responsible for vetting candidates, but things operated just a little bit differently on the Crescent. For an iconic train carrying passengers between two of the most prominent cities in the country, the management was six kinds of madness in a blender. For one, they had two ex-cons manning their mail car, the Pullman porters ran a gambling ring out of the caboose, and the fireman was a monkey. Apparently, the engineer, who had been an infantryman during the Korean squabble, had found the orphaned primate while stationed in Japan and proceeded to raise him as one would a son. As unbelievable as it sounds, I'd watched that monkey sit on the stool beside the engineer and throw out signals, blow the horn, and adjust the boilers. Once, while the engineer dined on a long overdue lunch, that monkey ran the Crescent out of Slidell, across Lake Pontchartrain, and into Orleans Parish with the same competency as his handler.

Meanwhile, as the unknowing passengers whiled away the time playing canasta in their berths and smoking cigars in the lounge, the crew of the Crescent bled her dry. My brother Johnson and I were some of the most egregious offenders. He was the foreman of the car and, therefore, responsible for properly handling all the mail on board. There were two more postal clerks on the same route, and to my knowledge, they were completely unaware of the felonious activity that was going on right under their noses.

Our job was to sort the mail, and we did just that. It was a fast-paced operation, as we were required to have the proper sack ready for dispatch as the train passed the station and the local office's outbound mail was retrieved by the catcher arm as we sped by. The sack was then immediately opened and organized into the dozens of various compartments within the car. Because it was such an expeditious task, it was exceedingly easy to exercise sticky fingers. By the time we reached the end of our section, we always had a small sack full of envelopes addressed to Sears or Montgomery Ward that were a little too heavy to contain personal checks. This financial bolster served me well, but it lacked imagination and thrill— after all, it doesn't take a rocket scientist to rob the U.S. mail. Regardless,

I stuck with it for a time and, before long, stumbled upon a far more lucrative opportunity.

The Crescent ran about 200 miles from Meridian to New Orleans, stopped an average of eight times, and collected from 26 post offices. Most of our towns, therefore, were roll-throughs, and locals would congregate at the post offices, rail crossings, or even in their backyards to watch the train speed by. The passengers nearly always found this endearing, and in pleasant weather, would have the windows in the coaches down so they could wave to the bystanders, and up ahead in the cab, the monkey would blow the whistle. There were a few retired railroad men who were staples of the route and would sit trackside whittling and gumming their navy plug, and, of course, there were wide-eyed kids, as I myself once had been, who would run shouting and whooping alongside the iron horse as fast as their little legs could carry them—and then there was Johnny B. Goode.

I didn't learn his name for quite some time, but I saw him nearly every day. He lived in a little wooden cabin with a sloping, mossy roof and concave walls beside the Pearl River station, where the speed restriction was about ten miles an hour. He was a good ol' country boy, about eighteen years at most, and as provincial as they come. I never saw him wear anything other than overalls, patched as necessity dictated, and if he owned shoes, never sported them. He was as skinny as a beanpole and around six feet tall. His jaw jutted out like a cypress knee, but he was otherwise a relatively handsome kid. And, if he wasn't colored, I would've been convinced that he was the progeny of Black Peter—because other than that satanic soloist, I've never met another individual so adept at playing the guitar.

Without fail, around breakfast time and then again at sundown, he'd be sitting out on a tree stump in the pine grove near the tracks with an old, weather-worn acoustic guitar in his hands. The passengers were completely enamored with him, and the train crew considered him to be as much of a landmark as the station signs and water towers. Unlike Black Peter or even Bobbie, the 'Git-Box Kid'—as we knew him—was a bit of a ham, and the more the passengers clapped and whistled, the more he'd show off. It did not take long before I'd concocted a scheme that'd pay off for both of us and was eminently more enjoyable than slicing open envelopes and stuffing my pockets with the hard-earned dollars of housewives and rural bumpkins trying to buy curtains and corn-shellers on time.

One sunny day in early spring, when I wasn't working in the mail car, I took the train up from New Orleans and got off at the Pearl River station. As usual, the Git-Box Kid was in his favorite spot in full view of the Pullmans, strumming away. I waited on the platform for the train to depart before approaching him. I'd ditched my starched thousand-miler and dirty boots for a pale gray seersucker suit and wingtip oxfords and acquired a leather attaché case which I carried under my arm with casual importance. Like any shrewd businessman, I dressed myself up to look twice as good as I was and acted twice as good as I dressed. The Git-Box Kid noticed my sharp threads as soon as I detrained, and when he realized I was walking in his direction, he was just about knocked out.

"What's your name, young fellow?" I called out as I hiked up a small knoll, careful not to step in the mud with my new shoes.

"Johnny," he answered, wide-eyed and enthusiastic, "Johnny B. Goode. Tha's Good with an E. The B stands for Beauford."

I shook my head. Of all the people with all the names in the entire world, I was becoming acquainted with somebody named Johnny B. Goode.

"Wha's you'rn?" he asked me. I could see the boyish curiosity just about oozing out of his ears.

"Johnny," I replied, "I'm Johnny too—except my name is Johnny B. Bad. The B stands for Ben, and folks call me Jack—Jack Ben Bad."

Johnny B. Goode stood before me and blinked heavily. "Aw shoot! Why, tha' ain't your right name, mister—cain't be so!"

I chuckled, "No, Boy, I am J. Sampson of the Crescent City Talent Management Company."

His jaw dropped open, and a horde of mosquitoes became fatally detoured into the gaping cavern by the force of the gasp that followed.

"Could'ya...would'ya mind introducin' yo'self once mo'?"

I repeated my assumed persona. "I often travel on the Crescent to and from New Orleans, and you caught my eye. You've really got something with that guitar of yours there. Would you mind showing me a little something more?"

He was so tickled, you would've thought I'd just gone and promised him one million dollars, and boy, oh boy, did he put on a little show for me there outside the Pearl River station. Not only did he pop off an impromptu version of Bing's *Mississippi Mud*, he turned that guitar around and played it left-handed, he played it behind his back, and he even laid it on the ground and played it with his toes! I was thoroughly impressed—and almost wished, for his sake, that I really was with a legitimate agency.

"Well done, Boy!" I applauded him. "I believe you are just what we are looking for. Have you ever been on stage? Played for a crowd?"

He was so visibly excited he was shaking, "N-n-n..no, Sir, only at church an' revivals. People likes what they heah. Tells me thin's like 'Johnny you's greater'n good!'"

"Folks have got a mighty good ear in these parts," I replied emphatically. "I'd like to make you an offer, Johnny—to come and play in the blues clubs down in New Orleans and up in Atlanta—maybe we'll even make a record."

Johnny B. Goode could no longer contain himself. "Pa!" He shouted at the top of his lungs before taking off and running toward the house, "Pa!"

I smiled silently to myself and strolled after him in the direction of the cabin.

I was presently received on the rickety back porch by a bewildered gentleman about ten years my junior who introduced himself to me as Johnny's father, Mr. Goode.

I explained my errand once more, and the euphoric man let out a whoop and a holler and started dancing all around that creaking porch. "Boy, I tole you, boy! Whuhdid I tell you, boy! You's gon' be a big stah, a big stah! Playin' in da big town—e'ry big town! Why praise de Lord—Mr. Sampson, Sir, d'ya think mah boy Johnny heh's got what it takes to lead one of dem dere big blues ensembles one day? Get to see his name all lit up in lights an' allah dat?"

I drawled out a professional reply, "The degree of Johnny's future success is, of course, something I do not have the means to guarantee you of at this time—but I can doubtlessly assure you that he meets and exceeds every qualification our company requires of new talent and is as well-mannered and personable a young man as any I have ever managed before. My associates and I would be more than pleased to mentor and guide Johnny in his musical career as far as he desires to take it."

More celebration was had by father and son, and then roles and conditions were discussed. I was to be Johnny's sole manager. I would be responsible for all booking and publicity and chaperone him during engagements. In return, I would receive a small percentage of his wages as compensation. I would be responsible for managing all of his affairs, financially and otherwise, and look out for his best interests at all times. It was a charming little agreement, and I made sure to write in a few clauses that favored me alone. I hoped that, like most men of humble means, Mr. Goode and Johnny would not hire a lawyer or read the whole document. In this, I turned out to be luckier than I could've ever imagined because both Johnny and his father were illiterate—and far more trusting in the business tactics of a stranger than anyone should ever be. They both signed without hesitation.

I returned to the Goode house the next day and collected Johnny at the station. He had gotten himself all duded up in his Sunday best and was wild and bright-eyed when I arrived. He had his humble guitar slung over his shoulder in a gunny sack. His father stood beside him, buzzing with excitement.

"Don' you worry 'bout a thin'," Mr. Goode told Johnny, "You jus' put yo' head to playin' and savin' up yo' money and makin' yo' ol' momma proud—Lord rest her soul."

Mr. Goode then turned to me, removed his hat, and thanked me profusely for the opportunity I had given his son.

I smiled and assured him the pleasure was all mine.

My favorite chapters in life have been anytime someone else did the work, and I reaped the reward. After my stint in Nevada—where I'd done all of the sowing and enjoyed none of the reaping, I thought it was about high time for that to change. I'd made the club circuit rounds with Black Peter, and I'd made the rounds with Bobbie McGee, and I was fully determined that the third time would be the charm. I knew the terrain, the rap, and the club owners—and they knew I brought in quality—albeit unusual—entertainment. With Bobbie, I'd gotten my foot in the door, and once I was in, with Johnny by my side, I took off running—and the boy did not disappoint. Where Bobbie had earned me a living, Johnny earned me a life.

Right away, I booked him appearances at any club that would have him—and after they had him once, they'd call me up to ask when they could have him again. The kid was outrageously talented, and he was a showman to boot. He may have been a bit slow on the uptake, but he never came off as dumb. In fact, his hokey, back-bayou mannerisms, coupled with his musical prowess, lent him just enough favors to make him appear quite charming, especially to the city slickers to whom he was quite a foreigner.

In those days, Bourbon Street and most of the French Quarter were governed by the iron fist of Jim Crow. Clubs were white only with one entrance where colored people could not so much as loiter, let alone be served, but upon nearly every stage—regardless of how strict the ordinances—eminently talented black entertainers could be found. Of course, in most of the smaller clubs and bars, they didn't have a colored dressing room or a segregated back room of any kind, so I'd bring Johnny in through the kitchen just a few moments before he was to go on and then usher him out the same way once he'd finished his performance.

The magnitude and customs of the city were absolutely mystifying to Johnny, and I do not believe he ever lost the sense of sheer amazement that overcame him when he stepped off the Crescent coach at Union Station. Such a reaction was to be expected. If you've never seen a city before—and even for many who have—New Orleans is pure culture shock. Populated initially by Parisian ex-cons and prostitutes, a sense of lawlessness and social freedom continues to persist. It's no wonder I felt at home there. Drink was subject to hardly any regulation whatsoever, the open exchange of products and services generally prohibited went largely unmolested by the law, and even friends of Dorothy found tolerant—if not welcoming—environs. But, if you were unfortunate enough to be black, you were subject to the same disenfranchisement consistent throughout the rest of the south. For a white manager of black talent, that complicated my life some, but not enough for me to give up the venture entirely.

In the early days, before he was offered regular engagements, Johnny played seven nights a week, sometimes at two or three clubs a night. I conducted all the necessary business and, in turn, lined my pockets with about ninety percent of his earnings. I ensured he had enough to keep a decent room, pay for his meals, and have a buck or two of spending money per week, but that was all. I figured as time went on, I'd have to give him a bigger cut, but Johnny never so much as mentioned the meager allowance. He so thoroughly enjoyed performing and living in the city and was so grateful for the opportunity that, to him, his success was payment enough. The kid was as happy as a dog with two tails. Club owners loved him, and their patrons loved him even more. It wasn't long before his name was in lights up and down Bourbon Street, and I spent my evenings in the audience with a free drink in my hand, watching my efforts pay themselves off with interest.

I tried to keep Johnny working and as near to me as possible to prevent him from getting any ideas of venturing out on his own and learning just how much he'd been taken for, but my concern was hardly warranted. Johnny was as loyal as a patriot, and above all, the poor bastard trusted me implicitly. It was a shame, really, but he was far too young and hailed from far too homegrown and trusting environs to realize the prevailing truth that everything in life is a graft until the money's in your hand.

—And the kid brought in some decent money. There's not a musician in the world who'd be able to bet against an oilman with the earnings he brought in from playing the blues in bars, but compared to his fellow performers—no matter what color—Johnny did well.

Johnny's popularity was bolstered by the fact that by the late 50s, Dixieland—the long-reigning southern favorite—was out, and guitar bands were in. Initially, he played that old acoustic article he'd brought from home, but as soon as he proved his potential, I bought him a new electric model Fender Stratocaster. The rest is history. Funny enough, Johnny really hit his stride after he started singing songs he'd transplanted from the revivals back home to the seedy bars of New Orleans. Those Baptists sure loved their gospel songs, even played in a club; they took their swinging God anywhere they could get him, especially the Negroes. And Johnny could lay down a rocking version of *When The Saints Go Marching In* that made the whole crowd go practically wild.

Johnny played to predominantly white audiences, but some clubs were exceptions. The Dew Drop Inn was a decided favorite, and no more than a few days passed in a row without an engagement there. The atmosphere was considerably more relaxed, as Jim Crow was not a customer. Most evenings, mine and Johnny's brothers could sit at the same bar and share a drink without any rumblings from the local officials. Once or twice during my residence in New Orleans, it got raided, but the efforts were mainly a power play intended to remind the darkies they'd best not get too comfortable with such casual integration.

However, in the city at large, the population did not dare mix at will. Even Johnny and I walking down the street side-by-side occasioned some crooked glances. Growing up in Denver, there was some skin trouble, but never to the extent that it existed in the south, and though I'd observed it all my life, I never got used to it. Johnny, on the other hand, was no stranger to Jim Crow, and though city living was often far more derogatory to Negroes than his hamlet on the river, Johnny weathered the abuse jovially.

Johnny lived in a segregated boarding house in Tremé, across from the Quarter, while I took up living on Bourbon Street with Loose Lucy—a voluptuous blonde-haired burlesque dancer from the 500 Club. She was catty, mercurial, and hardly older than Bobbie, but she loved my money, and I loved her assets. Somewhat akin to Bertha Steele, my fondness for her was tried quite considerably whenever she opened her mouth, but as I'd said in Reno, what is it for a man to live a life of luxury without a woman beside him? Although, I knew from the start of our affair that Lucy was merely a temporary filling and soon to be replaced.

Unlike every other epoch of my life, I put my head down and saved as much of the money Johnny brought in as I could. I veered away from gambling dens and poker tables like they were police stations, and when I did feel like losing some money, I frequented the billiard hall three doors down from my Bourbon Street apartment. When Bobbie left me, it seemed she'd taken with her more than just her one good man—she'd taken my mojo too. I couldn't draw better than a low pair or a kangaroo straight in poker and consistently rolled craps on the come-out. When I tried to finagle the odds in my favor, the touch I'd known all my life just wasn't there, and no matter how hard I tried, I'd end up losing—or worse, getting caught.

Even before Bobbie's sudden exodus, my ability was markedly lower and that of the up-and-coming gamblers infinitely superior—but now I'd just folded up completely. To the young bucks, all greased up in their Murray's and leather jackets, I was an old man. I talked like an old man, walked like an old man, and played like an old man. Their slang, customs, and swagger were all new to me, and my presence was scorned and derided. I could feel the glory days and big wins of my youth fading rapidly into my rearview. I decided that if I saved up enough money before the arrival of summer—when the oppressive heat and humidity make the Louisiana bayou practically uninhabitable—I would finally and irrevocably go back home to Bonnie Lee and do so with an ounce of my pride left intact. I thought about writing her and telling her that I was finally out of prison and on my way home, but I chose to surprise her instead. After all, the look on her face when she opened the door to see me standing on our front stoop at long last would be priceless—and doubtlessly worth the wait.

By the time the eminently profitable Mardi Gras season ended and spring came on—filling the markets with crawdads, the Mississippi with jumping catfish, and the streets with hungry tourists—I had saved up five thousand dollars—the combined total of Johnny's pay, supplemented by my various efforts—and I was anxiously awaiting my return to Mexico. Johnny was doing two shows a night at the Dew Drop Inn Monday through Wednesday, three shows a night at the Tiajuana Club Thursdays and Sundays, and a full set with encores at the Brass Rail over the weekend. I kept him hopping, and the boy liked the hustle—just as long as none of his engagements prevented him from playing with the choir at the Baptist Church down on St. Charles come Sunday morning.

During the six months he'd been at it, he'd lost much of his country naivete and had matured considerably. He dressed smart, had lost the heaviest notes of his bayou twang, and fallen in with a group of other colored musicians who spent much of their time drinking before and after shows at the Dew Drop Inn. Johnny, who stayed true to his pure Baptist roots despite his vice-soaked surroundings, never touched a drop of alcohol, nor did he involve himself with the wily and willing women of the evening or any of the other schemes, scams, and sins of the underworld. Many of his compatriots, however, kept their noses considerably less clean. I'd been introduced to a few of them, and they seemed to sniff around at me uncertainly—wholly unsure if I was a benevolent or a con, despite the laud Johnny heaped upon me.

They were an ambitious group of youngsters. Before long, Johnny was talking about joining in with a bunch of them and recording an album at Cosimo's and even the possibility of leaving New Orleans entirely and moving on to Atlanta, Memphis, or even Harlem. I knew right about then that it was time for me to make an exodus. The kid had a right to his own career—one that would flourish without my hand in his pocket—and he'd already come through in spades.

One fine spring afternoon, as the smell of mandevilla and gumbo filled the heavy May air, Johnny and I sat together on a quiet park bench in the Quarter and terminated his contract. The agreement, which had been stirring for weeks, was mutual and amicable. Johnny, as earnest and maudlin as country folks so often are, told me over and over again that he'd 'sho' miss' me' and that 'Nawlens sho' wunn't gon' be tha same widdout' me, but his eager, boyish excitement to be out in the wide world on his own was so great that it bled through his fiercest sentimentality.

According to our contract, of the 90% of Johnny's earnings that I'd conserved under the guise of exercising financial responsibility, 40% was to be released to him at the termination of my services. Of the five thousand clams that had survived my careless spending and been spared the vagaries of the gambling halls, that amounted to about $2,000.

Once I did the math, that's when I began to think. Johnny had far more promise, potential, talent, and time than I did, and I needed every dollar of that $2k. So, I wrote him a check. It wasn't a good check, of course, nor was it mine. I figured a personal check would arouse too much suspicion when he went and waved it around in front of his friends at the Dew Drop Inn, who would insist that he cash it immediately before I had the chance to skip town. Instead, I called up my Johnson friend, and through his shady network, he connected me with an innovative young man who made his slippery living forging cashier's checks. Nobody questions a cashier's check—and by the time the bank processed it and realized it was a fake, Johnny would have his money, and I'd be in Mexico with $5,000 worth of good American greenbacks.

Feeling quite self-satisfied, I sent Johnny off with a handshake and booked myself a ticket on the night train to Houston. I did not, however, tell Lucy. Such a conversation would have incited an utter meltdown on her behalf, and I had not the desire nor the energy to witness such theatrics. Therefore, I spent my last afternoon in our apartment reclined back on the divan, watching Carol Lawrence on the Ed Sullivan Show and waiting for Lucy to go out for the evening. About halfway through the program, Lucy, who had spent most of the day in her bedroom beautifying herself, slinked out in a besparkeled, hip-hugging, emerald green evening gown.

"Does this dress make me look fat?" she asked, pouting.

I rolled my eyes, checked my desire, and turned back to the television set. The woman had the figure of a 20th-century Aphrodite. The only fat Lucy had on her entire body was between her ears, and the only way you could make her look fat in an evening gown would be to stuff another girl in there with her. Yet, she insisted on asking me every time she dressed.

"Massive, Honey," I languidly replied, "You look like a blimp with legs."

"I do not!" she protested indignantly.

"See? You know you don't, so why ask me?"

"Take me out tonight, Jack!" She implored me, "It's my day off, and my girlfriends want to go to the 501 Club!"

"Oh, that gaggle of twits! All they do is spend my money and give me a headache. I'd rather spend a night in the county."

"But don't you want to take me out?"

"Sure, Honey, sure I want to go out with you, but not the rest of the Dionne quintuplets. I'll take you out next week."

"But I promised them!" Lucy stamped her feet like a child about to throw a tantrum.

"Alright then, go! I'd rather shoot pool anyway; I don't feel like going out."

"Oh, you and that damn pool hall! I don't think you really spend all that much time there. I think you're messing around with some other girl—maybe more than one!" she turned and folded her arms in a huff.

"Lucy, trust me," I assured her, my eyes trained on Carol Lawrence's legs, "with you around, the very last thing I need is another girl."

"Oh sure, that's what you all say. Damn you men, there ain't a good one in the whole bunch of you!" Angrily, she grabbed her purse and a package of cigarettes and stormed out the door, which she slammed behind her.

The force of the door was jarring enough, and her comment even more so. I soon lost interest in Carol Lawrence, shut off the television, and wandered down to the pool hall, where I'd remain until I left for the depot ahead of departure time. I shot half a dozen games, losing or scratching every one, and around eleven, I settled my debts and headed for the station. I didn't get very far. As soon as my feet hit the sidewalk, two mammoth hands clamped down on my shoulders like a vice and steered me into the nearest dark alley.

Before I could even think, my back was up against the stucco, and I was surrounded by three exceedingly disgruntled colored men. I recognized all three; they were Johnny's musician pals from the Dew Drop. The largest, most menacing of them was a towering trombone player named Rudy, and Rudy made Shannon Todd look like he had a hormone deficiency.

As it turns out, rather than flaunt his check before his envious friends, Johnny had run straight down to the bank. I'd thought I would have had a few days before the bank realized the check was a fake, but unfortunately, it appears that one too many of my young friend's forgeries had crossed the counter at that particular institution, and the bank insisted on investigating every cashier's check that was presented before they paid off. For the six months that Johnny had worked unceasingly, he had gotten not a red cent. He was distraught—and his friends were irate. The gig was up; I'd bet all in and lost the pot. And now I had to pay through the nose.

"C'mon now, fellas, listen," I stammered as the three men closed in around me, "There's been some kind of mistake. I don't know nothin' about no fake check, honest! I'll go right down to the bank tomorrow and get it all straightened out. You can all come with me if you want, Johnny too!"

"Ol' Man, you'll be luckeh if you live tah see t'morrow," Rudy growled, "an' if you does, you'd best do yo' livin' elsewhere—fo' if I sees you in Nawlens alive again, you ain't gon' be that way fo' long."

Once he finished drawling out his threat, Rudy lit me up with a Dutch winder to the ribs, sending my body back against that wall with the same force as a battering ram. That single punch was more devastating than any other I'd ever sustained. It felt like every rib I'd ever broken on my left side instantly fractured along faults that had healed long ago. The pain was indescribable. I used to be renowned as one of the fightingest men in Denver, but at that moment, I found that fight had left me—for I could hardly even defend myself.

If I'd been up against just one of them, the odds would have been poor, but with three, I was at their mercy, and they didn't have much of that. They didn't fight me three to one, either; instead, they took turns, and all three knew just how to hit in order to achieve maximum damage. When one guy got tired of punching me in the head, the next took his place. It was the worst beating I had ever endured in my entire life; even if you rolled all the others into one, they still would not compare—and I only remember quick, agonizing flashes of it.

Once I was on the ground, Rudy dug through my pockets and took from me every last earthly cent I possessed, every last dollar I'd fought to hang on to and bring back to my wife. Panting, helpless, and unable to even crawl, I watched him count it. Once he was through, upon finding the sum satisfactory, they gathered around and began to kick me. I suppose they did so until I passed out, but fortunately, my brain had bounced around so violently out of its pan by that point that those memories shook loose into the greasy pools of city sludge that I awoke face down in some hours later.

I felt like I'd been struck by a freight train—and my first semi-coherent thought was that another one was coming. If I remembered nothing else, I remembered Rudy's threat—and my palsied condition was more than adequate to prove his sincerity. Therefore, driven by the same fear which moves all beasts in this world, half-conscious and less than half-alive, I began to crawl.

—Or, at least, I tried to. My mind said, 'crawl,' but my body said, 'sorry, Jack, no can do.' My right arm was entirely void of usefulness and hung there like a chunk of aching vestigial flesh as I dragged myself pitifully on, propelled by my left forearm and knees.

A couple of lifetimes ago, the Mystick Althea had told me my future from a deck of illustrated playing cards. I remember one that depicted a man lying face down, pierced tenfold by glistening swords. Such is the sum of how I felt at that moment, except that fellow was dead and grateful for it, and I was alive and in agony. Everything from my waist up had been cut, pummeled, and left to bleed—and something in my belly had busted wide open. Call it shock or desperation, but the one and only thought that ran through my pounding skull was the urgent need to get the hell out of New Orleans—but I was getting nowhere fast.

The sky was purple and bruised with dawn by the time I'd dragged myself three doors down to Lucy's apartment. The drunken denizens of Bourbon Street continued to buzz about in gradually decreasing quantities as night waned, stepping over me and ignoring my torment. In those days, no one who had spent more than a few nights in the Quarter looked twice at a man face down on the sidewalk—whether he be drunk, dead, or writhing mad. And, certainly, nobody looked twice at me.

When I finally reached the downstairs door, it took every last iota of strength I possessed to knock loud enough to wake her. Lucy emerged what felt like an eternity later, wrapped in her silk robe with arms crossed— either entirely oblivious or utterly indifferent to the devastating extent of my injuries.

"Jack?" she asked to ensure that the swollen, twisted face caked with dried blood actually belonged to me, "What in hell happened to you?"

"They...jumped...me," I gasped in between shallow breaths laden with anguish.

"Who?" she asked, instantly suspicious, and before I got the chance to choke out an explanation, she started screaming at me.

"I know who it was! I know who jumped you! The boyfriend or husband of that girl you're seeing on the side! Uh-huh! I ain't the fool you take me for! I know you're running around! Well, it serves you right, Jack Jones, you rake!"

"Ain't...ain't no...other...woman," I struggled, "Gotta...get...outta...town. Need...money...need...money...to call...call me a...a cab."

"A cab!" she exclaimed indignantly, "I ain't calling you no cab!"

"Then call...me...an ambulance."

She must've, because the next thing I remember, I was in a heavily starched, heavily bleached hospital room, convalescing. And, let me tell you, the nurse I awoke to sure didn't help the process. She was no Rosalie McFall by any means—and whatever preconceptions she had of me seemed to indicate that she believed I had no right to recuperate in peace. Once I regained consciousness for good—after nearly a week, I was told—she'd wake me just about once every hour to take my vitals and ensure I wasn't in pain. I hadn't been, of course, when I was asleep, and when I did ask for some painkillers, she sure took her sweet time returning to my bedside.

The doctor, a highly respected Cajun gentleman just south of middle age, was far more compassionate. He informed me that I'd suffered four broken ribs, a ruptured spleen, a severe concussion, and a fractured right arm. When asked how such extreme injuries were sustained, I told him I'd gotten drunk and fallen down my apartment stairs. He didn't buy my explanation for a second.

"That flight of stairs had a mighty powerful right hook," he replied knowingly, but he did not press me for the truth.

As it turns out, when Lucy called the ambulance, she told the driver that I was just some random drunk who had knocked on her door—which meant that until I regained consciousness, I was John Doe. All my identification was in the billfold that Rudy had stolen, so when I was finally coherent enough for them to ask what my name was, I gave it as Robert McGee. Living under an assumed name is second nature to a lifelong con, but in this particular case, I wasn't concerned about John Law or Rudy and his band of avengers coming after me; rather, I was to be a fugitive from the collection agencies who would shortly be demanding the balance of the costly medical bills that I was currently racking up.

I spent three weeks in that hospital bed, underwent two surgeries, and just about emptied the dispensary of codeine. Finally, once I could get my legs under me and breathe without excruciating pain, I decided I'd been there long enough. My own clothing had been so badly torn and bloodied that it'd been discarded, but that of my roommate, who'd undergone an operation to repair a rupture, was clean and folded on the nightstand beside his bed. On a particularly hectic night, while he was fast asleep, after donning a shirt so large I swam in it and pants I needed to cuff twice to avoid tripping over, I snuck out of the hospital and into the sweltering New Orleans night.

It was less than a mile from the hospital to the railyard, but to me, it felt like twenty. In all my years, I've never boarded a train in such sorry shape as I did that midnight as I climbed into the cradle of a gondola hauling ballast west—likely from the penal institution in that city, which I had somehow been able to avoid. New Orleans was one of the few rail hubs in which I hadn't been the recipient of the sheriff's most gracious hospitality, likely because I'd never entered that city a bum—but through this most unfortunate reversal of fate, I was most certainly leaving as one.

And I would never return. Paying heed to Rudy's promise and my own tarnished memories, I boarded that freighter and never looked back. But, my mind had expectations far loftier than my broken body could fulfill.

I made it twelve hours and three hundred and fifty miles to Houston before I tapped out. It was nearly noon when I eased my gnarled and aching body over the rim of that searing black train car and trudged lamely out of the yards toward any establishment that promised air conditioning and hydration. I was denied entrance to five bars of varying degrees of seediness before one basement bordello let me in. I had no money, of course, so I drank the ice water I was served and relished in the cool and quiet without even offering a glance in the direction of the bawdy girls who were mulling around half-drunk and off the clock. My eyes were fixed on a bottle of Denver-distilled gin, but despite the fact it was a mere three feet away from me behind the bar, I was further from a shot of the stuff than I was from Bonnie Lee in Mexico.

There had never been a time in my life when I'd felt so helpless. I had not a dime—only the stolen, sweat-soaked clothes on my back—and no way of earning any more. I couldn't work if I wanted to. I couldn't push a broom, bus a table, or man the door. And I could forget entirely about splitting wood for the Salvation Army in exchange for a meal—I couldn't even shuffle a blame deck of cards! Nor could I steal the stuff, as I would've at any other time when I found myself broke. Even if I could sneak around the back of the bar while nobody was looking, I couldn't reach up high enough to grab it off the shelf—my aching ribs would never allow it. And, so, I remained there as long as they permitted me, crunching on ice cubes, my eyes locked on that bottle as it taunted me the way a cruel child taunts a lion in a zoo.

Shortly before sundown, I was ushered mercilessly out onto the street ahead of the crowds, and once more, I found myself alone with nowhere to go. Night came on soon enough, and with all other options long retreated, I found an empty doorway just inside the mouth of an alley and exhausted, hungry, and suffering bodily, stretched out for a restive, uncomfortable sleep.

The next few days that followed passed with selfsame advent. Defeat and despair dug their moldy claws into my unwashed back, but despite my insufferable condition, I flatly refused to starve to death in Texas. If I was doomed to die a bum, I was determined to do so somewhere that had better weather, at the very least. I wanted to get as far from New Orleans as possible, and Houston was far too hot—literally and figuratively.

After that last hop, I would have signed myself over to holy life immediately if it meant I never had to see another freight train again, but I knew I was entitled to no such luck. However, at least for a while, I could not bear the lurching, shuddering, and jolting of the flat-wheelers on the mainline, so once I made the decision to leave, I stood at the entrance to the freeway with my thumb pointed north, waiting for some good Samaritan to stop and offer to truck this crippled old hobo off to the destination of his next bout of misfortune.

I went the way of the driver each time one was fool enough to pick me up, and by the end of the trip, I was usually able to pry a couple of sympathy bucks or some spare clothing off of the fellow. Meals were procured by begging at the backdoors of restaurant kitchens in whatever town I found myself, and when handouts were sparse, I usually had a few dollars saved up in my sock to see me through. It was nearly always my objective to score the services of some over-the-road trucker who took advantage of the traffic-free nights to see himself out of the urban areas so that I could sleep without worrying about the local constables scraping me off of a park bench and depositing me in the city jail. For the most part, this policy paid off, as it was decidedly rare that any private citizen would stop for me.

After my fifteen years away, I found that there had been a nationwide push to clean house as far as homeless undesirables were concerned. The number of tramps on trains had dropped to a fraction of their former masses, and since the war, the number of trains themselves had decreased significantly as well. For those who still chose to ride the iron horses unticketed, the journey was more treacherous than it had ever been before. Steam and coal were rapidly being replaced by diesel-electric—making hauls longer, with greater speeds and fewer stops. Rail companies had tightened their regulations, and softhearted brakemen and 'bo money hardly bought you the miles they did in the past. Years of damages had resulted in a 'zero-tolerance' attitude toward the members of the floating fraternity, and their methods, too, had received an overhaul. Bulls were less likely to beat the dickens out of you when they snatched you by the collar off of one of their freights, but the penalties dished out by the law were steeper—longer sentences for the penniless and heavier fines for those poor bums whose government pensions Uncle Sam could dam up any time he pleased. Passenger trains, in particular, were almost entirely off-limits, railside jungles that once hosted populations larger than some rural towns were all but abandoned, and water towers—long-standing monuments to trampdom—had become mere relics.

In cities across the nation, there was a mass movement of governors and local politicians hell-bent on cleaning up their territory. Tramps, bums, cons, and every other strange varietal of social misfit who had previously found shelter on the road and in the various nooks and crannies of the underworld suddenly found themselves swept under the proverbial rug of civic gentrification. Even in Chicago—the one-time hobo capital of the nation—the word on the street was 'move up or move on.'

I had been living on the road far too long to be ignorant of the writing on the wall. My kind was being forced out. The hobo, the bindle-stiff, the traveling yegg, the jungle buzzard, the scenery bum—they were going the way of the buffalo and the free lunch. And I knew, whether I liked it or not, that if I didn't keep my wits about me, I'd soon join their ranks.

X

Wharf Rat

I didn't ride a freight train or enter a rail yard for nearly six months after I left Houston by way of an oil tanker. Instead, my thumb became my ticket, and for the first time in my life, I toured America by highway. And not just any highway; the interstate highway—freshly mapped, paved, and set upon by millions of Michelins.

My objective was the West, and after considerable hitchhiking, backtracking, and hard traveling, I found myself in the forests of the pacific coast, just outside of Portland, Oregon. I left that city of roses in early July on the back of a flatbed bound for the timberlands. My idea was a simple one. If I couldn't get over on the quick-witted townies anymore, I figured I'd try my luck with the loggers. I knew their type as well as I knew my own, and if there's any group of men whose favorite hobby on payday is throwing around their hard-earned cash to feed the follies of the flesh, it's loggers and ironworkers. Ironworkers are likely the more thoroughly mad of the two, but loggers have more patsies among them. My hopes weren't incredibly high by any means, but I wasn't going to make enough money to bring back to Mexico by begging on the street, so I decided to give it one last go.

I settled in a company town in Tillamook County, living on the outskirts down near the Wilson River in a shabby lean-to I'd constructed out of whatever refuse I'd been able to gather up. It was somewhat habitable during the summer months, but once the wet season came on in October, it provided no more shelter than a box of rain. I was one of a few opportunity bums who'd drifted in off the highways and possessed no capacity for work but pecked like buzzards at the drunken carcasses of the loggers who wassailed the town every Saturday night.

No longer did I get to partake in the casual joy of card playing or dice-rolling as I had in the days of my youth when confidence ran high and winning was a sure bet. Now, my hands trembled when faced with a big pot, and my rheumatism-bound fingers, once quicker on the draw than Wild Bill himself, slipped and fumbled, were often forced to deal honestly and, therefore, often forced to lose. I had a better chance of employing my graft in craps, but despite all the years of practice and surefire techniques I'd relied upon my whole life, I just wasn't quick enough to keep up with the men of tomorrow. The most I earned in one evening was $500, and the only good thing I'd rolled that night was a lush in the alley outside the bar. The money had been wrapped up in an envelope along with a letter to his wife back home in Vancouver and designated as a down payment on their first house. Perhaps some thieves allow sentiment to interfere with business, but I've never been one. After all, when a man acts as a careless fool, he resigns himself to a fool's lot—such is what he deserves. If man was wise, he'd take such misfortunes as an occasion to learn, but man hardly ever learns. As for myself, I slipped that $500 into my pocket without a second thought and carried on through town no more sated than before when I hadn't a penny. The first thing I bought was a bottle of gin.

I lasted there until the fall when the rains came and washed me right out of timber country like I was a rat in a drain ditch. I left Tillamook with $35 and lit out down Route 101, headed south to California. A timber lorry plucked me off the shoulder along which I'd been walking since early that morning, watching black woodsmoke curl like an adder above the trees on the mountains in the east where rangers conducted prescribed burns every year to abate the danger of the next season.

"Ever see one of those fires get out of control," I nonchalantly asked the driver after an hour or two of silence.

His expression was taut.

"Never one of those," he replied in a hollow voice, his unblinking eyes trained on the smoke that the clouds and fog drove down into the valley roadway, "but I was working with a logging gang on the Coquille River in '36 when Bandon burned."

I did not reply, but he continued anyway. "The fire started right in our camp. It was the driest summer I remember. The company didn't even want us smoking on the job, but we all tweaked a few puffs when the straw boss wasn't looking. By the time it was all over, the newspapers in nearby towns had chalked it up to a spark caused by the friction of one log being dragged over another. But that wasn't how the Bandon Fire started. I didn't tell anybody then, but it was my cigar butt that caught in the brush."

He paused several moments before rambling somberly on. "I went to Bandon after the fire burned itself out on the shore. It'd consumed everything in its path. There weren't more than half a dozen buildings still standing. The whole community was living in Red Cross tents on the beach. Every day a couple families would walk up the hill and rummage amongst the remains to see if they could salvage any possessions. Few were so lucky. The place looked like Hiroshima." He shuddered.

"I'll bet that cured you of cigars," I suggested wryly.

"Cured me!" he exclaimed, my attempt at humor lost on him, "I haven't been able to even so much as look at a cigar since...It was because I wanted a cigar that a whole town burned! People died!"

"Hey, you weren't the only one smoking. If it wasn't you who caused it, it would've been somebody else."

The driver turned toward me bodily, his eyes full and haunted. "But it wasn't somebody else."

The remorse-filled trucker reached his final destination in Medford, but I continued on, glad to be rid of such heavy company. Within a week, I found myself in San Francisco, and it was there that I chose to remain. It is much easier for a man to be homeless and jobless in a city than in a small town, and San Francisco offered me something far more lucrative than all the drunks in all the logging camps in the Pacific Northwest: a port. Sailors—or sea tramps as they are often known by denizens of the road— most often meet or exceed the careless extravagance with which men of any vocation carry on. Loggers, miners, and all others of equal station rush into town once a week to blow their pay. Sailors sometimes see port for no more than a day or two every few weeks—and accordingly, their lack of restraint makes them suitable marks for a man in such a delicate position as I.

In the city, however, there were far more men in such a 'delicate position.' Although the prospects in port were decidedly plump, they were divided amongst a much larger population—most of whom were desperate, half-starved, and ruthless when it came to a dollar. I once watched two bums beat the snot out of one another on a street corner while the hophead whose bankroll they were fighting over was roused by the clamor and crawled away unmolested.

Such senseless displays were commonplace on skid row—but more so in San Francisco than in any other city I'd seen. Part of the reason, at least, was an undeclared turf war between resident bums and newcomers. Round about 1959, urban renewal campaigns were responsible for the mass effacing of vagrants and other ne'er-do-wells out of the general proximity of the better neighborhoods in the city. South of Market, Howard, and Third had been the bums' ancestral home since before the begging ban went into effect, but since the arrival of steam shovels and cranes that leveled the slums and replaced them with what the town council so humorously called 'affordable housing,' the sleaze had oozed down the hill to the Embarcadero to meet the resentment and disdain of those vags already living there.

The wharves that flanked the city were infested by itinerants, which made for poor begging. One or two bums per block are to be expected in any city, and those men will often end a day of mooching with a collection of coins at the bottom of their can. However, when such unfortunates can be found along the sidewalks at the same regular intervals as light posts, most passersby will slip their money clips into their socks and hasten their step— hence the vulgarity with which the wharf rats regarded the skid row invaders. However, for the jobless, penniless, and hopeless, it was one of the city's last bastions where sleeping on the sidewalk wasn't a sure ticket to the clink, and I could count myself amongst its growing population.

I lived in a flop house in South Beach, half a block from the wharves. Board was 30¢ a night, and even that was a heinous price for the conditions offered within. The place advertised 'clean sheets' and 'comfortable cots,' but in reality, it was a front for a rat and louse breeding colony. The sheets were gray, the cots were rusty and prone to collapse, and there were rarely less than ten men to a room. It was nearly always full to capacity.

There were few respectable citizens found along the wharves. Other than the fishermen and trulls who emerged at dawn and dusk, respectively, the demographic was split relatively evenly between stevedores, tomato-can vags, and sailors who had been waylaid by the first bar in port and never made it any further. For most, that was the Marine Bar.

The Marine Bar stood on the corner of Main Street and Bryant, one block from the Embarcadero, and its flashing neon martini glasses and overflowing beer steins were more effective in entrapping parched men than a fishing trawl. Stale, lukewarm beer was 10¢ a pint, and a tumbler of unbranded whiskey could be had for the same price. The most oft-consumed potation of the regular crowd was Dago red, which could be procured for the whopping price of fifty cents a gallon. Purple, bloated winos occupied the stools along the back wall and were subject to rotation every twelve hours or so. Porthole windows fixed high on the wall were the only purveyors of sunlight, and electric light inside was exceedingly dim—likely to prevent those who walked in the front door from noticing the excrement which clung to the far end of the bar like barnacles on the bow of a ship. The haze of smoke helped as well—and cigars could be purchased for as little as a penny. To the unaware sailor standing at the door, the only evidence of the saloon's regular patrons on most days was the smell.

Quite a phenomenon existed there, and I watched it play out many a time. Men who walked in thirsty, hardworking, and fresh off the ship stopped at the corner directly across from the door for their first few rounds of drinks. As conversations got underway with those who'd taken up residence there hours earlier, these men often found themselves sliding further down the bar and into the recesses of the dark room. The evilest fun could be found about halfway down, where there was usually a whore or two waiting for an invitation and an open exchange of pills, powders, and solutions to send a man off in any direction he wanted to go. For those who lingered past this point, as drunkenness mounted and urged the imbiber toward sickness, unconsciousness, or both—the far end of the bar served as their final destination. As long as they retained enough money and consciousness to order a round every hour or so, they were permitted to languish there. Once they passed out, they were removed from the stool and lined up against the wall until they regained their faculties and stumbled out the back door under their own power or began turning gray and looked as if they were about to croak and were tossed out into the alley ahead of the reaper's arrival. The front door was locked between two and four a.m., but if you dared to brave the unlit corridor peppered with sleeping drunks and bodily fluids that led inside from the alley, the Marine Bar was accessible twenty-four hours a day.

I spent most of my time in San Francisco nestled somewhere around the middle of the bar, where men were early enough in their binge to still have some money but drunk enough to be careless. Rocky Mountain Euchre was my claim to fame, but I made more picking their pockets when they weren't looking. The bartenders were all women, most of them nothing to look at, as they were old and dried up ahead of their time, some of them doubling as periodic tenants of the middle of the bar during their off hours. However, there was one bartender whose shifts I never missed. She was an English girl from Carlisle and prettier than a daisy in May. She even had all of her teeth. I never learned her proper name, but everyone called her Jack-A-Roe.

Aside from the sunset, she was the most beautiful thing to be seen on the wharf, but her eyes were sad. She was married to a philandering sailor herself and remained in that den of sin in hopes that her man would come walking into the Marine Bar one day. Every time the door blew open and some salty, windswept wreck stepped up to the bar, her eyes would brighten—but for a moment only, as disappointment followed quick on the heels of her dreams.

She was a kind girl, possessing eternal patience and a depth of compassion rarely seen; far too good for the sea tramp to whom she remained faithful and true. She had sailed herself during the last war and seemed to enjoy listening to the mariners' rough talk and stories of storms and gales and ghost ships aplenty that echoed ceaselessly within the walls of the Marine Bar.

Just like tramps, here or the world over, no matter how much those sailors griped and lamented and cursed their captains, their ships, their mates, and the sea and all its power—after no more than a few days amongst landlubbers, they were off again to ride the waves to foreign lands. This was the fate of Jack-A-Roe's husband, as it was my own. Wanderlust, chronic and fatal, laid waste once more—and its casualties littered the Marine Bar like shipwrecks in a shallow harbor. If there's one thing I've found to be indubitably true, it is that a taste for freedom is equally dangerous to a man's future as a taste for liquor. I attempted to explain this to the pining Jack-A-Roe, but though she tried, she could never understand.

She could, however, make one hell of a cocktail. The gin they served at the Marine Bar was no fitter for human consumption than canned heat and tasted like turpentine, so Jack-A-Roe mixed it with bourbon and bitters, tossed a splash of ginger beer on top for good measure, and called it a Suffering Bastard. She told me it was a hangover cure from back in the old country, and it fully deserved its designation. It cured your hangover right quick because, after a strong one, you were drunk again. And, there was undoubtedly no more appropriate name for such a concoction imbibed there—for we were all suffering bastards, indeed.

One unremarkable morning after I'd finished off a few of them, along with the end of my funds, I rose from the barstool I'd occupied since the previous evening—relieved that I'd been able to escape the horrors of the flop house for a night—and set off to find a cheap restaurant at which to beg for a handout. It was December and decidedly cold. Mild the vast majority of the year, San Francisco reserves a terrible affliction for those who choose to remain there throughout the winter months. The fog, which sweeps over the city and keeps the summers pleasantly cool and the strength of the sun at bay, comes near to freezing in winter and imparts to the bones of an old man a dampness that is unmatched by the Denver snow, the Chicago wind, or the torrential rain of New Orleans. No matter how many layers of clothing you pile on or how many shots you take to warm yourself up, that dampness never fails to penetrate, making San Francisco a perfectly miserable city in which to spend the holidays homeless.

Hungry, I stepped out from the relative warmth of the Marine Bar, pulled the collar of my oversized, button-less coat up to my ears, and took to the bum-laden wharves. Subdivided packing crates, trash-lined hogsheads, and the odd canvas tent provided shelter for the tomato-can vags who burrowed into whatever refuse they could find to keep warm and dry. More often than not, their attempts were futile. Usually, a bum, or part of him, could be observed outside of these makeshift flops. The term 'bottom of the barrel' was coined because that is where such a type lives. Few beggars could be found amongst these booze-and-crumb-addled wrecks, as most resorted to crawling through dumpsters and raiding one another's camps when in need of food or a jolt. Some were junkies, but most were victims of liquor and, having little or no means of procuring it, were forced to drink its cheapest varietal—burgundy foot juice.

Now, there hasn't been a day in my life when I had the chance to belly up to some good liquor that I haven't done just that. Back where I came from, gin was as damn close to mother's milk as a man could get, and we drank it for just about every reason you can think of. We drank gin when we were celebrating, and we drank it when we were mourning. We drank it to go to sleep, and we drank it first thing in the morning to jolt ourselves awake. We drank it to get sick, and we drank it to get well—and just like Jack-A-Roe's Suffering Bastards, that old Rocky Mountain gin cured any ailment from hangovers to gout. I swear it. I had my first good, hard swallow of gin when I was just one day old. My Ma always told me that my brothers had just about dried her up, and since she had no milk, she nursed me on my Pa's gin. I've had a taste for gin since the cradle, but it never did get a taste for me. Some folks would call me lucky, but I believe it was an accident of birth—you see, I was born with a hollow leg, and I never could seem to fill myself plumb up enough for the stuff to get to my head.

The winos and alki-stiffs that lined the piers and upholstered the gutters did not share my good fortune. Most, if not all, suffered their fall from grace in faraway places and drifted into San Francisco for the waters, but no matter where they came from, it appeared the most hopeless eventually landed along the wharves south of skid row. The mechanics of this migration were clear. After all, it's dangerous to get drunk in San Francisco. If you tripped and fell while walking down a steep thoroughfare like Jones Street, you wouldn't stop rolling until you landed in the bay.

—And that appeared to be precisely what happened to the unfortunate soul who accosted me that afternoon. Up ahead, with his back against the seawall, rotted an old man under a pile of filthy, torn clothing. His hair hadn't been cut in years and was soggy and mildewed from the incessant fog, and his grimy face likely hadn't seen water since the last time it rained. His eyes were milky white and unfocused, scarred by cataracts, and he was missing half of one leg. The other was missing a foot. Sensing my approach, this straggly, bearded, unwashed heap reached out his gloved hand, clasped around a coffee can, and beseeched me for a donation.

"Got a dime for the blind?" he rasped in an old, broken, toothless voice.

"Ha!" I exclaimed sardonically, "I ain't got no dime. I ain't got so much as a green penny." I peered into the can where some change had already been thrown. "Hell, I'm broker than you!"

"I beg your pardon," he replied, "These old eyes are only here for show these days. What's your story?"

I had no desire to be sociable, but he seemed uncharacteristically polite for a man shattin' on his uppers, and I thought he might be inclined to share some of his take—or at least some of his wine.

"Agh," I spat in disgust, "It's too long and sad to tell."

"How old is ya?"

It'd been some time since I'd counted. "Fifty-four," I told him, but I felt like one hundred and eight.

"Me too," he replied, but he looked about three years younger than Moses. "It's hell gettin' old, ain't it?"

"It's hell livin'," I declared cynically.

"It's hell livin' like this," he clarified.

"At least you ain't gotta worry about buyin' shoes," I suggested wryly. "Left 'em on the tracks?"

"No, I've never hopped a train," he professed. "It was sugar trouble. I was in prison. Never got treated. After twenty years, they let me out on medical parole."

"San Quentin?" I asked.

"Florence, in Arizona," he answered.

"Kill a man?"

"No. But that's what they convicted me of. And I was as innocent as the day is long."

"I've heard every man in prison is innocent," I patronized him dryly.

"I've never killed any living thing with more sense than a steer," he lamented, his voice cracking. "And they convicted me of shooting a man— a living, breathing man; a living, breathing man who would've went right on living and breathing if somebody hadn't shot 'im. Shot 'im right in the back. Mister, do I look like the sort of man who could shoot another man in the back?" Agitated, he reached for his pint and took a long, palliative slug of Dago red.

I watched him without pity. "I'll tell you what," I assured him, "I'll bet you anything that if you took a shot off this pier, you couldn't even hit the water."

The wharf rat lowered the pint from his lips, then tremblingly extended his dirty hand out in the direction of my voice. "My name is August West," he told me, "What's you'rn?"

"Jack," I told him.

"Jack," he replied sincerely, "I'd like to thank you mightily for listening to me. Ain't many around anywhere who'll extend an unlucky man such courtesy."

That was probably the only time in my life I'd ever been referred to as courteous.

"I can't do much of nothin'," he rambled on drunkenly, "Can't see, can't walk. The other bums, they steal whatever I manage to get. Ain't nobody who wants to talk or be friendly. I'm alone, inside my own mind, and a man's mind can be a mighty ugly place to be sometimes—"

He broke off coughing—it appeared sugar trouble was not the only scourge he had left prison with.

"It's always been this way," he moaned, his chest rattling as he continued to wheeze, "If there's a god, he hates me. Ain't never had more than half a chance at anything, and I've screwed up all the rest. Half of my life, I spent doing time for some other fucker's crime. The other half found me stumbling around drunk on burgundy wine," he motioned disgustedly at the pint from which he suckled. "The only good that's ever come to me is my wife, Pearly—Pearly Baker, and I'll tell you that woman is as good as gold. She's been true to me. I know she has. Wrote me letters every day of those twenty years. Now she ain't got a place to send 'em, and I can't see to read 'em."

"I'm sure she's been true to you," I assured him, thinking of my own wife back home.

"I'll go back to her one day. I'll die in her arms. And when I meet my maker, I swear, I'm going to punch him right in the nose. Ain't got no right—ain't got no right making a man suffer this old way. Worked like the dickens as a kid—always stayed poor. Always been good to my Ma and Pa— and when they died, they left the farm to my brother. He lost it betting on the rodeo. Married up my woman Pearly—never had no others. Never raised a hand to her, never to my children. Never gambled like that fool brother of mine, always tried to be a good, honest man. Sure, I always loved my wine—but that ain't no sin. Ain't no sin—"

He broke off coughing again, and a few drops of blood escaped his mouth and spattered on the sidewalk.

Once he'd regained his composure, he continued, "One time, I had a chance to make a new start. Pearly's Pa died and left us his ranch. Price of cattle that year was $17.50 a head. Two years later, the price rose, and disease killed off half my herd. Whatever profit I made, I drank. Finally, I promised Pearly and the children I wouldn't touch it anymore. Not a drop until the bills were paid and we had no less than one hundred dollars in the bank. And I made good on my promise. For six months, I didn't touch it. Cattle prices rose again that year, and I made some good deals. In the summer of '38, I took a trip to Tucson to do some trading and pay off the last of my debts. The slip from the bank showed $97.00 in deposits. I was so right proud of myself that I went and bought a gallon of wine. I wasn't going to drink it; I swear I wasn't. I just wanted to have it to celebrate when I reached my goal. But the road home was long. I had a mouthful. And then another. And then I just couldn't help myself. I didn't make it home until daybreak—and when I did, that gallon was gone—"

Another fit of violent coughing punctuated his account.

"Didn't—couldn't let Pearly or the kids see me drunk like that. I'd promised. Couldn't—" his voice cracked with emotion, and he shook his head in shame, "I never went into the house. I crawled up into the hayloft and slept it off. I woke up to a marshal standing over me. He arrested me and took me back to Tucson without a word of explanation. It wasn't until they questioned me that I realized I was being charged with murder. Some old man had been shot on the road home from Tucson. Shot for no reason. He wasn't even robbed. Still had his billfold on him and everything. The killer had stolen my horse right out of my barn and left his old, lame mare and the gun he had used behind. The marshal had followed the horse's tracks right into my barn and pinned the crime on me. I had no alibi for the day before; I'd spent it drunk. I swore to my innocence. I swore that lame horse wasn't mine, and Pearly swore, and the kids swore—but I had no proof. My horse was never branded, nor was this one. My fingerprints weren't on the gun—but neither were anybody else's. The evidence was all circumstantial. The jury in Tucson sentenced me to life. And my life is just what they got."

August West retracted his blind, sorrow-laden gaze from the ground and looked me dead in the eyes. Blind or not, he still managed to find mine, and I couldn't seem to pull them away; I was rooted to the spot. My uncle's ominous words rang in my ears, and a chill colder than death ran through me. I haven't been able to shake it yet.

"Mister," he spoke avowedly, his voice trembling with unexpressed rage, "I've never killed anyone in my whole life, but I swear to you, if I ever meet the man whose crime I rotted in jail twenty years for, I wouldn't think twice. I wish these blame old eyes worked again just so I could see that fucker dead."

And—as if to consummate that point, he groped for the pint of wine and took a generous slug.

Suspicion had crept in slowly, but realization tumbled upon me in an instant. Dazed and shaken to my core, I stumbled away from him without a reply and walked hard and fast in the direction of the north shore. When I reached Fisherman's Wharf, I stopped, worn out and exhausted, my legs and back aching. I leaned against the pier and turned my wide eyes toward the water, and all of a sudden, this feeling came over me. It was as if I became aware—of the gulls winging their way over the waves, of the schooners with their lee rails down, cutting hard across the bay, of the stone walls of Alcatraz prison looming sinisterly in the distance—of my own heart pounding, my breath fluttering in my scarred lungs, gasping at the salty sea air, the twinge of hunger in my stomach, this strange tightness in my chest—and something else I could not identify. I closed my eyes, and all I could see was the twisted, haggard face of August West—the innocent man who had suffered twenty years for the crime I had committed.

I left San Francisco a week later, as the city had become unbearable. The cold had invaded my bones, and restlessness had invaded my mind. The vermin at the flop house staved off any hope of sleep, so I spent the majority of my time at the Marine Bar, trading any rogue coins I'd scraped up for Suffering Bastards. On one comparatively slow afternoon, while the bay wind buffeted the window dressings, Jack-A-Roe polished bottles, and I sat there gripping my glass and shivering, a conversation between us developed.

"Cold one today, ain't it?" I proffered.

"About tolerable," she replied, "It's only going to get worse from here on."

I shuddered, "Miserable, miserable weather. Cold and wet. Why do you stay in this city?" I asked her.

"Ain't all that different from Carlisle, you know," she replied with a naturalized smile.

"Don't that chill get to you?"

"Sometimes," she replied, leaning on her bar rag and staring past me out the porthole window, "but I've got love to keep me warm."

"When's the last time that old man of yours came back to you, anyway?"

Jack-A-Roe sighed heavily, "It's about two and a half years now."

"That's a long time."

"He's been longer. The longest was five years and two months. But he came back. He always comes back."

"And you ain't found anybody to take his place in all that time?"

Jack-A-Roe turned from the window to face me. "Couldn't even if I wanted to."

"How's that?"

"There's not another man like him in all the world. He may not be the most handsome or the smartest or the richest by any means—he may not even be wholly mine—but I love him. I don't love anyone else; I never have. Thought about it and even tried a time or two...but it doesn't work that way. I've tried to stop loving him; it hurts to love someone you can't be with. It hurts to have your heart stretched out thousands of miles over the sea, halfway around the world, and back again. But no matter how long he's gone for, no matter how many times he comes back and leaves again, I still love him the same."

I studied her face and considered the depth of her fidelity, "I've got a wife back home, just like you," I told her. "Her name is Bonnie Lee."

"How long have you been away?" she asked.

"Right around twenty years now," I replied. "Prison."

"Why aren't you there with her now that you're free?" she asked, somewhat puzzled.

"That's just it," I admitted. "I'm free."

"You'd rather be free and in this crummy old place than home with the woman you love, who loves and waits and has waited for you?" she questioned, her fair face creased with confusion.

"After fifteen years of breaking rocks, a man is entitled to a little freedom," I told her. "What's your man's excuse?"

"He loves the sea," she spoke in a pained whisper, "Even more than he loves me."

"That wanderlust can get quite a hold on a man," I explained, sliding my empty glass back across the bar, "No different than brandy or wine."

"I hope you go back to her," Jack-A-Roe cautioned as she mixed me another drink and gestured to the far corner, "Before this stuff swallows you like it has them. At least some of them, somewhere, have got to have people who love and miss them."

We both took a long look at the withering specimens of manhood drooling on the end of the bar.

"What if he never comes back?" I asked Jack-A-Roe.

"What?" she replied, startled.

"Your man, what if he never comes back?"

Jack-A-Roe turned her purple eyes away from the wayward unfortunates to meet mine. "If I never see him again in this life, then I'll meet him at the Station."

"What station?" I asked her.

Jack-A-Roe shrugged, "I don't know if it has a proper name. If it does, it's not one found on signs or manifests. I've come to call it Terrapin Station myself."

"Why?"

"Well, you know what they say, 'it's turtles all the way down.'"

I leaned forward and peered over the edge of the bar to see if she was hiding a bottle of her own. "Where is this station?"

"Not here. It's somewhere out there, far beyond this place."

"You mean heaven?" I blurted out incredulously, trying to make sense of her absurd description.

"Not exactly," she replied, "heaven is what you'd call a final destination. The Station is more like a waiting room."

"A waiting room? You mean purgatory?" I asked, prying some long-calcified Catholic vocabulary out of the attics of my life.

"No," she answered, grappling for the appropriate word. "The Station is...is, well, exactly that. It's a stopover."

"A stopover?"

"Yes," she answered, "Between lives."

"Between lives?" I echoed, "You mean that you think we come back and do all of this all over again?!" My voice cracked at the weight and preposterousness of such a suggestion.

Jack-A-Roe remained composed, seeming to understand my reaction but not moving to defend her statement. "Not the very same sequence of events, but yes."

I laughed heartily, "Ok, so let me get this straight. We live this life, then we go to some station in the sky, and then we live another life. What happens after that life?"

"Another life," Jack-A-Roe smiled, "And then another, and then another—it's lives all the way down."

"That's ridiculous," I told her. "The way I've suffered in this life, why would I want to come back and live again?!"

This time, Jack-A-Roe chuckled, "Jack, I hardly think it has anything to do with what you want."

"But what about heaven and hell and all that? I don't believe in them neither, but at least that makes sense—if you're good, you go to heaven; if you're bad, you go to hell. Why do you have to live over and over and over again?"

"To learn," she replied simply.

"I've learned enough in just one life—that life is a crock."

"How do you know this is your first life?" she asked.

I stared at her like she had three heads, all of them spewing nonsense.

"Have you ever had things happen to you that you didn't deserve or escaped some fate you may've been owed?"

"Of course, but who hasn't?" I replied bitingly.

"Ever thought about why?"

"Well, sure, life just ain't fair, that's why."

Jack-A-Roe's indigo eyes flashed in the dim light of the bar, "Life, Jack, is very fair. But, like spectrums of light, there's more to it than we can see all at once. Think about it," she urged. "What about that man who was wicked all his life and, on his deathbed, apologized to God and now gets to live for eternity in heaven. What about that woman who was born into the dregs of society and lived a life of sin and sadness because she never had the good fortune to know anything else and now must be tortured until the end of time in a lake of fire. What about that child who died at birth and never got to live—the jury is still out on what happens to him. Does any of that sound right to you? Does any of that sound equitable? Do the innocent really suffer without compensation? Do the wicked really get off scot-free? Doesn't it make far more sense that there's more to the picture than what we see in the frame—that all deeds are met with their equal reward in due time?"

"You're really asking the wrong guy," I stammered, all her conjecture entirely lost on me. "I don't believe in nothing. Never have. Don't wanna, neither."

Jack-A-Roe gazed at me the way I did her when she failed to comprehend my explanation of the tenacity of wanderlust. "So you think all of this is meaningless?" She raised her arms above her head and circled them around to indicate the whole world, "All you've ever done and made and felt and been? Do you really think life is a zero-sum game?"

"I don't know what I think," I told her, "but I know if anything comes after this, it most certainly cannot be any worse."

Jack-A-Roe met my eyes with a pained smile, "And you're sure of that?"

At that moment, a sailor pushed open the front door, allowing a frigid gust of wintery air to swirl into the room. For a man who was already freezing, such an unwelcome addition was intolerable. I wrapped my ragged coat around me and shuddered. "Yes, I'm sure that nothing could be worse than this," I promised her, laying my last dime down on the bar in exchange for a drink.

I did not go back to the flop house that night. Instead, I left the Marine Bar and headed straight down to the railyards south of Brannan Street. A southbound reefer freight was pulling out, and I heaved myself up on one of the passing ladders, promising my chattering teeth and aching sinews that we were fast bound for the land of beaches, palm trees, and shirt sleeves. However, in the meantime, my accommodations consisted of the empty ice hold of a reefer car. I laid my folded coat across the hatch to prevent myself from becoming trapped in case the lid slammed closed unexpectedly, then eased myself down the course net of wire inside and settled in for a long, unpleasant evening.

The ice compartment was a barrier to the biting wind, but the dampness and cold were only exacerbated inside the giant iron car. I drew my aching bones up into a gnarled ball, stuck my frozen hands under my armpits, and swore that this would be the last time I duked it out with the cold—as forty years of the same arrangement had doubtlessly proven that the cold always wins. I thought back to San Francisco and the bums that dotted the wharf. On a night like this, exposed and in poor health, many were sure to croak. I rubbed my sides and hoped like hell that my train reached its destination in good time so I would not share their wretched fate.

As the heavy train hit its stride and the cadence of the iron wheels thundering beneath me began to lull me to sleep, I closed my eyes. When I did, the old, pained face of August West stood out against the darkness. I shook my head in anger to dispel the image, but it remained—his gray beard fringed with frost, his murky eyes fixed and unblinking, his purple lips slightly ajar, his tortured soul flown. I thought of his faithful, waiting wife, and then I thought of my own. I reopened my eyes and spent the remainder of that endless evening wide awake.

Sometime the following afternoon, the freight pulled into the yards at Los Angeles, a city eminently unfriendly to bums. Down inside the insulated car, it was still just as cold as it had been the night before, but once I dragged myself up the wire net and poked my head out of the hatch, it was seventy-five and sunny—southern California at its best. When my stiff, frozen body met the dry desert heat, a tremor passed through me at once.

With the sun's warmth came a rush of relief, but that chill in my bones remained.

Eager to defrost, I cautiously eased myself up onto the roof of the car and crawled across the deck, keeping low and out of sight. There was much activity in the yards as hands worked, servicing engines, disconnecting strings of cars slated for local delivery, and making up another long-haul freight with the remnants. I had no intention of hanging around long enough to accompany my current chariot to its terminus. My train was soon to be inspected, and any hitchhiking hobos picked off like fleas by the cinder dicks. I peered over the bustling yard and saw that the nearest train was smoking hard and just about ready to depart. My odds weren't good of catching it out, and I had no idea what direction it was heading in, but I knew I was sure to be apprehended if I sheltered in place, so I made a run for it. Granted, a run for it at my age was more like an awkward, limping hobble.

I made it to the shadow of the boxcars unmolested and considered my options. The covert option was to ride the rods, but even along the shortest hop, with my shaky grip, such a mode of transport was too much of a gamble with death than I was willing to take. I knew that sitting fully exposed on the rear deck of a hopper car was risky, but it appeared to be the only recourse in which greasing the tracks was not a variable—so I boarded.

Miraculously, we were underway within minutes. Once the train was out of the yards and picked up speed, I leaned back against the hopper and exhaled. However, my good fortune did not last for long. Within minutes of my premature assumption that I was home free, the figure of a man appeared on the deck, and a brakeman in starched denim coveralls climbed down the ladder to stand before me. Years ago, I would've made a break for it and dove from the car regardless of the train's speed, but without that as a viable option, I moved not an inch and submitted to my fate.

"Where do you think you're headed, mister?" he asked in a voice that carried a distinct New York accent.

"I'm goin' wherever this train is goin'," I told him flatly.

"The hell you are. I would've thought you'd know better, Old Man," he rejoindered.

"Can't you shacks be a sport for once?" I asked wearily.

"Depends on whatcha got. The fare here is cash, grass, or the skin off your ass—nobody rides for free."

"I ain't got nothin'. Search me."

"Ain't got nothing, eh?" The brakeman sneered, "Well, I can tell you what you're gonna get when we make it to Cucamonga. It ain't a suite at the Hilton, but they feed ya' regular enough."

I didn't protest.

"Now up with you, come on now, you know the drill, that's right," he ordered me as I rose to my feet and we marched back to the caboose. The brakeman called ahead to the precinct in Cucamonga, and when we arrived in the yards, a patrol car was there waiting for me. I was stuffed down into the back of it by a member of the local police force and carted off to the station, where I was booked, measured, photographed, questioned, and left to languish in a holding cell until the judge could see me. That interview was conducted the following morning, and little to my surprise but much to my chagrin, I was sentenced to sixty days in the city jail for trespassing on railroad property.

If I were to account for it all, I've likely spent about one-third of my life in prison. Thinking back on the couple of long hauls and the innumerable short stints I spent in every kind and quality of institution, from provincial hoosegows to the federal pen, those sixty days in Rancho Cucamonga constituted the hardest time I have ever served.

In the nearly four years since I'd left Nevada, age had finally caught up to me, and being confined to the old 6 x 8 for two months, sleeping on that rickety bunk, and feeling the dampness of those stone walls made me into more of an old man than I'd ever been before. There was no work to be done at the prison, so for all that time, all I did was sit. It was the longest stretch I'd spent on my back in all my life, and let me tell you, it did nothing for my constitution. The only ways to pass the time were to sleep, read, eat, and pace. I confined myself mainly to the former and the latter, and besides the guards, I had no company for the entirety of those two months. We were fed in our cells, which were barred only in the front, the other three sides consisting of brick walls. There were no windows, and the only amenity besides a blanket, toilet, and sink that adorned the cell was a mirror that hung over the faucet.

In most places, mirrors are absent from jails, as a prisoner may be so inclined to break it with his fist and slit his wrists to terminate the boredom, but this mirror was an exception. It was mounted with narrow iron bars across it—not unlike the cell door—and let me tell you, what a dirty trick that was. Its presence and effect were intentional, no doubt, as the occasion for a man to see himself in his current predicament is both rare and striking. And, I can hardly imagine there is any vision more disheartening than one in which a man sees himself as the world sees him—barred from the society of free men, at the mercy and whim of the powers that be and branded as dangerous, misfortunate, or in my own case, simply unwanted. Seeing that old face behind bars in the mirror, wrinkled, weather-beaten, and framed by a shock of white hair quickly receding, made me wonder where all the time had gone. After sixty days of rumination, I concluded that I'd spent it, gambled it away, cast months and years into the wind with the same calm indifference with which a sharper tosses checks into the pot—and I'd walked away from that table dead broke, a veteran of forty years whose earnings in that time could not even cover the palm of my hand.

That face in the mirror haunted me. I shivered every time I looked at it. I tried not to, but morbid contemplation seemed to suck me in. It was the face of a stranger, of a long-suffering old man I did not know. But my eyes were the same. They were the same eyes that had shone in wonder as I'd listened to the rambling tales of hobos on the banks of the South Platte. They were the same eyes that had smiled upon the taking of hundreds of thousands of dollars over the course of my life. They were the same eyes that had glowed with love for many a woman and ached with despair when two of them left me. They were the same eyes that had cunningly read the backs of marked cards without giving away their secrets, the same eyes that had gazed upon the tracks of every railroad in the country. Those two fixed blue spherules were the same eyes that had looked out upon my whole mad life. They'd evidenced every expression from joy to anger, from larceny to curiosity. For hours, I stared into my own eyes in that dusty mirror, wondering what expression they'd borne when I'd driven a knife into the heart of Shannon Todd or when I'd shot those two boys dead in that Texas barroom. And whenever I occasioned to think of my crimes, all of which had been justified, another face arrived to occupy the forefront of my mind, and it lingered there morning and night.

By the time I was released in February, I'd long since decided that I'd had enough. I was tired; tired of running, tired of lying, tired of having to stay one step ahead of the law, tired of being broke. I was tired of prison digs, cheap food, cheap booze, and the women along the way. Forty years on the road was enough for me. I was going home, home to the woman who knew me better than any woman ever did and loved me for the scoundrel I was—despite all my efforts to convince her otherwise. I'd spent the last two months thinking, and I'd come to the conclusion that even if August West's patient, faithful wife never saw him again, and Jack-A-Roe shuffled off to her Station still pining for her love, penniless or not, I was going back to Bonnie Lee. And I was going to tell her everything: everything that'd happened, everything I'd done, regardless of what I thought her reaction might be. All I wanted to do was gather her into my arms and tell her how much I loved her and missed her, and apologize for all the foolish things I'd done. I wanted to get to know my son. I wanted to lay back in a home of my own without any concern for the rest of the world. I didn't care if I had to work some menial job for the rest of my days—just as long as I could spend them in Chino with Bonnie Lee.

Mexico had been that whisper in the wind every time a deal went sour, every time the weather turned, every time heartache set in. It was the call of home that had beckoned me in the wake of every misfortune for nigh on twenty years. I'd long ignored it, but now I was sick for want of it.

Homesickness, I've found, is largely a product of age. That longing for security, that captive desire to rest one's weary bones and weary mind in an atmosphere of familiarity, is a notion that rarely takes hold of a young man. Youth, oftentimes, is accompanied solely by wonder, risk-taking, and lust for life. Meanwhile, man has long since run out of wonder, taken more risks than he has earned, and traded lust of life for love—and the desire to keep living it. Beyond the safety, refuge, and serenity that Chino offered, it was the only home I'd known since I'd left Denver at fifteen. Its promise was one of renewal and peace, and for the first time in my reckless life of wandering, I could not wait to go home.

I left the Cucamonga jail as a man on a mission. I headed straightaway to Route 66, unhooked my trusty left thumb from my belt loop, and started walking. However, the Road was not going to let me go too easily. Not a single driver who stopped was headed south. By the time I finally got picked up by a Mack truck bound for Mexicali, I was nearly to San Bernardino, night had fallen, and a hailstorm that dropped ice balls the size of cherries had rolled in. The welts they left remained for days after I finally made it back to Mexico. I climbed into that cab breathless, exhausted, and smarting from the impact of several thousand hailstones. I thanked the trucker for rescuing me from the storm, but I needed to yell for him to hear me above the barrage of frozen rain bouncing off the roof.

With conversation rendered impossible, my final four hours in America were steeped in uncharacteristic reminiscence. I thought back on that very first freight I'd climbed aboard in 1920, a swashbuckling teenager full of fire and passion, curiosity, and enthusiasm, and I shook my head at all the changes I'd witnessed in the time that'd intervened. I thought of the rise and fall of prohibition, of coffin varnish and rum runners, of plush times and plush women. I thought of all the fast trains I'd caught out of slow towns and all the big pots I'd weaseled away from small operators. I thought of the thrills and the bills, of green door speakeasies and my part in it all. I thought of Tulsa, the town I should've left sooner, and the love affair that had ruined my life. I thought of Sherriff Steele, who'd arrested me, and upon whom my small act of revenge had been enacted as promised. I thought of my trial and the horror with which I had received my life sentence. I remembered the misery and toil of McAlester; I remembered my daring escape and all those snake-bitten unfortunates I'd left behind. I thought of all those years I'd spent on the run, how the big bull market had been slaughtered and left to rot, and the drought and privation that had followed. I remembered the dust storms I'd weathered, the lonely nights spent in crowded train cars, the uncertainty, the fear, the sickness, and hunger. I thought of that fated night in rural Iowa which only the aid of an angel had allowed me to see the end of. I thought of my first love, Rosalie, and the sublime spell I'd spent in her company. I thought of federal repeal and the way she died. I remembered the despondence that followed and the locales that had hosted my pain. I thought of the zealot Saint Stephen on the beach at Santa Monica, Althea the witch, and Cosmic Charlie, my mad employer. I thought of the shriveled rose in Black Peter's hand. I thought of my Mexican adventure and the first time I'd laid my eyes upon my wife. I thought of the vigor with which I'd pursued her, the consummate joy I felt when I finally got her, the perfect life we shared, and the cunning scheme Uncle John had employed to lure me back north. I thought of my late uncle and his acute influence on my life and its dastardly direction. I thought of his larcenous eyes, hearty laugh, and good intentions. I thought of our arduous journey through the desert, of that most propitious evening in West Texas when we struck gold without ever having to hoist a shovel or a pan. I thought of the fear-laden flight that followed and his most unfortunate, necessary demise. I thought of the year I spent as a rich man and the utter frivolity with which I had spent it. I thought of Annemarie and Tom Banjo, the man who had loaned me life on uncertain terms and collected fifteen regret-filled years of it while I languished in the Nevada desert, pounding rocks and digging coal. I thought of the years and vitality I'd lost to labor, to thankless slavery, and every aching bone in my body reminded me of how much it hurt. I thought of the sweet taste of freedom when it finally came one fair day in March, of my decision to rebuild my manhood, of the unexpected twists and turns my life had taken from there. I thought of Bobbie McGee, her gentle touch and terrifying eyes, and the manner in which she came and left. I thought of the City of New Orleans, the town that'd hosted such depths of comfort and love, and the train that had hosted the Johnny B. Goode matinee. I thought about that eager, bright-eyed kid I'd swindled and his hard-hitting band of friends who'd made me a pariah to the Big Easy. I thought of the bleak times that had befallen me of late, of the Oregon forests and the San Francisco Bay. I thought of Jack-A-Roe the Eternal and August West, the poor, blind casualty of my time. I thought of the countless jails in which I'd served, the countless meals I'd begged, and the countless trains I'd ridden. I thought of the countless water towers in which I'd carved my moniker, the countless jungles I'd inhabited in near about every state, and the countless strangers with whom I'd shared stories, food, and flame. I thought of the countless games of fate I'd dealt, the countless aces I'd drawn, and all the dollars that'd passed through my hands along the way. I thought of all that I could remember and all that I'd forgotten.

As we barreled south out of the storm toward the approaching border, I thought of America. I thought of the America I knew as a young man and the America I looked around at now. She was a short-lived piece of heaven but gone to the dogs now. Once a land of opportunity, freedom, and beauty, she's been run right into the ground. She's a heavy country now, weighed down by tax and expense, law and regulation, crime and punishment, pomp and circumstance. Gone now are wilderness, wildness, and wonder. Soon to follow is my own kind, to whom such sirens call.

I looked around myself at the 40-ton mechanical beast in which I sat, thundering past the fertile fields of southern California with all its electronic gauges and blaring CB radio. I looked out at the neon-electric signs and lights in the cities we navigated, crammed full of every make and model of automobile, blowing their horns and pumping out clouds of noxious fumes that clung to the towering steel buildings and blocked out the sun. I looked at the crowds that gathered in the storefronts to watch the six o'clock news on television. I looked at the Technicolor billboards that burst up out of the shoulder of the interstate and marred the scenery. I looked around at the suburban metropolises that skirted the cities—hundreds of thousands of American dreams in a box—populated by staid conformists who waved around their Diner's Club cards and built white picket fences on the lands they rented, never to own. I looked around at the stretch of desert beyond where the oil derricks pumped unrefined cash into the pockets of the fortunate few while the children of the men who operated them ran around barefoot in the dust and signaled for us to blow our horn. I looked at myself in the truck's side-view mirror and then turned away.

As the moon climbed into the sky and we crossed into Mexico, I said a final fare-thee-well to the American side, home of Rocky Mountain gin and yegg conventions, where freight trains cut across the verdant prairie like vast black scars and the hobo used to reign and set my sights on cold cervezas, mouth-watering mezcal, and the morning dew in which I would soon once again walk with my love. I didn't look back for a moment.

XI

Not Fade Away

One week later, John S. Jones came walking home. I arrived in Guaymas courtesy of a family of fellow ex-pats who were aiming to take advantage of the surf. It was after nightfall when they let me off in the city center en route to their hotel. I headed straightaway to the beach. At my last stop in Hermosillo, I'd slicked, shaved, and showered, cast off my dirty, ragged road clothes, and donned the finest I could afford with the little I could beg and steal. I'd gotten a haircut and a good meal, and by sacrificing the price of a bed, I would still have a little something in my pocket when I stood on my doorstep tomorrow and welcomed Bonnie Lee into my arms.

I was eager beyond anything to see my wife again and put the nightmare of the Road forever behind me—ready and willing to vow that if Bonnie Lee wanted to see proof of change in me, not only would I swallow a couple centavos, but the entire coin purse. However, as for that night, that last night in which I would count myself as a wanderer, as a brother of the floating fraternity, I was content to sleep out under the stars.

Armed with a hand-rolled marijuana cigarette that had been gifted to me by a local, I made a humble pallet for myself in the warm, clean sand and gazed out over the shrimp boats bobbing in the gentle gulf waves—more comfortable and at peace than I had been in a long while. Now that I was back and felt the solace that I'd initially found in that city twenty years ago, I wondered why I had resisted the urge to return for so long—and even why I had left in the first place.

In the soft light from the stars that glittered like diamonds cast across a sheath of black velvet, I extracted the worn and tattered photo of Bonnie

Lee and the infant Cassidy that she had sent me in prison and examined it longingly. I felt remorse and disgust welling up within me for the years I had allowed to pass without contact, during which I had permitted my injured pride to preside over my foolish decisions and damned trajectory. Straining my eyes, I unfolded the letter that'd accompanied it, yellowed and deeply creased by the years and sorrows it had weathered. I read it again, as I had countless times since I received it—once more reviving her confessions of love, promises of devotion, and desire for my swift and safe return that had sustained me throughout all my falls over the last two decades.

With a breath and a sigh, I returned the photograph and missive to my pocket, leaned back on my elbows in the sand, and looked up at the vast blackness above, punctuated by pinpoints of shimmering starlight. As they reflected in my wide, wondering eyes, I fixed my gaze upon a single one of them. In an uncharacteristic gesture representative of my boyish anticipation, I made a wish upon that star. I wished that I would never again set foot on the Road, that I would round out my years comfortably in my own bed in Chino, and that the love and life that Bonnie Lee and I shared would be every bit as joyous and idyllic as it had been all those years ago. As I repeated my desires aloud, that celestial orb I'd selected to carry them suddenly dropped and streaked out of the dark sky, crashing somewhere beyond the devil's mountains that ringed that coastal city—as if some eerie celestial hand had snatched it right out of the heavens.

A chill not unlike that which affected me in San Francisco ran through my body on that balmy Mexican night, but I refused to let such a delusional association perturb me. Instead, I chuckled to myself, glad that I—unlike so many others—did not believe in nonsense such as wishing upon stars. Otherwise, I admitted, such an occurrence would be considered an eminently bad omen.

I did not sleep very much that evening. I attributed my extended wakefulness mainly to raging anticipation, which refused to cease and desist and only intensified as the hours of darkness wore on. Finally, about an hour before dawn, I dozed off. When I awoke, I was freezing. The morning dew, which, in my earlier life, had signaled the end of the night for Bonnie and me, had drawn itself up into droplets and blanketed the entire coast. As the sun had yet to rise, this made for an exceedingly cold and wet arousal, and the northern chill, which had yet to leave my bones, rallied once again. In an attempt to distance myself from the bay breeze, which further cooled the dew and caused the eruption of gooseflesh over my entire body, I rose from my sandy bed, donned my damp coat, and headed back east in the direction of Chino.

The tantalizing smell of *desayuno* being cooked up in dozens of kitchens wafted down the streets and hastened my step toward my old home, hopeful that Bonnie Lee was amongst the early risers whose pots were warm and full of sustenance. Despite the considerable gentrification and building-up of Guaymas, I'd observed, to my satisfaction, that the neighborhood of Chino remained relatively unchanged. This made for simpler navigation and put me at ease—as if by walking those well-trodden roads of my youth, the twenty years I'd been gone for simply melted away.

When I reached the top of the street where Bonnie Lee had first brought me that fateful evening all those long years ago, I paused for a moment. I hadn't paid it much mind, but from the time I'd stepped off the beach and commenced my final journey home, my heart rate had gradually increased until it felt like it was about to pound right out of my chest. I felt like I'd just run down a passenger train with a pack of bloodhounds on my heels. I even felt somewhat dizzy. I contemplated returning to Guaymas and prefacing my grand return with a stiff glass of mezcal, but upon remembering the home bar that my teetotaler wife kept, I steadied myself with a few deep breaths, brushed the sand off of my coat, and carried on.

The degree to which my old neighborhood continued to glow with all its former glory invigorated and enchanted me. I felt like I was stepping into a photograph of a prior time. The sensation was so pervasive that I nearly expected to see my wife holding our infant son in her arms—that is, until mine and Bonnie Lee's former home drifted into view.

The first thing I noticed was the roses: there weren't any. The tangled web of climbing vines that had all but totally ensconced our little adobe shack were gone entirely—ripped right out of the ground by their roots. And, as I grew nearer, I saw that the whole place was in a state of disrepair. The window panes had all been broken or shattered by the wind, and any remaining glass rose in menacing crags while the curtains hung tattered and faded behind them. It was clear that it'd been long abandoned. The front door had been ajar long enough for weeds to grow on the threshold, and it creaked on its hinges as I pushed it open. Much of our furniture still remained just as I remembered it, albeit sun-faded and rain-damaged. However, the bar in the corner had been thoroughly pillaged, and any remaining bottles had been emptied and scattered around the dusty floor. The hair rose on the back of my neck, and I continued on through the house.

The rest of the rooms evinced the same condition. No valuables were left behind, nor any photographs or suggestions of the loving couple that had once inhabited that humble hubble. All the cupboards in the kitchen were open and empty, and in the bedroom, the drawers of Bonnie Lee's dresser stood agape. The only remaining vestige of my sweetheart was a length of ribbon laid atop the nightstand. Once red, the silken material Bonnie Lee used to tie up her raven hair was now faded and pinkish in color. Suddenly, the toll of twenty years had never seemed so stark.

Remembering the terrible fate of my first wife, I clutched the faded ribbon to my breast and fled from the empty house in a panic. Several denizens of Chino were mulling about, and I accosted them in turn, acquiring after my missing bride. The first few neighbors I canvassed in my broken, disused dialect knew nothing of Bonnie Lee; according to them, the house I referenced had been vacant since they'd moved in. I attempted to quell and rationalize my urgent concern by considering every reasonable explanation for her absence, but despite my efforts, the situation unnerved me.

Finally, after consulting about half a dozen residents, I approached a pair of elderly women who were chatting in the yard of a nearby home. One of the two was busy hanging up the wash, while the other had just dropped in, as evidenced by the basket of groceries on her arm. I vaguely recognized the former as someone I'd once known.

Again, I struggled to inquire as to the whereabouts of my wife. However, this time, when I said her name, the two women beheld me strangely and then exchanged a curious glance amongst themselves.

"*Sí, sé dónde vive Bonnie Lee. Bonnie Lee vive en Guaymas pueblo,*" the former replied to my cascading relief.

"*Escribe! Escribe* her address...*escribe la...la...*direction—*dirección! Por favor!*"

Understanding my request, the owner of the home strode inside to fulfill it, but not before turning toward her confidant and sharing a second questionable expression and a sentence in their native tongue that I could not comprehend.

I thanked her profusely when she returned with a piece of torn notepaper containing Bonnie Lee's address and set off toward Guaymas proper with a new sense of urgency. My fears of tragedy averted, I realized at once the narrow window through which I had viewed the future. For those twenty years, returning to Chino was a constant; however, I'd been far too caught up in my own woes to consider all the untold horrors that might've befallen my little family in all that time. Though, as I neared the neighborhood into which Bonnie Lee had moved, it became apparent that misfortune had not been the cause of her relocation. The community where Bonnie Lee now resided was one of the most affluent in the city. It was situated high on a hill overlooking the sprawling fishing village-turned-city below. Our old haunts in Chino were a mere thumbprint from such a vantage point, and the shores and harbors that stretched beyond glistened in the warm morning sun like glass. The five thousand dollars I'd sent her appeared to have gone further than I'd expected.

As I drew nearer to my objective, I grew increasingly anxious. When I finally reached the street to which I had been directed, I stopped. Heart pounding and out of breath, I paused for a moment. My hands, I found, were shaking.

Once I composed myself, I stepped off the curb, ready to traverse the last few meters to my new and final residence, when I noticed the establishment standing on the corner. The brass shingle hanging above its narrow windows designated it as a mezcal bar. My hand immediately traveled to my pocket, which held my last two dollars. For years, I had rallied with every ounce of my strength against the idea of returning to Bonnie Lee dead broke. But now, standing at the precipice of such a momentous endeavor, I thought little of the difference between returning to her with two dollars in my pocket as opposed to no dollars. Neither was the fortune I'd promised, and with my pride as no object, I knew that Bonnie Lee would not kick up a fuss—my presence alone would be enough to generously sate her. And so, with the last two American dollars I would ever possess close at hand, I stepped into that sumptuous mezcal bar in hopes that one of their potations would settle my apprehension.

My hopes were well-met. It was no secret to me at that point that Guaymas served up the best mezcal in all of Mexico, and that particular institution claimed to offer its most exclusive varietals. As I had not tasted the tantalizing, smoky delight of mezcal in what felt like at least two lifetimes and had the buying power of American money, I decided to splurge. I ordered myself a glass of the finest spirits I could afford and drank them down until my pockets were empty and the grandest imaginations of life to come danced before my eyes. The severely stunted capacity for sentimentality that I possessed was roused just long enough for me to express some sadness at the fact that I would not be returning to the first home that I had called my own, as I had so long anticipated, but my disappointment was soon displaced by the thrill of possibility. Every house along this palm-lined avenue was practically a mansion by Mexican standards, and I certainly had no qualms about living in such environs. I'd expected that I'd need to work some menial job to cover the cost of my vittles, but if Bonnie Lee could afford to live in such luxury, it seemed quite plausible that I'd very well need not do more than lay back in a hammock and become a reefer like the locals. Such ambitions offended me little, and I offered up my glass in a toast to *siestas* and *senoritas* before draining it of its contents.

The sun was high, and so was I when I stepped out of that mosaic-tiled mezcal wonderland, promising the bartenders that I would make it a practice to never walk by without stopping in for a drink. All but the last of that enduring chill had been shaken, tended to by good mezcal and the heat of the day. Above me, in the sparsely clouded sky, two eagles circled and called. The now-warm bay breeze swirled around me and brought to my senses the wondrous, intoxicating, unmistakable smell of roses. I turned from the bar and, after no more than a few steps, located the source of the aroma. About halfway down the street, between two other structures of like kind, was a large and stately stucco home. It was two stories high and painted white with a roof made from terracotta tiles. The front yard was full of ornamental shrubs and fruit trees and bisected by a walkway stretching down two stairs to the street where a low wall ringed the yard, the entranceway to such a palace singularly designated by an arbor of climbing roses. Before it was parked a long, sleek silver Cadillac. The street number matched that printed on the piece of notepaper in my hand.

Ready to permanently resign my commission as a knight of the road, I stood before the archway of roses, the blooming flowers the size of my fist. Having nothing else to present my faithful, waiting wife at the end of my extended absence, I reached up and picked the largest, finest, and most beautiful of the roses and held it before me as I approached the broad, wooden door. I marveled once more at the pristine opulence of the property, every last blade of grass manicured to perfection, and then raised my clenched and quivering fist and knocked three times. The hollow silence that followed felt like it lasted an eternity. My heart raced like a runaway engine on the mainline.

After what was likely no more than a minute, I heard muffled footsteps approaching from inside the house, and the door unlocked and pulled back, revealing the savagely tan face of a young man. Equals in height, we stood eye to eye, and although his handsome features were dark, his hair was thick and black, and his eyes were not blue, I knew without a doubt that the man who stood before me was none other than my own son.

"*¿Puedo ayudarlo señor?*" he greeted me questioningly, clearly surprised to find me standing on his doorstep, "Can I help you?"

"What's your name, son?" I asked, unable to contain my excitement as my heart swelled with the strange and unfamiliar sensation of paternal joy.

"Cassidy," he replied, still wary and unsure of who this strange old man calling on him really was.

"Cassidy," I repeated, the pride just about seeping out of my ears, "I'm your Pa."

With this, his eyes widened, his back stiffened, and he looked at me as though I'd just pulled out a revolver.

"I think you've got the wrong house, *Señor*," he responded severely.

"Beg pardon, but you're mistaken," I explained, "This is Bonnie Lee Jones' house, ain't it? For God's sake, son, I know I don't look like the pictures you've seen anymore with this white mop on my head, but I know my boy when I see him!"

He remained cautious and unconvinced, though if his eyes grew any wider, they would've fallen clean out of his head onto the front walk. "I think you'd better talk to her yourself," he told me.

Cassidy turned away, almost trancelike, from the door, and I heard him mutter under his breath, "and then I think I'd better...."

I'd expected, perhaps foolishly, a more enthusiastic reception, but I understood his shock and confusion. Twenty years is a long time for a boy to grow up knowing his father only from snapshots—and I was sure a hell of a lot more rugged, bent, and tired than I had been the last time I'd laid down beside my Love. But, for Bonnie Lee, I could not say the same. When she appeared in Cassidy's place, I nearly collapsed in shock. Time had never been kinder to a woman. Though she had half a century under her garters, she hardly looked older than her own son. Her curvaceous figure was dressed in a patterned velvet skirt, and her eyes shone forth from an uncreased face, her skin as smooth and youthful as it had been the day

I'd met her. Her black hair—though likely dyed—was wound up in a braid behind her head, and nestled behind her ear was a stark white magnolia.

For as much as I'd imagined greeting her with laddish composure, as soon as I saw her enchanting form step to the door like it had in so many of my dreams of yearning throughout years past, I just gasped her name and moved to embrace her. Uncharacteristically, tears of utter joy sprung into my eyes. I fell to my knees.

"Oh, Bonnie!" I moaned as I held her tight, "Oh, Bonnie, how I've missed you so! I swear to you, Bonnie, I'm here to stay. I ain't going to leave you no more, never! Your Jack is a changed man, Bonnie Lee, and you'll love me all the more for it! I have so much time to make up to you, so many years—and I'm dying to start. I want to show you all the love I've got for you—for all the years I've been away and ached and died inside, waiting to see you again! I've got so much love for you, Bonnie Lee, and I want to tell you—I want to tell you about the life I've lived, all my rotten sins—the years of waste and abandon that I've survived and the stories I've lived to tell and that have finally brought me back home to you. Oh, Bonnie, how I love you...how I..."

I ceased my panegyric when I realized she wasn't hugging me back. No warm, loving arms had entwined themselves around my trembling body, no sweet lips had been pressed against my sunburnt face, no tears of burgeoning relief fell from her alluring eyes. I might as well have been holding a statue.

When I released her and struggled to my feet, her eyes met mine with utter shock and not an ounce of excitement. If anything, as the astonishment of my unannounced arrival wore off, it was replaced by nothing more than cold realization.

"Jack..." she spoke my name with hollow disbelief, "you've been gone for twenty years...."

"I know, Bonnie, and for most of those, unable to write. But, I told you I'd come back as soon as I was able, and here I finally am."

"You're seventeen years too late, Jack," she replied, shaking her head in awe as if there was something in the circumstance that she just couldn't understand.

My breath caught in my throat, and my heart froze and dropped into my feet like a lead weight on the end of a line. "What do you mean?"

"Jack, I remarried in 1941."

The inkling of uncertainty that had begun to trickle in since my arrival in Guaymas hit me with all the power of a bursting dam, and immediately I began to drown. "You what!?" I cried.

"When you wrote me and told me you'd gotten ten more years for breaking out of prison, I couldn't wait for you. Our son needed a father, and he needed one then—not in fifteen years."

I pulled from my pocket her letter, creased and fragile with age, and held it out before her. "But you wrote me...you told me you'd wait for me, no matter how long! That your love for me was stronger than time! That no other man could fill the space in your heart! You assured me—you promised me!"

Her response was so hollow it practically echoed and so cold it probably froze her tongue on the way out of her mouth. "I told you what you needed to hear. If I'd told you I'd found another man, you would've come running after me and stuck yourself with another ten years—or worse. It was for your own good—and either way, it wouldn't have changed my mind. Even if you did get out in under fifteen years, I never thought I'd see you again. After that many years in prison, I figured you would've taken up with some young hussy and drank and partied and ran yourself out before you came back to a one-horse town and honorable living."

"What about Cassidy?" I choked out, "I know I never had the chance to be a father to him, but he's my son, and he didn't even recognize me!"

Bonnie Lee just shook her head, "As far as Cassidy is concerned, Miguel, my husband, is the only father he's ever known. You're as much a father to him as the grocer who sold me his formula. He never even knew that you existed."

A wave of dizzying horror overcame me with such unparalleled intensity that I staggered backward down the walkway. I reached out to steady myself on the rose trellis beside me, and as I did so, a thorn pierced my hand. In pain, I drew back and stumbled down the two steps, so distraught and dumbfounded that I was sick. I felt all that good mezcal turn sour in my stomach, and bracing myself on the low stone wall, I retched.

Once I'd composed myself and risen to my trembling feet, I ran my hand across my brow and felt that it was moist. I looked down to see blood oozing from where the thorn had pricked me. It was as red as the roses that grew there, as red as the roses she wore in her hair a lifetime ago when we danced to the song of love. But, with time, those roses faded, and our love along with it. And, so it is, as I was once told, in love as well as in life, a cut rose is doomed to die.

From where I stood supporting myself on the wall, I looked back toward Bonnie Lee's front door, now tightly shut and bolted. On the walk lay the perfect rose I'd intended to give her. It had fallen from my hand when she'd informed me of her blinding treachery, and trembling from head to toe in shock, I did the only thing I could think of: I strode forward to retrieve it. However, as I bent down to take hold of its thorny stem, a familiar chill ran through my body and quick-froze my heart. I held the crimson article in my bloodied hand before my disbelieving eyes and saw that, unlike when I'd picked it just moments before, it was no longer fresh and vibrant but shriveled, dry, and dead.

That afternoon had shaken the foundations of my whole world, and the weakness that seeped into the cracks in the aftermath was unprecedented. I left Chino immediately. My shattered heart could not bear to spend another night in Guaymas, nor could I bear to wake to the settling of the morning dew, once a talisman of our love, that now set upon me as nothing more than a cold remembrance of all I'd once had and all I'd now lost.

I boarded the first freighter I laid eyes upon. It made no difference to me where it was headed. I cared nothing about the concerns of petulant brakemen or cinder dicks. I cared nothing about another stint in prison. I cared nothing for a dollar or my next meal. I was hollow. Frozen. Shook to the core. And, every time I closed my ravaged eyes for want of a moment of reprieve, all I saw was the blind face of the man whose vain hopes had roused my own.

The figurative crossroads where I'd suddenly and unexpectedly found myself standing was nothing more than a statute of cruel irony. For the first time since I'd been a boy, I had all I'd ever wanted: pure and unadulterated freedom. I had nowhere to go and nowhere to be, nobody after me and nobody I had left to pursue. I had nothing and nothing left to lose. But, now, I didn't want it. I wanted no part of that freedom for which I had sacrificed all I'd ever owned. I'd been set against myself by my own ambition and crucified by my own desires. I'd lost at the very game that I'd taught myself to play. I was now to sleep in the bed I'd made—not in my broke-down palace, but on an old potato sack on the back platform of a Mexican Central caboose. I was sleeping in the bed I'd made, alright, and I was sleeping alone.

SEA GUDINSKI

I stayed on in Mexico for as long as the locals would have me. Since leaving Chino, I'd been reduced purely to a beggar, as all cleverness and skill no longer took form in my defeated mind or was dealt out by my gnarled old hands. I drifted along, directionless, until I made it to Acapulco, about two-thousand kilometers south of Guaymas. Here, I found myself seeking alms from tourists—who equaled sailors in their apparent dislike of money but rarely disposed of any great quantity of it in my hands.

At that time, Acapulco was at the height of its golden age and practically overrun by wealthy Americans honeymooning and vacationing at all times of the year. The city itself was a monument to natural beauty flocked to by film stars and millionaires and filled by lush private clubs, villas with swimming pools the size of small lakes, and its beaches hosted sunsets so surreal that even the most staunch nihilist would be forced to admit the existence of something greater than himself, just for gazing upon them. The weather was eighty-five degrees and sunny every day. The streets were clean and mostly free of ruffians like me, and even the refuse was gourmet. I slept on the beach every night.

I remained in Acapulco for three months and was miserable every second of every day. It's a cruel sort of humorous, isn't it—how it's so much easier to be miserable in gay environs than when surrounded by the same element? I've spent half my life on cold pavement, cold steel, and behind cold iron bars—and at no time did any of those locales, with all their blatant suffering and vogue discomfort, even begin to approach the soul-gripping misery that can be found alone in a dimly lit nightclub surrounded by couples in high voice and celebration while you feel like some colossal, unbearable force has reached into your chest and is squeezing the life out of you. The same goes for beautiful surroundings. Have you ever gazed upon a 14,000-ft peak or a tropical shoreline while afflicted by heartbreak? It's even worse than sitting in jail, facing a steep sentence. Worst of all is when such afflictions strike in a place of fond memories. No knife cuts deeper than the grave turning of a memory, especially one that has sustained the bearer through so many years of uncertainty—one that has single-handedly supported the notion of a future exempted from the pain of loneliness and grave hurt.

Needless to say, I left Acapulco before very long, eager to get back out on the road. In all honesty, out on the road was the very last place I wanted to be, but having few other options, I consoled myself with the fact that, at the very least, I'd be amongst my own kind.

That being said, however, traveling in Mexico is hardly the same as traveling through the U.S. There are vast tracks of nothingness in America, across all of which I've passed numerous times—but in Mexico, those swathes are more expansive, more desolate, and all in all, more dangerous. In my youth, I would have fared fine against the desperados and yeggs roaming south of the border, but just as I would have looked upon my present form as a vulnerable old man, so did they. The odds of finding myself dead alongside the tracks, robbed of the handful of pesos I had in my pocket, was a very real possibility. Besides, the roads just aren't the same, nor are the trains and those who ride them. Although the law allows the average vagrant more freedoms than they do up north, the road itself lacks a certain familiarity and sense of comfort. The songs sung around the campfires aren't the same, the stories are all in Spanish, and the gamblers there will shoot a cheater just as the ranchers will hang a horse thief. Therefore, despite my desire to rid myself of the melancholy that my time as an American tramp had brought me, I soon found myself back on the same roads I'd been traveling along for the last forty years.

Despondent, defeated, and every kind of tired a man has ever known, I crossed back into the U.S. in the fall of 1960. As I crossed over the Rio Grande at Piedras Negras on the rear platform of a hopper car, I reluctantly turned my back on Mexico and any hope of a future consisting of stability, security, and joy. As in any previous period in my life of luckless endeavors, the world had continued to move and turn while I was away, and time had continued to roll on like that big river. Once more, I found myself alone, and this time, I feared, for good. The Texas desert spread out before me like a vast, silent, unpromising stage for uncertainty. I knew every corner of it, but it did not know me. Here was return; here was all of life stretched out before me, reflecting like a grim mirror all of what I was and what I could have been. Neither was any too glorious.

XII

Goin' Down The Road Feelin' Bad

A man tends toward thinking when he's traveling, and of late, I have been no exception. I've spent many days and nights lying awake in fast rattlers, thinking about all the places I've been in this bastard life of mine. I've spent many a long ride studying about the people I've met and the things I've said and done—it's a real wonder that I've never once paid any mind to where I'm going. Perhaps that's why I've found myself in such dire straits. Perhaps it is indifference that has directed the course of this cursed life, or perhaps it is simply greed—the tempting call of ill-got gains, the lure of ease and luxury, the siren song of riches that has led me to so many falls, bordered by heights that a purely honest man can never know. Or, perhaps, it is the simple pleasure of the unknown, boyish curiosity, and love of adventure that has set me upon this nameless Road. But the journey is different now; I feel as if some sense of immunity has perished, as if something I've been accompanied by my whole life has flown away from me. Age has set upon me at once, and it has brought with it nearly sixty years of unpardonable conscience.

I never had very much of that 'good stuff' as they call it—that Rugged American Individualism. I never carried the red card of the Industrial Workers of the World; I made my way on my own. I never broke bread with Jerusalem Slim or asked him to make an exception for my sins. But I have been thinking, of late, that perhaps I should have. We all have a road to walk in this life, and no road is dead on both ends. All roads come from somewhere and go somewhere—and when you're standing in the middle, the one thing that's sure is that neither end is going to seem clear; that much I know is true. Perhaps hell is real as well as heaven—but I never concerned myself with such ends of the road. I sure ain't been no saint, but I've snubbed my nose and laughed at the idea of torment—as I've been punished more than enough in this life for all I've ever done. Still, that strange little English bartender in San Francisco has got me thinking, more than I ever have, that perhaps hell is not owed me for what I have done but for what I haven't. I've always been of the opinion that every man owns his lot—but sometimes, the dice just don't add up.

When I think of youth and bygone years, I often feel somewhat haunted by it all. It all passed by so quickly. This road of mine has passed through many different landscapes and taken so many twists and turns that it's a wonder I never got lost on the way to where I am...or maybe I did...I guess I'll never know. I know I felt more sure of myself when I was sitting alone in a cell than I do today. Maybe it's a casualty of age, this fear. I never used to be afraid of anybody or anything, let alone my own shadow. I never imagined I'd live to be an old man, but life is cruel; it makes you sit idly by and watch as it unravels before your eyes.

Rain wears away rock just the same as time wears away man. You wake up one morning eager and bright, ready to face the world as a force, and a few revolutions later, that same man is stumbling through an alley, climbing the walls, digging his dirty fingernails into the brick, and pouring his guts onto his shoes. It's an ugly picture of truth, but truth it remains to be. It's a truth that lingers, pokes, prods, and promises its grim imminence with a grin and a glance in quiet corners, on lonely nights, in moments of confusion and moments of doubt. We joke and jest and toast to our invincibility, but man can't win in the game of life. We are to sacrifice our strength to our fears. We are to lose our poise to our flaws and our indifference to our mortal weakness. Man is not the only creature that suffers and dies, but man is the only creature that cries.

I have never shed a tear for any man, least of all myself, but I haven't been sleeping all that well these days. I've been throwing salt over my shoulder ever since I left Mexico, but all I've been hitting is my shadow—for that's all that's there. I've heard old bums talk of the Shivers since I've been a boy, and now I've got them, and there ain't no cure except death. Death always seemed a fitting respite from the qualms and traumas of life. I've never wanted to die and have fought off death's agents time and again, but I still always imagined I'd be gone long before my time—that women would lament me, that men would honor and hate me, and yet here I stand, a bum of nearly sixty years. I've lived out my usefulness and my prime—

and for the first time, death appears to me not as respite but as imminent, slow, and fearful demise.

I've got no recourse other than to keep riding, just like I always have. But, moving, traveling, and riding onward with no destination somehow loses its comfort of mind when the only place you desire to return to has exiled you, body and soul—but there's nothing else to do, so you roam. When you've never known anything else, you just keep on. I'm too old to change my ways and too healthy and ornery to embrace inevitable death, so here I am. I sure don't know where I'm headed, but then again, I never did. I don't know where I'll be in a few years' time—hell, I don't even know where I'll be at tomorrow—but I can only hope that I keep on living because that old wharf rat has got me thinking: I'm an old man too, and if there ain't time left in my life to pay my dues, when am I gonna pay them? Do the wicked really get off scot-free?

Through years that roll along like waves, strung together by memories, here I stand—and now you know all of it: every hurt and every joy from which my life has been composed. This world is yours now, do with it what you will. I will fade out into the night before very long, another face to be seen no more along the great and troubled avenues of life. A few souls will remember me, but most are already dust. The day will come—and it will come right soon—when this heart will beat no more, and every thought of love and hate will be laid to rest. In just a few offhand moments, I've told you of my life—and you will soon forget, as no man remembers the words of his forebearers until it is far too late.

Do you remember what you said to me when you first climbed into this boxcar? When I asked you what you were running from and you said boredom? When I asked you where you were headed, and you didn't have a damned clue? When you climbed onto this train, you were looking at me with your eyes all wide like I was some kind of bum chieftain, but I ain't. I'm just an old man who has done more traveling, cheating, gambling, lying, and running than was my share. I ain't nothing to this world; I ain't nothing to this train, even. This here train could run me right down under her wheels and not know a thing. World's the same. If I died today, nobody would know the difference. I ain't built nothing up, and I ain't torn nothing down. I brought in a life who never knew me, and I took out a few who never knew me, either. There ain't nobody in the world who cares if I die. I'm just an old railroad son, there are thousands more just like me, and if you stay on this train, that's likely what you'll become too.

There are three evils in this world: booze, bums, and boxcars. So, before you go tramping out across the country half-starved, freezing your niblets off in the frigid cold, and lying flat on your back in some backwoods jail for sixty days at a clip, be sure the place you're running from don't already have all the things you need. I've found that a man don't need much in life. A man don't need more than just two things: something to eat and someplace to lay his head. Now, a boy, well, a boy needs plenty. A woman, of course—usually one that don't need him—and money—lots of it—and adventure—exciting, dangerous, foolhardy—and most importantly, trouble. Oh, yes, a boy needs trouble—it keeps his mind moving. It moves his body too, and a hell of a lot further and faster than he'd ever expect.

If I've got one bit of advice for you, boy, it's to get off this train. Get off this train at the next stop, and don't you ever get back on. When you hear that whistle blow, you just turn your head and start walking in the other direction just as fast as your feet'll take you. Riding these here rails ain't at all like it used to be in my day, and these old trains have a funny way about them. They've got a way of making your life the most ruinous and exciting thing you ever did think of.

Somebody once asked me what a good title for the story of my life would be. I remember replying, "Skulls and Roses"—because in my life, there's been quite a mixture of both. I've got more old wounds and battle scars than I've got hair left on my head, and after all those forty years, all I've got in my pockets are the same odd coins, marked deck, and weighted dice I had when I first started out. You'd expect a man who's been on the road as long as me to have feet just about worn down to a nub and a left thumb that don't do nothing but stand at attention, but in some ways, just the opposite is true. I ain't got no home in this world anymore and no destination besides, but I've got something well and owed me that no man can steal and I can't give away even if I wanted to. I've got a ticket, stamped and sure—a one-way trip on the Wabash Cannonball down to Terrapin Station. I don't know what time it's leaving, and I ain't got a clue from where, but one of these days, I'll cash in my chips, hang up my hat, and hit the Road for the last time.

There's a different song in my heart now. It's low, and it's soft, and it ain't so proud anymore. It sounds something like the blues, like a song I heard some time ago and now repeats long and low without warning, a complete and dismal summary of a life that's been everywhere and done everything but has left nothing behind but blood and tracks. I can't say I fully regret these roads I've gone down, but they've been long and unforgiving roads, that much is for sure. Sometimes the light's been all shining on me, other times I could barely see, and lately, it's occurred to me what a long, strange trip it's been....